GRAINS OF TERROR

The wind picked up, moaning and almost making a crying, painful sound. The sand whipped and bounced off the house, muddying the vision of the man and woman who stood, mesmerized, by the window. A roar filtered and flicked over the drone of the wind and the millions of tiny sand-crashes.

"Nothing human did that," Connie whispered.

"Call the police, honey. Right now."

She ran to the phone and punched out the numbers, shaky with fear.

When Mark looked out the window again, a cry of terror choked his throat and froze his tongue. He didn't know what he was looking at. He had never seen anything like it before. It was a sandman.

Blocky and stumpy and sand-colored—non-human. It stood upright on blocklike legs. There were holes where eyes should have been. A slit for a mouth. Holes where a nose would be.

Behind him, Connie started screaming. Mark ran and got the shotgun.

The thing was lumbering toward them, its thick arms outstretched.

Grunting sounds emanated from the hole in its face.

Mark jerked the sh
pulled the trigger. Th
from the creature and k
ing the hallway with b

SANDMAN
William W. Johnstone

ZEBRA BOOKS
KENSINGTON PUBLISHING CORP.

ZEBRA BOOKS

are published by

Kensington Publishing Corp.
475 Park Avenue South
New York, NY 10016

First printing: June, 1988

Printed in the United States of America

Dedicated to Jerry and Carolyn Dallman

BOOK 1

And hand in hand, on the edge of the sand,
They danced by the light of the moon.

—Edward Lear

ONE

"I hate you!" the boy hissed at his parents. His eyes shone with a strange, almost unnatural light, and through his hate and anger, he smiled, baring teeth, a cruel curving. His teeth were very white. "I hate you more than anything in this whole world. I wish you were all dead and rotting in the grave!"

He ran out of the cottage and onto the sun-caressed and sea-kissed beach before his father could catch him and give him a whipping.

"And I hate you, too, Janis!" he called over his shoulder. "I especially hate you. You damn bitch!"

"Paul!" his father shouted. "You get back in here, and I mean right now!" Mark looked over at the cottage where the newlyweds were staying. But they were nowhere in sight.

He marveled at their stamina.

"Dead! Dead! Dead!" the boy shouted over the soft whispering of the waves on the sand. "That's what I wish you all were—dead!"

"Little twerp!" Janis muttered, giving the running form of her younger brother a dark look.

"That will be quite enough of that, young lady,"

11

her mother told her, although sometimes, like today, she silently agreed with her firstborn's assessment of Paul.

She left Janis sitting and muttering darkly, and went outside to sit on the steps beside her husband.

Yuppies, it would seem at first glance. They were in their mid-thirties, very attractive people, trim and fit, each with a career that brought in six figures a year, and they lived very comfortably. Affluent would fit them nicely.

With two lovely children.

Well . . . one lovely child. Janis.

Janis was a sweet girl. Ten years old and blond and already showing signs of blossoming into a beautiful woman.

And there was eight-year-old Paul. A rotten little brat!

He was highly intelligent and cruel as a rattlesnake, nice-looking and a sneak. Paul could have the manners of a prince and then turn around and spew verbal venom as deadly as any cobra's.

Mark shook his head. "I just don't know what else to do, Connie." She could see the tears in his eyes. "I thought this vacation would bring us all closer. Iron out . . . whatever has been troubling Paul. Looks like I blew it again. I just can't get through to the boy." He wiped his eyes with a handkerchief and then blew his nose. "We've got a problem kid, my dear."

"I know. And if we're to blame, I'll take my share of it."

He cut his eyes to her. Serious and questioning eyes. "What blame, Connie? What have we done?

12

Believe me, I've searched my soul trying to come up with something we did wrong."

She opened her mouth to interrupt. He waved her silent.

"No, let me finish. I've got to get this off my chest. You know me, Connie—Checklist Charlie. That's me. Before we left, I sat down and made a ledger—things that we have and haven't done with and for our kids. Connie, we're not perfect parents—I've never met the perfect parent—but we've tried. We try to maintain a Christian home without being strait-laced about it. We've never been drunk in front of the kids. Never. And we've geared our work around our kids. We spend more time with Janis and Paul than any other parents I can name. We always do things as a family unit. I've watched other couples our age, our friends. They don't spend nearly as much time with their kids. Is that it? Have we spent too much time with ours? I don't think so. But our work and our lives are geared around them. We include them in nearly everything we do. I'm at my wits end, Connie. I don't know where to turn for help. I don't know what to do. And I don't like what I've been thinking lately. It scares me."

She wasn't at all sure she wanted to hear it. But then some of her own thoughts about Paul had not been filled with motherly love. "What have you been thinking, Mark?"

He sighed. He'd been doing a lot of that lately. "Connie, do you, well, believe in the bad-seed theory? That some people are just born bad?"

"Do you?"

They both looked around. Janis had left the main

13

room of the cottage and gone to her bedroom. The door was closed, music filtering out to them.

"Go on, Mark," Connie urged. "Say it."

He met her eyes. "The boy is bad. He's vicious, and we both know it. He's been that way since he was old enough to comprehend. And you know he did that at a very early age. Too early. We can't have a pet. They all disappear. You know why as well as I do. Paul kills them."

She went on the defensive. "We don't know that for a fact, Mark!"

"Come on." There was a weary note in his voice. "Who killed the lovebirds—tore their heads off? Who set the canary on fire? And thought it was funny? That little—" He bit back the profanity he would have directed at his own son. "We've had three dogs since Paul was four years old. They all disappeared. I found the bloodstains, remember? Disappeared out of a chain-link fenced back yard. And Paul doesn't have any friends. None. The kids hate him because he's a bully. Smart as a whip and mean as an aroused grizzly. And I might as well get it all off my chest: I just don't trust him."

Connie sat for a time in silence, even under these strained conditions enjoying their closeness. "He steals, too," she finally said.

"Yeah. I know it. I've watched him sneak into our bedroom and go through my wallet. And your purse. I've whipped him for it. But I can't whip him anymore. I just can't."

"He peeks in on his sister while she's undressing."

"I didn't know that!" He expelled breath. "Connie, we both come from families who used the belt

14

and the switch. Not often, but when we needed a spanking, we got a good one. Just the same, I don't want to whip the boy anymore. Not now. It would be out of anger and not out of caring. I'm afraid if I did whip him, I'd lose what little control I have left, and I'd hurt him.''

"I've marveled at your restraint the past couple of days, honey."

"Thank you."

"What are we going to do, Mark?"

"I don't know. Take him to see a doctor when we get back, I guess. But I do know one thing."

She waited, dreading to hear what she had felt in her heart for a long time.

"It just can't go on like this."

Again, she waited.

"He's sick, Connie. Paul is mentally ill."

"Hey, little mon!" The tall man with the pretty honey-colored lady caught Paul, swung him around, and deposited him gently on his feet, in the sand. "What you all upsot about?"

The boy jerked free and faced them, no fear in him. His eyes blazed with a wild light. "Get out of my way or I'll kill you!"

The man and woman laughed, but it was a strange-sounding laugh. Hollow and deep. The woman said, "Oh, will you now? *Non*, I don' tink so. I tink you need someones to talk to. Am I rat?"

The man wore no shirt or shoes. Only a pair of very clean and very white trousers. The woman was slender and pretty, dressed in very bright colors, a multicolored bandana around her head. She wore a heavy necklace of strange-looking amulets.

And Paul knew they were amulets.

He stared at the pair. "I haven't seen either of you around this place before. Where did you come from? And I'll tell you right now: I don't like you!"

The man laughed and laughed. He bent over and slapped his leg. "Ma mon, you too little to be speakin' to me lak dat. I'm a big black mons. You just a little white boy. Ain't you 'fraid of me?"

"Hell, no!"

Again, they laughed. Exchanged odd looks. Odd to Paul.

"How come you was in such a hurry, ma little mon?" the tall man asked.

Paul stepped back and studied the man and woman. He had not seen them as he ran. And that was odd. They seemed to have materialized out of the sand. That was even more odd. Paul had prowled the area around the cottage, at night and during the day, for at least a mile in every direction, except out to sea. But he had never seen these people before. He knew the cottages along this stretch of beach were very expensive, but he sensed the pair were not tourists.

"I'm running away," he finally admitted.

"Ma little mon, you can't run nowheres far. You on an island."

"I know that. But I can run for a while. Before I have to go back."

"Dat's de truth. And if you don't go back?"

"The police will come after me."

"How come you running so hard away from your parents, mon?"

"I never said it was from my parents."

"Dat's true. But I speak de truth, too, don' I, little mon?" His eyes never left Paul's face.

And both his eyes and the woman's eyes blazed with the same wild light found in Paul's eyes.

And Paul knew it.

"Yeah. OK. You're right."

"You won' sit down and talk to me and ma woman?"

"Why should I?"

The man shrugged. "Why not? You ain' got no ones else to talk to, rat?"

Paul plopped down onto the warm sand. But it felt different to him. Softer, more pliable. And . . . He struggled for the word.

Friendly.

The woman sat on his left side, the man to his right. "Your poppa done give you a lickin', huh?" the woman asked.

"Not yet. But he will."

"You been bad boy this day?"

Paul noticed the man was picking up handfuls of sand and allowing the grains to slowly trickle through his strong fingers.

"They say I have."

"But you don' tink so yourself, hah?" she asked.

"I am what I am," Paul said. "I cannot help being that."

"Dat's truth, too," the man said. He ruffled Paul's blond hair. "What you won' from us, little boy?"

Paul slapped the man's hand away, and cut his mean eyes from him. "I haven't asked you for a damn thing!"

17

The man laughed. "Hoo, but you did ax. Dat's why we come."

"Come from . . . where?"

The woman waved her hand around and around. The wooden amulets jangled with her movements. Paul could see she wore no bra under her dress. Her breasts moved, too. "From out dere, little mon."

Paul grunted.

"You ain't got no friends nowhere, has you, boy?" the man asked.

"I don't need friends. Nor do I want them. I hate people."

"You don't won' friends unless you can control them. Ain' dat rat, boy?"

"Maybe." Paul wondered how the man knew that. But not really. He thought he knew why, thought he'd known all along.

"Other peoples make fun of your birt'mark, don' dey, hey, boy?"

Paul sat very still. Now he knew. "I won't ask how you know about my birthmark."

"I tink you already knows," the woman said.

And Paul did.

It came to him in a wild rush. And his smile became a savage thing, ugly to look at.

But to the man and woman, it was beautiful.

"We was once lak you." The woman's voice was low-pitched, yet hollow sounding like the man's. "Long time back. We comes back now and den. When ones wit' us calls. Lak you done called las' night."

Paul thought about that. He had slipped out of the cottage last night, as he had done every night since

18

his arrival on the island, and walked the deserted beach, by himself. No fear in him. And as the sea breeze whispered around the boy, the waves licking at his feet like a warm blood-salty tongue, he had thought the darkest of thoughts. Evil.

And he knew he had come home.

At last.

"You see now, don' you, boy?" The man spoke, his eyes on the shore. "'Pose we could hep you, little mon. What would you do wit' de power you axed for las' night?"

"Did I ask you for anything?" Paul lied. He had, but he wanted to be sure of the man and woman. His father might have sent them, to trick him.

Paul sensed he was very close now, and he knew he must be very careful.

"Yeah, you axed."

"Yes. I did, didn't I?"

The man and woman waited.

"You've been in my dreams, both of you. You're the ones who told me to urge my father to bring us here."

"Rat."

"Am I special?"

"You special. Me and Nicole been waitin' a long time for you to come."

"You're Mantine." Not a question.

"Rat."

"You're dead."

"Rat. But I comes back whenever I wants. Me and de woman. You got to tell us, boy. What you won'?"

"I would have my way," Paul said savagely.

The woman began to chant very softly. Paul could

19

not understand the words.

Mantine began to strike the sand with the palm of his hand.

"I would recruit others to follow."

Nicole continued to chant.

Mantine struck the sand with his hand.

"I would serve, like I served hundreds of years ago."

The chanting became a dark voice. The sand-striking a drumbeat.

"I would destroy!" Paul damned himself as he had done in centuries past.

The chanting stopped. Mantine began to mold a pile of sand. He spat into it, moistening it. Then the woman leaned over and spat into the sand. Paul could see her bare breasts moving as the dress parted.

Paul spat into the sand.

He watched as tiny figures were formed in the sand.

"You got friends now, Paul," Mantine told him. "Dey do what you tell dem to do."

"How many friends?"

"How many grains of sand does you see?"

"Thousands."

"Den dat's what you got. Touch de sand, Paul."

Paul touched the damp sand. It was very hot to his fingers, almost unbearable. He grimaced against the pain.

Under his small hand, the grains began to move and glow. The glow became intensely painful, but Paul would not remove his hand. Then voices began to speak out of the glow. Screaming was heard. Profanity. The sounds of sexual assault, of depravity, torture, and more debasement than one could endure and still remain sane. It was horrible.

Paul loved it.

He was touching home. Touching the dark soul of his real father.

Mantine said, "You leave de islands in a short time, boy. But me and Nicole be rat behind you. De t'ree of us is togedder at las'."

"It's been so long, brother and sister."

"Yeah. But now dere ain't nothin' kin pull us apart no more."

Paul looked at Nicole's breasts. Felt an ancient stirring within him, and knew he had never been a boy. Not really. Only inside a child's shape and form.

"Dey's a bucket back yonder." Mantine jerked his head. "You fetch it, Paul."

Paul scrambled for the bucket. How he knew where it was did not enter his mind. He suddenly knew lots of things. Slobber leaked from his mouth as hot memories flooded over him. He was not worried about destroying the shapes Mantine had molded from the sand. He knew he could call them back whenever he wished.

And he would.

Soon.

Like . . . that night.

Paul laughed, a strange and evil, deep and hollow laugh. His blood ran hot within him.

It was good to be back home.

When he returned to the man and woman, they were both walking around and around the pile of sand figures.

Paul began to fill the bucket with the searing

hot sand.

He found a small piece of shell, and made a tiny cut in his arm, letting the blood trickle onto the sand.

Nicole started to hum and chant and dance.

Mantine sang: "Dance a little step. Mak' a little sound. Turn de eart' into a partner, and de sand into a mon."

Paul stood up and then whirled around and around, the mark on his arm burning and throbbing. Around and around, faster and faster, he whirled.

Mantine and Nicole began to fade.

Paul stopped.

Looked around him.

He was alone.

Sort of.

The bucket of sand was at his feet.

Paul knelt down. Dug his fingers into the searingly hot sand. Words poured from his mouth, words spoken in a language that had been dead and forgotten for thousands of years.

The words were filth. The man-boy cursed God. Spoke of unspeakable things he would do to his sister, his mother, his father.

The blue sky darkened; the wind picked up. And the waves were no longer gentle; they crashed angrily against the shore.

Paul stood up, clenched his hands into fists, and shook them at the sky. He screamed, a high-pitched dark-tinged cry of defiance.

Then he brought his fists down to his sides. The sky was blue once more. The waves gentled.

The boy looked around him. All appeared normal. He had not been observed.

He picked up the bucket of sand and walked back up the beach. When the cottage came into view, Paul changed direction, and came up behind it. His mother and father were on the porch. He looked into Janis's room. She was lying on the bed, listening to the radio. She wore only panties.

Paul licked his lips.

Silently, he slipped into his room and carefully filled up several socks with the sand. He packed them at the bottom of his suitcase. Then he filled a bottle with sand, packing it carefully so it would not break. He scraped the bucket free of every last grain of sand. He had a thumb-size pile left on a piece of paper.

He thought of the newlyweds next door, and laughed. He had slipped over to their cottage at night and listened to them make love. He'd do that again this night. With some friends.

Smiling, he walked into the kitchen and began to make a sandwich.

He heard his sister say, "He came back."

There was a definite note of disappointment in her voice.

You'll get yours soon, Paul thought.

He continued preparing his sandwich.

"Paul!" Mark called. "Come out to the porch, please, son."

Janis came into the kitchen, to stand and stare at him.

"What do you want, bitch?"

What's the matter with his voice? she thought. It sounds . . . weird. "Daddy is calling you, Paul."

"I'm not deaf. Just hungry."

Janis turned to leave. But she stopped and looked

23

at her brother.

Paul stared at her through eyes that shone with centuries of evil and hate and savagery . . . although Janis could not know that.

Yet.

She dropped her gaze and walked from the kitchen. Paul made her nervous. She didn't trust him, and never had. She knew something was wrong with her brother, but she didn't know what. He had never been a little boy. Never. He had always seemed so old.

And he was a sneak and a thief. There was one thing Janis and her friends agreed on: Paul Kelly was a turd, a nerd. And they were afraid of Paul.

She walked out to her parents on the porch. "He's fixing a sandwich."

"How does he look?" Connie asked.

"Like he always does." Hateful, mean, weird, she silently added.

Mark picked up Janis's thoughts by watching her face. "He is your brother."

The girl looked at her father. "He is?"

"Now, Janis, don't be silly!" Connie spoke sharply. "Of course, he's your brother."

"Then how come he has that stupid-looking mark on his arm and I don't?" She knew why; she just liked, in her own way, to agitate.

"It's only a birthmark, honey," Mark told her. "We've been through all this before."

"Yes, but you never told me how he got it." They didn't know she had overheard them talking about it one time, about how Paul always refused to let anyone, even his parents, look at the mark. Really pitched a big fit about it.

"It's just a skin blemish, honey. No one knows how they happen; they just do."

They all heard the shower running.

"When your brother finishes his bath, Janis," Mark told her, "your mother and I wish to see him. Please tell him that."

"I will not go into his room until he is out of the shower and fully dressed." Janis stood her ground.

"Why, honey?" her mother asked.

"Because he's a nasty little creep, that's why!"

Connie knew what her daughter was talking about, and with her eyes, she cautioned Mark not to pursue it.

He complied, with a sigh.

They all heard the shower stop. The cottage by the sea pulsed with silence.

"Go knock on his door and ask him if he is fully dressed," Mark said.

Janis shook her head. "That won't do any good, Daddy." She met his eyes. "He'd just lie about it, and hope I'd come in and see him naked."

Her father stared at her. "Let's just try him and see, baby."

They walked through the house. At Paul's door, Mark nodded at Janis, motioning for her to knock and ask.

"Paul, are you dressed?" Janis called. "Can I come in?"

"Sure, sister! Come right in."

Mark flung open the door.

Paul was standing naked in the center of the room, holding his penis in his hand. His face paled when he realized he'd been tricked.

25

"Get out of here, Janis," Mark told her. To Paul, he snapped, "Put some clothes on, boy!"

Paul slipped into shorts.

"What is the meaning of this intrusion?" he asked.

Mark stared at him, aware that his son's voice had changed. It was much deeper, kind of hollow sounding. And the birthmark on his arm seemed to be bigger.

Would it grow as the boy grew?

Mark didn't know. It didn't seem likely.

He shook his head. "Paul, I would like an apology from you. For the things you said this morning."

Paul laughed. "That'll be the day!" He had started to say When Hell freezes over, but that would have been too disrespectful.

Blind fury seized his father. He jerked off his leather belt and advanced toward the boy. But Paul stood in the center of the floor, not one bit afraid. "You arrogant brat! I'll beat your butt until—"

"Mark!" Connie shouted from the doorway. "You said you wouldn't!"

Mark yelled his reply, his voice shaking with anger. "Stay out of this, Connie. He's not going to talk to me like that."

Mark swung the belt, the leather popping against Paul's backside.

Paul reached out on the second swing. With a savage cry and amazing strength, he tore the belt from his father's hand. The buckle ripped the flesh of Mark's palm as he jerked it free.

"Oh, my God, Mark!" Connie cried, as blood dripped from his hand.

"If you ever try to hit me again, I'll kill you!"

Paul hissed.

Connie drew back, disturbed by the strange voice coming from the boy.

But Mark stepped forward and backhanded Paul with his good hand. Paul's feet flew out from under him and he landed on the bed, one side of his face swelling and reddening from the blow.

As he lay on the bed, he screamed filth at his father.

The fury suddenly left Mark. He looked at Connie. Opened his hand. His palm was badly ripped, blood leaking out with each heartbeat.

Paul continued to scream, gutter-profanity rolling from him in waves.

Mark ignored him. "It's going to need stitches, honey. Come on. Drive me to that clinic up the road." He looked at Paul and roared: "Shut up!"

The filth stopped abruptly.

Mark wrapped a handkerchief around his hand. "You and Janis will stay here, Paul. In the house. If I find you've left, I guarantee you a world of hurt. And that is a promise, boy."

Paul spat at him.

"But the ocean . . . !" Connie protested.

"I have no intention of entering that filth-ridden sea of sharks and tourists," Paul declared haughtily. "I shall stay in the house and pray that you bleed to death before you reach the clinic."

Mark looked at Connie and grinned. "Are you sure you picked up the right baby at the hospital?"

"Mark!" She looked at Janis. "Stay with your brother. I'll tell that young couple next door to keep an eye out for you."

Despite the throbbing in his hand, Mark joked,

27

"From their bedroom, honey? They're on their honeymoon, gal!"

"Oh, Mark—come on!"

"Your attempts at humor are pathetic," Paul told his father.

Mark sighed and tried to ignore the boy.

"Do I have to stay alone with creepo?" Janis asked.

"Yes," Mark told her, "you do. If he tries anything cute, pick up a lamp and bop him on the head with it. Maybe that will bring him to his senses."

"I hope you're joking." Connie looked at her husband.

"I assure you, I am not."

"Don't worry, Daddy-bear," Paul's words were infuriatingly mocking. "I shall stay in my room like a good little boy."

"That would be a welcome relief." Mark walked out of the room.

"Get a cloth and clean up the mess, Janis," Connie said.

"I'll clean it up myself!" Paul told her. "I would rather not have to look at her ugly face." He glared at his sister.

"Whatever," their mother said wearily.

She left the room and walked to the car, catching up with Mark.

"God! What's happened to his voice?"

"I don't know. Maybe he's caught a cold. But when we get back to the mainland, Paul is going to see a shrink."

"I think it's time."

Paul hissed at his sister, like a snake. "Get out of my room, you pig!"

"With pleasure, creep! You're lucky Daddy didn't stomp you."

Paul merely smiled at her and rubbed his crotch.

"God, Paul, you're sick!"

She slammed the door hard.

Turn de eart' into a partner and de sand into a mon; the words returned to Paul.

Smiling, humming the chant Nicole had hummed, he poured some sand onto the bloody floor.

As the boy began swaying back and forth, the birthmark on his arm glowed and throbbed, almost painfully. But Paul didn't notice.

The sand came together in a sticky glob, then coiled like a nest of snakes. The coiling ceased as figures appeared on the floor. Stretching their stubby arms and legs and soaking up the blood, they rolled in the gore, blindly seeking out every drop of blood.

"My friends," Paul whispered, "go. Become as one and seek them out. Then return to me."

Paul opened the window and the sand figures, like snakes, slithered from the bedroom and slipped onto the sand by the house.

On the way to the kitchen for the cleaning supplies, Paul ran into Janis in the hall. He wondered how long she'd been there, and if she had been spying on him.

"Get out of my way," he snarled at her.

"God, Paul, you are such an ass! You're so smart, but you're so icky!"

"Shove it, sister."

Her face crimson with anger, Janis ran outside, to the porch.

Paul's eyes followed her. "You'll die, bitch," he whispered. "After I've had some fun with you."

The birthmark on his arm throbbed.

Paul had always known what the birthmark looked like; but he had to look real close to see it. The lines were fine, as if they'd been painted by a master.

They had, of course.

The circle was almost perfect. Inside the circle, there was a five-pointed star. Behind that, almost hidden, was an upside-down cross. Paul hadn't been real sure what it all meant.

Until today.

He smiled.

Because of the birthmark, Paul almost never, even inside the house, wore tank tops or sleeveless T-shirts. And he never swam.

He had been taunted by others all his life because of the strange-looking birthmark. His gym teacher, high on the list of people Paul hated, made him undress in the locker room and expose the mark so people could laugh at him. But he'd soon get his.

Paul had a long list. But he was careful not to write it down. He kept it in his mind, feeding on his hate.

And the hate-fires never burned very low.

On the porch, Janis waved at the young couple in the next cottage. They waved back.

"Your mom told us about the accident!" the young woman called to her. "We'll be on the porch until they get back."

"OK!" Janis responded. "Thank you."

Her father had told her that was the way love was, what it looked like at first, when he was talking about the newlyweds.

To Janis, it looked kinda nerdy.

All that kissing and sitting real close all the time. She thought she'd get tired of that pretty quick. But they hadn't, not in the two weeks Janis had been watching them. And if they'd come down here for the sun, how come they spent so much time in their cottage with the blinds down?

But of course she knew. She just thought it was stupid. She had long ago learned that adults sometimes acted like they weren't playing with a full deck of cards.

Dean and Donna Mansfield. Dean and Donna. The names fit them.

Janis wondered if she should tell her parents about what she'd seen when she'd peeked into Paul's bedroom.

She decided not. She wasn't at all sure she'd really seen it.

Things like that just didn't happen.

She sat for a long time on the porch, trying to convince herself of that.

TWO

"They were a real cute couple," Janis heard her father say.

The girl yawned, stretched, rubbed the sleep from her eyes, and threw back the thin covers. Getting out of bed, she peeked through the blinds and saw several police cars parked around the newlyweds' cottage. She quickly dressed in shirt and shorts, and walked onto the front porch.

Glancing at her brother's bedroom door, she noticed it was, as usual, closed.

Her mother pulled her back before she could reach her father, who was talking with a tall, older man. Several policemen, black and white, all dressed in crisp white uniforms, were standing about the tall man who looked like he was in charge.

Janis wondered what in the world was going on.

"I do hate to ask this of you, sir," the tall man said to Mark. "It's going to be quite distasteful. But since you were neighbors, so to speak, I must ask if you would help us with the identification?"

"Sure," Mark said.

"That's good of you," the gray-haired policeman

said. "Have you had breakfast yet?"

Distinguished looking, Janis thought.

"Yes. About an hour ago," her father answered.

"Umm. Pity."

Janis found that a very odd thing for the older man to say.

She sat on the porch with her mother, and watched the men leave. "What's going on, Mom?"

"The young couple next door, Janis. They were murdered last night. Dean and Donna. Murdered! Right next door to us."

"Murdered!"

"Yes. Quite horribly, one of the officers said."

"I'm hungry."

Connie looked at her daughter. Children just don't understand, she thought. They watch brutality on TV every day while they munch on chips or eat a pizza. They just don't understand.

"Go fix some cereal, Janis. And don't—do not!—leave the house. Tell your brother to stay inside."

"He's still asleep."

"Must be the sea air."

No, Janis thought, he prowls all night. But she kept that to herself. It wasn't anything new. Paul had been doing that for several years. "Yes, ma'am. The sea air."

Before she could take the first mouthful of cornflakes, from the kitchen window, she saw her father rush out of the cottage next door and vomit onto the sand.

She dumped the cereal, and went back out on the porch, to sit beside her mother.

"Must be really gross in that house," she said.

"I'm sure it's horrible."

"Maybe Freddie left Elm Street and came to the islands," Janis suggested.

Connie looked at her daughter. "You may go inside now, and take your suggestions with you. That is not a request. Take your bath. We have to start thinking about packing."

"Yes, ma'am. What do I do if Norman Bates is in the shower?"

"Janis!"

"Just asking. I'm gone!"

Connie watched as Mark walked slowly back to their cottage. His face was very pale. She rose, and fixed him a glass of ice water. Lots of ice.

Mark sat down, took the ice water, and drank deeply. "Horrible. I can truthfully say I have never seen anything like it. And I sincerely hope I never see anything like it again."

He shuddered.

"Were they shot, Mark?"

"No. That would have been easier to take, I think. They were hacked to pieces, I guess. Looked to me like they were literally torn to bits. The bedroom is like a slaughter pen." His stomach rumbled. "Their . . . intestines were hanging everywhere." He belched. "Their heads were ripped off, or cut off, and stuck up on the bedposts. The walls were splattered with blood. Bits of sand were sticking to the walls and the sheets. Very bloody sand."

"Sand?"

"Yes. The inspector thinks they went for a midnight swim and were surprised by intruders when they returned. But what was odd was the

35

amount of blood. I mentioned that there should have been more, but the inspector just grunted. I'm sure there should have been more blood."

Connie looked over at the death house. "Will this delay our leaving?"

"I asked that. The inspector said he doesn't think so. He'll be over to take our statements and verify our address, but he made it clear that we're not suspects."

"That's nice of him," Connie said drily.

"He will go through our cottage, though, and check our possessions, as he put it."

"I suppose he has to do that."

"It's his job, honey."

The inspector was very thorough. Very. And very polite as he went about his business inside, while half-a-dozen officers poked and prowled outside and under the cottage by the whispering sea.

Neither the inspector nor his men found anything. "Not that we expected to," he hastened to add, with a smile. "It's just something we had to do, due to the proximity of the cottages, don't you know?"

"Right," Connie said. She wasn't sure she liked this inspector; but then, her associations with stateside police officers had been very limited. She was friendly with the chief of police back home, but Mike wasn't nearly so officious as the inspector.

But then, she finally concluded, maybe the man isn't officious. Perhaps he's just very good at his job.

"Now, then," the inspector said, "you are planning to leave day after tomorrow, is that correct?"

"That's right," Mark said.

"Ah, good! I mean, I'm not implying I'm glad to see you leave; it's just that there is a New York City police officer coming in. Correction, a retired police officer. Rather young to be retired. My word, he's only forty-three. But, no matter. He's coming in this evening. He's the brother of the slain woman. Donna. This man may wish to speak to both of you." He looked at Mark and Connie. "Is that acceptable to you?"

It was.

"Fine. After we remove the bodies, my men will seal off the cottage, and a guard will be posted. Someone will be close-by around the clock. For your protection." He smiled at Janis, then lifted his eyes to Mark. "I thank you all for your cooperation. I am, of course, dreadfully sorry for this awful business. We'll be seeing each other again. Oh, by the by, Mr. Kelly . . . how did you injure your hand?"

Embarrassed and red-faced, Mark told the inspector the truth of the matter.

Paul listened, a smug smile on his face.

The inspector smiled. "Yes, quite. I checked the clinic, of course. I never like to leave loose ends dangling. It's so . . . untidy, don't you know? Well, good day."

Paul smiled as he wolfed down his huge bowl of cereal. The inspector gave him a rather queer look, arched one eyebrow, and then left, without another word.

Mark and Connie did not catch the look, but Janis did, and she understood it. Paul was as cold-blooded as a shark; nothing about the awful murders had upset him. But then, Janis recalled, Paul had expressed his dislike for Dean and Donna several times. She had paid no attention to it, then, for Paul hated everybody.

"I bet it was bloody and gory and sloppy in that cottage," Paul said.

"I don't want to talk about it," his father said. "Good God, Paul, how can you sit there and grin about it?"

The boy's grin widened. "Can I have some bacon and eggs? Real runny eggs. With lots and lots of ketchup." He laughed strangely and rocked back and forth in his chair. Then his gaze locked with his father's. "How's your hand, Daddy?"

Leo Corigliano had pulled the pin on his career in the NYPD after twenty years on the job. He had risen fast: five years in uniform, and then fifteen years as a detective. He had retired a lieutenant. And not everyone was unhappy about his retiring. Leo enforced the law. Period. He rocked boats. It didn't matter a damn to him who he arrested. From Hizzoner's office on down. Get him on a case and you couldn't shake him loose. He never closed an unsolved file. He just made copies of the paperwork and took it home with him, to work on during his off-time.

He solved a lot of cases others gave up on, because the department was overworked and understaffed, or they were pulled off the case. Sometimes for political reasons, mostly for legitimate ones.

Leo tried to get on with Internal Affairs. But he didn't. Everybody knew he hated a dirty cop.

He had never married. His job was his wife, his

lover, his mistress. There had never been room in his life for a woman on any permanent basis. And though he always had girlfriends, he never got too serious with any of them.

He was of medium height, medium build, medium weight. Not a lady-killer, but not unattractive. His eyes were blue, his hair prematurely salt and pepper. He had killed two people in the line of duty, wounded four. And he'd spent two years in the Army. Two tours of duty in 'Nam, as an MP. He really did not have to work. His parents had died when he was twenty-one, and his sister, Donna, was ten. Leo had raised her. She had been more daughter to him than sister. Their parents had been moderately well off, and all the money and property had gone to Leo and Donna. Then it was discovered that the elder Corigliano had taken out an insurance policy on himself and his wife, many years ago. For half a million. Paid double if death was accidental. Which the Coriglianos' had been.

Leo found himself with a lot of money on his hands. He set up a trust fund for Donna, and played the market with his share. The broker got lucky, and Leo and Donna got wealthier.

Upon retirement, Leo set up a private investigation firm, and worked just as hard at that as he had as a gold shield. In less than a year's time, Leo had more business than he and his operatives could handle. They did no keyhole peeping.

Leo Corigliano. A tough cop. A loner. A man who appeared untouchable, cold.

"This Mark Kelly," Leo asked the inspector, "his

story check out?"

"Oh, yes. Clinic records support it. Mark Kelly owns a thriving business in some town with an incomprehensible and unpronounceable name, in Arizona. His wife is a well-known writer. Does those dreadful romance things. The American authorities were quite helpful in this. The Kellys are squeaky clean. All but one of them."

Leo waited. He had dealt with the British before. He knew they loved suspense.

"The boy, Paul. The police chief in this town, whose name I cannot pronounce, and I am astonished that anyone else can"—he spelled it out—"Tepehuanes is as close as I can get, was quite helpful. Seems the boy has given his parents trouble for years. And he's only eight. Almost nine. Nothing serious, mind you. He's just a disagreeable little tyke. I could get little more from the man. You Americans are so close-mouthed about your juveniles."

"Far too close-mouthed. There's no such thing as a bad kid, you know. It's all society's fault."

"Do you believe that, Mr. Corigliano?"

"Hell, no!"

"Good."

"What else did the chief say about the boy?"

"His words?"

"Yes."

"I finally got out of him that his juvenile officers had picked the boy up several times. Skipping school, complaints from other parents that the child was a bully, that he killed small domestic animals. The chief said he wouldn't trust the boy in church, and wouldn't believe what he said if he was in the

40

middle of a Bible factory."

"Sounds like a real nice kid. And, of course, the parents don't know how much of this is going on?"

"That is correct."

"Same old story." Leo patted his pockets, then remembered that he'd quit smoking. Again. "Got a cigarette?"

"Oh, yes. Dreadful habit I just can't seem to break."

The men lit up.

"I've quit a dozen times," the inspector admitted.

"Me, too."

Leo was told the why and how of Mark's hand injury.

"An eight-year-old tore the belt from his father's hand? What is this kid, half-gorilla?" He waved that away. "The blood on the bedroom floor . . . ?"

"Eh? What?"

"The blood on the bedroom floor, where Mark Kelly is supposed to have bled. You find any?"

"No. But I didn't expect to."

"You've lost me, Inspector."

"I made only a quick check of the floor. I plan to have a team in the moment the Kellys leave. You know as well as I do that no matter how you scrub, you can't get it all. It's still typeable."

Leo nodded. "Then you're not buying the Kellys' story?"

"Oh, I don't think the mother and father had anything to do with it. And it would have been physically impossible for the children to have done that."

"Children can lift a machete, too, Inspector."

41

"Oh, quite. But it wasn't done with a machete."

Again, Leo waited.

The inspector sighed. "This is not easy for me, Mr. Corigliano—"

"Leo, please."

"Very well, Leo. Stanford for me. Old family name. I . . . ah, would not recommend you view the bodies. They have been positively identified. By a number of people and by their drivers' licenses. They had friends here, Leo. They met here last year. You might not have known that."

"Were the Kellys here last year?"

"No. They have never been here. At least not under that name. Leo"—he leaned forward—"the Kellys didn't do it. Dean and Donna Mansfield were literally ripped apart. Torn apart. There was not a clean cut to be found. And not nearly enough blood."

"What happened to the blood?"

Stanford shrugged.

"What do you have on these islands with the strength to tear people apart in the manner you just described to me?"

"Nothing."

Leo decided to let that drop for a moment. "Prints?"

"Many. So far, they all belonged to the Mansfields or the cleaning people."

Leo stood up. "Let's go see the bodies."

"Now? Really, Leo! It's the middle of the night. And I'm bending the rules by asking you not to subject yourself to this unpleasantness."

Leo stared him down. The inspector sighed. Stood up. "Oh, very well. This way. We'll take my car." He looked at Leo. "Be advised, their heads were torn from their bodies and stuck up on the bedposts."

"Not cut off?"

"No. Torn off."

"Muscles and tendons stretched and ripped." It was not a question.

"Hideously so."

"Let's go."

Leo took it all without changing expression. The inspector watched his face and marveled at his control.

Either that, or Leo was an emotional brick.

Without taking his eyes off what was left of his sister, Leo said, "She was worth a lot of money, Inspector. So you'd better put me on your suspect list. She hadn't had time to change her will."

"In this day of computers, it takes about fifteen minutes to check someone's financial standing, when governments cooperate. We have an excellent rapport with the American authorities, so I put you on the list and then took you off in less than an hour's time."

"Yes, quite." Leo gently mimicked the inspector. "Drugs, you know."

"Yes, quite." Stanford understood that Leo was joking to hide his grief.

"That's the last of my family, Inspector. The end of the line. Except for some cousins I've never met and have no desire to know. I'm not even sure where they live." He was staring at his sister's head. The body had been more or less reconstructed.

43

Stanford said nothing.

"You can cover it up. When your people are through . . . well, we'll talk about shipment later." He looked more closely before the sheet covered her.

"What are you looking for, Leo?"

"Bite marks. But all I can see are bruises. And the body is blue-white."

"There is no blood, Leo."

"Drop the other shoe, Inspector."

"When I think you're ready for it."

"You're the boss. I have to accept it."

"Thank you."

Outside, away from the smell of chemicals and the smell of death, Leo breathed deeply of sea air perfumed by flowers. "It's a beautiful place, Stanford."

"It is that. And it would be more so if not for a recent resurgence of an odious and ancient rite."

"Oh?"

"Vodun."

"What's that?"

The inspector glanced at him. "Voodoo."

Leo did not meet with the Kelly family. He rented a car, bought a pair of high-powered binoculars, and found a place where he could observe them.

He had called his office. When he returned to the mainland, he would know everything there was to know about the Kelly family. He would know things about them they had forgotten.

He watched them pack, watched them leave; and he was waiting at the cottage when Stanford and his

44

team arrived.

"You don't mind if I watch, do you, Inspector?"

"Not at all."

The inspector set his men to work and then went over to Leo. Corigliano watched the team work for a few minutes, then nodded his head and walked away. They were as good a crew as any he'd seen.

"You decided not to interview the Kellys, Leo?"

"I'll catch up with them in Tepehuanes. I'd as soon they didn't know who I am . . . yet."

"They didn't do it."

"No." Leo spoke slowly. "I don't think they did either. But the boy makes the hair on the back of my neck stand up." He glanced at the inspector. "Do you know that boy, Paul, prowls half the night?"

"My man reported no such thing, and he was on guard both nights since the incident."

"The kid is slick. I was watching from the brush just above the cottage. He waited, both nights, until your guard made his walk-around. Then he slipped out his bedroom window and hightailed it over that little crest there." Leo pointed. "A dune, I guess you'd call it."

"Did you follow him, Leo?"

"I tried. But that little sneak is good. He lost me both nights. I do know he met a tall man and a very shapely woman. Just up the beach." He pointed again. "That way."

Stanford was silent for a moment. "A tall man and a shapely lady. Were they black?"

Leo scratched his chin. "I think they were. Yeah, I'm sure of it."

"And they did what, Leo?" The inspector was

45

writing in a small notepad.

"I couldn't get that close. I assume they talked. I don't know about what. I do know the man and woman Paul met are the quickest people I've ever encountered. Blink your eyes and they're gone. Damnedest thing I ever saw."

"So far," Stanford said ominously. He ignored Leo's quizzical look. "Was the man wearing a shirt?"

"Ah . . . no. He wasn't. And neither of them left any footprints, either."

"No. They never do."

"You know these people?"

"I know of them. They pop up now and again. Searching for something. Or someone. I think they've found that someone this time."

"Stanford, you're sounding a bit weird. You want to tell me what's going on?"

With a sigh, Stanford hauled out a box of cigarettes and lit up, offering one to Leo. Leo produced a pack of his own, and both men smiled grimly.

"The legend says the man and woman you saw were killed around the turn of the century. They were, and still are, so the stories go, the high priest and priestess of a voodoo cult. Very unsavory people. It is said they come from the earth, and can return to it at will. No prints in the sand. And because they come from the earth, that is where their executioners made their mistake: they buried the bodies instead of burning them and sealing the ashes. Louis Mantine and Nicole became one with the earth . . . again."

Leo was staring at Stanford as if the inspector had gone around the bend.

"You really believe that crap!"

"It isn't crap. Black magic works. I've seen it done. Seen what happens. But this is much more than black magic. The cult of the sand people has existed as long as there have been inhabitants on these islands. Hundreds of years. Maybe thousands."

"The . . . sand people?"

"Yes. They usually succeed only in frightening the wits out of people, but there have been other rather macabre murders—among tourists, that is. God only knows how many have occurred back in the interior and on the other islands, but I've run into two other such cases since I've been on the force. A young couple in 1960, and another murder in 1974. These were rumored to have been the work of the sand people." Stanford was silent for a moment, the muscles in his jaw bunching. His eyes had gone hard as flint. "The MO in all cases, including that of your sister and her husband, is identical. There will be few clues, Leo. Believe it."

"Now, wait just a second. Are you telling me that some sort of . . . creatures murdered Dean and Donna?"

"We don't know, Leo. We don't know what they are. No one has ever seen them and lived to tell about it. At least not that we know of."

"But you just said tourists have had the wits scared out of them."

"Rustlings in the night. Strange misshapen forms. Screams that have been recorded—animal experts say they don't come from human or animal sources. Elusive shapes that possess unbelievable strength, and seem to have the ability to vanish at will. Into the earth."

47

"I don't believe I'm hearing this from you!"

The inspector said nothing in rebuttal. He sat and stared out at the calm blue waters.

"All right then, Stanford, tell me this: Why hasn't this been covered in the press?"

"Don't be ridiculous, man!" Stanford cut his eyes to Leo. "Our economy depends on tourism. That's why."

"All right. I'll accept that. But I meant in U.S. papers."

"We usually sit on this news for several days. Perhaps a week or more. Sometimes forever. By the time American journalists learn of it, if they do, it's stale—according to the standards of American journalism. No one wishes to read old news. And this is only the third time such a thing has occurred in nearly thirty years."

"That you know of, or wish to tell me about."

"Yes. Quite right. There have been, ah, other unsolved murders. On the other islands. But you must remember this: There are over seven hundred oolitic islands—limestone—and more than twenty-four hundred rocks and cays in the group. In a seven-hundred-sixty-mile arc. God alone knows what goes on on the tiny islands."

"I hear that boats disappear along with their crews and passengers."

"Indeed they do. Not very often. But it does occur every now and then."

"And never a trace."

"Never a trace."

"Tell me, to lighten the moment, about the sand people."

48

"I assure you, Leo, there is nothing light about them. Do you think you were spotted by the man and woman, or the boy?"

Leo hesitated. "I'm . . . not sure. I got the feeling I was."

"If you felt you were, you probably were. So be very, very careful."

"You really believe in this hoodoo, don't you?"

"Yes, I do. And you'd better start believing in it, too."

Leo said nothing.

"Inspector!" It was one of the investigative team.

"What do you have, Jamison?"

"Nothing, sir. Absolutely nothing. Not one trace of blood to be found in the bedroom."

"Thank you, Jamison. Keep looking, lad."

"Yes, sir."

Leo looked at Stanford. The inspector's expression was thoughtful as he sat on the porch.

"You said there would be no blood. That means the accident didn't occur or it occurred in another part of the house or it occurred during the murders."

"Your sister and her husband were killed between midnight and dawn. They were seen having dinner at eight at the inn. Very happy. No signs of a fight of any kind. And the hospital records are very clear, as is the doctor's memory: Mark Kelly's hand was treated approximately fourteen to sixteen hours before the murders were reported."

"Who reported them, Stanford?"

"I was afraid you would ask that. You know I don't have to tell you."

"I'm aware of that. But why would you refuse?"

The inspector stood up and gazed out over the flat blue of the sea. He exhaled softly and faced Leo. "A young boy with a deep hollow voice, Leo. He did not give his name. His accent gave him away as American."

"Paul Kelly." It was not a question.

"In all probability, yes."

"And by now, he's boarding a plane in Miami, bound for Tucson."

"Probably so. I had no proof that it was the Kelly boy who murdered Dean and Donna Mansfield, so I had no reason to interrogate him. When I knocked on the cottage door, Mr. Kelly said he and his wife had been up for about an hour and the kids were still asleep. It was early. Sevenish. Oh, I suppose I could have mucked about, stirring up this and that, questioning the boy—all to no avail, of course."

"Now give me the real reason, Stanford."

The inspector smiled. "You're a good copper. Leo, when I looked into that boy's eyes, I looked into the depths of Hell. He's a ticking time bomb. The chief in that odd-named town told me the boy is in a very advanced class at school. Brilliant. He also told me, off the record, that in his opinion the boy is nuts!"

"You think that's so?"

"I'm no judge of that, but I'd wager that the boy is so intelligent he could fool the best of child psychologists."

"Uh-huh. So you just let him wing off, and handed the problem back to the Americans?"

"I say now, Leo! That's such a blunt way of putting it, don't you think?"

"Oh, I don't blame you, Stanford. Not at all."

"Thank you."

"I've done the same, with other states, many times."

"I rather thought as much."

"Besides, you knew I'd be going after the kid, didn't you?"

"I rather suspected it."

"And you want to come along, don't you, Inspector?"

"As I said before, Leo, you're a good copper. Well"—he sighed—"I have time due me. I haven't taken a leave in years. Besides, I've never been to the wild West. Yes, I might join up with you. Take a working vacation, you might say."

"You're holding back, Stanford."

"Oh, I want to be sure about the boy, that's all."

"Uh-huh. Would you bring your wife? I noticed your wedding band."

"My wife . . . died some years ago. I have been married to my work. And I am known as something of an expert on voodoo, the black arts. That might come in handy."

"For a fact, Stanford, the boy could not have torn my sister and her husband apart by himself."

"For a fact, Leo."

"He had to have help, if he had anything to do with it."

"Also a fact. And yes, he did have help."

"If he did it."

"He did it." The words were grimly spoken.

"You let loose just enough to keep me intrigued, Stanford. I'm curious to know what else you're holding back—other than your last name."

51

"It's Willingston. Leo, it will take me a week to ten days to get my leave of absence processed. If you go it alone before I get there, be very, very careful. You're a skeptic. I was born in these islands. I've seen sights and rituals that an outsider wouldn't understand. But I do. And I saw something in that boy's eyes that I've seen only once before . . . before I killed that person."

"What, Stanford?"

"Satan looking back at me."

THREE

Tepehuanes, situated on the banks of the San Pedro River, was an old, old town only recently discovered by those wishing to escape the city life of Phoenix and Tucson. It was located almost exactly halfway between, and just slightly east of, those cities.

The price tag was high for a home in Tepehuanes, but the residents didn't mind that or the drive to either city.

And the town soon became filled with people with incomes of six figures, professionals. Doctors, lawyers, upper-level management types.

The police department was one of the best in the state, and one of the toughest. But it stuck to the letter of the law. The chief would not win a popularity contest.

Each district of Tepehuanes had specified what it wanted in a police chief and what it would expect from the person chosen. And when a chief had been selected, from hundreds of applicants—a man who had given the governor a ticket and had put his own brother in jail for DWI—he'd been placed under a four-year contract. The contract practically gave him carte blanche when it came to enforcing the law. No brother-in-lawing, no old-boy stuff; no selective immunity.

A Phoenix reporter came to Tepehuanes to do a story shooting down the system of hiring police chiefs by contract and giving them a free hand in law enforcement. The reporter called the place a police state. But the article was never written because, when surveyed, ninety-two percent of the people in Tepehuanes thought the chief and his force were doing a fantastic job, and hoped he would stay on forever.

The word quickly went out: if you want to cause trouble, don't do it in Tepehuanes.

The local DA, Don Davis, was positively delighted with the chief of police and with his methods of enforcing the law. In fact, Davis and Mike Bambridge became good friends, and played golf together every Thursday afternoon.

But the county sheriff, who was elected, and therefore had to court everybody whether he liked it or not, was not delighted about the whole business. He became downright unhappy when his wife's brother was arrested and the chief and the DA refused to deal. His wife's brother served thirty days in the slammer and had his driver's license pulled for a year.

It was just about that time when the chief requested that his people be commissioned as county deputies, thereby giving them wider authority.

Then the sheriff's wife's brother was picked up again. DWI and no driver's license.

"Let's deal," the sheriff suggested.

"Let's don't," the chief replied. "I don't make

54

exceptions. Shall I call a press conference? I'm taping this."

Gritting his dentures and swearing, the sheriff signed the commission cards.

The sheriff and the chief were not real close.

Leo Corigliano read the reports during stops on the drive out to Tepehuanes. He concluded that the sheriff, while probably a damned good lawman, was also a politician; but Mike was Eagle-Scout straight, and busted anyone who broke the law.

Leo liked Mike and felt sorry for the sheriff even before meeting them, for he knew each man had a job to do, and a difficult job even under the best of circumstances. There were too few Mikes in law enforcement and too few communities like Tepehuanes to back them up.

And that, Leo knew, was the heart of the problem: the communities. They said they wanted law and order—but not when it came to their friends, their relatives, and their kids.

Inspector Stanford Willingston had not been entirely truthful with Leo, but he felt Leo knew that and accepted it.

Stanford knew he would be wise to just let the matter drop, for he sensed that Mantine and Nicole were no longer anywhere near the islands. He had a notion the long-dead voodoo king and queen were about to pop up in Arizona.

That would free the islands of them for a while,

and drop the entire matter into American hands.

But Stanford could not just turn his back on the matter. Leo Corigliano was too good a cop to face such a horror alone. And horror was what the good people of that unpronounceable Western town were about to experience.

How, and in what form, Stanford could not know. But the sand he'd found sticking to the walls in the death house had given him a pretty good idea of what to expect.

The prospect chilled him.

What better place than Arizona to continue the horror?

Another thing Stanford hadn't mentioned to Leo was that less than an hour after his flight took off for the States, the death cottage would be turned into a roaring inferno, after being soaked with gasoline. Then every scrap of charred debris would be carefully scooped up, towed far out to sea, and dumped in where the water was deepest.

That done, Stanford Willingston stood before his wife's grave and made a promise to the silence.

"I shall not fail this time, my darling. I shall have my revenge. And I shall set you free. I promise you."

A priest stood a few yards away, a worried look on his face. "Fourteen years is a long time to carry such hate in your heart, Stanford."

Without turning around, Stanford said, "Did you bring the materials I requested?"

"Of course. I put them in your car. Are you leaving today?"

"This evening. I have made provisions for her grave to be looked after, Simon."

"You speak as if you will not be returning."

The inspector merely looked at the priest and then pointed to a second stone, new and neatly in line with his wife's headstone. Stanford's name and the year of his death had already been chiseled into the marble. 1988.

Inspector Willingston shook the priest's hand and, without another word, walked out of the tiny cemetery behind the church.

Few were buried in the tiny space.

For a very good reason.

"Creep!" Janis whispered, after her brother had closed the door to his room.

She thought her brother had been weird before they'd gone to the islands. But now! God, he was acting so odd it was unreal.

Openly defiant to his parents, all the time, Paul was refusing to do anything they asked, right down to taking a bath. Most of the time he smelled bad. It was like he was, well, deliberately trying to pick a fight with his father and mother.

And that just didn't make a bit of sense to Janis.

She concluded that her brother was just being his usual jerky self. Only a bit more so.

She walked up the hall and into the indoor garden of the Kellys' spacious home, which was set on a mesa just above the town of Tepehuanes. From there she stepped into the den, then the dining room. She paused at the entrance to the kitchen, listening to her parents talk.

"His behavior is worse than ever." Her mother was

57

speaking. "It's World War Three just to get him to bathe. I don't see how he can stand himself. He stinks!"

"Yeah," Mark replied. "I can't help but notice." That was said so drily Janis pictured some of the ice in his drink melting. "I think if he walks through the garden one more time the plants will begin to die."

Connie chuckled at that, but humorlessly. "Do what you have to do, Mark." Her voice was weary. "I've run out of options."

"I don't know what to do."

"But I thought you wanted to take him to see a child psychologist."

"I did. I do. But he's faking all this, Connie. Have you noticed his behavior lately? Around other people? He's beginning to act, well, goofy. And *act* is the key word, love. He turns off and on like a faucet. He's up to something, I know it, but damned if I can figure out what it is."

"You don't think a doctor could pinpoint the cause? They're trained to spot things, behavioral patterns, that parents can't see. Maybe we're just too close to him."

"It's worth a try." Mark exhaled slowly. "I guess," he added.

The shattering of glass brought them to their feet; Janis was already running toward the source of the disturbance. She began to scream when she saw what Paul was doing.

He had taken a poker from the fireplace set and was smashing every window in the indoor garden, alternately laughing and howling insanely as he did so.

58

"Paul!" his father yelled, and ran toward him. "Damn it, Paul, stop it!"

The boy suddenly fell to the stone floor, and began to jerk spasmodically, drumming his heels on the floor. Slobber leaked from his mouth. His eyes rolled back until only the whites were showing.

When Mark picked him up, Paul was stiff, rigid as a board.

"Bring the car around, Connie. Janis, go next door and stay with the Matthews. Tell them we're taking Paul to the hospital."

"Well, folks," Dr. Thomas said as he joined the Kellys in the corridor, "physically, there is nothing wrong with the boy. He is, in my opinion, perfectly healthy." The doctor brushed at his coat. Grains of sand fell to the floor. "I don't know where I got that," he muttered.

"Then, I mean . . ." Connie groped for words. "What happened to him this evening? Something had to have caused this craziness?"

Maybe, Mark thought. And maybe it was all part of a carefully planned act. But if so, why?

"I don't know," Jack Thomas said with a smile. Confuse the Parents, 1 & 2. A required course. "I've ordered a CAT scan in the morning. But it's probably nothing more than a bug the boy picked up in the islands. You haven't been back that long, you know."

The deepening in Paul's voice began in the islands, Mark thought. His defiance heightened while we were there. Or is it all my imagination?

59

"This scan you're going to do, that will tell us something?"

"Oh, yes. Physically speaking. If he has a tumor, or if something is pressing against a nerve and cutting off or interrupting messages to the brain. But, personally, I think the boy is healthy as a horse. They have some strange maladies in the islands, folks. Downright weird! Now go on home and get some rest. Paul is in good hands here, I assure you."

"Can we see him?" Connie asked.

"Sure. But he's sleeping. After Dr. Clineman checked him for obvious neurological symptoms, he gave Paul a mild sedative, a muscle relaxant, and the boy went right to sleep. His BP is right on the button. Heartbeat is solid and stable. His eyes are clear and responsive. Why don't you both check back around nine in the morning? We ought to know something by then."

The tiny grains of sand crunched under the doctor's shoes as he turned and strolled off down the hall. He hummed cheerfully.

Mark slapped at his ankle as something bit him. "What is it, Mark?"

"Sand flea, probably."

Connie said, "He's been our doctor for ages, but I still can't get used to how damned cheerful he is."

They walked out of the hospital.

It was well staffed and well equipped. Tepehuanes was a town filled with affluent people.

"Paul is faking this," Mark repeated. "As sure as there is a moon and stars, he's faking it. I can sense it."

"But why, Mark?"

There was no anger in the question, just a mother's concern for her child.

"I don't know. Maybe I shouldn't have said that. There may be something wrong with the boy. In a way I hope it is something that can be corrected by medicine or an operation. I guess I shouldn't have said that either, Connie."

"I understand what you meant, Mark. I'm hoping there is some easy answer myself."

"Well, let's hope. Say, wasn't that the little Cauldman girl in the room across the hall from Paul?"

"Yes. Her mother told me she hurt her leg while skateboarding this afternoon."

"Break it?"

"No. They're just keeping her overnight for observation. She was flying, I was told. Downhill. She's lucky she wasn't killed. I hate those damned skateboards."

"She's a pretty girl," Mark said.

"Yes, she is."

Jenny Cauldman and Paul Kelly were both in the advanced class at school.

And they hated each other.

"Come morning," Mark said, "Jenny and Paul will be screaming insults across the hall. But in this case, I'll take Paul's side. Jenny is one spoiled little girl."

"Between you and me, I agree." Connie smiled.

They got in the car and drove back home.

In the hospital, Dottie Cauldman was brushing

Jenny's hair. "Just relax, baby," she said. "Close your eyes. The sandman is on the way."

He sure was.

"He'll be here in just a minute, Jenny."

Give or take an hour or so.

"He's bringing you a present."

Uh-huh.

"It's something nice."

Well . . . ?

"And when the sandman comes, everything will be all right, you'll see."

Doubtful.

Across the hall, Paul was wide awake.

He had spat out the pill, and faked sleep.

His eyes were open, and a light shone from them. A very unnatural light.

"Loudmouthed little slut," Paul whispered, looking toward the room across the hall. "More than your leg will be hurt come morning."

A shadow moved in the darkened depths of the hospital room. From the wavy lines of the murk, a voice whispered, "Hey, little mon. You quite the actor, you know?"

Paul grinned. "Yes, I know."

"I tought your sister was gonna be de fust to die?"

"She was, but I changed my mind. After serious thought, I realized her death would draw too much attention to me."

"You good boy. Smart lak me. Now what's your plan, my mon?"

"Now we have some fun."

"I lak your fun, Paul. We gonna have lots of fun, you and me and Nicole."

62

"I hope so."

"You know who you is now, don' you, Paul?" the shadows whispered the question.

"Yes. But why?"

A dark mist moved out of the shadows to hover close to the bed, invisible to anyone who might glance into the room. "Why? Why you his son? You been his son for centuries. You his natural son. You comes back when he sends you back. Me and Nicole now, we his, well, sort of adopted children."

"And if I had not met you on the beach?"

"Way you was goin', your parents woulda pro'bly put you in some crazy house."

"Yes. I see. But after we have our fun, that might not be a bad idea. You see what I'm getting at?"

"Yeah. You smart boy. I lak dat. But I wonder if you knows de shape you is in ain't yours?"

"I suspected as much."

"Look at dis." The voice, low and menacing, was filled with yet-unseen horror.

Paul cut his eyes and smiled, enjoying the sights that filled the room.

From out of the mist, a wavy creature slowly took form; it was grotesque, hideous. Its eyes were huge and slanted, its nose was but two dripping holes. Scales covered the upper part of its face, baggy skin, gray and mottled, the lower half. Its teeth were long and needle sharp, but stained yellow and green by filth and scum. And its tongue, forked and long, slithered in and out of a near lipless mouth, blood red and dripping stinking drool.

Paul stared at the creature.

"Who is that? Is that me?"

"In a way. It's your twin brudder, boy."

Paul grinned. "Hi, brother! You want to join the party?"

The living counterpart of Paul's evil smiled grotesquely.

The misty shape that was Mantine shuddered. He had never encountered such evil as the devil-child that lay on the bed before him. If the dead could be frightened, Mantine was experiencing that sensation.

He stared at Paul, knowing that this was the true child of the Dark One, and he, or It, must be guided and protected for a time.

"I wish to review my past," Paul said. It was not phrased as a request; it was an order.

Paul's brother slipped back into the darkness of the room.

"As you wish, Little Master. Look at dis."

It was, to Paul, like looking at a TV screen; but more than that. He experienced the sensation of going through the screen of life and death, of becoming a feeling part of it.

And he knew he was in a part of Hell.

Burning flesh and wailing humans, naked and torn and bloody; and eternal flesh-bubbling. Men and women bound and chained in the most impossible of positions. Sodomy and incest, and worlds upon worlds of depravity; inhuman sexual acts that defied description.

He knew the why of it. The lives they'd lived on earth, actual or wished, they were forced to endure forever.

Paul licked his dry lips, loving every scene revealed through the eons, wavering painfully out of the mist

64

of past life.

He saw humans caught in cruel animal traps, misshapen furry forms forever skinning them alive.

He witnessed naked men fighting to the death in round bloody pits, only to rise again and again, to fight and die over and over, forever.

Paul laughed, loving each scene.

And he watched himself, walking through the timeless, silently screaming horror. He was not in his earth-form, but he knew he was looking at himself. There was a tall and not-quite-visible shape by his side as he walked.

Paul tried to get a better look at the shape. But its form kept shifting and altering, making a clear image impossible.

Time shifted for Paul, spinning him backward over centuries, always with that dark shape close by him. Scenes of torture and rape and ugliness were seared into his brain. He had never, in his present life, imagined that human beings could be treated so and still manage to stay alive.

Forever.

So much, so quickly, was being returned to his brain, his very receptive brain, that it all soon became quite mundane to him.

And Paul accepted what he was and what he had been for countless ages.

He watched his birth.

Watched himself and his brother tear from the womb, change shapes, alternate back and forth.

Then he realized the danger of it all.

"One cannot live without the other," he declared softly.

"True and not true," Mantine said mysteriously.

"So I am what I am. But wouldn't it have been much easier just to tell me?"

"Dat ain't de way it's done, Master. De fodder has lots of children. But most of dem can't handle what dey sees. I been waitin' a long, long time for you, Master. A long time."

"Well, you've found me. Or I've found you. Or we have found each other."

"True."

"Now what?"

"You got a blank book, mon. De pages needs to be filled up."

"I have a free hand."

"True."

"But I am not immortal?"

"Not yets."

"I can be killed?"

"Not in no permanent way."

"Explain."

"He is your fodder. He can send you back if he choose to do so. He has sent you back to do his will."

"Ah! I might not come back in this shape."

"Dat's true."

"We'll have fun. Starting now, Nicole."

She laughed softly as she stepped out of the mist and walked to Paul's side. Her fingers found him; he felt the rush of cool air on his skin.

Nicole bent her head.

Paul began to scream silently as the dark mouth opened and consumed him.

FOUR

"Her mind is gone," Dr. Clineman announced to those gathered around the bed of Jenny Cauldman. The child had been strapped down to keep her from flinging herself onto the tiled floor.

Mrs. Cauldman, too, had been hospitalized, knocked out with a strong sedative.

Jenny just vaguely resembled the girl she had been a few hours before.

"Her hair is gray and old and brittle," Dr. Mary Fletcher observed. "She is nine years old going on a hundred and nine."

Jenny's face was lined and wrinkled, simianlike. The child was now an old woman.

"That is impossible!" Dr. Thomas blurted out, pointing to the creature that, a short time before, had been so young.

"She was raped," Clineman informed the already shocked gathering.

"Raped!" Mary Fletcher said. "In this hospital? In that condition?"

"Possibly before her . . . change," Clineman said softly.

"Could the rape have brought on the aging?" Thomas tossed out the question to anyone.

Clineman picked up on it. "I have no idea. I am not even certain this . . . creature is Jenny Cauldman. I've ordered tests run."

"Her mother is certain it's Jenny."

Clineman sighed in resignation. What he was seeing was impossible. But there it was.

Hideous.

Mind-boggling.

There was a knock on the closed door.

"Come in," Clineman responded.

The chief of police entered, dressed in plain clothes, his Western hat in his hands. He looked at the young/old person strapped down on the bed.

"Good Jesus Christ!" he whispered. "What in the name of God is that?"

"Nine-year-old Jenny Cauldman," Dr. Thomas informed him.

"The rape victim I called you about," Clineman added.

Mike Bambridge found a chair in the crowded room, and sat down.

Jenny babbled and slobbered and feebly fought the leather restraints.

Mike opened his mouth to speak—several times. Nothing came out. He had personally seen to the skateboard accident, had worked with the EMTs on placing Jenny in the ambulance.

He stared at the creature on the bed.

Finally he found his voice. "That is not Jenny Cauldman."

"I'm afraid it is, Chief." Clineman hated to admit

it. To himself and to the others. "And I think you will agree that news of this . . . development should not leak out. Not until we can pinpoint what happened, what caused this . . . tragedy. If we ever do," he added grimly.

Mike stood up. He did not want to look at the thing on the bed. He forced himself to do it. "I'll need a rape kit completed."

"I'll see to that," Dr. Fletcher said.

Mike looked at her nametag, among other things. Mary B. Fletcher. He wondered what the *B* stood for.

The doctor looked at the cop. An attractive man, she thought. Sort of hard around the eyes, but—she finally found the word—dependable-looking.

"Thank you, Dr. Fletcher. And I certainly agree with Dr. Clineman about keeping a lid on this thing." He reluctantly took his eyes from Mary and clamped them on Clineman. "We'll get to the rape in a minute. But what caused this?" He pointed at the slobbering figure on the bed.

"I honestly don't know, Chief."

"Some sort of reaction to a drug, maybe?"

The doctors, all of them, smiled tolerantly, and then Clineman said, "No, Chief."

"Why do you say that?"

"She's been in here twice before this. Both times for minor injuries. Each time she received the same pain medication. She received that medication yesterday, and once last night. It is commonly called aspirin."

"No other drugs at all?"

"No."

"Well, there goes that layman's theory." He looked at Jenny. "I have to touch all bases."

69

"I understand, Chief."

Mike nodded. "No one heard her cry out last night?"

"No one reported anything unusual. I've had a list made of all personnel on duty last night. It's ready for you."

"Thank you. I want the semen checked and stored—in case our rapist strikes again."

"Of course."

"When was the last time she was checked?"

"The floor nurse checked on her at four this morning. That's when she found her in her . . . present condition. The girl was unable to speak for about an hour, according to the nurse. I got here at about five-thirty. By that time, the resident had found the stained sheets. We called you about six."

"And nobody has reported hearing anything unusual?"

"No."

"Odd. That look on the girl's . . . the person's face. I've never seen anything quite like it. It looks like, well, she was scared out of her wits, and her expression has been frozen that way."

"It does look that way, Chief."

"Did you save the sheets?"

"Oh, yes. And the sand and what we found on the bottom sheet. They appear to be some sort of scales."

"Sand? And . . . what?"

"Scales. They look like reptile scales. But of course, that's nonsense."

"You saved the sand and the scales?"

"In the ME's office, Chief."

"Sand and scales," Mike muttered. "Weird." He

looked at Jenny, thinking that the changes in her were even weirder! He lifted his eyes to Clineman. "When may I speak with the girl, Doctor?"

"Whenever God decides, Chief. Right now, Jenny Cauldman is a babbling idiot!"

Mike sat in his office and studied the report from the county medical examiner's office.

The semen was neither human nor animal.

The scales did not match those of any known creature, living or extinct.

Mike leaned back in his chair and took another sip of coffee.

The ME had to be mistaken. Somebody had screwed up in the lab; that was all.

He turned off his lamp and went home.

Jenny's mother died during the night. She got up from her bed, ran naked, screaming, down the corridor, howling that a demon from hell was after her. Then she took a header right out of the third-floor window.

Dr. Clineman asked the ME to check whether she'd been raped.

She had.

The semen was checked.

It matched the semen found in her daughter.

Her bed was checked.

Sand and scales.

Dottie Cauldman had taken her dive at three in the morning. At three-thirty, a gritty-eyed Mike Bambridge was sipping coffee out of a paper cup and trying to wake up as he stood in the parking lot of Tepehuanes General, watching Dottie being scraped and peeled off the hood of a Porsche.

The chief had not yet been told about the sand and the scales.

"Chief?" a detective called to him.

Mike walked over to the blood- and brain-splattered car. "What've you got?"

The detective shone his light onto Dottie's head.

The hair was flecked with sand and bits of scale.

There was no way to sit on this story. The double rape made the front pages for a couple of days, but there was no mention of sand or scales. Mike and the doctors sat on that bit of evidence. Public interest waned after a couple of days, and the story faded out.

Every male who'd been in the hospital at the times of the rapes was given a PSE test by the best psychological stress evaluator operator in the state.

Naturally, they all passed.

No one had thought to give Paul Kelly the test. He was only eight years old.

There were no reports of strangers in the hospital on either night. Mike didn't think he'd find anything of substance there, for the hospital security was very good. Anyone coming in after nine had to log in and out.

Everybody already there was checked out.

Besides, what the hell were they looking for? Somebody who had scaly skin covered with sand?

Mike Bambridge and his people had hit a stone wall.

Leo picked up Stanford at the airport in Phoenix and they checked into a motel at the edge of town, on the highway to Tepehuanes. Leo had been in town for several days, so he brought the inspector up to date.

"The *houngan* has been busy, hasn't he?" Stanford remarked.

"The who?"

"*Houngan.* Means a voodoo priest." He smiled at the pained expression on Leo's face. "Don't make light of it, Leo. Mantine is very, very good. But actually, *houngan* is a misnomer. A *houngan* deals mostly in white magic. Good magic. Mantine is a devil. He was a master of the black arts long before such things were really known except to a small group in Haiti and the Congo. And he is even more powerful now than he was when alive."

Leo sighed. He didn't want to ask, but he knew he had to. "Why is that?"

"Because he's been on the other side of light for so long. On the Dark Side. He's been learning at the cloven hooves of Satan."

Leo lit up before answering. "You still haven't convinced me, Stanford."

"I won't, Leo. But Mantine will. Believe me. He's found a devil-child in Paul. Bet on it."

"A devil-child?"

"Yes. According to legend, Mantine has been looking for a true Devil's offspring. Actually the flesh and blood of Satan. The child is always marked. Left arm, very high up, near the point of the shoulder. Did you ever see Paul without his shirt on, Leo?''

"Come to think of it, no.''

"Neither did I. And I asked people up and down the beach whether the boy ever swam. He didn't. And he never once took off his shirt. Several bathers noticed. They'd thought it was odd.''

"Maybe he has a skin condition?''

"Maybe.''

"You want us to march up to Chief Bambridge armed only with rumors and legends about hoodoo and sand people?''

The inspector smiled. "It's far too early for anything like that. He'd probably have us committed. No, I have a better plan. We might use a child, or several children—''

Leo narrowed his eyes at that. "Ah, Stanford, if you walk up to some nine- or ten-year-old kid, a total stranger, and suggest the child spy for you, his parents are gonna flip out, call the cops, and have you arrested—if the father doesn't shoot you on the spot.''

"Leo, I wasn't going to be that obvious about it.''

"Fooling with juveniles is risky, even for cops. Most cops don't like to mess with kids.''

"Are you serious?''

"Very, man.''

Stanford was exasperated. "For God's sake, Leo! I have no intention of abusing the children.''

"I know that, and you know that. The cops don't. Not a good plan, Stanford; not unless you approach

74

the parents first."

Stanford muttered something very profane and highly uncomplimentary to Americans. "Then we have no choice but to go to the police. Good Lord! Can't an adult talk to a child here?"

"A stranger can't. Forget it, Stanford. Now stop cursing Americans and let's get on with it. What kids did you have in mind? As if I couldn't guess."

"Janis Kelly, for one."

"Good choice. But how do you know she would agree to spy on her brother?"

Stanford smiled. "Because he despises her and she is afraid of him."

Leo glanced at the inspector. "You came up with that after only a couple of visits?"

"Actually, no. I visited the Kellys several times, but I had a female operative on the beach. You'd be surprised what she learned in a short time."

Leo again glanced at the inspector, a smile on his lips and respect in his eyes. "You're a sneaky bastard, Stanford."

"Yes, I am. Thank you, Leo. It goes with the territory." He opened his briefcase and took out a folder. "Now listen. This is interesting reading."

"Nothing," Mark said. "I just can't believe it. The doctors found nothing wrong with Paul."

Paul was in his room, as usual, the door closed and locked from the inside. Janis was at a friend's house; she was sleeping over, with several other girls. Mark and Connie were enjoying martinis before dinner. Paul had already eaten.

The steaks were on the grill, the potatoes in the oven, the salad made.

"Honey, we've been over and over this. Let's put it aside, please? You'll have to admit, Paul has been much better since his little . . . episode. He's even taking baths now."

"I noticed he wasn't quite so odious. Episode? Yeah. That little episode cost us a thousand bucks in repair bills. And thank God for hospitalization. But what's going on with Jenny Cauldman? She's in isolation, under guard. Her father is suing the hospital, and ranting and raving—during his more lucid moments and when he's sober. He was at the club this afternoon, getting slopped."

"Poor man. I feel sorry for him. God, Mark! He's lost his entire family. I shouldn't say that; I don't know what's wrong with Jenny."

"The doctors do, and so does Chief Bambridge. But they're not talking; they're keeping mum and maintaining a very low profile. And Ralph is not talking on his lawyer's advice. All he'll say is that it's horrible, hideous, awful. Then he starts crying. Nobody wants to be around him anymore."

"That's terrible, Mark. And no suspects in the rapes?"

"I don't think so."

"You think Paul raped the girl and her mother?" Leo's expression was very doubtful. "But he's only eight years old."

"Almost nine. And I didn't say Paul did it. I said his other being did."

76

"Which I do not understand. Not at all."

"Understand this, Leo: If I'm right, which I think I am, the boy isn't, and never has been, one of us. He's not human. And if he is a devil-child, which I believe, he has an alter shape, a form. From his homeland—"

"Homeland? What homeland?"

"Hell. Don't interrupt. The boy is—"

"Hell!"

"Yes, Leo. Like in Hades. There is no hope for him. He's beyond redemption. He must be destroyed, as distasteful as that might seem to you."

Leo stared at the inspector. "You plan to kill an eight-year-old boy!"

"You have a better idea?"

"Confine him, for Christ's sake! Kill an eight-year-old? Stanford, we don't kill children in the United States. No matter what they've done, we don't kill kids. Not legally anyway."

Stanford shrugged. "The boy is not like us, Leo. Why can't you see that? His father is Satan and he is evil. You say confine him? How?"

Leo rose and paced the motel room. Occasionally he paused and glanced at Inspector Willingston and then shook his head. "Books and movie stuff, Stanford. Even if I believed you, which I don't, do you have any idea what this Eagle-Scout chief of police is going to say about this plan of yours?"

"I don't intend to march willy-nilly into his office and announce my intentions. I don't wish to end up in the loony bin."

"Then what will you do?"

"For the moment, nothing. We'll nose around a bit, perhaps ask a few questions, behave like tourists.

Perhaps Paul will strike again.''

"Strike again." Leo sighed heavily. "While we sit here doing nothing."

"But we can't go to the chief with what we think."

Leo sat down, looked at Willingston. "All right, Stanford, level with me. Everything. Don't leave anything out. If we're going to work together, we've got to be straight with each other. I know you didn't come stateside out of the goodness of your heart, so let's have it."

Stanford picked up the phone and punched the button for room service. He ordered drinks and sandwiches, then said, "Put your feet up, Leo. Take your shoes off. Relax. It's a long story."

As is the rule nearly everywhere in the world, the kids knew more about Jenny Cauldman's condition than the adults did. Little pitchers have big ears and all that.

"She's about a thousand years old," Carla Weaver said. "All wrinkled and old and gray."

Jean Polk grimaced. "And from what I hear, she went crazy, too."

"They've got her strapped down in the nut ward." Carol Hovey fitted yet another piece into the puzzle. "Something scared her so bad she went bonkers."

"And she slobbers and hollers a lot," Melissa Patterson said; her mother was a nurse at the hospital. "Mom didn't know I was listening when she and another nurse were talking on the phone. She's scared. I heard her tell her boyfriend she was scared. But she didn't say anything to him about

78

Jenny. She's real close-mouthed about things like that."

"Her boyfriend?" Janis whispered, looking around her.

"Yeah. Daddy finally left us. A couple of weeks ago. I didn't say anything about it. It's been coming for a long time. They thought I didn't know. He used to come home drunk and beat Mom up. It was pretty bad. I'm glad he's gone. I was afraid he was going to beat up on me, too." Melissa shrugged.

"Who's her boyfriend?" Carol asked.

"Mr. Harrison. One of the counselors over at the high school. I like him. She doesn't know I know about him, though." Melissa grinned. "I think he's a hunk."

The girls agreed that Mr. Harrison was, indeed, a hunk.

"Sorry to hear about your brother, Janis." Carla felt one of them had to say it, though she didn't mean it.

Janis made a terrible face in reply.

"He still a nerd?"

"Worse than that. That hospital bit was an act. He's trying to make people think he's off his rocker. I can't figure out why."

"That's kinda dumb," Carla agreed. "And I didn't like the way he looked at me when I was at your house this morning. And his voice. What happened to his voice? It sounds like he's talking from the bottom of a big ol' bucket, or a well or something."

All the girls agreed on that.

"I don't know what's the matter with his voice. It's been that way since the last two or three days we spent

79

on the island. Mother thinks it's just changing early, but I don't believe that."

"What do you believe?" Jean asked.

Janis knew exactly what she believed, and very strongly. But, though these girls were her closest friends, she just wasn't ready to admit her darkest thoughts to them. Not yet. For there was a chance she might be wrong.

But not much of one, she admitted to herself.

The girls sat very quietly, aware of the silence, watching Janis carefully.

With a sigh, Melissa went to her overnight bag and took out a book. She looked at it for a moment, then turned to Janis. "About six months ago, I went with my mother to a yard sale. It was supposed to be a big one over in Phoenix. A real old house. But there was just a lot of old junk that Mother bought too much of. That's where I found this book. It's real old. I didn't have anything else to do while my mother poked around, so I started reading it. Most of it is real boring, but when I came to a certain picture, I just about died. I bought the book and began to study it. You can't read it; you've got to study it.

"I wasn't ever going to tell you about it, or show it to you, Janis. But now, well, so many weird things are going on, and Paul is acting so gross . . . let me read you something."

She opened the book to a marked page and began to read: "There exists in the world today a little known but very real, although small, cult of devil worshippers. This cult is named after its founder, Louis Mantine. Mantine was killed, for the first time, around 1875 in the Bahamas, then again near the turn of the century, after twenty-five years of voodoo horrors. On his second death, his wife, Nicole, a voodoo priestess, was hanged with Mantine. A violent storm, perhaps a hurricane, prevented the villagers from burning the bodies. They hastily buried them, and fled to escape the storm. When they returned, Mantine and Nicole were gone from the earth.

"The pair still return occasionally, to search for a devil's child. The child, so it is rumored, must not yet be ten years of age, and must be marked by the Prince of Darkness himself. If such a child is ever found, and established on Earth, Mantine and Nicole will then be freed from their search, and will forever reign on Earth as a reward from Satan."

The girls sat, stunned, for a moment. Not one of them thought she was talking about anyone other than Janis's brother, Paul.

"What is the mark?" Janis asked.

"But there is a lot more!" Melissa protested, holding up the book.

"Later. What is the mark?"

"It's always on the left arm, high up, near the point of the shoulder." She turned the page and handed the book to Janis.

Janis looked at the illustration, then closed the book. No one protested; the girls knew what the mark would look like. They had all seen it before.

On Paul.

"I feel like I've got to throw up," Janis finally said. She suddenly felt queasy and uneasy. "But I'm not going to," she added. Once more, she opened the book and stared at the picture. It was very detailed.

81

She handed the book to the other girls so they could look at the drawing of the mark.

They did. Then Jean said, "But is this real? I mean, do any of us actually believe in this stuff?"

All were silent for a time. Finally, Carol spoke. "We all know there's a God and a Satan and a Heaven and a Hell. The Bible tells us that. And we know God rules the Heavens and the Devil tries to rule the Earth—right?"

The girls nodded solemnly, and Carol went on.

"And we know there's good and evil. I believe what's in that book. But what are we supposed to do about it? Our parents all tell us that stuff"—she pointed to the book—"is baloney. But I'll bet people said the same thing about anyone ever going to the moon."

The girls agreed with that.

"It goes back to what she said." Jean looked at Carol. "What are we supposed to do about it?"

"Yeah." Carla tried for a grin and just about made it. "Can you just see us going up to a cop and saying, 'Hey, mister, we know where there's a devil-child.' I can just see us doing that."

"Maybe that's it!" Janis snapped her fingers. "Yeah, that *is* it!"

"What's it? Us going to the cops?" Melissa shook her head. "No way."

"Are you crazy, Janis?" Jean asked.

"No, no. Not us going to the cops. Us becoming cops."

"You been into someone's stash, Janis?" Jean asked. "You want us to join the force?"

"Of course not. But we can investigate, snoop and

follow Paul. Why not? We've got all summer."

"Now wait a minute." Melissa held up one hand. It was slightly darkened by chocolate from the ice cream bar she'd been eating. "Let's talk this through. Janis, do you think Paul was responsible for what happened to Jenny and her mother?"

Janis answered without hesitation. "Yes, I do."

"Why?"

Janis exhaled slowly, then made up her mind. Might as well level with them, she thought. I got to tell somebody, and I can't tell my parents; they wouldn't believe me.

"Because Paul can do weird things. And he prowls at night. He has ever since he was very little, maybe . . . oh, three years old. Is that natural?" She answered her own question. "No, it isn't. Sometimes he prowls all night. He captures and kills little animals. It's like what we've seen in the movies— some sort of blood sacrifice. I watched him do it once. I got sick. He smeared blood all over him and danced around and looked up at the moon and howled. I haven't ever told anybody this before—not *anybody*.

"Remember I told you about Daddy's hand getting cut by his belt buckle and about all that blood on the floor? Paul said he'd clean it up. He thought I was in my room, but I wasn't. I'd slipped outside and was watching him through a crack in the drapes. He took sand out of his suitcase, where he'd hidden it, and poured it on the blood. Some little figures formed. I couldn't tell what they were."

The girls sat transfixed, listening.

"And I mean Paul didn't shape the sand. The figures just formed. After they soaked up the blood,

83

they disappeared, and there wasn't anything but a pile of sand on the clean floor. I watched as Paul put the sand back in his suitcase; then I beat it back to my room. But I didn't make it. Paul caught me in the hall. I don't think he suspected anything, though.

"And there's more. You all know how Paul always liked to be clean. Well, for about ten days, right up until he went to the hospital, he wouldn't bathe. You all smelled him, right?"

The girls wrinkled their noses and grimaced, nodding their heads.

"You told the cops on the island about this, didn't you?" Jean asked.

"Are you crazy? Who'd believe a story like that?"

The girls looked at each other. Then Melissa spoke for them all. "We do."

Janis nodded her head. "Thanks. But I didn't do you a favor by telling you all this."

"What do you mean?" Carol asked.

"Think about it. If Paul finds out that you know . . ." She let that thought taper off into deadly silence.

"You're right!" Melissa exclaimed. "Now we don't have any choice. We've got to stick together."

Outside, the wind picked up, flinging little bits of sand against the windows of the bedroom, sighing around the house. These were not friendly sounds. It was . . .

"Evil," Jean said softly.

"Come on!" Carol urged. "Knock it off, or we're all gonna be scared silly. It's just the wind, that's all."

"There was sand on the walls of that cottage," Janis said, her voice low. "Where that couple was killed. It was all mixed up with the blood and guts and stuff.''

The wind moaned, then seemed to speak in a dull voice.

The girls moved closer to each other.

"I heard the cops found sand and snake scales in Jenny's bed and in Mrs. Cauldman's hair," Melissa said.

"Snake scales!" Carol was horrified. "Yuk!"

They all shivered at just thinking about a snake being in bed with them.

Janis pointed to the TV. The sound was turned down. An old movie was just starting.

"Do you believe that title?" Carla's voice was barely audible over the whispering of the wind.

Blood on the Sand.

FIVE

"So Paul's sister has suspected something's wrong with her brother?"

"Apparently," Stanford said, laying aside the folder. "And according to the girl, her parents suspect something as well, but, being parents, they prefer not to think the worst of their son."

"Do you believe the thought of anything supernatural has crossed their minds?"

"Oh, I doubt it. But it certainly has crossed Janis's mind. The operatives she spoke with all say she's one sharp little girl—and she's worried."

"About Paul?"

"About what she thinks Paul might do to her. She's afraid of him."

"And you feel she'd cooperate with us?"

"Oh, yes. She'd probably consider that something of an adventure."

"Then the problem is how to approach her."

"I'm working on that right now."

"Of course." Leo rolled his eyes heavenward.

Stanford smiled. "Don't pout, Leo. It's unbecoming in a grown man."

"Would you be offended if I say that I am not convinced all you've said is true?"

"Not at all. You're going to have to experience it. Then"—Stanford smiled again—"if you survive it, you'll be a believer."

"Thanks a whole lot."

"You're welcome, Leo."

"I'm concerned about this storm, Mark. This is very strange weather." Connie rose from the table, walked to the window, and looked out.

Flipping on the floodlights at the back of the house, she squinted her eyes, trying to see through the swirling sand. Something was out there, moving around, but she could not make out what it was.

She stared. There it was. Something . . . But what? She stared harder.

Shapes moving through the wind-whirled sand.

"Mark! There's something out there."

"In this weather? God, who could it be?" He rose from the table and joined his wife at the window. Blowing sand pecked at the pane. Mark stared. "Yeah, there is something out there. I see it. But what is it?"

"There!" She pointed. "Right there. And there's another one."

"Another *one*, Connie? What do you mean by that?"

"Another whatever it is, honey." She looked up at him. "That's all I meant."

As he stared out the window, trying to peer

88

through the blowing sand, Mark felt something ancient and long forgotten touch him. The feeling seemed to spring out of his genes, where it had lain dormant for centuries.

He shivered, wondering why, and put his arm around Connie's waist. He held her close.

"What's wrong, Mark?"

"I don't know. And that's the truth. I just feel sort of, well, odd."

"Yes, so do I."

"Scared is a better description, I think. But what the hell am I afraid of?"

"I don't know," Connie whispered, her voice just audible. "But I'm scared, too." Again, she pointed into the sand-whipped night. "See them?"

"I see . . . something. Oh, hell, it's got to be kids playing some stupid game!"

"In this weather? I don't believe that, Mark."

One of whatever was out there stepped closer to the house and stopped its circling. It shook a stubby fist at them, and a grunting sound could be heard over the wind and the peck, peck, pecking of the sand against the window.

Suddenly, Mark became angry. He pulled away from his wife, and walked to his study. Unlocking the gun cabinet, he took out a double-barreled twelve-gauge shotgun, chambered for three-inch magnums. He broke it open and loaded it, put a handful of shells into his back pocket. Then he walked back to his wife's side.

Her eyes widened when she saw the shotgun and the angry expression on her husband's face. "Mark, those may be college kids out there, from some frat house. You know, they can do awfully stupid things."

"To hell with them. I'm not going to do a thing unless they—whatever is out there—do something I think is hostile. Damn it, honey, this is our property. It's all fenced in. Whoever that is has no right to be here, much less after dark."

Connie shivered, almost uncontrollably. It's unreasonable, she thought. Why am I so afraid?

In his bedroom, Paul smiled. He was sitting on the floor, the door to his room locked.

Everything was going according to plan. He now had a following among the locals; though they came from so-called "good families," his followers were trash. The girl was nothing more than a thirteen-year-old whore. Snap your fingers and she'd spread-eagle. But soon his father would be rotting in the grave, although quite susceptible to recall—Paul laughed at that thought. Then he would have his mother all to himself. And he could quite easily manipulate her, have her.

But the boy knew he must not move too fast. Each plan had to be carefully thought out. His true father had told him, and not through Mantine, that he had many enemies. Soon he would be watched, and by his stupid sister, of all people.

Paul found that amusing.

His sister . . . Paul knew he would eventually have to destroy her, whether physically or mentally, he hadn't decided. But first he would use her, humiliate her, make her scream and beg and cry out for mercy.

The boy listened to the wind and the pecking of the

90

sand against the house.

"Closer," he whispered. "Come closer. The earth is whirling about you. You are of the earth. You and earth are one. Come closer. Now!"

The wind moaned.

"They're coming closer, Mark!" Connie's words were almost gasped. Her fear was very great. "My God, are they bears?"

He looked, felt his stomach knot up, turn sour. "I don't think so. Where would that many come from?"

He knew they weren't bears.

But he didn't know what they were. Or, worse yet, what they wanted?

Ancient fears rose up within him. Somewhere, buried deep in him, was the truth.

He fought it back, mentally shoved it into ages past. And he gripped the shotgun so hard his hands began to ache.

The wind picked up, moaning and making a crying, painful sound. The sand whipped and bounced off the house, muddying the vision of the man and woman who stood mesmerized by the window, watching . . .

. . . waiting.

A roar filtered over the drone of the wind and the millions of tiny sand-crashes.

"Nothing human did that," Connie whispered.

Mark shook his head, freeing himself from an almost hypnotic spell.

"Call the police, honey. Right now. Nine-one-one. Do it, Connie. Hurry!"

The urgency in his voice was transmitted to her. She ran to the phone, punched out the numbers, then asked for help, her voice shaky with fear.

The wind began to moan, as if speaking in some ancient tongue now known only to those who walk on the Dark Side, and threatening death and damnation and eternal agony to all others.

Mark's eyes went to his wife. She was just hanging up the phone. When he again looked out the window, a cry of fear was choked off in his throat.

It was a scene out of Hell. A surrealistic vision of a madman.

Mark didn't want to believe what he saw. He had never seen anything like it.

Yes, he had.

It was a . . .

. . . sandman.

Blocky and stumpy and sand-colored. Nonhuman. It stood upright on blocklike legs. There were holes where eyes should have been, a slit for a mouth, holes where a nose would be.

Behind him, Connie screamed.

Mark whirled around, the shotgun coming up. His wife still stood by the phone, staring into the hallway of their spacious home. Mark followed her fixed gaze. A . . . thing was standing in the hall entrance. It began to lumber awkwardly toward them, its thick arms outstretched.

Grunting sounds emanated from the hole in its face.

Mark jerked the shotgun to his shoulder and pulled one trigger. The magnum load tore the arm from the creature and knocked it backward, splattering the hallway with bloody . . .

. . . sand.

Mark stared in horror. "Sand!" he whispered.

Connie screamed. "Behind you, Mark!"

He turned just as the window was smashed, a thick arm reached through, and blunt fingers clamped onto his shoulder. Waves of pain ripped through him as the fingers tightened, but, one-handed, he jammed the shotgun through the broken window and pulled the trigger.

The middle of the creature disintegrated, the legs going one way, the torso another. The legs began to run from the house, but the torso pulled itself along, using its fingers to dig into the sandy earth.

Connie, showing a presence of mind she did not know she possessed, grabbed up a camera, ripped open the case, began to take pictures as Mark reloaded and fired again at the manlike creature now stumbling up the darkened hallway, steadying itself by one arm as it lurched away.

The load struck the thing in the center of its back and sent it sprawling, sand flying in all directions.

Connie spun about to take pictures of the things running in all directions at the back of the house—and of the running legs and the crawling torso.

Sirens wailed in the wind- and sand-lashed night.

Then the storm abruptly ceased.

A flat calm lay over the desert.

Connie ran to the front door and jerked it open. The lead cop gave the camera a very odd look.

Within seconds, policemen filled the foyer. Connie pointed. "There's one in the hallway and several of them outside, in the back. Follow me." She started

93

toward the kitchen.

"One what, lady?"

"I . . . I don't know, officer! But be careful, they're dangerous."

"Is it human or animal, lady?"

"I don't know!"

"It's a mixture of both," Mark said, pain in his voice. He was leaning against the kitchen counter.

"Put that shotgun down, sir," a cop told him. "Right now."

Mark laid the weapon on the counter, his shoulder contracting with pain. It felt like the muscles were ripped and torn.

"Holy shit!" a policemen yelled from the dark hallway. "Get this thing off me. Eric!" he shouted. Then there was pistol fire, and a wild scream filled with pain and terror.

Three cops ran into the hallway, their .357s drawn.

But they stopped short, momentarily frozen. Not believing their eyes.

A sand-colored manlike creature with one arm and the middle of his back blown out was dragging the cop down the hallway.

The three cops fired simultaneously. The reports were thunderous in the hall. The slugs tore into the creature, and its head erupted in a gush of bloody sand.

One cop raced outside to call in for help. His voice was clearly heard by those inside. "Officer in trouble. One down. Shots have been fired. One-twelve Mesa Drive. Respond code three, and send ambulance."

The officer who was being dragged was abruptly released when the creature's head exploded.

But at that moment, somewhere out in the desert, dark laughter arose, taunting and evil and deep toned.

Then drums began to pound, beating out a savage rhythm in the night.

Eric looked down at his partner.

Andy's throat had been torn out. His head was hanging by only a slender piece of flesh.

"Aw, Christ, Andy!" Eric whispered. Then he jacked back the hammer on his pistol as a door opened on the dimly lit hallway.

A little boy stepped through it, his eyes wide. When he spoke, his voice trembled. "I'm scared, Mommie," Paul said.

Connie ran to him. Stepping gingerly around the dead man and the pool of blood, she pulled her son to her, holding him close; and Paul smiled secretly.

The drums stopped as Eric ran from the hallway and cut to his right. He disappeared into the murk of the night, after stepping cautiously through a shattered glass door.

Mark moved away from the counter, his shoulder aching. He grimaced as he tried to work his arm to keep it from stiffening up.

Flashing blue and red lights now filled the circular drive. Chief Bambridge, wearing civilian clothes and carrying a riot gun, was the first inside.

Mark used his good arm to point to the hallway. "One officer in there, Mike. I think he's dead. Andy, they called him. The others ran out after the . . . things."

"Things?" Mike waved the other uniforms on ahead.

"I don't know what else to call them. They were, well, made of sand, but they bled real blood." He felt like a complete idiot.

Mike was about to ask if he'd been drinking, but Eric stepped into the room.

"He isn't kidding, Chief. They were made of sand—and blood."

"Yeah," another cop said. He squatted down by the entrance to the hall. "But look at the blood. It's dark and it's old and it stinks."

"Get the lab boys in here," Mike directed, "and order all available units in, right now. Ask the county for help. But don't say anything of importance on the air. Remember those goddamn scanners are all over the place."

"I shot two of them, Mike." Mark walked over to the chief, massaging his shoulder. "I blew one of the things in two, right out there." He pointed. "Connie got pictures of it; the legs running off in one direction, the torso dragging itself off in another, using its hands and fingers. The pictures will back me up."

"I'm not disputing your word, Mark. Maybe this will give us something to go on . . . on another matter." He shut up.

Most of the townspeople already knew bits and pieces of what had happened at the hospital. Including the sand and scales.

Mark grimaced in pain. He could no longer stand to work his arm.

It was swelling badly, so was his hand.

"You'll have to go to the hospital for that, Mark. It looks bad."

96

"I can't leave Connie and Paul here alone."

"I'll station one man inside and two men outside. As a matter of fact, I'll stay inside myself. How does that sound to you?"

"Good. I'd feel better about it."

"Any idea why whatever it was singled you out to attack?"

"I have no idea."

"A lot of weird things have been happening since—" He'd started to say, since you got back from the islands, but he'd bitten it off.

Hell, Mark didn't have anything to do with what had been happening.

Mike put that out of his mind.

The next hour, controlled chaos reigned in the neighborhood, with police and deputies going from house to house, warning people to stay inside and lock their doors and windows.

The cops found several blood trails, all leading out into the desert. Then they stopped. Cold. Not even the most experienced tracker on the sheriff's department could pick up a thing, and he, born and reared on the San Carlos Reservation, had the reputation of being able to track a snake across a flat rock.

Peter Loneman had not been happy with what he'd seen, or with what he'd felt out on the desert. Peter, whose Indian name was Man Who Walks Alone, had sensed the Indian coming out in him while he'd tracked the . . . whatever in hell they were.

Now, at the Kelly house, Mike looked at Peter and commented, "What's the matter with you, Pete? You

97

look like you're about to cloud up and rain. Not that we couldn't use a good rain around here."

Pete smiled and shook his head. "I got strange feelings out in the desert, Mike." All the deputies got along well with the chief and the city cops. It was just the sheriff who still held a grudge, because of his brother-in-law. "Indian feelings. Hard to explain to you, Mike."

"Mrs. Kelly made a big pot of coffee and a platter of sandwiches, Pete. Let's go eat and talk this out."

Connie was with Paul, in his bedroom. Mark had already called from the hospital to tell her he'd be there for a couple of days. And Connie had called Janis, and told her to stay where she was. A sheriff's deputy was on guard outside Mark's door, and two city units were stationed outside the hospital. Mike had called all the men in, canceling all off-time and leave time.

Mike chose a ham and cheese. Peter, with a grin, picked up a peanut butter and jelly sandwich. "Never have gotten over my love for them," he admitted. Then his young face sobered. "I'm an Indian. An Apache. But I'm college educated, so I reckon that makes me a good Injun." He grinned around his peanut butter and jelly. "You know what I mean. Still, I'm an Indian. My grandfather insisted I go through all the tribal rituals. And some of them are not pleasant. The snake cave. The bear rite. The sweat. Each tribe's are different. You don't know what I'm talking about, and I guess it's better you don't. Do you believe in spirits, Mike?" Pete dropped that on him quickly.

Mike chewed for a moment. "I'm not from around here, Pete. I grew up in West Texas. My grandfather was Comanche. Full blood."

"I suspected you weren't all Anglo. Mike, when you saw that little girl in the hospital, what'd you feel—first thing?"

"Scared. And eerie. A lot of different sensations. What I felt frightened me more than the sight of the girl. I didn't tell the doctors that, though."

"That was wise. Well, I felt that way out in the desert tonight. I didn't lose their tracks out there, Mike."

The men stared at each other across the table.

"What do you mean, Pete?"

"They became one with the earth, brother. Do I have to tell you what that means?"

"No," Mike said quickly. "But, needless to say, we won't talk about this except to each other."

"Hey-ho, bro! I ain't no fool." Pete quickly sobered. "We got big trouble, Mike. And we gotta put a lid on it real quick. I'll go back to the reservation and talk to some people."

"Medicine men, Pete?"

"Yeah. But I feel in my guts that they won't be much help. Know what I mean?"

Mike nodded. He knew. He had that much Indian left in him.

"I'm having those pictures developed right now. The ones Mrs. Kelly took. When will you be back?"

"No later than tomorrow afternoon. I'll see what the old men have to say. If anything." He stood up. "See you."

Mike waved him off. Then he picked up his shotgun and walked outside to check on the men at the front and the back of the house. The wind had picked up again. It was singing songs to him. Songs of times Mike had never known, but they were a part of his soul, were deep in his genes. Some scientists said that was impossible, but Mike knew better.

He stood on the stone patio at the rear of the big sprawling house, listening to the natural sounds of night on the desert. The soft singing of the wind. The flapping of wings as night birds sought food.

Sand things. Sandmen. That was impossible. And even if it were possible, no one had reported any sign of scales, not his people or Connie and Mark.

What the hell! Was this county filled with mysterious monsters?

There had to be an explanation.

But damned if he knew where to find it.

The wind sighed around him. Danger out there, the warning came to him. Something you don't understand.

And it's going to get worse.

He felt that very strongly.

He had ordered his people not to talk to the press. He might get away with holding back this time, but if it happened again . . . ?

Panic.

"What are we up against, Chief?" the officer on guard at the rear of the house asked, breaking into Mike's thoughts.

"I wish I knew," he replied.

But deep inside, he didn't want to know, for he sensed there was something horrible out there.

100

Waiting. Watching.

From the earth.

Stanford woke Leo as soon as the morning papers were delivered to the motel. He pounded on his door.

Rubbing the sleep from his eyes, Leo reluctantly ushered the inspector into his room.

Stanford waved the paper. "I have coffee and sweet rolls on the way, Leo. They struck last night. At the Kelly home. The paper doesn't say it was the sand people, but I'll wager my pension it was."

Leo grabbed the paper, sat down on the rumpled bed, and began to read.

"We've got to see the chief, Stanford. Today." He tossed the paper aside.

Peter Loneman sat in the medicine lodge of his people and listened to the old men talk. They weren't being much help. And Pete didn't blame them.

Chief Bambridge tried to get a few hours' sleep before returning to work. When he finally did nod off, his dreams were filled with demons and monsters and unspeakable acts—all set in a swirling sand-storm.

Connie Kelly sat in her kitchen and drank coffee, waiting for the hospital to call.

Janis and Carla and Melissa and Carol and Jean read the morning paper, passing it around, each of them going over the short article several times.

"Do you think Paul had anything to do with this, Janis?" Melissa asked.

101

"I think he had everything to do with it. I think he wants Dad out of the way. He can work Mother, get her to eat out of his hand. I've seen him do it. And as soon as he gets Dad out of the way, I'm next. You can believe that. He hates me."

"You mean we're next, don't you?" Jean corrected. "We're all in this thing together, aren't we?"

"I hate to say it," Melissa put in, "but I think we've got to get some boys in on this."

"Who?" Janis looked at each of the girls.

"Bing and Roy for certain," Melissa suggested. "How about it?"

"Suits me." Janis shrugged. "But you might all do better by backing out of this."

"No way!" the girls told her.

The County Medical Examiner, Dr. Larry Carleson, whose offices and lab were in the hospital, checked his findings for the third time and then shook his head. It just was not possible. There had to be some mistake. Things like this did not occur. They were medically and scientifically impossible.

But there it was, right in front of him, and he damn sure couldn't deny it.

The sand held life, of a sort the doctor had never seen before. But the blood was dead. Medically speaking. Devoid of functioning cells and corpuscles. His tests had proved that nothing in this blood would support life. The protoplasm, platelets, erythrocytes, leucocytes.

But it was alive.

Damned if I know how, Carleson thought.

He looked at the pile of sand that the officers had sworn was once a humanlike arm. His people had tested it. It was sand. But not all desert sand. The samples had contained crystalline rocks, quartz, and pieces of coral, and of snail and clam shells. There was also evidence of basalt, the black rock from a lava flow.

In other words this sand was a mixture of sands found in various parts of the world. That didn't make any sense to him.

But nothing about the bizarre happenings of the past ten days made sense.

Something moved just within range of his peripheral vision. He turned his head. But there was no one in the lab with him.

Settle down, Larry! he told himself. Just calm down.

But the feeling that he was being watched would not leave him.

Larry looked down at his right forearm. "That's funny," he muttered. "I never noticed those bite marks before."

He dismissed the marks as ant or flea bites.

Disgusted with himself for his old-maidish feelings of fear, he expelled air sharply, rose from the stool, and walked to the door. He didn't want any more coffee, but maybe some fresh air would clear his mind.

Larry felt there was a perfectly logical explanation for all of this nonsense, and he was determined to find it.

Or die trying! The words popped into his head.

He shook them away.

Typing the blood had been crazy enough. A, B, and O. Combined. That in itself was wacky.

At the door, Larry once more experienced the odd sensation of being watched. He turned and gave his lab the once-over. Nothing was out of place.

With a snort of disgust, he shook his head and stepped out into the quiet corridor, scratching the bite marks on his forearm. The damned things itched.

As soon as the door had closed behind Larry Carleson, the sand on the table began to transform itself into a stumpy arm and hand. The fingers worked back and forth, as if the sand itself had experienced some sort of stiffness. Then the arm snaked itself to the edge of the table and, fingers grasping the table's edge, swung down and dropped to the tile floor. There the arm lay pulsing for a moment, as if seeking direction, but finally, using its fingers, it began to pull itself across the floor to the wall alongside the door.

It seemed to sense the door, and stopped, waiting on the floor, off to one side.

Only a few seconds passed before the door opened. A young orderly stepped in. He opened his mouth to call for Dr. Carleson, but before he could speak, he felt something fumbling at his ankle.

The young man looked down and opened his mouth to scream.

Some sort of hand had attached itself to his ankle.

His foot flew out from under him as the hand jerked, and Glen Holland hit the floor hard, banging his head. But that pain was slight compared to the torment in his leg, and it was spreading upward, to his groin, and into his belly. He felt a million ants were attacking him. He tried to scream, but only a grunting sound came from his throat.

He beat his hands against the floor, trying to get somebody's attention; he could not understand why he could not scream.

His mouth was dry and stuffed with something.

It was . . .

Sand.

Glen began to thrash about on the floor as excruciating pain engulfed him.

That lasted for only a few seconds, and then the young man felt nothing at all.

His seeing but totally uncomprehending eyes watched as grains of sand began to whip all around him, some of them seeming to come under the door, from out in the corridor.

One grain of sand can easily escape a broom or mop or vacuum cleaner.

Get up! the words popped into his head.

He clumsily drew himself to his feet, swayed for a moment, got his balance, and then opened the door to step out into the hall.

He stood for a moment, watching a few people, all dressed in white, like him, walk up and down the corridor.

Some of them spoke his name.

Glen jerked his head up and down.

He did not know what to do, did not know who he was, did not know where to go.

Kill!

Glen half-closed his eyes, and tried to understand what kill meant.

Destroy!

He thought he knew what that meant.

OK.

Glen thought that was a fine idea. But what? He looked around him. The corridor was deserted. He saw a door and figured maybe somebody was behind it, somebody he could destroy.

Weapon!

Glen's sandy brain was muddled. To his left was a door marked JANITOR. Maybe he'd find something in there.

He did. A hammer.

Smiling like an idiot, Glen once more stepped out into the hall. He lurched up the corridor and turned into the first door he came to.

A ladies' restroom.

The yelling and screaming and hollering and cussing made his head feel funny. Grains of sand dropped off of his face.

That made the women holler even louder.

And Glen did not like the way some of the women were pushing and shoving him.

So he swung the hammer and smashed one right between the eyes. Left a funny little mark on her head. Her eyes just rolled back and she fell down.

Glen laughed and laughed.

Now all the women in the little room were yelling and screaming, and they were crowded into one corner.

Glen lifted both arms, one hand grasping the handle of the hammer, and he grunted at the women.

One of them picked up a large metal wastebasket and held it in front of her.

Glen swung the hammer.

He looked down. Another woman was bleeding out of her nose and mouth and ears.

Stupid-looking.

The woman with the wastebasket swung it, hitting Glen in the face with one edge. It didn't hurt, but it knocked him down and he lost the hammer.

Then Dr. Mary Beth Fletcher entered the restroom. She stopped short at seeing Glen fumbling around on the floor, trying to find his weapon.

Then she kicked the hammer away from him and started screaming for orderlies.

Glen looked up at her.

He opened his mouth to speak, his jaw working up and down. But nothing that made any sense came out.

Just gibberish.

Fletcher noticed the flat dullness of the young orderly's eyes, the sandy snot that dripped from his nose.

Glen had always been full of life, joking and kidding with everybody; he was kind and gentle with the patients and would do anything a doctor or nurse asked of him.

The restroom was now crowded with people.

"Get her out of here." Mary Beth pointed to the injured woman. "And call Dr. Belline. She's got a fractured skull, possible brain damage." She looked at Glen. "Come on, Glen. Come with me."

Glen tried to tackle her, but Mary Beth was too quick for him. Several burly orderlies grabbed him and forced him out into the hall.

But Glen broke loose from them and lurched up

the corridor, knocking people away as he stumbled off.

He staggered into a room and locked the door.

A knot of doctors and technicians and nurses had gathered. "What the hell happened, Dr. Fletcher?" one of them asked.

The women who had been in the restroom came out and began talking, all at once. Mary Beth shook her head and walked a few feet from them.

Behind the locked door, Glen began to scream.

Security came running.

"Call the police," Mary Beth told one guard. "Tell them to hurry."

Glen's screaming became high-pitched, a one-note wailing.

A nurse touched Mary Beth's arm. "Doctor? That woman in the restroom just died."

"Damn!" The word exploded from Mary Beth's mouth.

At the far end of the hall, Dr. Carleson stepped out of his office. He was furious. Someone had just stolen his sandpile.

"You jerks!" he shouted. Everyone in the hall turned and looked at the doctor. "That's my sand and I want it back. If you don't return it, I'm going to hold my breath until I turn blue and just die!"

Slater, Clineman, and Belline had just rounded the corner, intent on seeing what all the fuss was about. They stopped cold when Dr. Larry Carleson plopped down onto the floor and went into a tantrum, kicking and yelling and beating his hands against the linoleum.

Mary Beth reacted first. She gestured to the

orderlies who had handled Glen.

"You men who touched Glen, go take hot showers. Scrub until you're raw." She pointed to a nurse. "Get gowned and gloved, and burn their clothing. Move, damn it!"

She turned to Clineman, who was kneeling beside Carleson. "Don't touch him," she warned.

Clineman nodded. "Ah, Larry," he said.

Larry stopped yelling and bouncing around, and looked at Clineman. "You old coot! You'd better gimme back my sand. I'll tell on you if you don't!"

Clineman blinked, shook his head. "Larry . . . who are you going to tell?"

"I'll tell Mommie and Daddy you took it, and I'll tell them you been peekin' into the girls' restroom."

Clineman stood up. "Get him to a bed," he told two male nurses. "He's had some sort of breakdown."

Larry kicked his feet and squirmed about on the floor, waving his hands. "Havenothavenothavenothavenot!"

Mary Beth noticed the red marks on Carleson's forearm. They looked like ant bites. She pointed them out to the other doctors.

"Some sort of reaction?" Dr. Slater said, a hopeful note in his voice.

"I hope that's all it is," Clineman responded. "Gowned and gloved before anybody touches him." He looked at Larry. "We're going to help you find your sand, ol' buddy."

"You promise?"

"I promise. Come on, get up."

Mary Beth walked to the ME's lab and pushed

open the door.

Larry stood up and cupped his hands to his groin. "I gotta weewee!"

Clineman pointed to the men's john. "Right over there, Larry."

"Toooo late!" Larry yelled, and lifted his hands. There was a dark stain at his crotch. "I had an accident, I had an accident!" he said in singsong; the grin on his face was a silly one.

"That's all right, Larry." Clineman reassured the medical examiner, a man rated tops in his field. A man who had just weeweed in his underwear after losing his sandpile.

"You gonna 'pank me?" Larry pouted, sticking a thumb into his mouth.

Clineman assured Carleson he was not going to spank him. Then Larry was led away, to the psychiatric wing. To be restrained.

Mary Beth walked up to the other doctors. "The sand the police brought in is gone."

"Gone!" Slater blurted out. "Who would take it? And why?"

Mary Beth looked down and her face paled. "Back up!" she told her colleagues, pointing to the floor.

A trail of sand led to the room in which Glen had locked himself.

"Dear God in Heaven!" Clineman whispered.

110

SIX

"How do you want us to play this?" Mike asked the group of doctors.

The research wing of the hospital had been cleared, but Glen continued his high-pitched wailing behind the locked door.

One of Larry Carleson's assistants had quickly put samples of the sand under a microscope.

It was alive. Sort of. In a way. But he didn't know what kind of life it was. He'd sure as hell never seen anything like it.

"However we handle it," Clineman said, "we must be very careful not to come into direct contact with Holland. I want all your officers to be masked and gloved."

"They've been schooled in the handling of AIDS patients," Mike assured him.

Clineman nodded his head almost absently, then turned to one of Carleson's staff. "Have you found anything that will destroy this life form?"

"Fire."

"Nothing else?"

"Not that we've been able to ascertain in fifteen

minutes," the researcher said curtly.

Clineman smiled and patted the young man on the shoulder. "Sorry, Bobby. It's a tense time for all of us. Please keep trying."

Bobby nodded and walked back into the lab.

Several officers were standing by, gowned and gloved and masked.

Mike hit the door several times. "Glen Holland. This is Mike Bambridge, chief of police. Come on out, Glen."

The wailing never missed a note.

"Do you kick the door in now?" Mary Beth asked.

Mike smiled. "That's TV and movie stuff, Doctor. Besides that, it's damn hard on the feet." He motioned to an officer. "Bust it, Charles."

The officer picked up a twelve-pound sledge hammer and walked to the door. He hit the knob one accurate blow and knocked it out. It hit the far wall, having flown through the air with the speed of a bullet.

The door swung open. The lights were on in the room, and Glen Holland was sitting on the floor, wailing sounds coming out of his mouth. Snotty sand leaked from his nose and mouth. The stench was awful.

Glen looked at the crowd. Then a wild light appeared in his eyes. He gripped a scalpel in his right hand. Slowly, he stood up.

"Drop the knife, Glen!" Mike warned, jacking back the hammer on his .357.

Glen charged, screaming.

Half-a-dozen pistols barked, the slugs all striking the orderly in the chest. He slumped back against the wall, bloody sand leaking out of the smoking holes in his stained jacket.

But he was a long way from being dead.

Mike took aim and shot him between the eyes. Part of Holland's head struck the wall behind him. Bloody sand gushed out of it, all mixed up with gray matter and fluid.

Glen slumped to the floor.

He smiled at the shocked cops and doctors.

He was still a long way from being dead.

One of the cops stepped into the room and tossed a blanket over Glen's head. Then he and several others wrestled Glen face-down onto the floor and secured him with restraining straps.

"We can't keep him in the hospital." Dr. Slater finally found his voice.

"No," Clineman agreed. "Ah . . . take him to that unused trailer out back—the old portable inoculation unit. House him there."

"After that, come back and scrub down, lots of soap and hot water. Your clothing will be burned," Dr. Fletcher ordered. "And this floor has to be sanitized." She looked at a shocked and pale janitor. "Get to it and be careful."

"Yes, ma'am."

Mark was not released from the hospital. The doctors could not bring down his low-grade fever, and his blood pressure was fluctuating and could not be controlled.

Dr. Larry Carleson was placed in isolation in the hospital proper, and Orderly Holland was strapped

113

down in the trailer behind it. His heart had been shattered by two .357 slugs, copper-jacketed hollow-noses. Both lungs, his stomach and liver and spleen had been hit. And he had been shot in the head.

But he would not die.

Medically, it was impossible.

Yet it was happening.

Anyone who went near Carleson or Holland approached them fully gowned and masked and gloved.

Everybody who had come in contact with the contaminated sand was checked for those strange red marks. But so far, only Carleson and Holland had been affected.

No one had thought to check Mark Kelly.

Yet.

And Inspector Stanford Willingston and retired NYPD detective Leo Corigliano requested a meeting with Chief Mike Bambridge of the Tepehuanes Police Department.

Mike looked at their credentials, grunted, and waved the men to seats in his office.

Leo closed the door; which did not go unobserved by Mike.

"The Chief Inspector of the Commonwealth of the Bahamas and a retired NYPD lieutenant who now runs a hot-shot PI agency. Now"—Bambridge smiled—"I got to wonder why an odd couple like that would team up and come to Tepehuanes?"

"Perhaps to offer our assistance, Chief," Stanford said.

"Why would I need your assistance, Inspector? Are you speaking of some specific case that is currently open in our files?"

Stanford did not mince words. "Voodoo, black magic, creatures that appear to be made of sand, and a child of Satan, plus murder. I don't believe you are fully cognizant of the enormity of the problems facing this community, Chief Bambridge."

Mike sipped his coffee. He wondered if these men knew anything about what had happened at the hospital that morning. Mike had gotten only a few hours sleep, but he felt refreshed and experienced a rush of excitement at the inspector's words.

He kept his face expressionless, though. "Voodoo? Black magic? Satanism? You believe in all that hoodoo, Inspector?"

"Oh, quite, Chief. Any leads on who attacked the Kellys? And why?"

Mike said nothing.

Leo picked it up. "Gunfire at the hospital this morning. Your people kill anything?"

"I could order you both out of my office and tell you to keep your noses out of department business, you know."

"Then, why don't you?" Leo met the chief's eyes.

"You got a jacket on me, Mr. Corigliano?" Mike looked at the folder in Leo's hands.

"Leo, please. Yes."

"May I see it?"

Leo placed the folder on Mike's desk and the chief quickly scanned it. He had to read only a few lines before he knew Leo had him pegged practically from the moment of birth. Quarter-breed Comanche had been highlighted.

"My Indian heritage of some special interest to

you, Leo?''

"I don't know. It might help."

Again, Mike grunted. "Maybe." For a reason he could not fathom, Mike liked this odd-couple pairing of cops. And with gut instinct, he trusted them. "I've got a deputy friend who is Apache. He's at the reservation now, meeting with medicine men."

"Wise move," Stanford said. "If the creatures have gone one with the earth, the old men might know how to deal with that—if they'll cooperate. Which I doubt."

Same phrase Pete used, Mike thought. And Pete had doubted that his people would be much help. "You gentlemen object to my recording this session?"

"Not at all." Leo spoke for both of them, after a quick glance at Stanford.

Mike set up a cassette/corder and adjusted the mike. "Interviewing Inspector Willingston of the Bahamian Police and retired NYPD lieutenant Leo Corigliano. This is in connection with the rape and death of Dottie Cauldman and the rape and aging of her daughter, Jenny Cauldman. It is also in connection with—"

There was a knock and the door opened abruptly. "Chief." A uniformed sergeant stuck his head in. "Sorry to bother you, but the lab just sent us the blow-ups of those pictures Mrs. Kelly took."

He handed Mike a large envelope and left, closing the door behind him.

Mike carefully opened the envelope and looked at the eight by tens. His face paled.

"Damn!" he said softly.

"Sand people?" Stanford guessed.

Mike cut off the recorder. "Yeah." He handed the pictures to Stanford.

"They are as awesome as rumor made them out to be," the inspector said. He handed the pictures to Leo.

"Jesus Christ!" Leo muttered. He appeared to be shaken. He shook his head and returned the pictures to the chief.

Stanford pointed to the recorder. "Would you please reactivate that machine, Chief."

Mike cut the recorder back on.

Stanford said, "I have taken the liberty of calling my offices and requesting that they send some samples of blood from a recent double murder on the island. One of the murder victims was Leo's sister."

That answers one question, Mike thought. Maybe two. He glanced at Leo. "I'm sorry."

Leo nodded in reply.

Mike turned his gaze on the inspector. "You think the . . . sand people committed the murders on your island?"

"I'm sure of it."

"The same ones? How'd they get to Tepehuanes, for Christ's sake!"

"I think, Chief, they can grow out of a very small pile of sand. I believe they were brought here in someone's luggage."

"They . . . grow."

"That is correct. And, according to legend, they cannot exist without blood. I would like to see if the blood you found at the Kelly house matches the samples my people took from the cottage where the

117

double murders occurred."

"How do you know I found any blood samples at the Kelly house?"

"Oh, come, come, Chief! Let's stop all this pussyfooting about in the lilies, for heaven's sake. You've got a problem on your hands and we can help. Besides," he pointed to the envelope containing the pictures, "one of the sand creatures is blown in two and the other one is missing an arm. Of course, you have blood samples. The creatures cannot exist without blood."

Mike thought of Glen Holland. "Is the blood contaminated?"

"We think so. According to legend, it is highly toxic; has a life of its own. But once exposed to air, the sand dies within hours unless it finds fresh blood." We think. He kept that to himself for the moment. Stanford cut the air with an impatient slash of one hand. "The sand people can be contained. That is not your problem, Chief."

"It isn't? You could have fooled me, Inspector!"

"No. Your problem is that a child of Satan is controlling the actions of the sand creatures. As long as the child is alive, the sand people will continue to multiply and kill on command."

Mike stared at the inspector. Blinked a couple of times.

"Kill a kid?" he finally managed to say.

"Yes," Stanford said, his voice devoid of emotion. "And we must find Louis Mantine and his wife Nicole, in human form, and destroy them. Again. Do it right this time. Burn them and seal the ashes."

Mike became agitated. "Who the hell are Louis

118

and Nicole Mantine. And what do you mean, destroy them again!"

"They've been killed at least twice, Chief."

"That is impossible!"

"Calm yourself. Nothing is impossible when one is dealing with the devil."

"The devil!" Mike shouted.

His intercom buzzed. "Everything all right in there, Chief?"

"Yeah. No. I suppose so." He cut off the intercom.

Stanford said, "Louis and Nicole Mantine. Voodoo priest and priestess. They found the devil-child on the island and brought his true father to him. You'll understand as we go along."

"Well, I don't so far." He snapped his fingers. "Devil-child. Oh, no, Inspector. Tell me it isn't true. You're the man I spoke with a few weeks ago?"

"That is correct."

"Yeah. Now I remember. You wanted a background check on the Kelly family. Sure," he said softly.

"You beginning to get a clearer picture, Chief Bambridge?"

"Some pieces are coming together, yeah. Paul Kelly?"

"Yes."

"We think," Leo added.

"The Cauldman girl and her mother were raped by a grown man. Or a grown something. Paul Kelly is just a child."

"What do you mean a grown something?" Stanford asked.

Mike explained about the scales.

119

Stanford thought about that for a moment. "He might be a shape-changer. Either that or he's summoned help from his father."

"His father?" Mike said. "Mark?"

"No. Satan."

Mike put his head in his hands and sighed.

"What the hell is a shape-changer?" Leo asked, before Mike could.

"A creature who has the ability to change or shift shapes," Stanford replied.

Leo looked exasperated. "Stanford! Give me a break. You might be used to dealing with these things, but I'm not."

"Count me in as one of the 'nots,'" Mike said.

"Actually, it is exactly what I said. A creature who has the ability to assume the shape of something else—human or animal."

Mike sighed. "So . . . and this is assuming I'm buying any of this . . . Paul could have changed his form before he raped the mother and daughter, right?"

"That is correct."

"Changed it into what? We found reptile scales that don't match up with those of any known creature, alive or extinct."

"He might have changed into a demon."

"A"—once again, Mike sighed—"demon."

"To be sure!" Stanford said cheerfully. "Or perhaps the boy has a brother."

"No. He has a sister," Mike explained. "Janis. Good kid. Pretty."

Stanford brushed that away. "No, no, no. A brother from the Dark Side."

By now, Leo was looking at the inspector as oddly as Mike was.

"The dark side of . . . what?" Mike asked.

"Hell."

Leo said, "Mike, I know it's early, but do you have a bottle in your office?"

"I sure do!" Bambridge opened a drawer and pulled out a bottle of bourbon. He found three cups, then looked at Stanford. "You want a slug?"

"Oh, surely. I'm on vacation. I can be a bit naughty and not feel guilty about drinking this early in the day."

The bourbon poured, Mike leaned back in his chair.

Stanford took a small sip and smiled. "Yes. Yes, the more I think about it, the more I'm inclined to believe Paul might have a brother; an alter shape. Mantine would have the power to pull him here. I sensed the boy was evil when I looked at him on the island. But I warn you both: This will be the most difficult case you have ever worked on. Take it from me. I've been working on one like it for fifteen years."

Mike looked puzzled.

Leo cleared that up. "Mantine was responsible for the death of Stanford's wife."

"In a way," the inspector said softly.

Mike drained his cup. "Boys, this is getting to be a bit much for a country lawman like me."

Both Leo and Stanford had noted the efficiency of his office, the high morale of his men, and the high-tech equipment. Neither man believed Mike Bambridge was a good ol' boy or a country lawman.

"Those photos should have convinced you of

121

something, Mike," Stanford said.

"Oh, I'm not disputing your word or denying anything you've said, Inspector. It's . . . well, my mind is having a hard time accepting it, that's all."

"Ignorance and skepticism have killed many a person, Chief. From this point on, take nothing for granted, be suspicious of everything. For if Mantine wishes it so, nothing will be as it seems. And the boy will be growing stronger and stronger each day. Bear in mind that he is not human."

Mike lifted his eyes and stared at Stanford for a moment. "How do you kill something, someone, who is already dead?"

"Simple. Catch him in his human form and make the first shot count."

"A silver bullet?" There was only a touch of sarcasm in the man's voice.

Stanford chuckled. "No. Nothing that dramatic. Just a blessed bullet."

"You have one?" Leo asked.

"I brought a box of them."

"Fifty?"

Stanford smiled. "Marksmanship never was one of my strong suits."

Mike stood up. "You've leveled with me; I might as well level with you. You people seem to know a lot more than I do about what we're after."

"It won't take you long to learn, Chief," Stanford told him. "You'll either do that, or die."

When it came to introductions, Mike simply introduced the men as Stanford and Leo, and he said they were assisting in the investigation.

The doctors gave them some odd glances, but said nothing.

On the tour of the hospital, Stanford almost ran into Janis and her mother, there to see Mark. The inspector winked at the girl and held a finger to his lips.

Janis grinned and returned the wink, screwing up the entire side of her face. Then she nodded her head.

No one noticed the exchange.

Dr. Fletcher and Dr. Clineman showed Glen Holland to the men. Glen's head had been bandaged, as had his chest wounds.

"I don't understand what's keeping him alive," Mary Beth wondered aloud.

Stanford's only response was a grunt.

Holland's legs were covered with what appeared to be hundreds of savage insect bites.

Actually the living sand had entered his body through these small wounds.

Carleson's only red marks were on his arm. The man was busy and happy in his room.

Playing jacks.

"How much do they know?" Stanford asked, indicating the doctors.

Mike's eyes sought his. "You mean about last night?"

"Yes."

"Nothing."

The inspector frowned. "It's time for the truth, Chief Bambridge. There is no point in maintaining a

123

pretense now."

The group had been joined by other medical personnel.

"You spoke of skeptics, Inspector?" Mike jerked his thumb toward the doctors.

"Inspector?" Mary Beth looked up. "I can tell you're British by your accent. Are you from Scotland Yard?"

Stanford drew himself up to his full six feet, four inches and bristled. "Scotland Yard, madam, is not the only law enforcement organization in the world. To answer your question, no! I am not from the Yard."

"Well, excuse me!" Mary Beth retorted sharply. She looked at Leo. "And you?"

"I'm from New York."

"What's going on, Mike?" Clineman asked. "Now, damn it, man, we've got something loose in this hospital—this community. If you can shed some light on it, we must know what it is."

Mike visually passed the buck to Stanford. The inspector pointed to the rear of the hospital. "That man you have housed in the trailer . . . he must be destroyed."

The doctors all started talking at once, angrily. Stanford stood calmly, waiting for the hubbub to fade away.

"What do you mean?" Dr. Slater finally demanded.

"Dr. Carleson's minor . . . infirmity will pass. Give him twenty-four hours, and he'll be fine. I've seen several dozen cases like his over the years. But you are faced with a real medical and ethical problem

124

with Holland."

The doctors remained silent. Each knew there was absolutely no hope for Glen Holland, yet none of them had ever seen anything like what had happened to the orderly.

"I know you're all frustrated and baffled by what has happened," Stanford began. "I've been frustrated by this very thing for years. But think for a moment. That young man, Holland, is beyond help. His vital organs are shattered. His brain is dead. He's straight-lining, and you all know it. He has literally been eaten alive by living sand. Now why isn't he dead? Oh, he is. But worse, his soul is lost."

"This is ridiculous!" Dr. Thomas said. But there was uncertainty in his voice. "I don't profess to know what's happened, but I doubt the Devil had anything to do with it."

"Who said the Devil did?" Leo asked softly. "None of us did, so that means you must have thought about that before we arrived."

The doctor's face flushed. But he kept his mouth closed.

"Are you going to tell us the . . . Devil had something to do with Jenny Cauldman?" Clineman broke the silence.

"Oh, yes. Quite. She was probably frightened so badly she lost her mind."

"And aged?" Slater's tone was scornful.

"No, that was done deliberately. I've been giving that some thought. Was the girl quite pretty?"

"Very. Beautiful, I'd say," Mary Beth told him.

"The boy's alter shape would not be human. It could not take human form. Only the boy can change shapes. The alter-shape would be hideous to look at. That's probably your answer."

The doctors were rolling their eyes; some were smiling, openly contemptuous.

Stanford ignored them, as best he could. He turned to Carleson, who was busy playing jacks. "Treat the doctor with antiseptic, on his arm. Not enough entered his system to do him any lasting harm."

"Not enough what, Inspector?" Mary Beth asked.

But she knew.

Sand.

"Oh, the man is a crackpot!" Slater stated. He glared at Stanford. "Just who do you think you are?"

The inspector withered him with a frosty look. "Young man, I have tolerated just about all of your snippiness I can for one session. Suffice it to say, you may be able to lance a boil or remove a wart, but you do not know what this community is facing. It may be difficult for you to comprehend, but there are matters that fall far outside the range and scope of medical science. I'm sure your Maker will take your arrogance and stupidity into consideration on Judgment Day."

Leo smiled.

Mike chose that time to step in and cool the situation. "Is there some sort of private conference room here in the hospital?"

"Of course." There was a note of relief in Clineman's voice. He had expected the inspector to retaliate further against Dr. Slater. "Yes, I think that would be wise. It isn't very professional of us to be standing out in the hall and arguing. Please, let's all just settle down and listen to what Inspector . . .

126

ah . . . ?" He looked at Stanford.

"Willingston. You may call me Stanford." The inspector turned to Slater. "You may not."

Flushing with anger, Slater said, "If what you suggest will help the patients, I'm for it."

They adjoined to a conference room, and coffee and soft drinks were sent in. As Stanford began to speak, he was very aware of the hostility in the eyes of about half of those present. This time, he did not allow that to upset him.

He would save the pictures until last. After that, it would be up to the doubters as to whether they lived or died. They would have to be shown the power of Mantine, of Paul the shape-changer and his alter form, and of the sand creatures.

Stanford concluded with: "Keep an open mind until this evening, when the blood samples from Dean and Donna Mansfield arrive and can be matched with the blood Dr. Carleson took from the sand found in and around the Kelly house."

"And not a word of this leaves this conference room," Mike told them. "If I have to do it, I can get a judge to sign a gag order on you all."

"You really think there is something to all this talk of voodoo, Chief?" Clineman asked.

"The pictures, Mike," Leo suggested.

Mike tossed the envelope onto the table.

The doctors looked. And looked again. They stared in undisguised horror and disbelief at the blown-apart sandman, the torso going one way, the legs and lower part another.

Then Stanford capped off the effect of the photograph by placing a flat packet on the table.

127

"Eight by tens of what remained of Dean and Donna Mansfield. As you view them, note the circled spots. Those are blobs of sand stuck in the blood."

The doctors looked. Paled at the carnage.

Thomas asked, "If what you say is true, Inspector, why didn't this sand"—he pointed to the circles on the blow-ups—"become alive, for want of a better word, that is?"

"And I have a question," Mary Beth said. "If this Mantine person has returned from, ah, the grave"—she was amazed at herself for even saying it—"surely he has created other sand people over the years. What happened to them?"

Stanford nodded his approval of the questions. "Fair inquiries. Addressing the first one: I don't know. Perhaps the sand did not absorb enough blood to function; to activate. That's only a guess. But I can assure you all, when something of this nature occurs on the islands, we take no chances. The death cottage was destroyed by fire; very carefully burned. The ashes were taken far out to sea and dumped. In containers. We have, ah, followed this procedure several times over the years."

He looked at Mary Beth. "To your question. Certainly Mantine has created many sand creatures. But they must have blood to survive. Human blood. It is our belief the creatures tend to stay away from groups of people. They seem to have an animal sense of survival. And I don't know how long one of these things can survive without blood. Days, probably. We theorize they simply return to the earth after that."

"Dormant, but still alive?" Clineman asked.

Stanford shook his head. "No, I don't think so. I think without blood they die. If they didn't, the islands would be filled with them. We also believe—again, this is only theory—that Mantine alone cannot call these creatures. He must have help. Unfortunately, I believe he has found what he's been searching for in the devil-child. The houngans I have spoken with recently also believe this. They are both afraid and glad because Mantine has left the islands."

A cop stuck his head into the room. "Inspector? The blood samples you requested are on the way. We'll pick them up at the airport this evening."

"Thank you, officer." Willingston waited until the door had closed. "Now, as to Holland, what I am going to suggest will be met with revulsion and objections, but believe me, it is the only way to deal with the problem. As long as he remains alive, the living sand within him is growing stronger. You can't remove it and save him. You have to accept this as fact: Holland is dead. Medically and spiritually, he is dead! And what remains is very dangerous. His shell has to be destroyed."

Mary Beth shook her head and sighed. "I will concur; Glen Holland is dead. His brain, liver, heart, and lungs do not function."

The others agreed. Even Slater.

Clineman then said, "I believe this hospital should, from this moment on, take only emergency cases. Unless we have reason to believe the incoming have already been contaminated—and we should brace ourselves for that eventuality—they should be transported to Tucson or Phoenix. Any scheduled surgery, unless it is emergency work, should be done

129

away from this facility."

The others agreed. Reluctantly.

"Glen Holland." A doctor tossed that out.

"I shall take care of Mr. Holland," Stanford stated. "What faith is he?"

"Catholic."

"Then I suggest you contact a priest, immediately."

"And pass the buck to him?" Slater asked, once more challenging the inspector.

"No. To bless Mr. Holland before he dies. To perform the last rites."

"I thought you told us he was already dead," Dr. Belline said.

"He's dead physically. But I have to assume that the priest would want to pray for his soul—which the young man lost through no fault of his own. I'm not qualified to handle that part of it."

"I'll call Father Gomez." Clineman looked at the others, and they nodded their heads in agreement. "He's a young priest. Probably thirty years old. But well liked and highly educated. It's rumored that he was trained, if that is the right word, to be an exorcist." He shrugged. "That is only rumor, mind you."

"Good," Stanford said. "I hope it's more than rumor."

"Why?" Mary Beth asked.

"Well, that would mean the good father has some understanding of and belief in the supernatural. He'll be an asset."

Slater could not quite conceal his contempt for the entire proceeding. He was a good doctor, but impatient and often arrogant. He professed to be an agnostic.

"More mumbo jumbo," he complained.

Mary Beth gave him a look that warned him she wasn't going to take much more. "We're all in agreement, Dick; so why don't you just knock it off, huh?"

Mike hid a smile. He liked this lady's style, and other things he could not help but notice.

Slater flushed and closed his mouth.

"About Glen Holland, Inspector . . . ?" Belline asked.

"When the priest gets here, he and I will chat for a time. While we do, I want a truck hitched onto that trailer and made ready for travel. Preferably far out into the desert."

"I'll see to that," Mike said. "We'll use one of the department's trucks."

"Fine. And bring along about twenty gallons of gasoline, Mike."

"Right."

The doctors stirred uneasily in their chairs, and Belline finally said, "Inspector, exactly what are you going to do?"

"The only thing you can do when dealing with something like this. Destroy it by fire."

SEVEN

Janis waited on the couch outside the little room that housed the soft-drink and candy machines. Her dad just didn't look good at all. Not to Janis's way of thinking. His color was real bad and it seemed like he couldn't get enough water.

And his shoulder—her mother had said only that they'd had a break-in—was all bruised, swollen, and red-looking.

From where Janis sat, she had a pretty good view of the corridor the hospital had closed. Roped off. She had seen Inspector Willingston go down it, and she figured he had to come back out this way.

Something big was happening in Tepehuanes; something evil, she was certain of that. And she was equally certain that it centered around her brother, Paul.

Paul. His voice had continued to deepen in tone. It even had a little echo in it now. And his eyes were just plain crazy looking. If Janis had been leery of her brother before, now she was flat-out scared of him.

And all of a sudden, right out of the blue, Paul had friends. He had never had friends before; nobody had

133

ever wanted to be around him.

Until now.

That in itself was weird.

Those turds from over on the next block—all older than Paul—Rex Grummen and Frank Emerson and Lane Holcomb, were all hanging around the house.

Janis didn't like the way they looked at her.

Not one bit.

And that trashy Lisa Arnot was hanging around with them. She'd been in trouble ever since she was born, practically.

Lisa was pretty, in a slutty sort of way, but she had a real bad reputation. She was mean and sneaky, and she carried a knife . . . and had used it more than once, so all the kids said.

She'd just never been caught.

Janis couldn't figure it. All the kids now hanging out with Paul were her age or older; yet they were all taking orders from Paul, like he was some sort of little . . .

God!

Janis sipped her Coke and thought about it.

It had all happened so fast. Like overnight. In a matter of hours, the three turds and the slut had showed up, like they had been . . .

Summoned.

Of course, parents being what they are, sometimes stupid, her mother and father had no idea of their bad reputations.

They seemed happy that Paul had friends.

Janis wondered if, when she got old like her parents, she'd be so dumb.

She rose from the uncomfortable couch and

walked back to the empty bottle rack. She and Stanford spotted each other at the same time. She jerked her thumb toward the couch, and Stanford smiled and nodded his head.

Once seated, he said, "How are you, young lady?"

"Fine, sir. I guess. Daddy's been hurt."

"Yes, I know. I'm sorry. How is he?"

They were alone in the small visitors' area.

"The doctors say he's going to be all right. But I guess they say that about everybody, don't they?"

Smart girl, Stanford thought. "I suppose you're wondering why I'm here in Arizona?"

"I know why you're here, sir." Her eyes never left his face.

"Oh? Do you now?"

"Yes. My brother, Paul."

"Perhaps. You don't like your brother very much, do you, Janis?"

"You know I don't, sir."

"Now, how would I know that, young lady?"

"Because you sent those ladies to talk to me down on the beach, didn't you?"

She smiled at him.

Stanford returned the smile, vowing that he would never underestimate the astuteness of children. He decided to take a chance. "Yes, I did, Janis. And I thank you for talking with them in spite of that."

"That's all right. I can't tell my parents how I feel about Paul. They wouldn't believe me. It was nice to have someone to talk to."

Stanford waited. He had a few minutes before the priest was due to arrive.

"Me and my friends have agreed to spy on Paul and

135

his new friends. Do you want us to do that? I mean, we're going to do it anyway."

She's staying one step ahead of me, Stanford thought. "Paul now has friends. That's odd. I thought he didn't like people."

Janis shrugged. "Three punks and one slut."

Stanford winced inwardly at her bluntness.

"He never had friends before. And you're right: He doesn't like people. He doesn't like anybody." She looked over at the candy dispenser and then remembered she'd left her purse in her father's room, with her mother, taking only enough change to buy a Coke.

Stanford noticed the direction her eyes were taking and he stood up, digging in his pocket for change. "Have some candy on me, Janis." They walked to the dispenser. "Which do you prefer?"

She pointed out sour balls, and Stanford dropped the change in and punched the button. Janis popped one into her mouth and offered one to him.

He declined, politely but firmly. He'd eaten one of those things before. Only one. According to Stanford's reckoning, one could get the same effect by sucking on a green persimmon.

"These new friends, Janis, what are their names?"

She told him, in between crunches, and he jotted down the names on a small notepad. "How are they behaving?"

"Weird."

"Ah, could you possibly be just a bit more descriptive, Janis?"

She chomped down on another sour ball, and Stanford shuddered. "They're all older than Paul.

Bigger and tougher. But they're all taking orders from him."

Converts, Stanford guessed. Probably all very cruel youngsters, born bad, and easily led by someone of higher intelligence.

Especially if that someone had help from the darker side of the veil.

"Janis, I want you and your friends to be very careful. Don't get caught alone by any of your brother's new friends. That might prove to be very dangerous."

"I already figured that out. But it's gonna be kind of hard for me. I live there, remember?"

"Quite. Does your bedroom door have a secure lock on it?"

She shrugged. "It has a lock. I'll head for my room if I have to."

"How old are these kids?"

"One boy is twelve. Big for his age—mean. The other two are thirteen. Lisa is fourteen. And I think she and Paul are . . . well, you know."

"Yes, I know." It all fits quite neatly, he thought. He had seen the pattern develop before. "Are there drugs involved?"

"I'm sure of it. But Paul wouldn't take any himself."

"But . . . ?" Stanford pressed.

"Oh, if he thought they'd help, he'd give them to others, if he had them."

He has them, Stanford decided. Mantine would see to that. "I'm at the Country Inn, Janis. Room 144. Don't hesitate to call me if you get in trouble. If I don't answer, call the police station. They'll know

137

where to find me. You understand?"

"Yes, sir."

"And I want you to be careful, you and your friends. At first, I'd intended to ask you to do a bit of cloak and dagger work for me. I have since rejected that idea. It could be too dangerous for you."

Just try and stop me! Janis thought.

"You might get hurt, or worse. Do you understand, Janis?"

"Oh, yes, sir. We won't try to follow Paul or any of the others."

Sure you won't! Stanford had raised two children. And even though his kids had grown up and moved away, one to New Zealand and the other to England, he hadn't forgotten that kids love excitement, and dying is unreal to healthy children.

"I mean it, Janis."

"Yes, sir."

"Very well. I know you are a child that minds her elders."

She didn't meet his eyes on that one. Just crunched another sour ball.

"Is there anything else about Paul that appears to be different?"

"His voice. It's real deep now, and hollow sounding. It's scary."

It should be. It's coming from the other side of the grave.

"Why has it changed so?" she asked.

Stanford did not know what to tell her. As far as he knew, at least on the islands, Mantine had always failed in his efforts to enlist children. Why that was so, Stanford had no idea, and he was at a loss to explain what had happened to Paul.

How does one tell a child that her brother is a child of the devil?

"His voice," Janis pressed. "Why has it deepened and become so hollow sounding?"

"He's just growing up, Janis." Stanford felt like a traitor for saying that. The girl was in grave danger; but he did not know how to tell her that.

He felt her eyes on him, and was uncomfortable under her gaze.

He cut his eyes from her, and she smiled.

"No, sir. He's not just growing up. He's growing evil."

Deputy Peter Loneman caught up with Mike at the hospital. He was introduced to Leo and Stanford.

"What'd you find out, Pete?"

"Not much, I'm sorry to say. The old men said what the gods bring forth, the gods destroy. That's an Indian way of saying they don't know what's going on."

The others smiled at the expression on the deputy's face.

"Or," Pete continued, "they're telling me, in double-talk, that this is a white man's problem, and who gives a damn what happens to the white man? Personally, I think it's a combination of both."

"They didn't seem at all concerned?" Stanford asked.

"No. There's something else you've all got to understand, and I hope you won't take it the wrong way. When trouble faces an Indian, he's going to deal with it like an Indian, not like a white man. We are all—every Indian is—a lot closer to the earth and the elements than ninety-nine percent of the whites. Your ancestors were once like us, but that was lost, for you, hundreds of years back. Not so for us. We are still basically a warrior race. We haven't, and we never will, fully embrace the white man's ways." He shook his head. "I don't think I'm saying this right."

"Yes, you are, Peter," Leo told him with a smile. "Mantine—"

"Who?" Pete interrupted.

Mike quickly brought him up to date.

The deputy looked at Leo. "OK. Go ahead, please. Mantine . . . what?"

"Mantine must know that he is taking a terrible chance, a risk, in leaving the islands and coming here. It's not clear to me why he did it. Maybe we'll never know. But I think what you're saying is that when he makes his move, he'll be making it against a people who are soft and settled and unaccustomed to facing and handling any serious problem alone and without the aid of laws and lawmen. Am I getting close?"

"Very close," Peter told him.

"And maybe," Leo continued, "that might be the way to defeat this . . . thing." He looked at Stanford. "Do you understand what I'm getting at?"

"To a degree, yes. But in dealing with the supernatural, don't get complacent about anything; overconfidence can get you killed." He caught a glimpse of the young priest walking up the corridor. "That must be Father Gomez."

Peter looked. "Yeah. That's him. He's a nice guy.

140

But he's tough as a boot; don't ever doubt that. He was a street punk until he was about fifteen or so. His parish priest finally got enough of his lip and took him out behind the rectory. Then he proceeded to knock some sense into him. Turned Dan right around. He became a straight-*A* student, went off to college, and became a priest. He's, ah, well, it's rumored that he's the man you want if you're dealing with the Devil, face to face."

"We are," Stanford said grimly. "Come on. I have something very unpleasant to attend to."

Peter looked at the expression on the inspector's face. "What?"

"I have to kill a living dead man."

Stanford spoke to the priest for fifteen minutes, practically nonstop, with Mike and Pete and Leo and the medical personnel involved listening.

Father Gomez's expression did not change during that time.

When Stanford had finished, the priest sat for a moment in silence. Then he shocked everybody present by saying, "So Mantine finally thinks he's strong enough to leave the islands, huh?"

"My word, Father!" Stanford finally said.

The others just stared at the priest, none of them having expected Gomez to know who Stanford was talking about.

"Is there any truth to the rumor that you are an exorcist?" Slater asked.

Daniel Gomez shifted his dark eyes and smiled. "Do you believe in God, Dr. Slater?"

"I am a man of science, not one given to putting much stock in superstitious nonsense."

"Well, Doctor, I have a hunch you'll be a believer before all this is over, one way or the other."

Slater frowned and looked away from the piercing black eyes of the priest.

"The Devil is a son of a bitch," Gomez said. "I've been as close to him as I am to any of you, and let me assure you, it is not a pleasant experience. Look at my hair; I'm almost totally gray. Five years ago I did not have a gray hair on my head. I'm thirty years old, going on a hundred. You think Satan doesn't exist, Dr. Slater? He's real, bet on that."

"He might be real in your mind, Gomez"—Slater clung to his fantasies—"but not in mine."

"Then I feel sorry for you, Dr. Slater. You'll probably be among the first to go."

"Go where?"

Gomez smiled sadly and stood up. "Let's go see this Glen Holland."

"Are you going to answer my question?" Slater asked. "Go where?"

Gomez glanced at him, but said only, "I will pray for you, Doctor."

Masked and gowned and gloved, the men and women stood around the bed on which Glen Holland lay, strapped down. His eyes were wild, and contained an inhuman light. He fought his straps and mumbled in a language no one could understand.

Gomez bowed his head and prayed silently.

Outside the trailer, the wind picked up, lashing the metal structure with sand. The wind sang in a low, moaning voice.

It was unnerving to several of those present.

Gomez sprinkled Holy Water onto the face of Glen Holland.

Holland began to scream as the blessed water burned into his flesh, and a foul stench filled the trailer as yellow smoke rose from the seared holes. Then small bloody rivers of sand began to ooze, like pus, from the holes.

Slater vomited behind his mask, and rushed from the room.

Holland screamed even more wildly. He spat great bloody globs of sand onto himself and the bed. The globs that landed on his chest began to eat their way back into his flesh.

Dr. Fletcher turned away from the hideous sight, and when Mike slipped his hand into hers, she took it gratefully.

Gomez said, "Let's get this show on the road, people. There is nothing more I can do. He's got to be destroyed, and it's got to be done quickly."

"I'm still opposed to this . . . this barbaric practice!" Dr. Thomas protested.

"Shut up!" Gomez's voice was sharp. "If I get sick in body, I'll come to you. If you get sick in spirit, you go to a priest or a minister or a rabbi. This is out of your field of expertise. Let's go, folks. Move it!"

Riding out into the vastness of the desert with Leo and Stanford, in Mike's city unit, Gomez said, "How come nobody asked me how I knew about Mantine and Nicole?" He was smiling very faintly.

"My wife was Catholic," Stanford said. "I'm a convert. I've made friends with several priests on the island. And with several Protestant ministers who believe as we do. There are more than the average laymen might think. The priests told me something about some of the things they studied."

"Mantine has been around for a long time." Gomez was looking out the window. Ahead of them, a pickup truck, driven by a cop, was pulling the trailer that contained Glen Holland. Behind Mike's unit was a station wagon, filled with doctors. "He's been causing trouble for a lot of people over the years. And he's been responsible, directly so, for the deaths of several priests and lay people. He's ruined marriages, ruined lives. Just for the dark fun of it." The priest was silent for a moment. "I want to catch him in human form. Just once."

"You might very well die when you do," Stanford reminded him.

"Death does not frighten me. I've faced it too many times. I just want my death to be worthwhile," Gomez retorted.

They bounced along in silence for several miles.

Then Leo turned in his seat to face Stanford. "What about those other kids Janis told you about? The bunch that's hanging around Paul?"

"It bothers me," the inspector admitted.

"Why?" Gomez questioned. "That doesn't bother me at all. Ten years ago, it would have. I wouldn't have said that. But ten years ago, I didn't understand the Devil or the people who worship him."

The Galiuro Mountains loomed up in front of them, still some miles distant.

"God will forgive almost anything." Gomez's words were softly spoken. "But He is very clear about worshipping false gods. Very clear about his opinion of Satan. Some people are born bad. Branded with the mark of Cain. Born to serve the Dark One. It isn't some supernatural spell they've fallen under. The Devil didn't force them to follow him; Satan is not making them do anything. They're doing it because they have the Devil in them, and have had since the moment of conception. You can call it the bad-seed theory, if you wish to."

"Doesn't that fly in the face of exorcism, Father Gomez?" Leo asked.

Gomez smiled. "A name like Corigliano and you don't know about exorcism?"

Leo laughed. "I'm a backslider, Father."

"Hell, Leo!" The priest laughed. "You're not a backslider—you've fallen plumb off the horse!"

Leo grinned as the others had a good laugh at his expense. It was worth it; they had all been wound up tight.

Gomez looked first at Stanford, then at Leo. "I shall expect you both at church first thing in the morning. To hear your confession. And I want Father Gunter to bless us all. That is not a request, gentlemen."

"Yes, Father," the cop and ex-cop mumbled.

"As to your question, Leo—no. Being possessed is quite another matter. All that means is that during a moment of weakness, a moment the subject might not even have been aware of, the Devil took over. Most of the time, the human spirit can shake off Satan's influence without outside help. A few quiet

145

moments spent reading God's word, meditating, sharing what you have with someone less fortunate . . . or just sitting in church. That's usually all it takes. Only in extreme cases does it ever come to an exorcism. For me, there is no help for the ones born bad. They are beyond redemption. Many exorcists are split on that subject, however. Another priest might give you a totally different viewpoint. My theory is that one does not attempt to pet a rabid animal. There is no cure. You just kill it."

"You are a violent fellow, aren't you, Father?" Stanford said.

"You don't think Satan is violent, Inspector? You don't think Satan worship is violent? Do you believe that it doesn't encourage violent and inhumane and perverted acts and actions? I think you are far too intelligent to even think that, much less believe it. And aren't you here to kill, Inspector? Isn't that a violent act?"

Stanford sat, a stunned look on his face. "I never told you that, Father. You could not have known."

"Let's just say I know what Mantine forced you to do, Inspector, and leave it at that."

Rex Grummen rubbed his crotch and grinned at Janis from Paul's bedroom door. In his room, Paul laughed and Lisa giggled.

Rex licked his lips in a very suggestive manner.

Janis shot Rex the rigid digit, and stepped back into her bedroom, slamming the door. She looked at the lock. Wasn't much of one. But she'd never felt the need to lock her door before.

She locked it.

"Creep!" she muttered. "They're all creeps."

She had come home only to find Paul and Lisa naked on the bed.

She had screamed at Lisa and the girl—young woman really—had only lifted her head from Paul's belly and laughed at her.

Whore!

This was a mistake, Janis silently admitted. I should have gone directly to the Matthews' house like Mother told me to do.

Now there's no way I can get out of here.

I'm stuck! Trapped.

She walked to her phone and picked it up, intending to call one of her friends.

But as soon as she put the phone to her ear, she knew someone was on an extension, listening in.

Verbal filth rolled into her ear.

Sickening. Disgusting.

She knew the voice. It belonged to one of Paul's new friends. Lane Holcomb. Twice, the police had picked him up for rape. But the girls, at the last minute, had refused to testify against him.

Everybody knew why: Lane had threatened to kill them if they did.

And everybody knew he would.

She dropped the phone back onto the cradle. Looked at her clock. She sighed, knowing her mother wouldn't be back for several hours.

Stupid! Why hadn't she done what her mother had told her to do?

Janis caught movement out of the corner of her eye. A piece of paper being shoved under the door.

147

She walked over and picked it up.

It was a pornographic drawing. Depraved and sewer-dirty.

She looked at it, then, red-faced and getting mad, wadded the piece of filth up into a tight ball and slung it across the room. It hit the rim of her wastebasket, rolled around, and dropped in.

"Two points," she said automatically. "Maybe three from this distance."

What those people had been doing in the picture was impossible.

She guessed.

Laughter came from the other side of the locked door.

Then the boys began calling out things they'd like to do to Janis.

"No way, creepos," she muttered.

She went to her closet and got a coat hanger. Straightening it out, she went back to the locked door, and, kneeling down, put one side of her face to the carpet. Through the crack, she could see several pairs of bare feet.

She had a hunch they were all naked.

The smaller feet, with painted toenails, belonged to Lisa.

Unless one of the boys had turned funny.

The biggest set of feet, she guessed, belonged to Lane Holcomb. They were dirty.

"Hey, baby!" Lane hollered. "I got something nice and hard for you. I'm holding it in my hand. Why don't you open the door and you can kiss it."

Kiss this, you jerk! Janis thought, lining up the end of the coat hanger with one of Lane's big feet.

She jammed it. Hard.

Lane screamed and squalled, and she could see him jumping around in the hall. Peeking out under the crack, she could see drops of blood on the beige carpet. She grinned, knowing she'd gotten in the first good lick of this battle.

"You lousy bitch!" Lane yelled. "I'll get you for this! You'll be sorry you ever done this to me, you . . ."

Janis tuned out on all the things he was going to do to her.

And he finally wound down.

"Why don't you go stick your foot in Lisa's mouth, Lane?" Janis yelled. Actually, she had another part of Lisa's anatomy in mind, but she didn't want to say that.

She heard Lisa tell Lane to go with her because she'd put something on his foot.

Janis jumped onto her bed and grabbed the phone. No one on any extension. Quickly, she punched out Jean's number, got her on the second ring.

"Jean! Paul and his creeps have me cornered in my room. Get the gang and come over here real quick. Get Bing and Roy—and hurry up!"

"On my way!"

Since "the gang" lived only a few blocks apart, she knew they would be over in about five minutes.

Providing they could get permission to go out.

She sat on the edge of her bed and waited.

"What is this place?" Stanford asked, looking

149

around him at the desolate spot.

"Where we burn dope," Mike told him. "Been enough grass burned in this spot to get the entire state high for a week. Nearest resident is miles away. Right over there"—he pointed—"is our shooting range." He glanced at Father Gomez. "You ready?"

"I am. But I'm not so sure about the doctors. Or the three of you for that matter."

"What do you mean?" Leo asked.

"This is not going to be pleasant. You'll see. Come on."

"Come in, come in, come in!" a deep, hollow-sounding voice urged. It floated across the hotness. "We're about to have a barbecue. And I'm going to be the guest of honor."

"What the hell . . . ?" Belline muttered.

"Brace yourselves," Gomez warned them.

The only person who was not visibly shocked by Glen Holland's condition was Father Gomez.

Holland was lucid. He lay placidly in bed, not fighting his leather restraints.

And his voice was deep and firm, yet it had that strange hollow sound.

Gomez started praying.

"Oh, stop that mumbo jumbo, you stupid spic!" Glen said. "You're wasting your time."

Gomez stopped praying. Lifted his eyes to meet the savage dead eyes of Holland.

"You're all fools!" the voice rumbled.

It was not Glen Holland's voice.

"Who . . . ?" Slater opened his mouth.

He closed it after a hard glance from Gomez.

"Why are we fools, Glen?" Gomez asked.

"I'm not Glen!" the voice rumbled out of the mouth of Holland.

"Yes, I know that. But who are you?"

A hissing sound emanated from the mouth, followed by laughter. Evil, taunting laughter. Well-hollow. The odor that rolled in waves from the mouth was putrid. It fouled the nostrils of all present.

Father Gomez looked at Slater. "Dr. Slater, meet the devil."

Slater's face, under the mask, was pale. His eyes had a haunted and confused look.

Laughter once more rose from the bullet-mangled head of Holland.

"You have anything else you'd like to say?" Gomez asked.

"Yeah. Stick your Bible up your ass!"

Gomez picked up a can of gasoline.

"Going home, going home!" Holland sang. "In the heat of the day I'm going home."

Gomez doused the soulless being with gasoline, and profanity flooded from its mouth.

Mary Beth turned and walked out of the small trailer. In the hot, breezeless air of that arid place, she removed her mask and gloves and walked over to the dubious shade an old ramshackle building provided.

The voice continued to taunt her, follow her, throwing profane suggestions at her. She wasn't sure whether she was truly hearing the words or if they were in her mind.

Peter Loneman left the trailer, and took off his gloves and mask and gown. Then he took cans of gasoline from the back of the pickup truck. He glanced over at Mary Beth.

"Goes against everything you were ever taught, doesn't it?" he called.

She looked at him. Nodded her head, not trusting herself to speak. Not just yet. She walked over to him.

Peter looked up at her as he was twisting off a gas cap.

"For God's sake, don't light a cigarette."

"I don't smoke."

"Good. You know, what's really bad about this whole . . . mess, is that little kid."

"What little kid?"

"Paul Kelly."

"What about Paul Kelly, Deputy?"

They could hear the low sounds of Father Gomez praying.

"Oh, shut up, you asshole!" The voice ripped through the air.

Gomez continued to pray.

"I thought the inspector leveled with all you people?"

"I thought he did, too."

"Come in here and sit in my face, baby!"

"Our Father, who art in Heaven . . ."

"Will you knock off that fucking shit!"

". . . hallowed be Thy name."

"You haven't seen the last of me, bitch! I'll come back and kill you. Slow. I'll make your dying last and last and last."

". . . Thy kingdom come, Thy . . ."

The voice began to curse. And it gradually became the voice of the real Glen Holland.

"Paul Kelly?" Mary Beth asked.

"He's a devil-child, Doctor. The inspector trailed him all the way from the islands," Mike explained.

"A . . . devil-child?"

"Yes, ma'am."

"Oh, my God!"

"That pious puke won't help you, baby!" The voice cut through the hot air. "But I've got something that'll really make your day."

The voice was so loud Mary Beth wondered how those remaining in the trailer could tolerate it.

Loneman looked at her. "What's the matter? Other than the obvious, that is."

"Paul's father," she whispered. Peter had to strain to hear her. "I don't think he was checked for those strange red bites. Oh, God!"

"Too late, baby!" The words were blasted out over the hot landscape.

The others were leaving the trailer.

"Douse it, boys," Mike called.

Gasoline was poured in, under, and on the trailer.

Then they all backed up and waited until the gasoline fumes had dissipated.

"You shitheads think this is the end," Holland yelled. "But this is only the beginning. You'll see. You'll all see."

"Light it," Gomez said grimly.

The trailer went up with a whooshing sound that rocked them all back on their heels. The metal turned red-hot, the wood became an inferno, the plastic melted and dripped.

Gomez bowed his head and prayed softly.

Mary Beth suddenly screamed and pointed at the blazing trailer.

153

Eyes stared in disbelief, horror.

Glen Holland lurched out of the flames, his arms held out in front of him, cooked strips of flesh dangling from them. Wild laughter ripped from his now-lipless mouth.

All could hear the sickening sounds of raw flesh bubbling and sizzling as it cooked.

A ball of flame, he staggered toward the knot of lawmen and doctors.

Laughing hideously.

EIGHT

"Yeah, Frank"—Janis heard Roy Weaver's voice—
"you sure are gonna let us in. 'Cause if you don't, I'm
gonna stomp your head off. Now what's it gonna
be?"

"You get away from this house!" Paul shouted, his
deep voice carrying to Janis. "Or I'll call the police!"

Janis unlocked the door to her room and slipped
out. In the hall, she got a broom from the closet and
walked through the house to the front door.

"There she is now!" Bing Shelton called, pointing
at Janis.

Grim-faced and angry, Janis walked up to her
brother and swung the broom. The flat, tightly
bound straw caught Paul smack in the face, sending
him sprawling on his back in the foyer.

Janis then turned and kicked Frank Emerson right
in the balls. When he screamed and bent over, Bing
gave him a knee on the nose and Frank was out of the
game for a time, his nose dripping blood.

Carla and Melissa jumped on Lisa, and rode the
bigger girl to the floor, pinning her there and
holding her arms down so she could not grab the

knife they all knew she carried.

Bing, having wrestled Rex to the floor, was sitting on him.

Jean and Carol and Janis had cornered Lane. Janis was beating him with the broom.

"All right, all right!" Lane hollered. "Lemme alone!"

"Now that we got 'em," Roy panted, "what are we gonna do with 'em?"

Paul was sitting on the floor, his back to a wall. Janis looked at him and the light in his eyes chilled her to her very soul.

"I don't know," she said, brushing back hair from her face. "I just know I'm not gonna go on living where trash like this are welcome."

Paul opened his mouth to speak. He closed it as a familiar shadowy mist formed in a far corner.

"You trying to do too much too soon, mon," Mantine's silent words formed in the boy's head. "Jus' let tings take dey own course. Don' draw de cops to you, OK?"

"Yes," Paul said. "You're right. Thank you for reminding me."

Janis and her friends all wondered who he was talking to.

Paul remained on the floor, but he looked at his sister. "Janis, I apologize for the actions of my friends. This will not happen again. Let them up and they will all leave peacefully."

Janis hesitated, then nodded her head. "OK, Paul."

Paul's friends were released.

At a nod from him, they left, but not before giving

Janis and her friends looks that promised this was not over. Not by a long shot.

Janis noticed with grim satisfaction that Lane was limping.

Paul rose to his feet and, without another word or glance, walked up the hall to his bedroom. Once inside, he closed the door and locked it.

"Will somebody please tell me what's goin' on?" Bing asked.

Janis peeked out the side window by the door. Lisa and her thugs were pedaling away on their bikes.

"Let's get some Cokes and chips." She led them toward the kitchen. "We'll sit in the den and I'll explain."

Gomez grabbed up a rotting two by four and ran up to the lurching, howling, laughing blaze. He hit the devil's fire in the chest, knocking it to the ground. Then he hammered at the form, yelling, "Get some boards and brush; anything that will burn. Throw it on him."

The men and Mary Beth began to grab whatever would burn. Peter even jerked boards loose from the old building. Soon, the sheer weight of the things tossed on him prevented the creature that was once Glen Holland from rising. The howling and laughing and struggling became weaker, then stopped altogether.

All were sweaty and sooty and scared.

Even Slater.

Especially Slater.

The doctor walked away from the group and the

blazing pyre, and sat down in the sand. He stared numbly at nothing for a moment. Then he put his hands to his face and began to weep uncontrollably.

Mary Beth dropped the stick she held in her hand and walked toward him. Gomez's voice stopped her.

She turned to the priest.

"Let him alone. This is something he's got to work out by himself . . . for a time. He's full of doubts. After a while, he'll have a hundred questions to ask. But let him come to us."

They stood for a time, watching the fire burn down.

The only reminders of Glen Holland were a few scraps of cooked meat and bones. A charred skeletal hand protruded out of the dying fire.

Dr. Belline stared at it. "What I just saw was impossible. Yet . . . I witnessed it. I can't deny what I saw."

Mary Beth remembered Mark Kelly and told the others what she feared.

"I'll get on the horn," Peter said, "alert the hospital."

But it was too late.

"They released him about twenty minutes ago," Peter informed the group. "He left with his wife. All of a sudden his temperature and BP leveled out, and he felt fine. Said there was no reason to keep him any longer. And his shoulder was healing nicely."

The doctors looked at one another. Clineman broke the silence.

"Now what?"

"We pray that his miraculous recovery wasn't the work of a darker power," Gomez said.

"But—"

The priest interrupted Mike. "Don't count on it," he said shortly.

Roy and Bing, both twelve years old, had listened to Janis's story. They now sat on a sectional in the den, and stared at the girls.

Bing tried a smile.

It faded before the serious faces of the girls.

Roy sipped his Coke and looked at the picture in the book Melissa had brought over with her. No doubt about it; that was the mark on Paul's arm.

Roy always had thought Paul was somewhere on the south side of squirrely.

Bing rose and looked up the hall toward the bedrooms. Paul's door was still closed.

He sat down. "We're in trouble, gang."

"No kidding!" Roy looked at him, his sarcasm evident. "My, what a surprise. You got anymore monumental statements to make?"

"How'd you like a fat lip?" his friend asked.

"Knock it off!" Janis told them, putting an end to the bickering. "If we start fighting among ourselves, Paul will like that."

"Speaking of Paul," Bing said, "why don't we just go beat the hell out of him?"

"I don't think that would be allowed," Janis told him.

Roy looked at her. "Who around here would stop us?"

"I don't think he's from around here, Roy."

Roy got it on the second try. He opened his mouth

to speak. Several times. Nothing came out. His face became a little paler.

Carol looked around. "Here comes Paul."

The boy appeared, walking in a stately manner toward the kitchen. He stopped abruptly when he saw the book lying open on the coffee table.

Even from a distance, he could clearly see the picture.

He looked at his sister. Spoke in that deep hollow-sounding voice. "Don't go away. I feel it's time that we talked."

His sister nodded her head.

Paul went into the kitchen, but returned in a few moments, carrying a huge sandwich and a glass of milk. He sat down on the sectional, keeping his distance from the others, staying to one end.

"All growing children should have their milk." Jean stuck the needle to him.

"Screw you," Paul told her with a smile. "But then, you'd probably like that, wouldn't you?"

Jean half rose. "I'll slap your dirty mouth," she retorted.

Paul took a bite of his sandwich and chewed contentedly for a few seconds. "No, you won't. Because all I have to do is tell Lisa and Rex and Lane and Frank what I want done, and they'll do it. And I have a very vivid imagination."

The silence pulsed.

"What do you want, Paul?" Janis broke the almost tangible muteness.

Paul looked at his sister. He put down his sandwich and reached over, tickling her under the chin.

When she slapped his hand away, he laughed at her and retrieved his sandwich.

"I really haven't made up my mind yet, sister. But I do think I can truthfully say that it's going to get very interesting around here, very soon. Oh, my, yes. We're going to have a lot of fun." He laughed. "At least, I will."

"The inspector from the islands is here, Paul," Janis said.

"Yes, I know."

"How do you know!" She practically shouted the question. "I didn't see him myself until this morning."

"I have friends you cannot see, sister dearest." He grinned. "Yet."

"Devil-friends, Paul?"

"But of course!" His reply was given cheerfully, boastfully.

"How come you're telling us all this, Paul?" Melissa asked.

"Why not? What can you do? Go to the police with some totally preposterous story about me being in league with the devil? Go ahead, I wish you would. Then the cops will mark you all down as a bunch of kooks and they'll never believe anything else you say." He pointed to the phone. "Go ahead. Call them."

No one made a move.

He's right, Janis thought.

Paul took a big bite of his sandwich and a big gulp of milk. "Fucking makes me hungry."

The girls blushed and the boys looked very uncomfortable.

161

Paul cut his eyes to Bing. "Would you like to have Lisa, Bing?"

Bing blinked. "Ah . . . no!"

"Liar. Of course, you would. Well, if not Lisa, who would you like to have? Just tell me. I can easily arrange it."

Janis tossed cold water on that, knowing it would make her brother mad. "Of course, all he'll have to do is give up his soul, right, Paul?"

Paul's eyes turned mean. "Why don't you just butt out, bigmouth?"

Janis pointed a finger at him. "You listen to me," she yelled. "By now, all the doctors at the hospital know about you. The chief of police knows. And several of the cops and deputies—"

"You lie!" her brother screamed. "No one knows about me. They wouldn't believe it."

"I'm not lying, Paul. Inspector Willingston and I had a long talk at the hospital. They know a lot more than you think they do. So you'd better back off and think about what you're doing."

Paul rose from the couch to stand over his sister and glare down at her. Then he threw the contents of his glass into her face.

He left her sputtering on the couch, milk dripping off her face and onto her blouse, and walked up the hall to his room. At his door, he turned and shouted, "You're all dead. Damned! And worse! All of you!"

Paul stormed into his room and slammed the door.

Janis wiped her face, then went to change her blouse. When she rejoined her friends in the den, Bing said, "I think he means what he says." He didn't look too happy.

"I think we'd all better start being real careful from now on," Carol put in.

Janis looked up the hallway. It was empty. "Problem is, we don't know what he's going to do next. Or when."

Their talk was cut short when a car pulled into the garage that was connected to the house. They could hear Connie and Mark talking as they entered the kitchen.

"Well, that's a relief," Carla said. "At least you and your mother won't have to be alone with that creep."

"Yeah," Janis agreed. "He can't work Dad the way he works Mother."

In his room, standing over a wastebasket, Paul spat on a picture of his father.

"And Mark just got better, all of a sudden?" Dr. Thomas asked a resident.

"Everything was normal, Doctor. His appetite had returned. The swelling and redness in his shoulder had vanished. His BP was normal. There was no reason to keep him any longer."

Mark had not been admitted as anybody's special patient, so the resident had had the authority to discharge him.

"I'm not criticizing, Dave." Jack Thomas smiled. "Just curious, that's all."

The young doctor walked away, puzzled, but glad he hadn't gotten chewed out. Something very big was happening in this hospital, and he was just a little annoyed that he hadn't been included in whatever it was.

Just been told to be on the lookout for strange red bite marks.

"Fastest recovery in medical history," Mary Beth said quietly.

"Yeah," Jack agreed. "Let's go see about Larry."

Larry was much better. Most of his faculties had returned to him, but he couldn't remember anything about his brief journey into never-never land.

He recalled leaving his lab after feeling that somebody or something was watching him. After that, nothing.

Clineman brought him up-to-date, and despite all the horrors around them, Larry could not help but smile as he did so. The two men, friends since their college days, delighted in sticking verbal needles into one another.

But it wasn't much fun this time.

"I did what?" Larry asked.

Clineman told him.

"Sweet Jesus Christ!" the ME muttered. "Where are my clothes? I've got to get to work."

"Not yet." Clineman pushed him back onto the bed. "Maybe tomorrow."

Then he told him about Glen Holland.

The ME closed his eyes, and said a short prayer. "My people also had access to that sand, remember?"

"Relax. They've been checked. They're clean. And we've closed the hospital except for emergency cases. You in agreement with that move, Larry?"

"God, yes! Have you set aside a special wing for

anyone who comes in with suspicious-looking bite marks?"

"Good thought. No, we haven't."

"I'll take care of that right now." Jack left the room.

Mary Beth smiled and patted Larry on the shoulder. "Welcome back," she said.

"Are there any Doubting Thomases left?" Stanford questioned, his gaze touching on all present.

Mike's top people had been brought in and briefed, and they had agreed to keep a lid on the story for as long as possible. Once it leaked, the press would jump on it like a hungry hound on Alpo and blow it up to gargantuan proportions; then the department would have armed citizens shooting at everything that moved.

"But the people do have a right to know," Stanford countered, playing devil's advocate with a smile.

"Better a half-dozen die than half a hundred," Leo said coldly.

"Or more," Mike added.

Mike was dressed in honor-guard blues. He and a contingent from the department were to attend Andy's funeral at four that afternoon.

"Anything else?" Mike looked around the table.

The door to the room opened, and a uniformed cop, a worried look on his tanned face, entered. "Sorry, Chief, but we got a problem."

"What is it?"

"Andy's body, Chief. It's gone!"

165

Mike jumped out of his seat. Sat back down, his mouth open. "Gone? What do you mean, gone? Gone where?"

"Hell, Chief, I don't know. The funeral home just called and said they can't find the body. It was in the viewing room about an hour ago, they said. And Mary is about to go bananas."

Andy's wife.

"It will reappear," Gomez said, after looking at and receiving a slight nod from Willingston. "I was curious as to whether Mantine would pull something like this. He's having a devil's-own laugh at this."

Mike thought about that, and a look of horror came to his eyes and face. "Oh, no!"

Gomez nodded.

"You're not serious!" Mike almost yelled.

"Very," Willingston said.

The cop who delivered the message said, "Ah, Chief? I'm missing something here. Somebody want to tell me what is going on?"

"Get it from the assistant chief, Bobby. He's going to brief you all later on this afternoon."

"Ah . . . yes, sir."

The cop backed out of the room and closed the door. He wished somebody would tell him what was happening.

Mike stared at the priest. "All right, Dan, level with me. Where's the body?"

"I have no idea, Mike. My guess would be it's hiding in some darkened building, waiting for night."

"You're not following me, Dan. How did the body

166

get out of the funeral home!" he yelled.

"Walked out," Willingston said calmly.

"Walked out!" Mike shouted. "You mean . . . I mean . . . like some . . . ?" He just could not say the word *zombie*.

"Precisely, Chief," the inspector said. "And calm down, man. Watch your blood pressure. This type of work is stressful enough without overreacting."

"Calm down!" Mike retorted. "I've got spooks and haunts and sand-creatures to contend with, and now a dead officer who's a zombie . . . and you want me to calm down! What's going to show up next? Werewolves, maybe?"

"That is certainly possible, Mike," Gomez told him. "You must bear this in mind: we are dealing with the Devil here. Anything can happen."

Mike put his arms on the table and laid his head on them. He closed his eyes for a moment. Lack of sleep and being wound up like an eight-day clock for hours was taking its toll on him. With a sigh of resignation, he opened his eyes and raised his head, his gaze briefly touching on each man seated around the table.

"I don't know what to do," he admitted. "I'm at a total loss and I don't like the feeling."

"It will get worse," Gomez warned him.

Mike blinked. Sighed. "Thank you, Dan. That was exactly what I didn't need to hear at this time."

"You're welcome."

The door opened, and the uniformed cop who'd just left stuck his head inside.

"Inspector Willingston? Phone call for you on line four."

"Thank you." Stanford lifted the receiver and punched the line open.

"Inspector?"

"Here, Janis. What's the matter, dear?"

Briefly, and quite succinctly for a child, she told him what had happened at her house that afternoon.

"Thank you," Stanford said. "Now listen to me: Can you have one of your little friends stay over for a few days?"

"Oh, sure."

"Do that, dear." He thought for a moment. "Hold on, Janis." He looked at Mike and quickly recapped the other end of the conversation. "Can you spare a walkie-talkie for her? I think she's a very responsible young lady, and won't use it unless there's a real emergency."

Mike nodded. "Sure. No problem. But how do we get it to her without that brother of hers finding out?"

"I have a hunch Mantine is listening to every word we're saying anyway," Father Gomez said. "So what difference does it make?"

Mike and Leo could not help themselves; they looked around the conference room. Then, realizing what they were doing, they grinned sheepishly.

"Tell her we'll get it to her as quickly as possible."

Stanford relayed the message and hung up.

Mike muttered, "I've got one of the best departments in the entire Southwest, and it's all coming down to a ten-year-old with a walkie-talkie out to catch a bunch of spooks!"

*   *   *

Janis called Melissa, who said she couldn't have picked a better time. Her mother was going on vacation with her boyfriend, and she'd been worried about leaving Melissa alone. This would work out fine.

Janis didn't worry about whether it would be all right to have someone over. The house was so huge her friends never interfered with the day-to-day doings of her family.

Several times she'd had friends over for the night and her parents hadn't even known it.

Janis looked out back. Her father was sitting by the pool, enjoying the late afternoon sun. Connie was sitting with him.

At first, Janis had been excited about her dad's return. Then she had looked into his eyes, and her excitement was replaced by a cold feeling.

Something was very wrong with her father.

She didn't know what.

But she could make a pretty good guess.

And it scared her.

Her father's eyes were dead looking, and his voice was a dull monotone. He had joked and kidded only until Janis's friends had left.

Then he had abruptly changed.

Into what, Janis didn't know.

But she had a hunch things were about to go from bad to worse.

Maybe that night.

The girl glanced up the hallway. The door to Paul's room was still closed.

Janis opened the sliding doors to the patio, and joined her parents, by the pool. "Why don't you two

169

just relax and I'll cook Mexican for dinner?" she suggested.

Mark did not even acknowledge his daughter's presence.

Connie smiled. "That's sweet, honey. We'll take you up on that." When she looked at her watch, Janis knew there was something on her mother's mind. "Just go easy on the hot peppers this time, OK?"

Mark scratched himself absentmindedly.

Janis nodded at her mother, and went back into the house. She got a big package of ground chuck out of the freezer and put it in the microwave to defrost. Then she began to gather up onions and peppers and lettuce and cheese and tomatoes.

She wished she could get those disturbing thoughts about her father out of her mind.

But they would not entirely leave. They remained, crouched in a dark corner.

And she did not like the sensation of them being there.

She busied herself getting ready to cook her specialty: tacos.

Melissa was dropped off, said hello to Mark and Connie—Mark only grunted a greeting. Then the girls busied themselves in the kitchen, staying out of Mark's way.

"What's wrong with your dad, Janis? Just a few hours ago he was laughing and joking and acting like he was really up."

"I don't know. You wanna grate the cheese? Something's very wrong, though. You seen Lisa or any of the others since this morning?"

"Naw. Talked to Bing and Roy though."

170

"And . . . ?"

"They both took some money from their savings and went down to the hardware store. Bought hunting knives. You know, the kind you wear on your belt, in one of those leather cases."

"That might not be such a bad idea." Janis told Melissa what she was getting from the police.

"Awesome!"

"Cool it. Here comes Paul."

No greetings were exchanged. Paul just looked at what she was fixing and grimaced.

"You don't have to eat it, you know," Janis reminded her brother.

He smiled very sweetly. "Of course, I'll eat it, sister darling. Why, for me not to come to the table and be a part of the family on Dad's first night home from the hospital . . . heavens!" He feigned great shock and consternation, putting a hand to his forehead. "What kind of son would that make me?"

Janis had a pretty good idea, but kept her response to herself.

Melissa was standing back, away from the boy, watching him closely.

"What are you up to now, Paul?" Janis asked him. "I know you're pulling something."

"Why, sister! How could you even think such a thing? Oh, when you're ready, call me. I'll be more than happy to help set the table."

He walked out of the kitchen, humming a popular rock song.

Melissa watched him until he closed his bedroom door. "I thought he liked serious music."

"Yeah. He does. He's gonna do something nasty. I

171

just don't know what. Or when."

Melissa, like Janis, wondered what Paul was up to.

"He's gonna pull something. I just know it. I wonder what it is . . . ?"

Nothing.

Nothing at all. Paul was a perfect son that evening. He helped set the table. He poured the iced tea. He helped serve. He was a joy to his mother.

He was a fraud and a pain in the neck to Janis.

If Mark noticed his son, he made no mention of it.

He merely picked at his food, although he loved his daughter's Mexican cooking.

And he rarely looked up from his plate.

Then he excused himself, saying he was tired, and went to the bedroom.

"I guess Mr. Kelly is still kinda weak from staying in the hospital, huh, Mrs. Kelly?" Melissa asked.

"I'm sure that's it, Melissa," Connie replied with a smile. But she had something on her mind.

Janis picked up on it, and figured from the smug smile on Paul's face, he knew what it was.

"What's wrong, Mother?"

Connie patted her daughter's hand. "I have a slight problem. I was supposed to speak to the Tucson Writers' Guild this evening. But I hate to go off and leave you with your father."

"Oh, we'll be all right, Mother. The Matthews are right next door. And Daddy's here. Go on." She looked at her watch. Just a bit past six. They had eaten early. "Besides"—this was directed at Paul— "the police have increased patrols in this area, remember?"

Did Paul flush?

She thought so.

"You're sure?" Connie asked. "You know how your father can be when he doesn't feel well. He can be a bear."

"Oh, we'll be just fine, Mother," Paul assured her. His charming little smiles looked like a shark's grin to Janis. "You go on and have a good time."

Connie returned his smile and gently ruffled her son's hair.

He hated that! He felt like reaching across the table and slapping her silly.

But he smiled and tolerated it.

Connie left the table, intent on bathing and dressing.

"I think I'll call Roy and Bing, and ask them if they'd like to come over." Janis was looking directly at her brother.

"Yeah!" Melissa said. "I think that'd be a really neat idea."

Janis rose from the table.

"Sit down, sister," Paul said.

Janis sat.

"There is no need to do that. Look at it from my point of view. I can't stand the heat, so to speak. If you don't understand that, let me put it another way: It would be stupid of me to cause any more trouble so soon. Around here. You get my drift?"

"I get your drift, Paul. I just don't trust you. Not at all. Not after all the things you've admitted to."

"Well, that is entirely your problem, sister." Paul wolfed down the remainder of his food and stood up. "I'm going to my room and listen to some music, and perhaps read a bit. Then I shall bathe and retire for the evening. Good night!" He almost spat the last two words at them.

The girls watched him go. Glad he was leaving.

Paul caused goose bumps to rise up on Melissa's flesh.

But then, he always had.

She said, "Every day, he talks more and more like some college professor, Janis. Not like a kid."

"I noticed. But he isn't a kid, Melissa. He's a hundred, a thousand, a million years old."

"I don't follow you."

"He's as old as evil!"

Melissa shuddered.

Leo and Stanford dined at about the same time Connie was en route to Mesa Drive, to lecture would-be writers about the pitfalls of getting published.

"Lovely time of day," Leo observed, to break the pall that enveloped them, even in the busy dining room of the motel.

"Yes." Stanford looked up from his food. "Leo, I am not looking forward to this night, although I doubt we have to worry about the children. I think the boy has thought things out, or Mantine has warned him to go slow."

Leo waited for the other shoe to drop.

"I'd wager, for a time, Paul will content himself with mischief rather than murder. I've seen this occur several times on the islands."

"And the missing body?"

The inspector shrugged. "I'm only guessing—and

hoping—that the deceased officer won't make a deadly appearance. Not yet. Mantine will want the heat to die down."

"Let's hope that you're a good guesser, Stanford."

Willingston's smile was thin. "Yes. Let's do that."

Mike Bambridge and Peter Loneman sat in Mike's office. They were bachelors and neither one wanted to return to an empty house that evening.

Not yet.

Even though Mike was tired, the adrenaline was running high and fast.

"Have you talked with Sheriff Sandry yet, Mike?"

"Not yet. I know I should, but I just haven't got in mind yet what I'm going to say."

Pete had to smile. "Should be a very interesting conversation when it occurs."

"Yeah."

"He's a good cop, Mike. He's a politician, but still a good cop."

Mike nodded.

"Want to cruise the town?"

"Beats sitting around here staring at the walls."

"Well, we could go pick up some women."

It was an old joke between them. Both men had suffered through some disastrous love affairs, and their emotional scars ran deep.

Just the same, Mike was once more experiencing those old familiar pangs whenever he looked at Mary Beth.

And he had a hunch that Pete knew it.

He had changed out of his blues into street clothes.

He stood up and clipped his holster onto his belt, checked his .38 Chief's Special. Looked at it with some degree of disdain.

"I don't know why I carry it. Am I supposed to kill a spook with this?"

Peter's smile was somewhat forced. "Let's roll."

Father Dan Gomez knelt in front of the altar and prayed for strength to see them all through the ordeal to come.

The priest sensed Satan all around him.

Even as he knelt, he sensed the presence of the Dark One. He felt the Prince of Darkness was silently mocking his prayers and pleas to God.

And he fought to concentrate, to keep his eyes downcast, to resist the almost overpowering urge to look around him and search the dark corners and pockets of the church.

Dan knew the Lord of Filth was close; but he wasn't about to give him satisfaction by showing fear.

Though he certainly was experiencing a touch of it.

Facing the Dark One was nothing new to the priest. But this time he felt the danger more strongly than ever before.

And it filled him with a myriad of emotions. These, too, were stronger than any he had experienced. Anger. Hate. Disgust. Loathing. Fear. And the primitive urge to kill. To destroy.

But he knew that he alone could not destroy the evil that slithered silently about the town.

He also felt that not one of his new allies would, or could, kill a child. An eight-year-old boy. Ten thousand years of evil contained within a child's form. Paul. Yet killing him went against everything all of them had been taught since childhood.

They couldn't do it even if he convinced them that Paul was totally, undeniably evil. The epitome of wickedness. A monster. The Son of Satan.

Inspector Stanford Willingston . . . ? Gomez felt the man was hiding some dark secret in his past. Yet the inspector just might be the one person with the insight to see beyond the boy's innocent façade, to look past the mortal shape and see into the darkness beyond.

Maybe.

But if it came down to Dan Gomez, and he knew the boy had to be destroyed, would he have the strength to do it?

The priest didn't know.

But Gomez, despite his doubts and fears, was certain of one thing: He was going to have to meet the boy, face to face.

A lowly and humble, and very mortal, man of God meeting the child of Satan.

Gomez wasn't looking forward to that either.

He bowed his head and prayed.

Mary Beth Fletcher was restless. Rising from her chair, cutting off the TV, pacing the confines of her nice home. She paused often to look outside.

It would be dark in about an hour.

The central air conditioner spewed forth its

artificial coolness, filling the house.

But Mary Beth felt something else creeping around her, touching her—something as intangible as the cooled, pumped air.

She didn't know what it was.

Yes, she did.

She just wouldn't admit it.

Not yet.

But soon.

Her chin set in determined defiance, she walked to the wet bar and fixed a light gin and tonic. Clicked on the stereo. Spun the dial. Could find nothing she liked. She flipped through her records and tapes. Same thing.

She turned off the stereo.

The silence pulsed around her.

Like a heartbeat.

Heavy. Thudding. Slow.

She heard a giggling.

The house creaked.

The giggling stopped.

She heard a rattling. Looked around her. She could see nothing.

"Damn!" The word exploded from her mouth.

The rattling grew louder.

She looked down at the bar, at her glass of ice and gin and tonic.

The glass was moving. Shaking from side to side. Slopping out the liquid. The ice cubes banging against the side of the glass.

Impossible.

But there it was.

She grabbed for the glass. Missed. The glass had

178

side-stepped her hand. She tried again. Caught the moving glass.

She immediately turned it loose and fought back a yelp of pain.

She looked at her fingers.

They were reddening and beginning to blister where the icy, moisture-coated glass had burned her.

Burned her!

That was impossible.

But the throbbing in her fingers, the blistered flesh, mutely told her it had happened.

The glass had ceased its movements.

The giggling could not be heard.

The house grew silent.

Controlling her shaky nerves, Mary Beth walked to the bathroom and tried to open the medicine cabinet to get some salve.

The mirrored door would not budge, no matter how she tugged and jerked at it.

She looked into the mirror, then screamed at the sight staring back at her.

Snakes.

Hundreds of coiling, open-mouthed and fanged serpents, piled on top of one another, greeted her eyes. They seemed three-dimensional, ready to leap out at her.

She felt something tugging at her jeans.

Looked down. Didn't want to look. Afraid of what she might see.

Her fears were confirmed.

A dirty human hand and part of an arm were protruding out of the commode, the fingers clutching at the denim.

179

She screamed in pure terror, kicking at the hand and arm, dislodging the fingers from her jeans. Then she ran, in blind panic, from the bathroom. Ran into the hall wall in her haste. Stumbled. She could hear the snakes hissing in the bathroom, the hand and arm flopping around on the tile. It was a wet, oozing, slimy sound.

She ran up the hall and into the kitchen, grabbing her purse and fumbling in it for car keys. Then she tore through the door to the garage, slammed it shut, and ran to her car.

Something grabbed at her behind, catching on a pocket.

She howled in fear.

Looked around.

It was only a broken handhold on a garbage can.

She jerked free and managed to get into the car. Fumbled with the keys, but got them into the ignition.

Something moved on the back seat.

There was a sickening sweet odor in the car.

Smelled like . . .

Death.

The door from the kitchen to the garage was slowly opening.

She heard that wet, slapping, slimy sound.

The arm and hand.

She lifted her eyes to the rearview mirror.

Met the eyes of the cop, Andy. She could see where the mortician had repaired his mangled throat.

He was dressed in uniform.

Grinning at her.

He put his hands, pale and lifeless, on the back of

her seat and slowly pulled himself forward.

She could feel his stale breath on the side of her face as he came closer.

She could not move, was frozen in the seat.

In the mirror, she watched the corpse open its mouth, saw stitches tear out of dead lips to dangle down like tiny black worms.

His breath was horrible.

Andy put a dead hand on her shoulder.

The kitchen door banged. Cutting horror-filled eyes to it, Mary Beth could see a slime-trail, like a large slug would make, glistening behind the arm as the fingers pulled it along.

Andy's hands reached over the seat.

And Mary Beth's mind clicked off. Darkness drifted over her, red-tinged darkness.

She dropped into unconsciousness, slumping over the steering wheel.

NINE

Dr. Dick Slater walked into the kitchen to ask his wife if he could help with dinner.

But it wasn't his wife standing by the sink.

His wife was pinned up against a wall. About two feet off the floor. Pinned and held there by some unseen force. Her face was a horrible mask of terror. Her mouth opened and closed with no words coming forth.

No words, no sound, no nothing.

She was naked. Her clothing lying in tattered rags beneath her dangling feet. They appeared to have been ripped off.

Dick Slater stood rooted to the floor, staring at the impossibly grotesque creature by the sink.

Washing dishes.

One of his wife's aprons tied around its waist.

The creature had the head of a huge-jawed and bug-eyed dog. Its upper torso was thick, its arms muscular, almost human, hairy. The hands of the thing were clawed. The legs were birdlike. The feet were lizardlike.

It was smoking a cigarette.

It looked at Slater through snake eyes.

It pointed one long finger, with a curved, clawlike nail, toward a dish towel, and said, in a high thin voice, "Would you dry, please?"

Then the creature began to laugh.

Judy Slater dropped to the floor, released from her pinned position.

The creature vanished. The dish it had been holding hit the floor and shattered. The apron fluttered in midair for a moment, and then settled gently to the floor.

Judy found her voice and began to howl insanely.

Dick Slater stood paralyzed.

He finally found the will to move his legs, and stumbled toward his wife, knelt down, put his arms around her familiar nakedness, calming her, soothing her.

"What in God's name was that thing?" she screamed at him.

"I don't think God sent it, Judy," he managed to say.

Dick Slater was no longer an atheist.

The two drifters sought refuge for the approaching night in a ravine, or barranca, as they are called locally.

A big ditch.

In the fading light, they spilled their just-stolen money onto the sand. It came to twenty-two dollars and some change. All the kid hitchhiking had had on him. After they'd robbed him, they'd beaten him, stripped him, and then left him naked, bleeding, and

184

unconscious in a ditch.

As a final gesture of their complete contempt for decency and morals and law, the men had stood over the kid and urinated on him.

Now they counted the money and split it between them.

"Enough for a couple bottles of booze and some food," the one called Harold said.

"Yeah." His partner laughed.

The shadows thickened, deepened into dark purple pockets in the barranca. A slight breeze found its way in. Bits of sand kicked up around the men. Neither man noticed.

They finished off what remained of a pint of wine and ate a can of beans and some crackers.

"We'll stay here the night and save the money for tomorrow. Wait 'til we get some ways down the road."

"Why?"

"You're new to this area. People like us don't wander too close to Tepehuanes. The cops there'll roust your ass hard, brother."

"Lay the leather to your head, huh?"

"No. Not so much that. They'll just move you along real quick and tell you not to come back."

"And if you come back?"

"Depends on whether you get lippy with them. You get smart-mouthed, you get busted upside the head and land in the pokey. And you get rolled out at six in the morning. Breakfast at six-thirty. Then you work all day. Thirty minutes for lunch. I mopped the same fifty-five-foot corridor eighteen times in one day. We stay out of Mike Bambridge's town."

"Pigs!"

"Yeah."

A shuffling, grunting sound drifted to the pair of drifters.

"What was that?"

"Who knows? Who cares? Probably a dog lookin' for something to eat." He pulled a filthy, flea-ridden blanket out of an equally filthy knapsack and rolled up in it. "Get some sleep, partner. We'll pull out about four in the morning. Too hot to move much during the day."

"Yeah."

"Goddamn wind. It's hot."

"Yeah. And the sand. I hate sand."

The odd shuffling and grunting sounds came closer.

The drifter tossed his dirty blanket to one side and sat up, looking around him.

He blinked his eyes. Rubbed them. His partner was also sitting up. Both of them were frozen in place by fear and disbelief.

They were surrounded by the impossible.

"Holy shit!"

Blocky, stumpy, stubby manlike forms stood around them, staring at them through empty eyeholes, slowly swinging thick arms back and forth.

The drifters shook their heads. Blinked. Harold said, "Kids in costumes." He shouted, "You kids get the hell outta here. What's wrong with you, anyways?"

The creatures lumbered closer.

"Ah, them ain't kids, Hal."

Closer.

"Sure they's kids. What else could they be?"

He was about to find out.

Most unpleasantly.

Harold stood up and walked toward the sandmen. He picked up a stick. "I'll bust your heads, you punks."

The odd shapes grunted some sort of reply.

When he drew close enough to take a good hard look, Harold stopped. His heart thudded heavily in his chest. He knew fear. Real fear. He took a step backward. Turned around and started to run.

He screamed as he had never screamed before in all his worthless life when an earth-heavy hand fell on his shoulder, stopping him. The hand squeezed. Harold's collarbone shattered; the muscles in his shoulder were crushed amid the crunching and his screaming.

His arm flopped uselessly.

The sandman tore it off and tossed it to another of his kind.

Blood poured from the ripped shoulder.

Harold's partner stood in silent, mind-numbing horror; his feet felt as though they were rooted to the ground.

Harold's wild screaming prodded the drifter into motion.

A world of pain now enveloped Harold.

His partner found he had no place to run. He was surrounded by the . . . things.

Blunt stubby fingers worked at Hal's face, digging in, gaining a hold.

His flesh was jerked off. Peeled like the skin from a tangerine.

187

The manlike form popped the bloody, whiskered, and hairy skin into his mouth-hole and chewed and smacked contentedly.

Harold had passed out from the hideous pain. He was dropped to the now-bloody sand.

The creature knelt beside him. Put his mouth-hole to Harold's eyes and sucked them out.

Harold's cohort in worthlessness turned to run. Right into the outstretched arms of another creature.

Nose to nose-hole with it.

Partner howled and shrieked as the sandman began to crush the life out of him. Blood poured from his nose and ears and mouth. And a ropy coil of intestines protruded, gray and slick, from his mouth.

The sandman sucked them into his mouth-hole.

The sounds of bones being crushed joined the breeze-whipped minuscule sounds of sand particles bouncing around the bloody earth-stage, mingled with the low moaning of the wind in the barranca.

Partner's gurbling and choking sounds were cut short as fingers dug into his head, popping the skull open. Brains gushed forth and other sandmen gathered around, sucking them up greedily.

The sandman holding Partner in his last embrace began eating his face, then tore off limbs and dug out organs and flesh from the trunk of Partner.

Crunching and slurping, lipless smacking and toothless chewing drifted on the breeze.

Those who could not find the strength to partake of the feast seemed to melt into the hot sand, once more becoming a part of that which they had once been.

They were ignored.

But a few thin lines of sand stretched out from the mounds to suck at the blood and tissue and scraps of flesh tossed away.

The shadows grew a darker purple as dusk lifted her skirts and settled gently over the bloody landscape.

And when night dropped its curtain over the land, the shapes lumbered away from what remained of the carnage, leaving behind scattered bones, scraps of flesh still clinging to their stark whiteness.

One of the sandmen carried a hipbone in its hand as it lumbered away into the darkness, melting into the night.

There were fewer of them now, but those that remained were bigger, stronger.

They had no thinking process; not as humans or animals know it. Their sole purpose was to kill, eat, survive.

They lumbered away to a safe place. There, they would stay until the need for food and blood brought them out again.

Soon.

Mary Beth opened her eyes and looked up into the face of Mike Bambridge.

She blinked a couple of times, bringing him into clear vision.

"Easy now," Mike told her. "You're all right. Neighbors heard the horn and phoned the police. The call went out, and I got here first. Peter and me. Are you hurt anywhere?"

"I don't think so," she managed to say. She sat up,

worked her arms, and moved her legs. "No. I seem to be all right."

"Can you tell me what happened?"

She told him. From the rattling glass to the dead cop. Then she pointed out the long slime-trail leading from the kitchen, across the garage floor, and then out into the back yard.

Mike looked at Peter. "Get a team out here to take some samples of that . . . whatever it is."

"You want me to call Leo and Stanford?"

"Yeah. Good idea." He looked around. A lot of neighbors had gathered in their yards. "Have someone tell them Mary Beth surprised an intruder. He's gone—we hope—and she's all right."

Uniformed cops began walking toward the neighbors, and Mike went into the house and used the phone.

His radio was squawking as he walked back to his car.

"Sheriff Sandry's in the office, Chief. Says it's very important he meet with you. Pronto."

"OK. That's ten-four. It's time. Have a unit bring him out to the Fletcher residence. I'll wait here for him."

"Ten-four, Chief. He's on his way."

Mike waited for a moment, watching as Mary Beth walked back into her house, unassisted. Peter approached the car. Informed him about Sandry's coming over. "This going to get you in trouble with the sheriff, Pete?"

"I don't think so, Mike. I really don't care whether it does, or not." He grinned at Mike. "You got an

190

opening in your department?"

"For a damn Injun?" Mike returned the grin. "Always, Pete. But I can't see it coming to that."

"Dr. Fletcher says she isn't hurt; refuses to go to the hospital to be checked. I asked your department to call the hospital and send a doctor over here to have a look at her. Just in case."

"Good thinking." He sighed heavily. "If this is any indication, Pete, I have a hunch it's going to be a very long night."

"I have the same feeling." Loneman could not suppress a shudder. "This is book and movie stuff, Mike. Stepping right out of the pages and off the screen."

"Don't remind me," Mike said glumly.

Leo and Stanford met Sheriff Burt Sandry. The sheriff looked at their credentials, and returned them without comment.

Then the men stood by Mike's unit and talked for several minutes, with Stanford doing most of the talking.

In the middle of it, Sheriff Sandry had to sit down.

The expression on his face would have been priceless, had it not been for the gravity of the whole situation.

Watching Sandry, it was all Peter could do to keep from laughing; even though he was well aware this was no laughing matter.

The sheriff sat for a few seconds in silence. He blinked a few times. He opened his mouth to speak, then closed it.

Mike said, "Everything they've told you is true, Burt."

"You burned the body of a hospital orderly?" Sandry managed to croak.

"Yes."

"Because you thought he was the Devil?"

"Possessed by the Devil, Burt."

"Did he grow horns and a tail?" the sheriff said sarcastically.

Sandry was no newcomer to the field of law enforcement. He'd first been a city cop in Tuscon, then a member of the state police. After being shot twice and decorated many times, Sandry took early retirement and ran for sheriff. He was a good sheriff.

Sandry looked up at Mike. "Mike, are you nuts, man?"

Stanford said, "Carleson's people have matched up the blood samples just flown in from the islands, Sheriff. They match with the samples taken at the Kelly house."

The sheriff looked skeptical. "Same blood type, Inspector?"

"Same blood."

The sheriff closed his eyes, and mumbled something under his breath. Opened his eyes. "Inspector, that is impossible!"

Stanford smiled. A little. "When one is dealing with the Devil, Sheriff—voodoo, black magic; call it what you will—nothing is impossible. Absolutely nothing."

Burt Sandry cut his eyes to Mike. "Let's put this . . . hoodoo on the back burner for a minute.

You missing a body, Chief?"

"How'd you find out about that?"

"No supersleuthing on our part, Mike. Several of my officers were to attend the funeral. The director got all hinky when my people asked to see the body, so one of my deputies slipped around to the viewing room. Empty casket."

Mike nodded. "Yeah. Andy's body is gone."

"That's disgusting. Anybody that would steal a body ought to be horsewhipped. Publicly."

"It wasn't stolen, Burt."

"What do you mean, it wasn't stolen? What happened to it?"

"We, ah, think he just got out of the casket and walked away."

Sandry did some rapid thinking and blinking, but he kept his mouth closed for the moment. Wondered if maybe he should call the boys and girls in white coats with butterfly nets and restraints.

He looked at the men gathered around him. They sure looked serious enough.

Maybe it was just a joke. Peter was a prankster from the word *go.* Yeah, that was it. They were all putting him on.

"OK, boys. You've all had your joke at my expense. Joke time is over. Now what's really going on around here?"

No one laughed.

"We're leveling with you, Burt," Mike said.

"Mike . . ." Sandry got out of the car and faced the Chief. "Andy is dead, goddammit! Dead people don't just get out of caskets and walk off!"

Mike reached in the car and got the packet of

pictures Connie had shot of the sandmen. He handed them to the sheriff.

Sandry visibly paled as he eyeballed the blow-ups. He cleared his throat a couple of times. He looked at the pictures Stanford had brought from the islands—pictures of the death house on the beach.

Taking great care, he slowly replaced the pictures into the Manila envelope.

"We need to talk at length, Mike."

"Agreed."

"This place secured?"

"Yes. I've left a couple of my men here. I'm running short of personnel, Burt."

Sandry shook his head. "Not anymore, you aren't. My people are available as of now." He glanced at Peter. "Get on the horn and get a team in here, Pete. Right now. They take their orders from Chief Bambridge. Got it?"

Coffee cups and sandwich wrappers littered the conference table at the hospital. Unless they wanted to use the civic center, this was the biggest room available.

Still, it was fogged with cigarette, cigar, and pipe smoke.

Sheriff Sandry drained his coffee cup and expelled breath slowly.

Mind-boggling.

Looking at his cup, he asked, "What's the latest on Dr. Fletcher?"

"She's resting comfortably," Clineman said. "She was badly frightened by . . . something."

194

"And you all believe the . . . Devil is behind all this?"

"I believe that something, well, supernatural is behind it, yes." Clineman really spoke for them all.

Dr. Slater was not present. No one knew where he was. His phone went unanswered.

Sandry slowly shook his head. It was all just too much. Everything thrown at him had had a mind-numbing effect. But the part of him that relied on logic cried—screamed—out that he should reject what he'd heard.

Yet deep within him, in that part of him—the primitive inner entity—that runs deep and goes back to the caves . . .

. . . he believed.

He didn't want to believe.

But he did.

"That slime-trail leading from the Fletcher house?" Sandry asked.

"Traces of excrement, urine, chlorine, and the thousand other elements found in any sewer line," one of Carleson's assistants informed the sheriff.

Sandry shuddered. Made no effort to hide the shudder. Goose bumps appeared on the sheriff's arms. The short hairs on the back of his neck seemed to him to be standing straight up.

"This Kelly kid—bring me up to date on him."

"You know all that we know," Mike answered. "And we're in a bind where Paul is concerned. He's an eight-year-old boy. Can you imagine the uproar the press would create if they got wind of us planning to move against a small child? Accusing him of being in cahoots with the Devil?"

"We'd all be out looking for new jobs," Belline said. "And damned lucky to be able to find one."

"At all costs"—Leo eyeballed everyone around the table—"I believe we must keep our suspicion of Paul from the press."

All agreed.

The thought of doing real harm to a child was totally repugnant to the sheriff. Although there were some kids he'd like to take a paddle to.

Sandry spread his hands. "Then . . . what do we do?"

Stanford spoke the damning words that no one wanted to hear. "Kill the demon."

"Who among us would do that?" Dr. Thomas asked. "I know I could not."

No one volunteered.

Everyone sat silent for a time, carefully avoiding anyone else's eyes.

Father Gomez spoke up. "It isn't that easy, anyway." He looked at Stanford. "Is it, Inspector?"

Stanford shook his head. "No." The one word was very softly spoken. "It isn't. You'd be fighting Mantine all the way, for one thing."

"What's the other thing?" Sandry asked.

"More than one thing," the priest declared. "You'd all best plant it firmly in your minds that we'll be fighting Satan. If this is truly the Devil's son, his own demon-child, we're in for one hell of a fight. No play on words intended. And, be assured, Satan's minions will surely take a hand."

"Minions?" Belline asked.

"The town of Tepehuanes probably contains a hundred or more lost souls. Ninety-nine percent of

196

them unaware of it. But if Satan calls, they'll answer."

"Jesus!" The word exploded from Clineman's mouth.

"I'll take Michael," Leo said.

"Don't blaspheme." Gomez grinned at the man. "But in a fight, you're right. Michael is God's mercenary."

"I never heard a priest say anything like that before," Sandry said.

"I'm an unusual priest." Gomez put his hands on the table. "What's occurring here in Tepehuanes happens more often than any of you know. Or could imagine. Why do you think the demon-child is a child, and never an adult? Think about it. Over the centuries a hundred—a thousand—communities around the world have faced the same problem we are now confronting. In one way or another. The sand creatures are a joke—"

"An ugly joke," Mike broke in.

"Wrong word choice," the priest admitted. "The sand people are merely a distraction on the part of Mantine." He looked at Stanford. "Do you agree?"

The inspector nodded his head.

Gomez went on. "The real danger is the boy, and what he is capable of doing. He converted the young punks who now follow him in only a matter of hours. That tells me that Satan picked this town a long time ago, and planted the seeds. Only God and Satan know what the boy is planning at this moment."

*　　　*　　　*

"How's your dad?" Melissa asked.

"Asleep. Asleep real deep it looked to me."

"Paul?"

"Still in his room. I wouldn't go in there for a million bucks."

The girls sat in the den. The wide-screen TV was on, but they were paying no attention to it.

Earlier, they had split up, Janis going one way, Melissa going the other, checking the windows and doors.

All were securely closed and locked.

It was only a minor comfort to the girls.

A part of Janis wanted to believe what Paul had said, about not wanting too much heat, that nothing was going to happen this close to home.

Wanted desperately to believe it.

But she didn't.

Somewhere in the house, a door opened.

Janis looked at Melissa. She had heard it as well.

The girls listened for any following sound.

Nothing.

Something in the house creaked and both girls jumped.

The sound was not repeated.

Headlights swung into the drive, the lights reflecting off an inside wall.

Janis went to the door and peeked out the side windows. The man was one of the cops who had stayed as guard with her mother and Paul and Chief Bambridge.

She opened the door and stepped outside before he could ring the bell and alert Paul.

"Where is your brother, Janis?" he asked, holding

198

up the walkie-talkie.

"In his room. That the one you're going to lend me?"

"Yes. It's fully charged and easy to use." Quickly, he added, "Use it only in an emergency, Janis. And don't turn it on until you're ready to call in. That saves the batteries."

She thanked him, and he drove off slowly.

Then she quietly closed the door behind her, locked it. Looked up the hallway. Paul's bedroom door was still closed.

She showed Melissa the walkie-talkie.

"Neat. You going to tell your mother about it?"

Janis thought about that. "No. Not yet."

Melissa opened her mouth to protest.

"Don't ask me why not. I don't know. I've just got a hunch, that's all."

Janis hid the walkie-talkie in the linen closet, way in the back, under some sheets her mother never used. Connie swore that someday she'd tear the sheets up and use them for rags. But she never did.

Janis didn't want to keep it in her room because she knew that sometimes, when she was out of the house, Paul went through her things.

Something else she'd never told her mother.

The girls settled down back in the den, in front of the TV.

There was a real good horror movie on Showtime. But neither Janis nor Melissa wanted to watch it.

Both of them were wondering what Paul was going to do next.

*　　　*　　　*

The priest had been wrong, as had Stanford and several of the others, in thinking that Mantine was ever omniscient. And Paul had practically no seerlike powers. Though Mantine could slip between the veil, it was not as easy as snapping one's fingers. Once in his human form, he was very vulnerable, so he and Nicole preferred to stay in the shadow-world of the netherland.

Mantine had no idea at all what the doctors and the lawmen and the priest were talking about.

And Paul did not know about his sister's walkie-talkie.

But Mantine and Paul could call out evil—at will.

Against anybody.

At any time.

They could create illusions.

But both preferred reality.

It was so much more fun. It produced real panic in people.

Neither of them had a grand plan to take over the world or the country or the county, or even the town of Tepehuanes. Nor did either of them have the power to accomplish such a thing. Or the inclination, for that matter.

Their sole function for existing was very basic, very simple: *evil.*

To create evil one must enlist and recruit, and Paul was doing that.

With kids.

Adults had such a lazy evil in them.

Kids were much more inventive.

Mantine's role had been fulfilled. He had found and cultivated the demon-child. Now Paul could be

200

left on his own, and Mantine and Nicole were free to go, to return to the islands to walk free upon the earth.

But Paul fascinated the devil-couple. Neither Mantine nor Nicole had ever seen a child with so much unleashed power, or with so much evil in him.

It was awesome.

And entertaining.

Mantine and Nicole had decided to stick around. It would be risky for them; they were vulnerable here. But they decided they might be able to help whenever either felt it necessary.

But mainly they stayed to watch the fun.

Paul had progressed so rapidly, falling back into his true role with ease.

As he had done, so the Master had informed them, several times over the rolling ages.

It had been a difficult birth for Paul's mother. For a time, she had come close to death.

And why she didn't die was a mystery to Mantine until the Master explained.

Interference from . . .

Up There.

Mantine had shuddered with undisguised disgust at just the thought of . . .

Up There.

It had almost made his flesh crawl.

If he'd been in his human form, it certainly would have.

Paul would be difficult to kill now. It was possible, but highly unlikely.

For Paul to truly die, the demon alter form would have to be killed along with him.

And that would take some doing.

No, Paul was safe, Mantine felt.

A scant seventy-two hours before, Mantine would not have believed that. He would have said no small form such as Paul could contain such pure evil.

Now he would willingly admit to being wrong.

But he was certainly not going to tell the boy, for a couple of reasons: Impetuousness was the brother to carelessness, and carelessness was trouble.

Paul could have a lot of fun in this town. But he would need a bit of guidance for a while longer.

Mantine knew he was taking a chance; nevertheless he'd stick around for a time.

It was all going to be such fun!

"You mentioned other communities, Father Gomez," Dr. Belline said, "so you obviously have some knowledge of how they handled the situation. Would you share that knowledge with us?"

Gomez looked at his empty coffee cup for a moment. Then he sighed. "Somebody usually volunteers to destroy the demon child."

No one seemed overly surprised at that. In their hearts, they'd been expecting it.

But no one volunteered to do the deed.

The group waited for a time, Belline finally urging, "And . . . ? One doesn't just kill a human being without attracting some attention, somewhere along the line. How is that handled?"

Gomez lifted his eyes. "I'll correct part of that. We are not dealing with a human being. We are dealing with a demon in human form." He waved that off.

"But I see your point. When it . . . happens, the child is listed with the law enforcement people as missing. More often than not, the police are directly involved. If it is an adult, he or she has been kidnapped, or has just left home. Sometimes there's a horrible, never-to-be-solved murder. Occasionally a priest is called in. But usually, by that time, people have waited too long; it's far too late. All we can do is suggest options."

The group digested that bit of information.

"Have you ever killed a demon, Father Gomez?" Dr. Thomas asked.

The priest stirred uncomfortably in his chair. "I cannot reveal any part I might have played in such a situation. I would be breaking a sacred oath. Please understand my position."

"I killed one," Stanford said, his voice very low, and very emotion charged. "It was the most bloody awful deed I have ever done."

Leo glanced at him, knowing he was about to fit together the final part of the puzzle surrounding the inspector. "Who, Stanford?"

In a voice filled with memories, choked with long-suppressed anger and hate and love and revenge, Stanford said, "My wife."

TEN

The girls both jumped about a foot off the couch at the crashing sound just behind the house.

It was followed by an animal-like grunting.

Janis and Melissa suddenly got real close on the sectional.

A shadow flitted across the windows facing the vastness and darkness of the back yard. The back yard faced the desert, which stretched, seemingly endlessly, toward the faraway mountains.

Both girls could clearly hear the strange gruntings and shufflings coming from the back yard.

And something brushed up against the house.

"Paul lied!" Melissa whispered hoarsely.

"What else is new?" Janis replied.

She slipped from the couch and walked to the row of light switches by the back door. Clicked on the outside flood lights.

The area was filled with harsh light.

Melissa started screaming and pointing.

Janis turned. Stared in disbelief.

It was her father. Mark was standing, stark naked, in the back yard. He held an axe in his hands.

He moved to the windows. Pressed his face against the glass. Grinned at the girls. Slobber leaked from his wet lips, staining the glass. His breath, a pant, fogged the pane.

Mark stepped back, lifted the axe, and smashed the glass. Wild grunting sounds ripped from his mouth. He screamed obscenities at the girls.

Crouched naked on the sill, drool dripping from his lips, he directed sexual threats at them.

Then he climbed in, moving like an ape, springing to the den floor, broken glass slashing his legs and feet.

But he paid no attention to the cuts or to the blood that flowed from the wounds.

He lifted the axe above his head, and slowly advanced toward the girls. He was grinning.

Then he screamed and charged them.

The girls darted behind the sectional just as Mark brought the axe down, smashing a coffee table, wood and glass flying through the air.

He paused for a moment, staring at them.

They moved back as one.

And he began to stalk them, his bloody feet leaving slick trails as he walked.

His eyes were very bright and very wild and very insane.

Janis and Melissa ran around the large den. Mark slopped through his own blood, following them, swinging the axe from side to side. His words had once more turned into gruntings. He slobbered and drooled and grinned insanely at the frightened girls.

But it was clear to them what he intended to do.

Before he killed them.

They were only ten years old, but not stupid.

"We gotta split up," Melissa suggested. "That way one of us might make it."

Before she could reply, Janis caught movement out of the corner of her right eye. Paul, standing under the archway leading to the den.

It's all over now, she thought. Paul will finally get his wish. I'm finished. And Melissa along with me.

That was only partly true. And not in the way Janis thought.

"Father!" Paul yelled. "Stop this! Have you lost your mind?"

Mark turned to face his son.

Janis could not believe what she had just heard. What in the world was going on?"

"Janis!" Paul called. "Get to the phone. Nine-one-one. Call the cops."

Paul moved to his left, his father turning slightly to keep the boy in full view, and hiding his eyes from his daughter and Melissa.

Mark screamed at his son as Janis ran to the phone and punched out the numbers. She spoke quickly, her voice trembling, fear in it, but gave all the correct information.

"Run, Janis!" Paul yelled from the other side of the huge den.

Janis just got clear. Mark had charged her, swinging the axe, smashing the phone.

Mark turned, his wild bright eyes now on Melissa. He grinned at her.

She darted away.

Paul shouted and jumped up and down, forcing his father to look at him.

Screaming from mind-clouding rage, Mark charged his son, holding the axe high above his head. The boy ducked, the axe head knocking a huge chunk of paneling out of the wall.

Mark worked the axe free and turned.

Then Paul threw books, vases, ashtrays, and anything else he could put his hands on at the bloody, axe-wielding man.

The girls quickly got into the act.

Mark was battered backward.

An ashtray struck him in the face, bloodying his nose and snapping his head back.

He roared his rage as red and blue lights suddenly flashed outside.

And he turned and jumped through a window, shattering it and pocking his already bloody body with still more cuts and slashes.

But he held firm to the axe.

Janis ran to unlock the front door before the cops shot the lock off as they do on TV and in the movies.

Only on TV and in the movies.

The foyer filled with uniforms.

"It's our father!" Paul shouted. He pointed toward the shattered windows. "He's gone crazy. He tried to kill us all with an axe. He jumped out back, through that window. Be careful."

The cop who had delivered the walkie-talkie to Janis looked strangely at Paul, then cut his eyes to Janis.

She shrugged.

The policeman found the back door and ran out into the flood-lighted yard.

It got real quiet in the bloody, wrecked, and littered

den. Janis and Melissa stared at Paul.

"How come you suddenly got so concerned about our safety, Paul?" Janis asked.

"Why, sister!" the boy exclaimed, wide-eyed, "what kind of brother would I be if I refused to come to your aid?"

Chuckling, he walked to a chair and sat down, after brushing debris from it.

"I love it!" Paul said.

The girls stared at him.

True, he had saved their lives.

This time.

But what was he saving them for?

"Lost the crazy bastard!" A cop's voice came through the broken windows.

"He couldn't have gone far. Keep looking. But be careful, he's got an axe."

Paul sat in the chair and smiled.

Paul had gone directly to his room after being questioned by Chief Bambridge. He'd said he was emotionally exhausted and distraught about his father.

At a signal from Mike, Leo and Stanford entered the house and sat down. Mike turned to Janis. "How much does she know?" He cut his eyes to Melissa.

"Everything. So do Carol and Jean and Carla and Roy and Bing. They're carrying knives now."

Mike questioned both the girls. Their stories were the same as Paul's.

"The boy is setting things up quite well for himself," Stanford said. "No way on God's earth

209

could we convince anyone outside of our group that Paul is anything other than what he appears to be, a brave little boy who came to the rescue of his sister and her friend."

Father Gomez appeared in the doorway.

The invisible impact stopped him there. Hit him in the face and chilled him.

He knew without stepping closer that he was facing a power much stronger than he had ever faced before. He could sense the evil presence of the Lord of Darkness.

He felt real fear.

His collar was suddenly much too tight.

Sweat popped out under his shirt.

Satan was here. In this house. Very near.

The average priest would never meet him.

Many exorcists would never meet him.

Those that did almost always died.

But Father Gomez knew it was his time to meet God's oldest enemy. Face to face.

The Antichrist.

He wondered if the boy knew it?

He hoped not.

Gomez fought his emotions under control, aware that all in the den were staring at him. Then he stepped through the door and into the foyer, went down the stone steps and into the den. On impulse, he turned to his left.

The powerful sensations grew stronger.

He fought back panic.

He touched the cross around his neck.

He felt better.

He changed direction, walked toward the officers

and the girls, and the sensation eased.

He spoke only one sentence, then turned around and walked out of the house, into the warm night.

"I've got to see the bishop."

Leo watched the priest leave. "Now, what was that all about, do you suppose?"

Stanford felt chilly sweat trickle down his belly. "We're in trouble. Very big trouble."

The cops searched the rest of the night for Mark Kelly. But somehow, he had slipped out of the neighborhood.

Maybe out into the desert.

To die.

They hoped.

But no one believed it.

They had all been briefed. They knew what they were up against. But a lot of them had not believed it.

At first.

Until they were shown the pictures.

Lots of true believers in blue then.

That evening, a lot of dusty Bibles had been dusted off, and passages read. A lot of priests and preachers had been visited.

None of the cops had spilled anything. They were all tough and capable men and women. They knew what they did not need was panic. So they just asked for a word or two of blessing.

Then they went back to work.

Connie had entered the house, taken one look at the

wreckage and blood, and had collapsed.

She very nearly fainted again upon hearing who had caused the mess.

But she had waved off the suggestion that she go to the hospital. She preferred to stay in her own home.

Officers were posted outside it, and Leo and Stanford volunteered to spend the night inside.

"You don't mind?" Mike asked.

They shook their heads.

"You're going to need some pieces."

Both men opened their linen jackets, exposing pistols in shoulder holsters.

Mike smiled. "You can get arrested for carrying those, you know?"

The pair returned his smile.

"Good God, man!" Mike was speaking to Leo. "What is that hand cannon?"

Leo slipped his pistol from leather. Smith and Wesson, model 624. Four-inch barrel. .44 special.

"Stop a freight train," Mike said, returning the cannon to Leo.

Stanford carried a .38. Colt. Loaded with the bullets the island priest had blessed.

But he knew, after looking at the face of Gomez, that he'd be lucky just to slow the demon down with the bullets.

Much less stop it.

Killing it was very nearly impossible.

But that howitzer Leo was packing might make the demon think twice.

At least Stanford hoped it would.

Though he knew from personal experience that a gun alone would not kill a devil's spawn.

212

And if Paul's alter self was here . . . ?

Stanford didn't even want to think about that, didn't know how to visualize it. Ugly. Awesome. Hideous. Dangerous.

Indescribable.

"Odd look on your face, Inspector." Mike handed him a walkie-talkie.

Stanford nodded his head absently. He was wondering what Mrs. Kelly's reaction would be when she learned of his presence in the house.

He and Leo had deliberately stayed out of her sight upon her arrival, and after she had been revived from her swoon.

Stanford looked up the hallway toward Paul's bedroom. His sensors were not as finely tuned to evil as those of the priest, but he could, nevertheless, sense the raw evil in the house.

He knew the sensation. Had experienced it firsthand.

Could still feel the hot stickiness of blood on his hands.

Blood from the only woman he had ever loved.

He fought back the memories. Fought them back as he had managed to do over the years. Struggled to return his thoughts to the present.

He watched as several officers brought in sheets of plywood and hammers and nails.

"Let's get busy closing up those windows," Stanford said shortly. He walked toward the shattered panes.

"I'll get a broom," Janis suggested.

"Good girl."

"He ever tell you how he killed his wife, Leo?"

213

Mike asked.

"No. Not yet. Maybe he never will. He's a very private person."

"Children?"

"Two, I think. They're grown and gone from the islands. He doesn't give out much about himself."

"I get the feeling this is a personal thing with him. A vendetta, I suppose."

"I think you're right."

Mike started to walk away. He stopped, and looked back at Leo. "You know anything else about Stanford?"

"No. But I have a gut feeling."

"And that is . . . ?"

"I think he came here prepared to die."

Leo, with Janis's help, was fixing breakfast when Connie walked into the kitchen. Melissa was still sleeping. Paul was in his room.

Connie had not yet seen Stanford. He had taken his morning tea outside, to sit quietly by the pool, alone with his thoughts.

She managed a brave smile and sat down at the table, accepting a cup of coffee from her daughter.

"I haven't seen you before," she said to Leo. "Are you new to the force?"

She really wanted to ask about her husband, but was not sure how to bring up the subject.

She was afraid he might be dead.

And somewhat afraid he might still be alive, although she didn't understand this feeling.

Her thoughts were confused and jumbled. Too

much had happened in too short a time, and she did not believe it was due to coincidence.

Leo placed a breakfast plate before her. Bacon and eggs, hashed browns and toast. Set out another plate for Janis and one for himself.

Leo introduced himself and took a chair. "I'm a retired New York City cop, Mrs. Kelly."

"Connie, please, Mr. Corigliano."

"Leo. It'll save time. Takes a minute and a half to pronounce my last name and then people usually don't get it right."

She smiled at him. Liked him right off. But he didn't smile.

"And you're just helping Mike out, Leo?" She tasted her eggs and found that they were good and she was hungry.

"You might say that, Connie. Donna Mansfield was my sister."

For a moment, that didn't register. When it sank in, Connie laid her fork on her plate and stared at Leo.

He met her gaze. Really a very pretty lady, he thought. Classic beauty. Delicate bone structure. Looks like Catherine Deneuve.

Connie picked up her fork. "I wish we had never taken that trip."

"It wouldn't have made any difference, Connie." Leo knew he was now treading on dangerous ground. But he felt he had to know where the woman stood; how much she knew and how much she suspected, if she suspected anything.

And would talk about it.

Janis sat at the table and kept her mouth shut, just

215

listening to the exchange. She liked Stanford a lot, but there was something about this quiet New York City man that she liked even more. She got the impression that Leo was hard as Charles Bronson and tough as Clint Eastwood if he ever got going.

"Odd thing to say, Leo."

Leo decided to let that cool. "No sign of your husband yet, Connie."

But she wouldn't let it drop. "Does our trip to the islands somehow tie in with all that's been happening around here, Leo?"

"I think you know it does."

Connie noticed that Janis kept cutting her eyes toward the pool area. She rose from the table and walked to the window over the sink. Glanced out and saw Stanford just getting out of the deck chair.

She narrowed her eyes and walked back to the table, taking her seat. She looked at her daughter.

"You might have told me he was here, Janis."

"He's been here for several days, Mother. I mean, not here in the house, in town."

"I . . . see. And you chose not to tell me?"

"Yes, ma'am."

"Why, Janis?"

"I, uh, we made a deal."

"A deal. How nice for you both." Connie picked at her food, eating a bite of this and that. As she nibbled on a piece of buttered whole wheat toast, she lifted her eyes to Leo.

"You believe my husband killed your sister and her husband, Mr. Corigliano?"

Lost ground. Back to Mr. "No, I don't believe that, Connie."

216

Now she was puzzled. Before she could ask anything else, Stanford came in and poured another cup of tea.

He smiled at her. "Good morning, Mrs. Kelly. How do you feel?"

"Inspector. Taking into consideration all that's happened, and the mystery surrounding certain events"—she looked at first her daughter and then at Leo—"I'm feeling rather well, thank you. Please sit down and join us."

"Thank you."

"Want some breakfast, Inspector?" Janis asked. "Leo and me fixed plenty."

He smiled at the girl. He liked her. "That would be very nice, Janis. Yes, please."

"The plot thickens with your presence, Inspector." Connie tried a smile that almost made it. "Should I be taking all this down in anticipation of a book?"

"I'm afraid none of this will ever be made public, Mrs. Kelly. Or should I say, it should not be made public?"

"As a writer, I don't believe in censorship."

Stanford smiled. He thanked Janis as she placed the breakfast plate in front of him.

"Really, it isn't a question of censorship, Mrs. Kelly."

"Connie, please."

"Thank you. Stanford, here." Awkward, he thought. Very awkward. How does one go about telling a mother that she has conceived a demon-child? That she has bathed and burped and powdered and changed a devil-child? "Are you a religious

217

person, Connie?''

"To some degree. We attend church. Not as often as we should, I'm sorry to say. Why do you ask, Inspector? I really do not understand where all this is leading.''

"What church?''

"Episcopal.'' There was a note of impatience in her reply.

"Ah! Very good. Yes, indeed. Is your priest in town?''

Connie sighed and stared at the man. "No, he isn't. He's on a sabbatical this summer. Area priests are taking turns filling in while he's gone. Why are you asking these things, Inspector? And what in the world has all this to do with my husband?''

"Well, I merely felt that in this moment of personal anguish and crisis you might like to consult with your minister, that's all.''

"Really?''

"That is correct, Connie.''

Connie stared at him. Narrowed her eyes. Smiled. Stanford dropped his fork when she said, "Inspector, that is a great big crock!''

Janis giggled and Leo managed not to choke on a mouthful of hash browns.

Stanford regained his composure. Blinked at her a couple of times. Then a smile creased his face. "Yes. Yes, it is, Connie. Quite right . . .''

Before he could say anything else, Paul walked through the huge den and up the steps, past the main dining area and into the modern and gleaming kitchen. His expression did not change when he looked at Stanford. Mantine had been at the hospital when the inspector had made his appearance.

The boy kissed his mother on the cheek, surprising her, for he had not done that in a long time.

"Any news about Father?" Paul asked, in that odd-sounding, deep, and well-hollow voice.

Stanford had not heard the boy speak since just before he'd left the islands.

Now Paul's voice chilled him. The evil cold penetrating to the marrow. He placed his fork on his plate and put his hands in his lap. He did not want the demon-child to see them trembling. Looking at the devil in human form, Stanford literally felt his flesh creep and crawl. His skin felt soiled.

"No, dear. No news as yet. Sit down. I'll get you something to eat."

Paul patted his mother on the arm. "Keep your seat, Mother. I'll get it myself. I'm really not very hungry. It's the tension, you know." He looked at Stanford. "Good morning, Inspector. This is quite a surprise."

No child left in him, Stanford thought. He neither walks or talks or behaves as a child. He's shed the first layer. He is a thousand years of sin. Old as time.

"Paul. Terribly sorry about your father."

"Yes. A tragedy, to be sure. I'm really quite upset about it."

"I'm sure you are. Wish there were something I could do." Other than taking out my pistol and putting a bullet between your eyes.

Do it! he told himself. Right now! Kill him while he's vulnerable. Do it!

219

But he could not.

Stanford fought back primitive emotions. Calmed himself.

He noticed that the mark on the boy's arm had enlarged, reddened. What he could see of it, that is. And he knew the boy was growing stronger by the hour.

To wait much longer might well mean the end for them all.

Leo turned in his chair to look at Paul. Smiled at him. The smile was not returned. The boy's eyes held an unfathomable darkness. "That was a very brave thing you did last evening, Paul."

"Thank you. Do I know you?"

"I'm Donna Mansfield's brother." Leo dropped that on him and watched for a reaction.

Paul's left eye twitched. His cheeks flushed just a bit. His small fingers tightened on the edge of the plate he was holding.

That was it.

Leo could feel the hate shining at him. It was so intense it almost burned his flesh.

Then Paul's lips curved in a slight sneer. "Is that supposed to mean something to me, sir?"

Connie stepped in, even though she did not understand the tangible friction between the man and the boy. "The lady who was murdered on the island, Paul."

"Ah! Certainly. Now I recall. Well, what brings the two of you to this part of the country?"

Like Stanford, Leo had noticed that the boy now spoke like a well-educated adult.

"You might call it curiosity, son."

The sneer changed to a knowing smile. "I'm not your son. And curiosity got that cat in trouble, didn't it?" Paul turned and fixed his attention on his plate.

His mother gently admonished him. "That's not a very nice thing to say. These gentlemen guarded us last night. Volunteered their time."

Paul said nothing.

Melissa wandered into the den, rubbing sleep from her eyes. "How come you didn't wake me up, Janis?" she called.

Janis laughed, and the laughter felt good to her. She hadn't had very much to laugh about in the past few days. "'Cause I didn't know which end to grab to shake you. You were burrowed under the covers like a mole!"

The adults smiled at that.

Paul did not.

He took his plate into the den, passed Melissa without acknowledging her presence, and sat down, as far away from the others as possible.

The TV news was on. There had been a terrible plane crash. A hundred or more people killed. Paul smiled at that. To him, that was good news.

Maybe he could arrange for something like that to happen closer to home. That would be fun.

All those ripped and mangled and torn and smoking bodies.

He'd work on that for sure.

His mother rose to answer the ringing of the doorbell.

Chief Mike Bambridge.

"'Morning, Mrs. Kelly." He smiled at her. But she noticed the smile did not reach his eyes. They looked very tired and very serious. "I've got some good news for you. My people found your husband about an hour ago. They took him alive. He has a few bumps on his head. I'll level with you. They had to club him down. But he's alive. He's at the hospital."

"Thank God!"

Stanford was watching Paul. He saw the boy's lips form a sneer of pure disgust.

ELEVEN

Mike drove Connie to the hospital, advising her on the way not to expect too much at first from her husband. He was in restraints and had been sedated.

Leo and Stanford stayed at the house with Janis and Melissa. Paul had gone to his room. By the set of his shoulders, Stanford knew the boy was highly irritated, and he knew why.

Paul's plans had not worked out. Stanford felt sure the boy had counted on the police killing his father, with no suspicion placed on him.

Stanford also knew that Sheriff Sandry and Chief Bambridge had given firm orders to their forces to take Mark Kelly alive—if possible.

Just don't get yourselves killed in the process, both men had added.

Stanford felt it would be most interesting to see what the little demon would do next.

Dangerous and quite possibly deadly, but still interesting.

Paul certainly was aware by now that his every move would be observed. He was under a magnifying glass.

Leo answered the doorbell, admitting Father Gomez.

Both men noticed that the priest seemed much more relaxed than the last time they'd seen him.

Gomez carried a small box in his hand. He sat down, was introduced to Janis and Melissa, and opened the box.

Gold crosses and chains.

"I had them blessed last night," the priest explained, giving each person a cross. "Give these to your friends, Janis. Make certain you do that. And give this one to your mother. You, personally, place it around her neck. Will you do that?"

"OK, Father."

The priest leaned back in his chair. "That coffee smells good. Could I possibly beat you out of a cup?" He smiled at the girl.

"You got it!"

Melissa went with Janis, to make some toast.

When the girls were out of earshot, Leo asked, "Did you come to meet Paul?"

The priest nodded. "If he'll meet me. It's time. I want to see his reaction when we come face-to-face."

"And what do you anticipate that reaction will be?" Stanford inquired.

Gomez shrugged. "Who knows? This early in the game, I doubt it will be anything dramatic. But then, he may decide to kill me and have done with it."

"You can talk in front of us, Father Gomez," Janis called from the kitchen. "We know all about it. Me and Melissa and the gang."

The men smiled, Gomez calling out, "Sorry, Janis. I suppose it is an adult's inclination to be protective of the young."

Laughter drifted out of Paul's room, floating like an evil invisible vapor up the hall and into the den and kitchen.

"He has extraordinarily good hearing," Leo noted.

"Yes. But that's about as far as it goes," the priest replied, accepting a cup of coffee and a plate of toast with thanks.

The others waited for an explanation of that statement.

"I spent most of last night in study and consultation with the Monsignor in Phoenix." He glanced at Janis. "Would you turn on the stereo, dear? A little noise would be most helpful."

She got his drift and smiled. Just like in the books and movies, she thought, walking to the bank of electronic equipment that made up a complete entertainment center.

But this is real, she reminded herself. I've got to keep remembering that.

She touched the cross hanging around her neck.

With the stereo set on a loud rock station, Gomez motioned the little group to come closer.

"Mantine is vulnerable. Don't worry, neither he nor Nicole can hear us. But Paul probably can. I was wrong about some things. They are not all-knowing and all-seeing. To put it plainly, they're on our turf now. Oh, they still hold a good hand, so far; but that is subject to change, and soon. I hope," he added grimly.

"But Paul is still dangerous, isn't he?" Janis asked, a part of her not wanting this adventure to end.

225

A larger part wishing fervently that her brother was on the moon.

Or even farther away.

"Dangerous doesn't even begin to describe him, Janis," Gomez stated quietly. His eyes were very sad as he looked at Janis. "You do believe that Paul was responsible for what happened to your father last night, don't you?"

"Yes, sir."

"Do you fully realize what has to be done to your brother?"

She stared at him. "I know what they do in books and movies."

"And . . . ?"

She side-stepped that for a moment. "He's my brother, Father Gomez. So I've got a question. Maybe two or three. First, could I turn out to be like Paul?"

Gomez's sigh was painful. He'd been wondering when the child would ask that. "I don't know, Janis. I can't answer that; not with one-hundred-percent certainty. But I would say that you are perfectly normal, and be ninety-nine and nine-tenths percent certain of it. I wish I could give you a better answer."

She nodded her head, her expression serious. "Can the demon inside my brother be destroyed without killing Paul?"

As she spoke the damning words, she knew what must be done.

A heavy burden for a child.

Gomez shook his head. "No, dear. That's impossible. Again, I'm sorry."

"I see. All right. Answer me this: could Paul have prevented this from happening? I mean, to him."

"Perhaps in the beginning. But you see, we don't know when the beginning was. You see, Paul is . . ." He paused, searching for words that would best explain to a young girl that her brother was beyond redemption. That an innocent-looking young boy was, in reality, evil incarnate. A monster in human form. The Son of Satan.

Janis found them for him. "Paul is not eight years old, is he? He's old, very old, right?"

"That is my belief, Janis. And we really don't know why your mother was chosen to birth him. These things just . . . happen, that's all."

"So it wasn't anything that my mom did, right? I mean she isn't looked on as being bad. By God, I mean? You're saying it wasn't her fault, right?"

"That's correct, Janis."

With a very adult sigh, the girl stood up and looked up the hallway. Paul's door was still closed, as best she could tell from her angle of vision.

"These aren't questions, Father Gomez. I'm just talking out loud. Paul killed those people on the island, or had them killed, somehow. He did something to Jenny, and then did it to her mother. He was responsible for . . . whatever happened to those people at the hospital. And he caused the death of that cop, right there"—she pointed—"in the hall. He even set up our dad, made him go crazy. But even if the police could prove he did all those things, Paul is in a child's body, and the courts won't do anything to him. Paul knows that. My brother isn't just bad, and he isn't nuts. He's just evil. The Bible says that evil must be destroyed." She looked at Father Gomez. "Does that answer your original question, Father?"

227

"Yes, it does. But the important thing, Janis, is this: Are you certain in your own mind?"

"Yes," she replied in a soft voice. "I am. I always knew something was wrong with Paul. I always did. But you're going to have a hard time convincing Mother. And there is this: I don't want to be around when . . . what we're talking about happens. Mother is going to have to be away, too."

"I understand that, Janis. But you might not have a choice, either of you," Gomez cautioned, "even though we'll do everything we can to keep you out of and away from . . . the final act."

"But . . ." Janis's voice revealed her anguish and fear.

Stanford averted his eyes and shook his head.

Leo said a silent little prayer for a child with such a heavy load on her young shoulders.

Melissa looked around her, her eyes touching all of them, then fixing on Janis. She did not really understand what was going on.

The priest met Janis's eyes. "There is a possibility that you might have to finish what we are unable to."

"I don't know if I could do that, Father. You're asking an awful lot of me."

"Hey, what are you talking about?" Melissa asked.

Janis waved her silent, not taking her eyes from the priest's.

Melissa got it then. "Aw, come on! Paul is her brother!"

"That is precisely the reason, child," Stanford told her.

Janis's shoulders slumped.

Janis looked at the shattered and boarded-up

228

windows of the den, the bloodstains still on the carpet in the hall. Her mother had already ordered new carpeting.

In his room, Paul laughed and laughed. The sound was ugly and evil and taunting as it drifted to those seated in the den.

"If it has to be"—Janis's words were just audible over the blaring of the stereo and her brother's wild laughter—"then I guess I'll find the strength to do it."

Gomez bowed his head and began to pray softly.

A breeze picked up suddenly on the desert, kicking up grains of sand, hurling them, ticky-tacky, against the house.

"One by one!" Paul's voice came hurtling at them, deep and well-hollow and evil. "You'll all know the coldness of the grave. One by one!"

His laughter cut at them.

The house began to stink as a foul odor drifted about those in the den. And thin tentacles of yellow smoke snaked about their ankles.

Paul's laughter was now louder than the music blaring from the speakers.

"You know me, and I know you!" His words came to them. "But I'm just a little boy," he taunted. "There is nothing you can do to me."

"Yes, there is, Paul," Janis whispered, her words unheard by the others. "And if that's the only way, I'll do it."

BOOK TWO

This is the Black Widow, death.

　　　　　　　　—Lowell

ONE

"Open the door, Paul. I want to talk to you."

Father Gomez waited in the hall, in front of the locked bedroom door. He listened. Thought he could hear movement behind the door. But he couldn't be sure, although he had been told that Paul was in his room.

"Paul? Come on. Open the door. Talk to me," the priest urged.

"Fuck you!" the deep, well-hollow voice retorted at last.

"Come on, Paul. Let's talk. There is no reason for you to be afraid of me."

Laughter from behind the closed door. "Afraid of you? Don't be silly. That is the most absurd thing I have ever heard."

"Then why don't you open the door and talk to me?"

At the priest's urging, Stanford had taken the girls outside, to sit by the pool.

Leo was standing at the hall entrance, listening, watching.

Gomez heard something behind the door. What,

233

he could not be sure. But it sounded faintly like a quiet roaring; a gathering of wind, perhaps.

In Paul's room?

Gomez tapped on the door once more. "We must meet, Paul. You know that. It's time."

The sounds of laughter. "All right," Paul said. "So you want to talk to me, heh, Holy Roller? Well, then. Come on in."

Gomez heard the door being unlocked.

He knew Paul had used his powers to do it.

Leo had walked up the hall, to stand beside the priest. "What's that roaring sound?"

"I don't know."

The men exchanged glances.

"I don't trust him," Leo said quietly.

Gomez only smiled. He turned the doorknob and pushed open the door.

The roaring sound both men had heard became a dark-tinged maelstromic vortex. The whirling winds grabbed both men, sucked them through the doorway and into the room, then spun them around and slammed them against a wall, almost knocking the breath from them. They were picked up, as if by invisible hands and shaken, as a parent might shake a naughty child.

Each man felt an invisible hand slap him across the face.

The bedroom door closed. Locked.

Gomez and Leo were slammed hard against the wall, their heads bumping against the paneling. Then they were shoved to the floor, to land on their bottoms.

The part of Leo's brain that was not in shock, that

could still register and record events, noted that not one book, one piece of paper, or record cover—nothing else in the room—was being affected by the winds.

Only he and Gomez.

And Paul had not been alone in there.

But what in God's name—Leo felt that only He might be able to explain it—was that thing . . . creature . . . that hideousness crouching by the bed, beside Paul?

The creature began to change before the eyes of the wind-held men. A metamorphosis that both would rather not witness.

While Paul sat Buddhalike in the center of the bed and laughed demonically. Insanely. The boy's eyes were wild, his lips peeled back grotesquely. And his teeth were very white, the cuspids long and needle-pointed. Slobber leaked from Paul's mouth.

He was hideous-looking.

But not as horrible as the creature now standing by the bed. The metamorphosis had produced a standing snake, a snarling deformed caninelike beast, a great cat out of prehistoric times, a winged serpent, a half-man/half-beast, and a scaly creature that defied description, but whose sight would produce terror in even the bravest of person.

Then it became what it was.

A demon.

Both men knew it. Leo without knowing how. Father Dan Gomez because he had been born to, someday, face it.

That day had arrived.

The priest whispered a prayer that could not be

heard by human ears over the wailing of the funnel-like wind that held the shocked men in its embrace.

The demon's eyes were huge and half-mooned, slightly slanted. Two holes in the center of its ugly face dropped green-yellow stinking slime. Scales covered the upper part, mottled and loose skin the lower part of its face. And its long, needle-pointed teeth were stained and crusted with scum and filth. A long, forked tongue flicked in and out of its lipless mouth. That mouth, open and hissing, was blood-red and expelled an olfactory-insulting odor.

Leo and Gomez were jerked to their feet by the forceful hands of the demon's wind. Banged against the wall. Then the wind ceased abruptly. The cessation was so abrupt that both men were slammed to the floor in a sprawl of arms and legs.

Leo's hand snaked under his jacket, his fingers touching the butt of the .44.

His mental confusion ended when the snarling, hissing, walking foulness started to move toward them.

"Mine!" Paul screamed. "Damn your souls to the pits of my father."

Gomez began to pray.

Paul began to laugh.

Leo jerked out his .44, earing back the hammer.

He gave the demon a taste of Smith and Wesson.

The roaring of the big .44 was enormous in the closed room. The demon was slug-struck in the shoulder. Picked up off its big, flat, dirty and clawed feet, and tossed to the floor. A stinking gush of red, yellow, and green pus and blood flew from the wound.

The demon screamed in pain.

But its wound healed as rapidly as it had opened.

And the room filled with a putrid, yellow, sulfuric eye-smarting mist.

Before Leo could swing the muzzle of the .44 toward Paul and pull the trigger, which was exactly what he had in mind, he was jerked off the floor, turned around in midair, and—legs straight out in front of him—hurled against the bedroom door, the force of the impact tearing the door from its hinges and dropping Leo to the carpeted hall floor, still holding onto his .44.

Stanford and the girls came running into the hallway just as Father Gomez was tossed out of the room. He landed on his butt beside Leo, and was just as confused as the ex-cop.

The door was picked up, placed back into the frame. The cracks vanished. The pins were dropped into place. The lock clicked.

The wind died into silence.

But that thin stinking mist oozed out from under the door to softly lick at human feet and ankles as Leo and Gomez were helped up and steadied for a moment.

"Would you holster that cannon, please?" Stanford requested of Leo.

Shaken, Leo slipped the pistol back into his shoulder holster. "I hit it. I got in a fair shot. I should have taken my time and killed the goddamn thing! What was that in there?"

The men were led up the hall and into the den, then seated.

Melissa and Janis were pale and clearly scared.

237

Stanford noticed and gave them something to do. "Get them glasses of water, please, girls."

The girls took off for the kitchen, glad to have a mission.

Gomez looked at Leo. "You wouldn't have killed it if you'd emptied your gun into it. Didn't you see it heal almost instantly? And what was it? Some relation of Paul's, I would imagine."

Gomez flexed his left arm; he had struck the wall hard with his left shoulder.

Leo shook his head. "Relation!"

Gomez leaned back in his chair. "At least we now know our worst fears are confirmed."

"We do?" Leo took his .44 from leather, punched out the empty brass, and reloaded.

As the girls brought glasses of ice water, Stanford met the priest's eyes. "He's the Devil's own?"

Gomez nodded. "Without a doubt. And he's powerful. What happened just a few moments ago was Paul's way of showing us a sample of what he can do. Believe me, the worst is yet to come."

The inspector stood up and took his service revolver from its holster. He looked down at Janis. There was sadness in his eyes.

Gomez rose to face him. "No, Stanford. Not here. Not now. Not yet."

Leo stood up. "I'll go with you, Stanford. Between the two of us we ought to do it."

"No!" The priest's voice was harsh.

"Why not?" Stanford demanded. He held the pistol muzzle-down, by his side, his trigger finger resting on the trigger guard. "He's shown us what he is. The battle lines have been drawn. I see no point in

238

delaying what you and I know is inevitable."

Gomez opened his mouth just as the doorbell sounded. Janis answered it. The gang. Carla and Carol and Jean and Bing and Roy. She waved them inside and down the steps to the sunken den.

Stanford had turned and quickly holstered his pistol.

"Gonna be big doings down at the civic center," Bing said. "That Dr. Slater and his wife have just called a press conference for late this afternoon. The TV people are comin' in, and a bunch of newspaper reporters. We just heard it on the radio. You know what's goin' on, Janis?"

"Not really." She looked at the men, one by one.

"I'll get on the horn to Mike." Leo moved toward the phone. "See if he knows anything." He quickly punched out the number of the hospital, figuring Mike would still be there with Connie.

It took the switchboard operator about a minute to track down the chief.

Leo turned as he waited, to look up the hallway. The door to Paul's room was closed.

Gateway to Hell, Leo thought.

He was having a very difficult time accepting all that he'd seen in that room, though he knew damned well he'd pulled the trigger on something.

And that something was not of this earth.

But then, he thought . . .

. . . neither is Paul.

Mike came on the line. "Chaos is about to break loose, Leo. Dick and his wife had some sort of encounter, last evening, I guess it was. He's turned in his resignation at the hospital. Says he's going to bust this thing wide open, that it's his moral duty to put a stop to it."

"Now how does he figure he can do that by blabbing to the press?"

"Beats me, buddy."

"Hang on." Leo handed the phone to Gomez.

The priest listened, his face tightening as the words rolled into his ear. "Listen, Mike . . . see if you—or somebody—can dissuade Slater. If you don't, he'll die. I'm convinced of that. Paul will never let him talk. The boy knows he can't stand that kind of publicity. And for that matter, neither can we. Slater has got to be stopped—right now. See what you can do."

"Too late, Father. Dick and his wife are holed up in their house. They're not seeing anyone, nor are they answering the phone. The statement they issued jointly says it will all be explained late this afternoon, at the civic center."

"They're fools. All right, Mike. Thanks. How is Mark Kelly?"

"Last report is that he's not good. Mentally or physically. The doctors don't think he's going to make it. And they don't know why. His cuts were not that serious, neither were the bumps on his head."

Gomez briefly, and in low tones, explained what had happened to him and Leo.

Shocked silence on the other end. Gomez could sense the man was having a tough time getting a mental picture of it all.

Finally, with a grunt, Mike said, "You should have let the inspector shoot him."

"That wouldn't have been countenanced, Mike."

240

The priest stretched the telephone cord to its full length, and moved away from the young people. "Mike, you do understand that this is all a game, don't you?"

Again, a long silence. "A game, Father? What are you talking about?"

"Dark humor from the Dark One. Satan is just having fun. This is all a joke to him. A long-running, ageless joke. But I think that old abomination has a very definite plan in mind."

Mike waited.

"I think he wants Janis," Gomez whispered.

After Father Gomez left, heading for the hospital, Janis looked at Leo and Stanford.

"You don't have to stay. I'm not afraid."

"Speak for yourself!" Melissa said, her eyes wide.

She glanced at the gang, back to the men. "No. Think about it. Too much has already happened in and around this house. I'm low on Paul's list now. And I have a funny feeling that he's changed his mind. I don't think he's going to kill me. I don't know how I know that; I just do. I think something . . . well, bad is going to happen to me. But when—or if—it does, it won't be in this house. I think it'll be out there." She jerked her thumb toward the outside.

Stanford felt he knew what Paul had in mind for his sister. But he kept quiet about it. They were, after all, brother and sister.

He cautioned himself not to forget that.

"Perhaps," Stanford replied. "But, Janis, you

must keep in mind that you are in constant danger." He looked at the group of young people. "Are you all going to stay here with her?"

They were. All day. And that was a promise.

Stanford met Leo's eyes. The New York City man shrugged. Then both men walked to the door. There, they paused to look back at the girls and boys. Both wanted to say something, anything that might help. But they couldn't find the words.

Paul had remained silent, in his room. In that passageway to Hell.

Both men wondered what the little demon was plotting in his evil brain.

With a parting nod, they left the house, closing the door behind them.

The kids seemed to relax after the adults had gone. Stanford and Leo were OK people. But they were adults. And you had to be careful what you said around adults.

Bing sniffed the air. "I could swear somebody fired off a gun in here."

Janis explained.

The kids, as if operating under the control of one brain, all turned and looked up the hallway, as if expecting to see the yawning gates of Hell open before them, the fiery entrance to be filled with howling demons, writhing in a frenzied mass of teeth and tails, and mouthing threats of burning in pits forever.

It didn't make any of them feel better when Paul stepped out of his room and walked up the hall, toward the group in the den.

Bing and Roy touched the stag handles of their

sheathed hunting knives. They'd stuck the knives in their socks before leaving home, to conceal them from their parents, and had slipped the leather loops through their belts after they'd gotten out of their houses.

But Paul did not step down into the sunken den. He stood for a moment at the railing, looking at the gathering below him, and smiling. His eyes flicked over the hunting knives, and he laughed.

"Mighty warriors all, hey?" Paul sneered at the boys. "We'll see." He glanced at his sister. "I'll be out for a time. Perhaps all day. Goodbye, sis!"

The boy walked out of the house, slamming the door behind him.

After a soft expulsion of breath that signaled her relief, Carol said, "Maybe we'll all get lucky and he won't come back."

"I wish," Janis agreed. Then she remembered the inspector standing up and taking out his gun. The way he'd looked at her. Sad. Father Gomez standing up, stopping the inspector from . . .

The phone rang.

All the young people jumped at the sudden jangling. Then they grinned and looked around, embarrassed.

Janis turned to the coffee table. But the coffee table was gone and so was the phone, thanks to Daddy and his axe.

She ran up the steps to the kitchen, and stilled the ringing.

Connie.

"Is everything all right, Janis?"

"Everything is . . . just fine, Mother." Why didn't

243

she go ahead and tell her mother about Paul? Easy answer to that one. Her mother wouldn't believe it. "How's Daddy?"

"Not . . . very good, honey. But let's all be brave about it. Where is your brother?"

"He's outside. Playing."

That was as good a reply as any, Janis supposed.

"I've decided to stay with your father, Janis. At the hospital. They've provided me with a room next to his. I'll be here several days, probably. I'm going to call Linda and see if she can stay at the house with you while I'm gone. I'll call now, then come over at about five or so to get some clothes. So I'll see you later on this afternoon. Is that agreeable with you, Janis?"

"Fine, Mother. See you later."

Janis hung up and then turned to the gang. She gave them a rundown on the conversation, and grinned along with them.

Linda was OK people, a decent babysitter.

And she had the greatest collection of horror videotapes and books in the whole world. She was really into the supernatural and all that stuff. She probably knew more about ghosts and creatures and vampires and werewolves than anybody in the county.

Maybe the whole state.

Yeah. With Linda coming over, things were definitely looking up.

Sort of.

The woman opened her red-rimmed eyes. The room

244

was shrouded in darkness. The curtains drawn. Something had awakened her. But what?

She lay on the bed and listened for some sound. She heard nothing.

Mentally, Mary felt she was standing on the ragged edge and was about to topple over into some dark abyss.

First her husband, Andy, had been killed answering a trouble call. Then his body mysteriously disappeared from the funeral home.

And nobody from the department would tell her anything, except that some kids probably took the body.

She didn't believe that. Not at all.

What next?

She turned her face toward the pillow and tried to cry. But she was finally all cried out. Her eyes felt sore and tired. No tears came.

She froze, prone in bed, as a bumping sound came from the hall. It was sort of a stumbling footfall kind of noise. Staggering.

Then she realized that it was probably their lone ranchhand—her lone ranchhand—if that was what one could call Old Jake.

It was even stretching it to call this place a ranch. Most wouldn't.

A few cows, a few horses, stuck out in the country.

That bumping sound again.

Mary sat up in the bed, clutching the covers to her. She was naked under her thin housecoat, and something about the odd sounds made her anxious and caused her flesh to creep.

Bump.

"Jake, is that you?"

Stumble.

"Jake!"

Lurch.

"Jake, come on now! If you're drunk again, you can just get on out of this house."

A grunting sound. Animal-like. But not any animal Mary had ever heard.

Bump.

Suddenly, Mary felt—knew—that it wasn't Old Jake in the hall.

But she didn't know what it was.

She fumbled in the nightstand for her pistol. Andy had insisted she keep it there, living like they did, way out in the country.

Bump. Grunt.

Out in the shack that was laughingly called a bunkhouse, Old Jake had just finished polishing off a half-pint of rye whiskey.

He raised up and peered out the extremely dirty window just above his bunk. Must have been his imagination playing tricks on him, he thought. But he could have sworn he'd seen someone . . . or something . . . stagger across the yard just a few minutes ago.

Guess not.

He lay back on the bunk and reached down into the paper sack on the floor. Broke the seal on another bottle of rye and took a slug.

After he stopped coughing and hacking, he sputtered, "Goddamn, but that's good!"

Then his thoughts turned maudlin.

"What a way for a real cowboy to spend his last days," Jake muttered. "A goddamn handyman on a rawhide outfit that's owned by a missing dead man."

Old Jake was partly correct in that. Dead, but not missing.

Not anymore.

Jake took another slug and wondered what had really happened to Andy's body?

Bunch of kids probably stole the stiff. Goddamn kids nowadays didn't have no respect for nothing.

Jake lay back and took another slug.

Thought of better days. . . .

Mary's heart began to hammer as the bumping and staggering, the lurching and stumbling sounds stopped.

Right outside her bedroom door.

She jacked back the hammer on the single-action .45.

Shaking, she watched the doorknob slowly turn.

"I'll shoot you!" Mary yelled. "Go away. I'll kill you. I mean it."

The door was inching open.

Mary leveled the .45 as best she could. Taking a two-handed grip like Andy had taught her.

The door swung open.

Andy stood there, grinning at her.

Mary screamed, her eyes rolling back in her head. Then darkness took her. She slumped back on the bed, unconscious, the cocked .45 landing beside her.

Andy moved closer.

In the bunkhouse, Old Jake snored on.

"Put him in jail," Sheriff Sandry suggested. "Trump up some charge until we can talk some sense into him, beg him to lay off this foolishness." He sighed and waved his hand. "Aw! Forget I said that. That would really tip off the press people that we're trying to cover up something."

Once again, they had converged at the hospital, in the conference room.

"I've got an idea," Peter suggested. "But I'd hate to do it to Dr. Slater. He's always been an all-right guy."

"Let's extol his virtues at some other date," Dr. Clineman said. "Tell us what you've got on your mind, Deputy."

"We go clean, one hundred percent. No one around to back up Slater's story."

"Fine, Peter," Sandry said. "But how?"

"First of all, for it to work, Jenny's going to have to be moved. And I mean away from this area. To a private sanitarium."

"That's easy," Belline said. "We can arrange that in twenty minutes. Go on."

"And Jenny's father is going to have to be taken out of town, kept out of sight for a few days. Along with his attorney."

"There's no problem with Ralph," Mike said. "He's drunk most of the time anyway. We'll just get him drunker and carry him off. He'll never know the difference."

"Getting the lawyer out is not going to be as easy," Sandry told them. "But I know he's got a client over in Tucson facing a murder-one charge. We could get word to him that his client wants to see him. Like right now. He'd have to go. It's weak, but it might work."

"Agreed," Mike said. "That'd get him out of town for this evening anyway."

"Then what?" Mary Beth asked Pete.

"We plant people in the audience, to start laughing Dick down as soon as he starts talking about creatures and ghosts and demons. Laughter is infectious. It might work."

Belline nodded his head. "I hate to make Dick look like a fool, but we've got to do something. All right. Let's do it."

"I'm for it," Carleson said, looking around the table. "Unless anybody has a better suggestion."

No one did.

Belline pushed back his chair. "I'll make arrangements for the Cauldman girl to be moved. That private hospital up near the border would be best, I think. That agreeable with you all?"

It was.

Belline left the room.

Sheriff Sandry looked at Peter. "Get a couple of folks to ease Mr. Cauldman out of town. Take him to the safe house we use on the Aravaipa. I'll be out later to talk to him. And get somebody working on getting the lawyer out of town."

Pete nodded and left the room.

"Are we forgetting anything?" Mary Beth asked.

"I'm sure we are," Mike said. "It'll come back to haunt us. No play on words intended." He grimaced. "Well, the S.O. and the P.D. will keep their mouths shut. I'll have someone file a report about the theft of Andy's body, and let the press take a look at it if any reporters ask to see it."

"We're forgetting Glen Holland," Dr. Thomas reminded them.

"Right. But he wasn't from this area," Clineman answered. "I'll do a report stating we shipped his body back home. He was from Chicago. It'd take anyone weeks to wade through the red tape."

"Anybody got anything else to add?" Mike asked.

No one did.

Mike stood up. "All right. We'll all wander into the civic center, separately. Interested citizens and all that. See you all there."

Mary came out of the darkness to a familiar sensation. Very pleasant. The feeling of Andy's body next to hers.

But his flesh was so cold.

Then Mary remembered that Andy was dead.

She opened her mouth to scream.

A hand, also cold to the touch, quickly covered her mouth.

She struggled to maintain her sanity. That couldn't have been Andy standing in the doorway. Impossible. She was being molested by some drifter.

She managed to twist her head and get a one-eyed look at her assailant.

Andy.

His cold hand covered her mouth, preventing her from squalling out.

He continued his assault.

Something broke in Mary's mind. A part of her drifted off into marshmallow land.

In the dim light of the bedroom, the only illumination filtering through the partially open door, Mary could see that the makeup had come off of Andy's throat, exposing a horrible gash.

The stitches that had held his lips together had come loose. They were hanging down over his lower lip like tiny wriggling black worms.

Andy removed his cold hand from Mary's mouth, and bent his head to kiss her.

In the grip of terror and disgust, of near madness, Mary twisted her head, pressed her face against the rumpled sheets, to avoid the kiss from that dry, dead, cold, wormy-looking mouth.

"Mary." Andy's voice was dull and deep. It echoed around the bedroom, making Mary's tortured mind see a spirit rising from the grave, out of a dark mist, twisting and entwining amid dew-wet tombstones that seemed starkly real.

She vainly fought to keep some part of her lucid by telling herself that none of this was real.

It was not happening. It could not be happening.

"Mary." That voice. Dead. Grave-deep and hollow, it nudged at what was left of her sanity.

But she could not deny his presence.

Andy bent over her and she felt a sharpness, a pricking sensation on her neck.

Then a cold tongue began to lick it.

A warm stickiness oozed down the side of her throat.

She experienced no pain as Andy began to suck and slurp at the trickle of blood.

Her head felt very light.

Another bit of lucidity left her.

Andy's mouth began working at the other side of her neck. That very slight pricking sensation. That warm sticky ooze flowing down the side of her throat. Andy's tongue, not so cold now, licking and sucking the flow.

"No!" she yelled, her fingers, clawed now, digging into the sheets.

He laughed.

Profanity rolled in waves from her mouth.

She cursed God. Jesus. Mary. Joseph.

In her mind, Andy had turned into a creature from Hell, clawed and scaled and hideous.

Yet suddenly he was beautiful.

He was speaking in some language that, at first, was alien to her.

Then she began to understand the ancient words.

She agreed with them. Agreed to follow the rules. Agreed to everything.

Yes. Yes. Yes!

Lost her soul. Gave it up willingly. Mentally watched it rip from her and flap away, carried in the great beak of some dark reptilian-appearing creature with wings of darkness that completely obscured her mind. The creature soared out of sight.

She was lost.

His mouth sought her throat.

Mary willingly, on command from a new master of evil and darkness and pain and perversion, moved her head, allowing Andy access to it.

He bit into her throat. And blood flowed into his mouth and up and through his long, sharp, hollow teeth.

Another darkness took her.

She made no effort to fight the fall.

Together, the twin undead tumbled into a pleasant fire, the flames touching them, but producing no pain. Skeletal hands reached from the smoke and ash and fire to touch them as they fell.

The fires of evil licked their flesh, searing and bubbling and marking them.

Jake opened his eyes. He could have sworn he'd heard someone screaming. But it wasn't no squall of fear or terror or nothin' like that.

It had sounded to Jake like some woman in the throes of ecstasy.

He must have been dreaming about sex. That must have been it.

Unless Mary had some man in bed with her.

But Jake doubted that.

He lay back in his bunk, unscrewed the cap from his bottle of rye, and took a good pull. Moments later he fell asleep.

TWO

"Promise not to tell, Linda."

The sixteen-year-old smiled at the serious face of her charges for the next few days and nights. "All right. I promise. Now what's going on that's so big it's got to be kept hush-hush?"

"You're not going to believe it," Janis warned her. "But since you're going to be staying with us, you've got a right to know."

Linda looked at the shattered window, still all boarded up. Janis had shown her the bloodstained carpet in the hall. She had noticed the knives Bing and Roy had attached to their belts, the tenseness the young people were exhibiting. And she had, of coures, heard the rumors going around town about strange happenings.

But they were just rumors.

Dismissible.

And she had been baby-sitting since she was thirteen. Knew kids pretty well. Knew what was trivia to an adult was often of monumental importance to kids.

Linda waited. And as she did, she noted that the

usually bubbly Janis seemed tense and serious.

Then Janis started talking, slowly at first, hesitantly. When she warmed up, her words came out in a verbal torrent.

Linda looked at the book Melissa handed her.

Felt numb.

That picture was just like the mark on Paul's arm. For sure. She'd seen it many times.

She made Janis slow down, back up, take it from the beginning and go slow.

While Janis talked, Linda walked around the den, taking in the shattered and boarded windows. She walked up the hall and carefully inspected Paul's closed bedroom door. When she tried the knob, she found the door locked, and totally without damage.

Paul always had been a strange kid, she recalled. The other kids didn't like him, didn't trust him, and were wary of him.

And he was a little snoop.

Still, that didn't make him a demon.

But she couldn't deny the bloodstains on the hall carpet, or the fact that Mr. Kelly had gone bonkers, or the picture in the book.

It was identical to the mark on Paul's arm.

Linda didn't know what to believe.

But she was going to major in parapsychology at college, and most definitely believed in the supernatural, in abnormal and unexplained phenomena.

She decided to go with the kids' story.

She rejoined them in the den. "OK, gang. Let's take it from the top once more. Then we'll make a plan of action. If what you've told me is true, I've got my thesis already written!"

"We've got to start dealing with Janis's followers."
Paul gave the order to those faithful to the Dark
Ways.

They crouched in the empty lot and listened,
grinning with evil anticipation.

He smiled back at them, knowing that his true
father had thousands of willing and anxious and
waiting servants on this miserable planet, ready to
serve, regardless of the cost.

Young and old and in-between.

Lane smirked. "I got something I'd like to give
Melissa."

"Then give it to her," Paul told him. "I really
don't care what you do to them. Just as long as you
get them out of circulation."

"Dead?" Lisa asked matter-of-factly. She was
holding her very sharp knife.

Paul shook his head. "That might not be wise at
this stage of the operation." His voice had deepened
even more. "I would suggest banging them around
some, perhaps breaking a bone or two. But whatever
you do, I want no harm to come to Janis. Do all of
you understand? No harm must come to Janis!"

They all understood his words, though none of
them understood the why of them.

But they would obey.

They did not have to understand. They never
would. Until it was too late.

These were the expendable troops. Throwaways.

257

Which was exactly what Paul intended to do with them, when they had exhausted their usefulness.

Lisa slid her knife into the clip-on sheath in her boot. "Have you lined up others, Paul?"

"The town is filled with them. They will all come when I command." He looked at each of them, directly in the eyes. "Through the Master."

They all dropped their gaze.

They understood.

Finally.

This was what they'd been placed on earth to do. There were thousands like them. Usually, they fulfilled their evil purpose in mundane ways, as thieves and murderers, in acts of petty evil, which were heartbreaking to their victims.

Few ever fully realized their true purpose.

These would.

Paul said, "Old Man Gillette is a caco. And he knows it. So do many of the others in the area."

Gillette was totally evil.

Without a semblance of redeeming social value.

Worthless.

"What's a caco?" Rex asked. "I don't think I ever heard that word before."

"There are many things you have never heard. You will learn. A caco, in modern language, is nothing. But in my father's domain, a caco is an evil person, capable of doing great damage if called upon to do so."

Lisa grinned. "And you're going to call."

"Correction. I have already called."

"What about this big-deal meeting at the center tonight?" Frank asked.

258

"There will be no meeting. I have seen to that. Now go. Deal with my sister's friends."

The Slaters, Dick and Judy, heard the car pull into the driveway and its door clunk shut. Whoever it was could just go away. Neither Dick nor Judy were about to make any statements until the press conference that evening. Then they were going to tell everybody about the terrible things happening in the town. And about the police and the sheriff's department and the doctors conspiring to cover them up, and ignoring the safety of the citizens.

Dick and Judy were no longer skeptics. They had seen. They believed.

They were prepared to be laughed at. Expected it. But if only one reporter believed them, that would get the story out.

The doorbell rang.

"Go away!" Dick shouted.

The chiming continued.

"Stop ringing the bell."

"It's Ralph Cauldman, Dr. Slater. Jenny's father. Please let me in. I have to talk to you. It's very important."

Back in his office, the lawyer who was representing Ralph lay on the floor. Dead. His heart had just stopped beating.

Dick and Judy looked at one another.

"Please, Doctor, talk to me. I have information you can use at this evening's conference. Please let me in."

"It might be something we can use," Judy said.

"They've taken my daughter away from the hospital, Dr. Slater. I don't know where she is. They won't tell me. I'm about to go crazy. Please, open the door and talk to me."

Neighbors began to gather on their front lawns. Listening.

"Those heartless bastards!" Dick jumped to his feet, headed for the front door. "I should have guessed, should have known they'd pull something like this. Damn them all."

He jerked open the door.

Ralph Cauldman stepped in, a big wide grin on his face. "Hi, sucker!" he said.

He reached inside his jacket and pulled out a pistol, jacked the hammer back.

"No!" Dick managed to say. He held out his hands as if they alone could stop the slug about to come at him.

They didn't.

Ralph fired once, at point-blank range, the slug hitting Dick in the chest and penetrating his heart. Dick fell backward and slid down the foyer wall to the floor, dead.

Screaming, Judy jumped from the couch and ran out of the room, Ralph right behind her, waving his pistol.

He fired once. Missed. The slug knocked a chunk of paneling from the wall.

Screaming his rage, Ralph charged up the hall, trying to catch her.

Judy ran into a bedroom and slammed the door. Tried to lock it. Ralph's shoulder hit it before she could. The door flew open, inward, the side of it hitting Judy in the face, breaking her nose and knocking her back.

Ralph lifted the pistol and shot her, the slug striking her just above the bridge of her swelling nose, and exiting out the back of her head.

Judy flopped once on the carpet, then lay still.

Ralph ran out of the house and into the Slaters' front yard.

Neighbors, who had gathered on the street, stood staring for a few seconds. But they ran wildly in all directions when they saw the gun in Ralph's hand.

"Wait!" he yelled. "Wait. I won't hurt any of you. I promise. You've got to listen to me. Slater did something to my little Jenny. It was all his fault. It was his fault."

He fired into the air to get their attention.

He did.

Pandemonium reigned.

People started jumping behind parked cars, hitting the ground, hollering and screaming and squalling, and running for their lives.

"It was all Slater's fault!" Ralph yelled. "I had to kill him. Don't you understand? Don't you see? Sure, you do. I had to have revenge for what he did to my wife and daughter. Slater raped them both. Jenny and Dottie. You can understand that. You've got families of your own."

"Look at me! Look at me!" Ralph hollered.

Then he stuck the barrel of the Make-My-Day .44 Mag into his mouth.

And pulled the trigger.

The slug jerked Ralph's head back. There was a very strange expression on his face, but for a few seconds, he stood upright. Then he slowly tumbled backward as the bullet came out just above his ear.

Ralph Cauldman jerked once and died.

In the confusion, no one seemed to notice the handsome honey-colored man and his lovely wife as they drove by in a car driven by the caco, Gillette. Mantine and Nicole were sitting in the back seat.

Mantine smiled at the chaos. "Ver' good. De boy done handled it ver' well. I tink we could leab him on his own any time."

"Dat's good. I am ready to go bak to de islands. We go bak now?"

Mantine thought about that for a moment. "No. I don' tink so just yet. I won' to see more. De boy intrigues me. I tink we mus' see de end of dis."

Nicole shook her head. The wooden amulets around her neck jangled and clacked with the movement. "I don' lak it when we visible lak dis. Too much can hoppen to us dat we don' haves no control over."

Mantine patted her knee. "You worries too much, ma baby. Relax. We gonna have us a good time. Lots and lots of fun. People gonna die in all sorts of funny ways. It gonna be fun to watch. You'll see."

Behind the wheel, Gillette laughed evilly.

The press converged on the hospital like sky-darkening locusts settling on a wheat field. The doctors agreed to meet with them in an informal press conference on the side lawn of the institution.

The first question was tossed out. Why was the hospital admitting only emergency patients?

Clineman fielded it smoothly. "Because we have two suspected cases of Legionnaires' Disease, and we don't want to endanger anyone else."

Everybody knew about Legionnaires' Disease. The press could accept that. OK.

What about the murders of Dr. and Mrs. Slater?

"A terrible, terrible tragedy. It was just awful."

All the doctors agreed, with much shaking of heads and clucking of tongues.

Why did Dr. and Mrs. Slater call this press conference?

"I have no idea," Clineman told them. "After speaking with colleagues, I find that none of us has the foggiest idea what Dick was going to say. He offered no explanation for turning in his resignation. It came as a great shock to us all. Dick Slater was a very fine doctor, and was well liked."

What about Ralph Cauldman's daughter—Jenny?

"Well, perhaps Dick blamed himself for that. He was her physician. Come to think of it, Dick was behaving a bit strangely of late."

Why? Because of the girl?

"Possibly."

What happened to her?

"She lost her mind."

How?

"We don't know." Belline took the mike and the hot seat. "And we probably won't know for some time. If we ever do find out."

Is she still here at Tepehuanes General?

"No. She has been transferred to a private institution, where she'll receive better attention."

Why better?

"The hospital is better equipped to deal with her type of illness."

Where is this institution?

Sheriff Sandry took the mike. "According to the juvenile authorities, we cannot divulge the location at this time. Come on—she's just a little girl! For God's sake! Hasn't she suffered enough? Give the kid a break."

The reporters asked a few more questions, then packed it in.

A deputy took Sandry to one side, motioning for Leo and Stanford to come along.

"What do you have, Wally?" Sandry asked.

"That creep Gillette. I saw him about an hour ago with two blacks in the back seat of his car. Handsome man and a knock-out lady. I laid back in my unmarked car and followed them. Sheriff, at no time—no time—did Gillette stop and let those people out. Yet, when he stopped at the post office, they were gone from his car. I didn't believe it. I walked up and looked in the back seat. Empty. Except for . . . well, this sounds sort of stupid. . . ."

Sheriff Sandry's sigh was audible. "So what else is new, Wally? Zombies and sand creatures and hobgobbins are normal? Go on . . . except for what?"

The deputy shuffled his feet. "Well, sir, the back seat . . . the whole car! It smelled funny. First I couldn't place it. Then it came to me. It smelled like the sea at low tide."

Sandry had a pained expression on his face. "In the middle of Arizona?"

Stanford smiled grimly and the sheriff noticed it. "What do you find amusing about all this, Inspector?"

264

Stanford looked at the deputy. "This man and woman, they were both light-skinned? Call them honey-colored, perhaps?"

"Yes, sir. They were a nice-looking couple."

"Mantine and his wife, Nicole. Both in their human shapes . . ."

Sandry sighed again and rolled his eyes.

Stanford asked the sheriff: "What does this deputy know of the situation in here?"

"Everything that I know about this lash-up. He's part of the Tach Team I ordered in here."

The inspector nodded. "Deputy, the next time you see that couple—and you pass this word on to everybody else—no matter where they might be, you walk up to them and kill them! You shoot them dead on the spot. That's the only way—or rather, the easiest way—to get the job done."

"Sir!" Wally recoiled.

Sandry stepped closer to the inspector. "Now you wait just a minute, Willingston!"

"No, you wait!" Stanford cut him off. He waved his hand. "All right, Sheriff. All right. This Gillette person, he's rather a despicable character, I take it?"

"That's not the word for Gillette," Mike put in. "He's a convicted child molester. A dealer in kiddy porn. But we can't get enough on him to take him to court."

"He's a caco," said the inspector.

"He's a what?" Leo asked. He was always, or so it seemed, learning something new about the supernatural. "What is a caco?"

"The simplest way to explain that is to say that a caco is a very evil person. Some of them are not even aware that they are minions of the Dark One, subject to his call at any time."

Sandry looked Heavenward and muttered something under his breath.

"You mean the . . . Devil is making them do what they do?" Wally asked. "Don't let a defense attorney hear that. What a defense that would make."

Stanford quickly nixed that. "Absolutely not, Deputy. These people do what they do because they want to do it. Not because of some trumped-up reason. They are born with the bad seed in them."

"I think I might like you after all, Stanford," Sandry told him. "But be that as it may, my people can't just walk up and shoot someone. As much as we all bluster and brag about wanting to do something like that, I wouldn't have a man on my department who could do it. I think you understand that, Inspector."

They still don't understand, Stanford mused. "All right, Sheriff. I suppose you and your people are going to have to witness some horror before you'll be able to act."

Sandry didn't know quite how to take that, so he offered no response. He cut his eyes to the ex-cop from New York, and knew Leo felt the same way as the inspector. But the sheriff would not allow his people to cold-bloodedly kill.

Not yet.

Leo said, "If you guys had been with Father Gomez and me, in Paul's room, you wouldn't have any reservations about letting the hammer fall on some of these people."

Sheriff Sandry's expression was unreadable. "Be that as it may, there will be no wholesale killing in this county. So with that understood by all, I hope, what's next for us?"

Stanford glanced at him. "If you will not order the destruction of these lost beings, we have only one other choice in the matter."

"And that is . . . ?"

"We wait for them to strike. To kill again. Maybe then you'll do something." Stanford turned his back to the group and walked away.

Sandry quietly reassessed his previous evaluation of the inspector.

Janis called the rectory and got in touch with Father Gomez, asked him to bring over another cross for Linda and to talk to her. The priest said he would be over as soon as possible.

"Hurry," Janis urged.

Paul still had not returned.

And the mood was changing. Not just the mood, Janis thought. Something else. Something almost unexplainable. There seemed to be a heaviness in the air. Some invisible force that was touching them all, and silently working on them. On how they felt, behaved, thought.

They had discussed it, had agreed to fight it and to bring it up whenever the feeling became too much for them to cope with alone.

Late afternoon, the sun fading, creating inky pockets of unknown depth and content throughout Tepe-huanes and the area surrounding it. In a few dark splotches just outside town, odd-shaped and lumpy beings stirred and rose in the purple shadows. Soon it would be time to resume the hunt for those who had not joined with the earth, those who had grown stronger.

In the medicine lodges on the reservations, a drumming began. A warning beat, to anyone who understood it; to those who knew that on this borrowed earth, anything was possible. That there were Gods many—most—did not recognize or accept.

But after this night and those directly following it, there would not be so many skeptics.

No, there would not.

Satan laughed.

God frowned.

Michael raged and shook his mighty sword.

God told him to sit down. This fight was ageless. The faithful would survive it. They would live and be the stronger for it.

The rest would fall.

God smiled at the ageless mercenary of Angels. He would have to keep an eye on this mightiest warrior of them all.

When it came to getting into a good scrap, Michael could be sneaky.

And in the bunkhouse, Old Jake opened his bloodshot eyes. Something had awakened him. But what?

He listened.

Nothing.

He reached down toward the sack on the floor beside his bunk and found a half-pint bottle. He looked at the contents. Just about one good slug left.

He uncapped and gulped it down. Coughed. There, that was much better.

That sound again.

Jake hauled himself up in the bunk and looked out the dirty and fly-spotted window. His eyes widened in shock. He blinked a couple of times.

No. By God, that just couldn't be.

But there it was.

There was Andy, buck-assed naked, stumbling and—Jake struggled for the right word—yeah! lurching toward the corral, a saddle in each hand, the stirrups dragging the ground as he walked. His bare feet kicked up little pockets of dust.

Old Jake slapped his forehead with the palm of his hand. Andy was dead! Everybody knew that. It was in the newspapers. He'd even heard it on the radio.

But wait a minute . . . if Andy was dead like everybody said he was . . . what was that out yonder?

Shore looked like Andy.

Old Jake cut his eyes to the back door of the main house, as it opened.

What appeared in it really got his attention and held it.

Mary. In all her glory. Except for her neck, which was gory with blood.

Blood! Jake looked closer. Blood.

She didn't have a stitch on.

What was goin' on around this crazy place?

Jake lay back on the bunk and tried to reason things out. Came to the conclusion that he needed a drink. He felt under his bunk. He always kept a spare bottle there—for emergencies. And he figured this was an emergency for sure.

He leaned so far out of his bunk he lost his balance and fell over the side, onto the floor, landing on his belly, the wind knocked from him.

But he found the spare bottle of rye. A pint. Full. The seal unbroken.

Hands shaking, Jake fumbled through the dust and cobwebs, and pulled the bottle to his chest, cradling it like a baby for a moment.

He peered under the bunk and came eyeball to eyeball with a small scorpion.

"Find your own bottle, you ugly son of a bitch!" he muttered.

The scorpion scurried away, disappearing through a hole in the floor.

Jake broke the seal and took him a long wallop.

Felt better.

His nerves calmed, he capped the bottle and, pulling himself to his feet, chanced another look out the window.

Nothing out there. The corral was empty. The wind kicking up little dust devils in the dirt and sand.

"Naturally," Jake muttered. "My old eyes was playin' tricks on me, that's all."

He took another swallow, capped the bottle, and stuck it in the back pocket of his jeans.

Then he got to thinking. And just on the off chance that Mary was wanderin' around out there in her birthday suit . . .

Jake stepped outside and looked warily around

270

him. Nothing in sight. Then he heard a slight shuffling sound, and stepped quickly around the corner of the bunkhouse. He peeked out around the rickety building.

And almost lost it.

Mary and Andy were coming out of the lean-to that served as a stable for the horses. Both of them were still buck-assed naked.

But Mary's nudeness produced no feelings of lust in Old Jake. Not now. He could see much better than when he was looking through the dirty window of the bunkhouse. And what he saw almost scared him to death.

Mary's throat and neck were a bloody mess.

Jake's stomach turned sour as Andy and Mary walked closer and he could make out what appeared to be bite marks on her throat.

Bite marks?

He squinted his eyes.

Yep. No doubt about it. Bite marks was what they were.

All kinds of horrible thoughts ran through Jake's alcohol-soaked brain. Of vampires and zombies and werewolves.

He pressed closer to the bunkhouse wall, just part of his face and one eye sticking out as he watched the awkward-moving naked pair.

The horses were saddled up now. And Mary and Andy stood in the center of the corral. They seemed to be communicating with each other. But no words were coming out of their mouths. Weird!

Jake's legs felt so weak he knew he didn't dare risk

stepping away from the side of the bunkhouse. He didn't think his legs would support him without help.

A drink. He needed a drink. Bad.

Jake carefully pulled the bottle out of his back pocket, uncapped it. He took a long pull.

Easing the bottle back into his pocket, Jake chanced another peek around the corner of the bunkhouse.

Andy and Mary were in the saddle, riding off toward the west, into the sunset, just like in the movies. But the only way this thing was gonna have a happy ending was if Jake could get gone and never see them two again.

He hobbled toward the lean-to. Managed to saddle his own horse, and swing into the saddle. He bumped his head coming out of the low-roofed building and lost his hat. But he didn't want to try to retrieve it; he might not be able to get back into the saddle.

He walked his horse to the open corral gate and stopped, uncertain as to his next course of action. He didn't know whether to follow Andy and Mary or hightail it into town and tell the cops what he'd seen.

But sweet Jesus! Who would believe him?

Jake's mind was made up for him as the sounds of hooves striking the ground came to him. He looked up, fear in his eyes.

Andy and Mary were galloping toward him, coming out of the sun.

When they drew close enough for Jake to see the savage looks on their faces, he got into action. He slapped his boot heels against his horse's sides and wailed in fright. He yelled the only phrase that came into his mind: "Hi-yo, Silver!"

The horse tore out of the corral and through the open gate, Jake holding on for dear life. The pint bottle of rye whiskey in Jake's back pocket impacted against the cantle and busted. Shards of glass dug through Jake's jeans.

He chanced a wild-eyed look behind him. Andy and Mary were not fifty feet away.

Jake could see the unnatural red of their lips and tongues. And their teeth were so very very white in the fading sunlight.

Fangs.

They were grinning at him.

Jake screamed.

Andy and Mary began to laugh.

Then they moaned in unison behind him, their ghostlike mouthings reaching Jake's ears over the pounding of hooves and the pounding of his heart.

Jake was a drunk, all right. He had never denied that. And maybe he wasn't as good a hand as he used to be. But the one thing he'd always prided himself on was keeping a good horse. And his paint pony, Cochise, was just that.

And drunk or sober or in-between, Jake could always sit a saddle.

"Jake!" Andy called.

"Come back, Jake!" That was Mary.

"No way!" Jake yelled over his shoulder.

The naked couple were close. Jake could almost reach back and touch their horses' noses.

When Andy and Mary closed the distance, Jake looked to his right. Mary was beside him, grinning at him.

She reached for him.

Jake let out a squall of terror, and the paint pony gave a jump that would have been the envy of any horse that ever ran in the Derby.

Jake could see the faint glow of the lights of Tepehuanes, miles away. He knew the main highway was only a couple of miles away, straight ahead.

"Go, Cochise!" Jake yelled.

They galloped on into the fading light of dusk.

"Sweet Jake!" Mary called. "Please come join with us, Jake."

"Leave me be. Please leave me be," Jake muttered.

"Join us, Jake!" Andy moaned.

Jake leaned over, his face pressing against the horse's neck. "Cochise, you get me outta this mess and I'll fix you up with that filly over at the Two-Rivers Ranch."

The pony seemed to understand. It lengthened its stride, pulling away from the naked man and the bloodied woman.

The cries and moaning began to fade.

A mile later, Jake slowed his pony and twisted in the saddle, looking behind him. His ghostly pursuers had given up the chase. They had turned around and were heading the other way.

Jake walked his horse on, letting it cool down; then he stopped and let the animal blow and rest for a few minutes, always keeping a wary eye on his darkened surroundings. When he came to the highway, he waited. Finally, spotting a deputy's car coming toward him, he dismounted and flagged it down. It hurt him when he moved. The glass from the broken whiskey bottle was now firmly embedded in his flesh.

The deputy walked toward Jake—everybody in the county knew Old Jake—then stopped abruptly after taking a deep breath. He fanned the air and backed up.

"I know I don't smell like no rose, Deputy. But you just listen to me for a couple minutes."

"I'll listen, Jake. But you ain't getting any closer than you are right now."

The deputy had been briefed as to what was going on in and around Tepehuanes. But as he listened, he opened and closed his mouth a couple of times, his eyes wide. He finally waved Jake silent, and walked back to his car to call in.

"I hate to think what the sheriff is gonna say about this," he muttered.

Father Gomez had come and gone from the Kelly house on Mesa Drive, leaving a blessed cross hanging around Linda's neck. It was utterly dark now, and a heavy oppressive feeling lingered, thick in the air. Almost tangible was its touch on the flesh.

"Evil," Melissa said, after stepping outside and quickly returning.

The girls had all gone out, accompanied by the boys. They had all felt the same thing.

Paul had returned. "Lovely evening," he'd announced to them all. "The air has a nice touch to it, doesn't it?"

They had just stared at him.

And he'd laughed.

Before going to his room and closing the door, he

had noticed the crosses around the necks of the young people, and had smiled.

Bing's and Roy's parents had called, asking the boys to come home.

But neither boy had wanted to leave.

Their parents had insisted. Come home. Now!

The boys had protested. "But Linda's here with us. We're all right. Honest."

Now!

Bing and Roy walked slowly through the invisible murk that had settled over the streets of the town.

"The girls are gonna get in on all the action," Roy complained.

"Yeah. But there's some big doings at the country club tonight, and the day wasn't a total bummer."

"This night sure is, though."

"It isn't over yet."

A block away from the Kelly house, Bing and Roy walked into an ambush.

"Hi ya, punks!" Lisa called out, stepping from the shadows.

"Oh, no!" Roy muttered.

"You wanted some action," Bing reminded him.

Both boys noticed that the ranks of her gang had swelled. There were two more girls, Sally and Maggie, and three more boys, Red and Dave and Clark. All of them thirteen or close to it.

Bing and Roy looked at one another. Nine to two was lousy odds any way you cut it.

"Get out of the way, Lisa," Bing told her. "Tell your people to move and let us pass."

His voice sounded flat in the strange evening air.

She laughed at him, her laughter seeming even more evil in the strange oppressiveness that clung, invisibly, around them. "And if I don't? If we don't wanna move? What do you think you're gonna do about it?"

Both boys touched the hafts of the hunting knives on their belts.

Lisa noticed the movement, and grinned at them. Her teeth seemed unusually white in the gloom. "I think they're lookin' for trouble, gang. What do you say we just give it to them."

"Yeah," Sally said, excitement in her voice.

More laughter in the thick night. Evil laughter. Not a trace of nervousness in it. Hard, dangerous laughter from the mouths of the Unforgiven. The Damned. Worshippers of the Night. Young people who had willingly given their souls to the Prince of Filth. The Master of Darkness. They had been born to serve him. The bad seed implanted into the genes of their ancestors hundreds of years back.

A foul odor sprang up from the invisible murk.

"What's that smell?" Roy asked.

"Smells like rotten eggs to me," Bing told him.

"What the hell's the matter with you two?" Lisa challenged. "That smells good!"

At first, both boys thought she had lost her mind. Then they knew why the rotten-egg smell was good to her.

And knowing terrified them.

Lisa grinned, the nastiest grin either boy had ever witnessed. "Wouldn't you guys like to get to know us better?" she asked.

"No thanks," Bing and Roy replied in unison.

Lisa's face tightened as she realized she was being rejected.

"We're not good enough for them, Sally," she said, her words venom-laced.

"Let's get 'em!" Maggie whispered hoarsely.

Lisa's gang began to slowly encircle Bing and Roy. Clubs in their hands. Their eyes were flat and hard looking, an odd light shining from their depths.

When they got close, Roy suddenly kicked out, the toe of his tennis shoe catching Clark in the crotch. The boy cried out and doubled over, gagging and puking as pain rolled over him.

Rex jumped at Bing, club in hand, raising it to strike. He screamed as Bing's knife, honed to razor sharpness, flashed in the murky night, then dripped crimson. Rex wailed as he dropped the club, his arm hanging useless, cut from elbow to wrist.

Then bright lights from a car caught them all in a blinding glow. Red lights flicked on, adding color to the scene. And the squawk of a police radio could be heard.

"Run!" Lisa shouted.

She and her gang split, leaving Rex and Clark moaning and bleeding on the sidewalk.

Peter Loneman jumped out and ran up to the scene, made eerie by the revolving red and blue lights from the police car. The city cop who'd been riding with him raced after the kids. He lost them. Smaller and quicker, they vanished into the night.

"Stinks out here," Peter said.

"Hell," Bing told him.

The deputy looked up from where he was doing

some fast emergency work on Rex's arm. "Beg pardon, son?"

"That smell. It's from Hell."

Peter said nothing. Personally, he felt the boy just might be right.

The city cop returned, panting, and called in, alerting the hospital that their ETA was about ten minutes. Two kids hurt.

The city cop rode in the cage with Rex and Clark. Bing and Roy were up front with Peter.

"Janis and the girls are alone with Paul," Bing whispered. "Well, not quite alone. Linda is with them for a few days."

"Who is Linda?"

"Marlson," Roy told him. "We got to go home, Deputy. Our parents are expecting us."

"Yeah," Bing added. "We don't show up pretty quick, we're gonna get it."

"Don't sweat. We'll call from the hospital and I'll clear it for you," Peter assured them. "Which one of you cut the kid and why?"

"I did," Bing confessed. "And you know why."

"Maybe. We'll talk about it later. Just relax; you're all right. You're not in any trouble."

"Maybe not in any legal trouble." The boy spoke softly.

"I know." Peter's words were just as soft.

"It's a funky night," Roy said, looking out the window. "Something is really bad wrong in this town."

And going to get worse, Peter thought. He did not put that into words.

He didn't have to. They all felt the same way.

279

"You can't do a goddamned thing to me, pigs," Rex shouted from the back seat. "I'm just a kid." Then he laughed and laughed, holding his cut arm.

His words and laughter caused the short hairs on the back of Peter's neck to rise.

"Yeah," Clark piped up. "We're minors. You can't do a thing to us."

Peter gritted his teeth and said nothing. He slowed to avoid a drunk staggering across the street. He had never before seen a drunk in this elegant part of town.

A whiskey bottle smashed against the side of the police car. It was followed by an obscene yell from out of the darkness.

Peter did not brake to see who might have hurled the bottle. He gritted his teeth and drove on.

"It's going to be an interesting evening," the city cop said from the back seat.

Rex and Clark laughed almost insanely.

THREE

Sheriff Sandry sat in Mike's office and stared at Jake. The man smelled like a sewer, but he was completely sober as he retold his story.

Sandry sighed heavily and looked at Mike.

The chief said, "Take him to the hospital and get that glass dug out of his butt. They may want to keep him. If so, post a guard outside his room."

"I know what I saw, Chief," Old Jake said. "I was tight when it all started. But by God, I was sober when it ended. And you can believe that."

"We believe you, Jake."

Jake and the cop gone, Sheriff Sandry let his feelings show. "You . . . mean"—he was stuttering —"you mean . . . you want me to believe . . . that we got two zombies riding around naked, on horse-back!"

"It sure looks that way. It may sound funny, but I don't think anyone who comes in contact with them is going to see the humor in it."

Sandry closed his tired eyes for a moment. Without opening them, he said to a deputy, "Get a team out to the ranch. Go over it. And please"—he opened his eyes—"be careful."

Mike's phone buzzed. The chief answered it. Peter. He listened for a moment, then hung up. Turned to Sandry, Leo and Stanford who were sitting quietly in the office, waiting and watching and listening.

"Some young punks just jumped Janis's friends, Bing and Roy. The punks came out on the short end of the stick. Pete's got them at the hospital. Come on. Let's go pay them a visit."

"Always bearing in mind"—Stanford stood up—"that they are precious little juveniles and must be treated with kid gloves."

Sandry looked at the Inspector of Bahamian Police. Sometimes, he thought, this man is a real jerk. Accurate in his assessments, but a jerk. "Right, Inspector."

"Let's go," Stanford said cheerfully, then turned and walked out of the room.

Becky Matthews stepped out of the back door to stand on the stone patio. Her house was next to the Kellys' on Mesa Drive.

She thought she had seen something from her kitchen window. Something that shouldn't have been there.

Now she could see nothing. But she could sense something . . . intangible but still present. Something heavy and oppressive in the night air.

Her eyes swept the dark forest. Nothing. She wished her husband, Sam, would hurry up and get back from the city. She looked at her watch for the fifteenth time in as many minutes.

It would be hours before he arrived on the red-eye from Los Angeles.

The wind moaned and kicked up bits of sand around her, tickling her bare ankles.

Becky rubbed one against the other as she stood in the near darkness behind the house. The only light was that which managed to filter through the glass doors leading to the patio.

She glanced over at the Kelly house. Wondered how Mark was doing. She had spoken with Connie earlier. Connie Kelly had not sounded very optimistic.

Becky turned to reenter the house. Heard a low grunting sound. She turned around, attempting to peer into the darkness.

Nothing.

Nothing except that odd, almost dirty feeling that clung in the air.

A slight odor. Like rotten eggs.

Becky loved the desert. Had loved it from the moment she and her husband had deplaned from Pennsylvania, Sam having just been promoted by his company. The Matthews made lots of money. Were young. Had no kids. And Becky loved Tepehuanes. Loved the security of the neighborhood. Loved the quiet loneliness of the empty vastness behind their beautiful home.

Until now.

She had never been scared before.

Now she was terrified.

And she couldn't understand why.

There was nothing to be afraid of.

Was there?

She quickly stepped back into her house and closed the sliding doors, locking them. She pulled the drapes tightly together, then walked to the wet bar. Maybe a drink would help.

She heard—or thought she heard—something bump against the outside of the house, in the rear, just as she was fixing a jug of martinis. Becky willed herself not to look around.

It was a losing battle.

She broke out into a chilling sweat as she saw—or thought she saw—a lumpy shadow on the patio, outlined against the drapes across the sliding doors.

The shadow stopped, seemed to be trying to look into the den.

The chiming of the front doorbell gently jarred her into welcome movement.

She peeked through the eyehole, and breathed a sigh of relief.

Her neighbor, Jane Harvey. Becky jerked open the door and waved the older woman inside.

"Jane! I'm so glad to see you. Something very strange . . ."

She noticed the pistol in Jane's hand. The muzzle was pointed at her belly.

"Jane—"

"Shut up!" the woman snapped. She stepped aside, motioning with her free hand toward the open door and the yawning darkness outside. It was pocked only by widely spaced street lamps. "Let's go over to my house, Becky." Jane Harvey grinned. "We're having a party. You're invited."

"A party?" Becky began to smile. "Oh, I get it. It's a joke, right? Some sort of gangster party, and you're

284

Belle Starr, right? That's funny, Jane. You really had me going there for a minute." She frowned. "But if you're Belle Starr, why aren't you dressed Western?"

Jane slapped her across the face, the blow reddening the smaller woman's cheek, knocking her back on her heels. Becky felt the pain in her face spread, involuntary tears in her eyes.

"Move!" Jane commanded. "Right now. And don't open your mouth again unless I tell you to. Do you understand all that?"

In his room, Paul Kelly sat on the bed and smiled. It was going to be such a fun night.

For some. Not for others.

Becky managed to nod her head in understanding. She was almost numb with fear. She moved through the door and into the night, walking across her yard toward her neighbor's house.

The two women entered through the back door, into the den. On their way, Becky discovered what she thought she'd imagined hearing and seeing had been reality.

Several of her neighbors, in various stages of undress, entered the house behind her.

The sliding doors closed. The drapes were pulled shut. Tightly.

Becky stood in the well-appointed den and stared in shock and disbelief.

There was Mr. Yardly, owner of a local real-estate office. He was sitting on the couch beside Mr. Simpson. They were both naked. They grinned at Becky.

She didn't really have to look to see what was causing the grunting sound coming from her left.

But she looked anyway.

Marie Operman was bent over a chair, the Reverend Nils Masterson on top of her.

Becky noticed that Masterson's socks were mismatched.

Pure, raw, gutter profanity rolled, in shocking waves, out of Marie's mouth.

Jane's husband, Todd, walked into the den. He, too, wore nothing. He grinned at Becky.

"We're having a party here tonight, Becky baby. We thought you might like to join us."

"Well, I don't," Becky managed to say. "I want to go back to my house." Anger overrode her fear. "What is the matter with all of you? Have you lost your minds? I'll call the police and have you arrested for kidnapping."

They laughed at her.

Then, slowly, they came closer.

"Goddamn you all!" Becky yelled, trying to fight off Betty Jordan's hands as they roamed over her body, fondling this and that.

She tried to run, to escape. But she was ridden down to the floor. Hands ripped her clothing from her. Air-conditioned coolness fanned her flesh. She tried to fight them off.

"No!" Becky wailed. "Please, no!"

The long night began.

"I could have sworn that was Jane Harvey walking over to Becky's house," Melissa said. "And I still say that was a pistol in her hand."

"Mr. and Mrs. Harvey are proponents of gun control, Melissa," Linda reminded her. "They're on the committee to ban handguns in Tepehuanes. Now come on! She probably had a cake or something."

"Some funny-looking cake." Melissa was not convinced.

With a sigh, Linda shook her head. She had allowed her own imagination to run rampant after listening to the kids' stories. Some of their fear had been transmitted to her. Now it was time to calm down and think this thing out.

That was a good idea. The problem was, Linda was still just about as scared as the kids.

That odd smell was getting to her. And Paul's voice . . . God! it was eerie.

"Well"—Linda stood up—"I think I'll just walk over to the Matthews' house."

That statement was met by a loud and very determined chorus of "Oh, no!"

The phone rang.

Linda stilled it. Bing. She gave the phone to Janis.

Janis listened for a moment, said a few OKs, then hung up. She turned to the group.

They had agreed that since Lisa had a gang, they would have a group.

It sounded better.

"Lisa and her pals tried to ambush Bing and Roy." Janis was aware that her brother was probably listening. "Lisa's bunch didn't do too good. Rex got cut pretty bad, and Clark—that must be the Clark over on Temple Street—got kicked in his parts. Bing

287

and Roy are with Deputy Loneman. As soon as Rex gets stitched up, the cops are taking them in to be questioned."

"Did Bing call his mother and father?" Linda asked.

"Yeah. They're uptight. So are Roy's mom and dad. And Bing says there's some big doings over at the hospital. Something about some old cowboy seeing zombies."

"Zombies!" they all blurted out, including Linda.

"Yeah. Bing didn't know too much. But he overheard some cops talking." She turned and punched out the Matthews' phone number and let it ring and ring.

No answer.

"I don't like that," she said, placing the receiver on the cradle.

She motioned for Linda to come closer. Held a finger to her lips. Whispered to her.

"Get a poker from the fireplace. I made a club out of a broken table leg. We're going over to the Harvey house. I've got a feeling something bad is going on there. You don't wanna go—I'll go myself."

Linda looked at Janis. She wasn't accustomed to taking orders from children . . . still, something in the girl's eyes and manner quieted any objections she might have wanted to voice.

Linda nodded, walked to the fireplace, and picked up the poker.

Janis took an old table leg from the closet, then whispered to the other girls. Carol nodded and turned on the stereo. Rock music filled the room.

Janis moved toward the door at the rear of the den,

Linda right behind her, holding the poker. Outside, the wind sighed gently, blowing over the dark desert.

"Spooky," Janis said.

"Stinky! Phew."

It was all of that. And more. Neither girl could put her feelings into words, but the night was somehow different. They listened. The wind was different, too, not only the night murk.

The desert was no longer friendly. Now it seemed ominous and dangerous. A place to be avoided and feared.

Both girls tried to tell themselves that it was all in their imagination, that nothing was wrong. That the added murk of the night was not real. But the attempts stuck in their minds. Silent lies.

Something was very wrong. And not just here. All over Tepehuanes.

Janis stopped abruptly and Linda bumped into her. Both girls almost jumped out of their sneakers.

Janis waited until her heart had slowed its frantic pounding, then whispered, "Getting to you, huh? I know the feeling. And it's been getting worse, harder to deal with every day."

"You want to explain that?"

The girls, speaking in whispers, stood in the yard between the Kelly house and the Matthews' house. The murk seemed to surround them. But it was not protective.

Its touch was somehow ugly, leaving both girls desperately wanting to take a long hot bath.

They rubbed their bare arms.

"Ever since we got back from our trip. It's just . . . well, I don't know . . . hard to explain. A

289

feeling I have. It's kind of like a pressure cooker, you know? I guess that's the best way to describe it. It's just been building and building. Never seems to stop."

"And when do you think this thing is going to reach the blowup point?"

"Real soon," Janis said, a dead quality in her voice. She moved forward, making her way through the stinking and unnatural darkness.

Linda stayed close behind her. She no longer felt stupid carrying the poker.

They passed the rear of the Matthews' home. All was silent. Both could sense the house was unoccupied. They exchanged silent glances in the darkness, and slowly moved on.

As they drew nearer to the Harvey house, they could hear music bulling through the stinking air. Hard rock music. Heavy metal. Its harshness surged at them, the undecipherable howlings and wailings containing messages of a most Satanic nature. Somewhere in the house, a man laughed. That was followed by a woman's shuddering, Sybaritic cry of pleasure.

Another woman screamed in pain.

"That sounded like Becky Matthews," Janis whispered.

"Yeah."

"And that music. That's odd. The Harveys don't listen to music like that. They have all those records from the old days. Sixties' stuff."

Linda nodded her head. "That sure isn't Elvis or Jerry Lee," she agreed.

They slipped on, making their way onto the

Harvey property, through the open gate in the fence.

Then a shadow seemed to rise directly out of the ground, in front of the girls.

"Well, now." The man spoke. They could see his hard grin; could smell his unwashed body despite the stink in the air. "Would you just take a look at who's here? Come join our party!"

Both girls reacted as if by reflex. They did not say a word, just swung their weapons; Janis on the left, Linda on the right of the man.

And they were not a bit gentle.

Janis's heavy table leg conked the smelly man on one side of his head just as Linda's poker bonked him on the other. The odious figure dropped to the ground without another sound.

"Did we kill him?" Janis panted.

"I don't know. And I really don't care."

"Me, neither."

The girls willed their hearts to stop racing. They took deep breaths, relaxed their grips on the poker and the table leg, and so eased the pressure on their whitened knuckles. And they silently requested their legs to stop trembling before their knees started knocking.

They could hear the man breathing.

"Guess not," Janis said.

"He's gonna be out for five or ten minutes," Linda guessed. Her voice was shaky. "And probably disoriented for that long when he wakes up." Her breath came hard. "Come on. Let's see what's going on in that house and then get out of here."

"I'm with you."

They moved closer to the Harveys', almost at a

crawling pace. The night and the strange wind, the smell, and the crash and thud of the music wrapped around them like a shroud. Both girls felt dirty.

They reached the house and pressed against it for a moment. Linda peeked through a crack in the drapes covering the den window. She could not contain a gasp of rage and fear and anger.

"What is it?" Janis whispered.

Linda shook her head. "Let's get out of here."

Janis tried to see inside, but Linda pushed her away. "Don't look!" she said.

Janis struggled free and peeked in.

She felt sick to her stomach.

"I warned you."

"So next time I'll listen." She fought away the nausea but could taste bile. "Come on. Let's get back to Becky's house and call the police."

They walked much faster now, on leaving.

The smelly man was still unconscious as they passed him. Janis stopped. Raising the table leg, she gave him another knock on the head.

"For luck," she explained, the words containing a hardness that belied her age.

The girls slipped into the Matthews' house, through the garage door. Janis ran to the phone, punched out the number of the police department. Mike was not there, she was informed. Very quickly, she explained what was going on at the Harvey house.

"You girls stay right where you are," the dispatcher instructed them. "Don't leave that house. A unit is on the way."

They left the house, of course. Both of them felt

vulnerable in there. Trapped.

They were standing in the shadows cast by the tall shrubbery at the front of the house when the police cars pulled up. They arrived silently: no lights and no sirens. The girls ran out to meet them.

Peter Loneman was in the third car, riding with the city cop who had brought Janis her walkie-talkie.

Linda said, "Becky Matthews is tied face down over a pool table in the den. She's naked and she's all bloody."

"Stay with them," Loneman said to one of his men.

Then he and a burly city cop carrying a sledge hammer ran to the front door. The doorknob was knocked out with one blow, the dead-bolt lock shattered with another. The door swung open. Several naked men and women tried to run out the back of the house, through the sliding doors.

They ran right into several cops, waiting with night sticks. Hickory impacted heads.

Janis and Linda watched as more police cars pulled up, Mike and Sheriff Sandry in the lead vehicle, Leo and Stanford right behind them. The girls hurried over to them.

"Jesus, it stinks out here!" Sandry remarked, wrinkling his nose.

"Makes your skin crawl," Mike added.

"Put in a call for an ambulance!" a cop shouted from the shattered doorway. "This woman's been tortured as well as raped."

Neighbors began to gather on their front lawns, standing in tight, silent little groups, their presence highlighted by the flashing red and blue lights of the police cars that had pulled in last.

Linda put her arm around Janis's shoulders, held the younger, smaller girl close to her.

Janis's world began to spin in multicolored hues as metallic-sounding words spewed out of a unit's radio that was set to broadcast out of the speaker set in the light bar.

"Advise Chief Bambridge that Mark Kelly just died."

Janis awakened on the couch in the den of her home. Linda was bathing her face with a wet cloth. A paramedic was standing over her, smiling down at her. Her group gathered around her, their faces solemn.

"She'll be all right," the EMT said. "If she starts feeling bad, give us a call."

He left the room and Janis looked at Linda. "I didn't dream it, did I?"

Linda shook her head. "No. You didn't. But I'm sorry you had to hear it the way you did."

"It wouldn't have made any difference," the girl said pragmatically. "Would it? My daddy would still be dead, wouldn't he?"

When no one responded to that, Janis sat up. She felt all right. Maybe just a little weak. "Where is Mother?"

Linda answered. "She just called. She'll be here in about an hour. She asked me if I'd stay on for a few days. I said I would."

"Paul?"

"In his room. He knows about his father."

294

"How did he react?"

"He just smiled."

"He would. Those people at the Harvey house?"

"The cops took them away. The man we bashed on the head has a concussion, the medic said. Becky's been taken to the hospital. The cuts on her looked a lot worse than they really were; that's what the medic told me."

"What kind of cuts?"

"Someone took a real sharp knife and made a lot of cuts on her body. Stars and moons and other shapes. But they weren't very deep."

Janis accepted a Coke from Melissa. "How long have I been out?"

"'Bout ten minutes."

"Bing and Roy?"

"I don't know what's going on down at the police station."

"Fuck you!" Rex told the cop. "I don't have to tell you a goddamn thing."

"And that goes for me, too," Clark said.

Outside the interrogation room, the booking area was filled with half-dressed and loudly protesting men and women, all from the Harvey house. Astonished lawyers were trying to figure out exactly how this had happened to outwardly successful and decent men and women.

The detective questioning the boys resisted an almost overwhelming impulse to slap the daylights out of both of them.

He had to keep telling himself that this was all in a

day's work; just part of his job. The attitude of the boys was nothing new.

But it wouldn't wash. Something was terribly wrong with these two kids. Something the detective had never before encountered. Usually boys were outwardly scared or they tried to put up a false front to hide their fear.

Not these two.

They weren't afraid. Not even a little bit.

"And you still maintain that Lisa and the others were not with you when Bing and Roy were attacked?"

"Hey, man!" Clark grinned at him. "We didn't attack them. They attacked us."

The detective knew none of these answers could be used in a court of law. The boys' parents were not present and neither was an attorney. But Mike had told him to question the boys.

Clark leaned forward, putting both elbows on the table. He spat in the detective's face.

The man rose from his chair and walked out of the room, barely holding on to his temper.

Behind him, just before the door closed, both boys laughed.

The detective walked over to a coffee pot and poured a cup.

He had never seen anything like these two.

Peter approached him. "Sol. What'd you get out of them?"

"Attitude and arrogance." He sipped his strong coffee. "They're not afraid, Pete. Looking at them, I have to keep reminding myself that they're really just boys—and human!"

Deputy sheriff and city detective locked gazes.

The detective's hand, still holding the cup of coffee, began to tremble.

"You don't believe that, do you, Pete?"

Loneman stared at him.

Sol got the unspoken message in Pete's eyes and a thin trickle of sweat formed and wormed its way down his forehead.

"They're just kids, Pete!"

"Yeah. You just keep on believing that. I'm goin' to take a run over to the boys' homes. Me, Mike, Leo, and Stanford. We'll get back to you, Sol."

"So what do you want me to do about it?" Clark's father asked.

He stood shirtless in the doorway of his expensive home. He had not asked them inside. His manner was both hostile and belligerent. And he smelled bad. The men could see his wife lying on the couch in the living room.

She was nude, and had made no attempt to hide her nakedness.

It was embarrassing.

She opened her legs wide, and smiled at Mike.

Her husband laughed at the expression on Mike's face.

Mike composed himself—with an effort. "We would like you to come down to the station and get your son, sir."

"Oh, yeah? Well, why don't you just send him on home? He'll get here directly, I reckon."

Mike sighed. "Mr. Mahoney, your son was involved in a very serious incident earlier this evening. Don't you even care?"

The man shrugged his shoulders. "Sure. But he ain't hurt is he?"

Mike shook his head.

"Then send him home."

"Sir," Leo spoke. "What do you have to do that is more important than seeing to the needs of your son?"

Mahoney blinked and then grinned. "Well, me and the old lady was plannin' on having some fun."

On the short trip over to the home of Rex Grummen, Stanford, who was sitting in the back with Leo, said, "The boy has to be destroyed—and quickly. Surely you can all see what's happening here. Townwide. His power is growing at a phenomenal rate. If we wait much longer, there's a possibility he could become invincible. Do I have to tell you what will happen then?"

No one said anything.

"You must understand," the inspector persisted. "This is an open pool of raw filth, growing and growing, spewing disease in all directions. Unless one neutralizes the filth, it just keeps on contaminating everyone and everything around it. Surely, after the events of this evening, you can all see that."

"I can't cold-bloodedly kill an eight-year-old boy, Stanford." Mike spoke without taking his eyes off the road.

"Nor can I," Peter said.

Stanford's sigh was loud. "Satan is laughing at your predictable attitudes."

No one spoke again until they reached the Grummen home. It was almost a repeat of what they'd seen and heard at the Mahoney house.

Rex's father answered the door, in his underwear. "Oh, yeah?" he smirked. "Well, goddamn! I guess that makes the kid just a chip off the old block, huh?"

"You won't come down to the station and pick up your son?" Mike asked.

"Naw! Just let him go. He'll get here when he's good and ready, I suppose."

Mr. Grummen got a good laugh out of that.

Even though Rex was only thirteen.

Mike and Peter knew that, just hours before, Mr. Grummen had been a well-respected member of the community; a devoted family man, a churchgoer, a solid citizen.

As they rode back to the station, Peter said, "Two successful businessmen. Car-dealership and furniture-store owner. Both of them upper middle class. Nice people. Neither of them had ever been in trouble before. Did you smell them? It seemed neither of them had been near soap and water in days. But I know that's impossible. I was in Grummen's store day before yesterday. I've got a question: Why them and not us?"

Not one of the men in the car was terribly religious.

Finally Stanford said, "It isn't over yet."

"'Til the fat lady sings," Peter retorted.

No one laughed.

Mike pulled into the parking lot of the police station, his headlights picking up Lisa and her gang, sitting on the curb. He walked over to them.

"What are you kids doing here?"

"Sittin', man," Lisa told him, looking up. "Waitin' on Rex and Clark to get out of your bucket. Is there any law against us doin' that?"

Mike tried to stare her down. He could not. Her eyes, young/old/evil locked into his. "What makes you think I'm going to cut them loose?"

"Hey, man!" Lisa grinned up at him. "What are you going to hold them on? The other boys attacked them. We seen it. Your move now."

Mike wished his next move could be to blink his eyes and have all that had happened prove to be a dream.

He blinked his eyes.

Nothing had changed.

Lisa and her gang rose as one and walked out of the police parking area. They crossed the street and sat down on the curb.

"So much has come unglued the past few days, Mike. These kids—why has this happened to them? I know their families attend Nils Masterson's church. Is that part of it? I don't know *what* to think anymore." Peter Loneman shook his head.

"You mean you think they'll have to die like Paul?" Mike asked.

"Not . . . like Paul," Stanford said.

"They're just kids," Mike said wearily.

Leo tactfully changed the subject. "Speaking of Nils and his . . . followers, what are you going to do with them?"

"Do with them? I'm going to hold them. Rape, kidnapping, torture, crimes against nature. Anything else I can come up with."

Sheriff Sandry had walked up. "No, you're not, Mike."

The men turned to the sheriff.

"Why not, Burt?" Mike demanded.

Sandry took a long breath. "I don't like this any better than you do, Mike. But here it is. Becky Matthews is not pressing any charges. She just made that statement from her hospital bed. She now says she was a willing participant."

"It can't be!" Leo exploded.

"He's just getting stronger and stronger," Stanford muttered.

"Who is getting stronger and stronger?" Sandry asked.

Before Stanford could reply, Mike ripped off his cowboy hat and threw it down on the concrete. He kicked it across the parking lot, cursing as he did so.

Across the street, Lisa and her gang laughed.

The wind picked up, sending bits of paper and other scraps flying through the downtown streets.

And Inspector Stanford Willingston shook hands with all the men, then walked silently away, into the night.

FOUR

Mike had no choice but to release Jane and Todd Harvey and the others found at their house. There were some minor charges he could have held them on, but to keep the press at bay for as long as possible, he released them all. Jailing a respected minister and other pillars of the community would have brought the press in at full gallop. As it was, the local paper was probably going to give the whole situation front-page space.

Mike said to hell with it, and went home to try to get some sleep.

Sheriff Sandry drove back to the county seat, saying he'd return the next day. Call him if anything else weird happened.

"You can expect a call," Deputy Loneman said with a grin.

Sandry's reply was a disgusted grunt and a wave of his hand.

As Rex and Clark walked out of the police station, Leo and Peter watched them link up with Lisa and her gang, then wander off into the murk of the night.

Mark Kelly's body had been taken to a local

funeral home.

Bing and Roy were driven home in a police unit.

The police and the sheriff's deputies were edgy and frustrated and uncertain as to what they might be facing as the night dragged on.

They soon found out.

Incidents of family violence went up astronomically, and no cop likes to work domestic trouble.

"Any of you guys want to tell me what is going on?" a young reporter for the *Tepehuanes Guardian* asked. The *Guardian* was a small daily.

"Full moon," he was told.

"Right," the reporter said drily, as he heard yet another family fight called in and the dispatcher rolled a unit.

Connie Kelly, given a strong sedative before she left the hospital, was out on her feet by the time she arrived home. She fell into her bed, and was asleep in thirty seconds.

Mercifully, her sleep was dreamless.

Every doctor who worked at Tepehuanes General was called in that night to help in the emergency rooms, patching up and stitching up men and women who suddenly seemed to think beating each other about the head and shoulders was the best way to settle minor marital disagreements.

It seemed to the doctors that at least half the town was involved in family squabbles.

Father Dan Gomez spent the night alternately sleeping and praying.

Leo tossed on his motel bed. He was worried about his friend, Stanford, in the next room. Sleep did come

304

to Leo, but it was slow in arriving.

Stanford cleaned his pistol and carefully loaded it. Then he made his peace with God. He asked forgiveness for what he was going to do come the dawning.

Peter Loneman drove the lonely roads that led back to the place of his birth. At the edge of the reservation proper, he stopped and got out of his unit. Stood on the road, listening to the drumming in the night.

"It's no longer my world," he muttered. "I don't belong there anymore."

After a time, he slid under the wheel of his car and drove back to town, putting the drumming behind him, knowing the hideousness could not be avoided, but must be faced.

Nearly everyone concerned longed for the light of day.

A salesman, whose home base was in California, unfortunately had elected to spend the night in Tepehuanes, and was having trouble sleeping. He stepped out of his motel room for a breath of air. He had never been in Tepehuanes before, thought it a pretty little city. Except for that awful smell. And the lack of whores. If he could find some action that might help him sleep.

He sniffed. Phew! Must be some industry here that fouled the air, he guessed.

But the brochure he'd picked up had mentioned nothing about heavy industry.

He concluded that it was too late to go barhopping, turned back to his motel-room door and ran into a lump, sandy smelly thing!

It grunted at him.

The salesman had only a few excruciatingly painful seconds to ponder what on earth had grabbed him.

But he would never know.

Neither would his wife and four kids back in San Bernardino.

Powerful arms crushed his chest and broke his back while a lipless slit of a mouth ate his face.

Another sandman jerked off one arm and munched on it, as if eating an ear of corn, while yet another lumpy creature reached inside the salesman and pulled out his intestines, stuffing them into its mouth.

What was left of the salesman was hauled off, to the rear of the motel, into even murkier darkness. A slick trail of blood marked his journey.

Soon nothing remained except for a few cracked and sucked-dry, white bones.

The lumpy shapes drifted away into the darkness, content for the moment.

In his hospital room, on his bed, there more for drying-out purposes than for any injury, Old Jake moaned in his sleep. He dreamed of being pursued across the desert by naked zombies on horseback.

About fifteen miles outside of town, for Mona and Darrel Lewis, Old Jake's nightmare was fast becoming hard reality.

Mona had awakened out of a deep and dreamless

sleep to sounds of sucking and of her husband thrashing about on the bed. She had opened her eyes and turned her head. When she recovered from mind-numbing shock, she opened her mouth to scream.

A cold mouth covered hers.

At first, she thought it must be a mustached mouth, for she could feel whiskers scraping her upper lip. Then, when her attacker raised his head, Mona could fully see the horror descending on her.

She passed out.

When she awakened, the horror had intensified, going far beyond any nightmare she had ever endured.

She was being sexually assaulted.

And she was cold. So very cold. Oddly, the cold was a pleasant feeling. Her neck felt slick and wet. A very strange sensation.

And in her mind was a new awareness. The awakening of evil. Long buried and suppressed, the need to do evil had now come to the fore.

Mona welcomed it. She felt as though she had just been released from prison.

She cut her eyes to her husband's side of the bed. Darrel was flat on his back, and Mary, her mouth red and sticky with blood was on top of him. His face and neck were bloody, too.

But that did not alarm Mona. It all seemed very natural to her. She felt it was meant to be. An occurrence she had long been waiting for.

Mona screamed as she experienced a climax like one she had ever felt. She pulled the dead, cold, stinking, and bloody mouth of Andy to her own lips and kissed him.

The four of them rested in the bed for a time, a sprawl of living dead. Until the desert began calling them in a silent voice. Then they rose, naked and bloody, and walked out of the house. Burrs and rocks dug into the soles of their feet. But they felt no pain. They felt nothing at all.

Except the primal urge to kill. To destroy. To gain souls for their new master.

The moon hung full and heavy in the sky.

Andy threw back his head and howled.

The others joined him, howling in voices that were born in the burning pits.

Joyful howlings.

The four of them walked to the garage, Andy and Darrel getting into the front seat of the luxury car, Mary and Mona into the back.

The men looked at each other, communicating without words.

Andy grinned, a macabre curving of the stitch-hung lips.

Darrel cranked the car's engine, dropped the shift into R, and floorboarded the pedal. The heavy car roared out of the garage, demolished a bird bath, flattened a lawn mower, and tore away part of the stone fence around the front yard before Darrel could find the brake pedal and bring it under control.

But the four of them found the wild ride exhilarating and highly amusing. They grunted and slobbered their laughter in the closed car, their lips very red and full in their pale faces.

After bouncing and spinning across the yard, they wandered around in the desert before finally finding the road that would lead them to Tepehuanes.

They did not know why they should go to Tepehuanes. It just seemed the right thing to do.

Several miles down the road, Darrel brought the car to a tire-squalling halt when Andy spotted a car parked on the shoulder of the highway, a young couple standing beside it. The hood was raised, signaling car trouble.

Andy lowered the window and the young man stuck his head inside, smiling.

"Boy, am I glad to see . . ."

His eyes widened, the words jamming up in his throat as the bloody nakedness of the car's occupants registered on him. He opened his mouth to wail in terror. But Andy rammed his hand into it and grabbed his tongue.

The young man tried to pull back, to get away from this obscene horror. He couldn't. Andy's hard fingers dug into his tongue and held on. With his free hand, Andy reached up and poked out one of the young man's eyes.

The wild pain-filled shrieking that collected in his throat was cut off by the hand that filled his mouth. The corners of his lips were split from the widening, and blood leaked down from them.

The young man's feet did a strange dance on the shoulder of the road.

Andy and Darrel and their ladies thought it amusing. They grunted and hooted and slobbered and clapped their hands.

Andy thought he'd never had so much fun.

He ripped out the young man's tongue, and swiftly grabbed the back of his neck, with both hands, dragging him halfway into the car.

309

The young woman who'd been standing by the disabled car finally broke free of the paralysis that had rooted her there, and fled. She ran, screaming, across the desert, Mona and Mary right behind her, grunting and calling for her to stop.

Her young man had been dragged all the way into the car. Two sets of mouths with very sharp teeth punctured his neck, and sucked the hot flow of living blood.

In the moon-splattered desert, the young woman tripped and fell, heavily, the impact knocking the wind from her. Naked bodies pounced upon her, ripping the clothes from her, forcing her to stand up.

She screamed until her throat was raw.

But Mona and Mary marched the wailing, weeping, near-hysterical naked young woman back to the blood-splattered car, forced her into the back seat.

All semblance of reason left her when she saw the pale and bloodless face of her young man.

His breathing was a wet gurgling, pushing out of his bloody mouth. His throat had been gnawed at.

Blood spattered the windows, the dash, the floorboards, and the upholstery of the luxury car.

She was pushed onto Andy's lap, in the back seat. She screamed, shrieking even louder as he bulled his way inside her.

Darrel shoved the bloody young man over the seat into the back, so the women could have something to drink after their race across the desert.

As they lapped greedily at the open, still-pumping throat, Darrel pulled out onto the pavement, and they motored along at a sedate forty-five miles per hour.

The lights of a truck drew closer behind them. An eighteen-wheeler whose driver was based in Alabama. South Alabama. He pulled out to pass, took another startled look at the antics going on in the back of the car, then swung back, reaching for the mike to his CB.

"Breaker one-nine for anybody. This is the Goose talkin'."

"Come on, Goose," his speaker crackled. "You got the Lone Arranger here."

"They's a-fuckin' up yonder!" Goose radioed, his four-watt CB jacked up to a hundred watts . . . at low output.

"Who and where, you dumb hillbilly?"

Goose searched for a highway marker. None to be seen. "I'm about six or eight miles outside of Kearny. Southbound."

"If you're all lit up like a Christmas tree, Goose, then I'm right behind you."

"That's me. Come on."

"I see you, Goose. Hold what you got. I'm givin' her all she's got."

"So is that ol' boy in the back seat. Good Lord God Almighty! There ain't a stitch of clothes on none of them people."

Lone Arranger pulled up close. "Lemme by! Lemme by! I wanna look."

"I was here first. But I can't figure out what that stuff is all over the back window. Looks like something splattered."

"It looks like blood to me."

"Blood!"

Mona and Mary chose that time to twist around in

the back seat and look out the blood-splattered rear window. They grinned at Goose.

The sight of their wild eyes and bloody mouths and faces just about caused the Goose to lose it all. He slammed on his brakes and the Lone Arranger had to do some fancy driving to keep from climbing Goose's donkey.

The Lone Arranger cut around the Goose's tire-smoking rig, his trailer swinging wildly for a moment. When he got it under control, he grabbed for his mike and started cussing.

"You stupid asshole! What's the matter with you?"

No reply from the badly shaken Goose.

"Goose! Where are you, Goose?"

Nothing.

"You'd better talk to me, you hillbilly!"

"I'm right behind you, Lone Arranger. Look here. You take a good long look when them two gals grin at you, boy. Then we got to call the cops."

"Call the cops! Have you lost what little brains God give you? Man, I ain't wrote in my little book since some time yesterday."

"I don't even know where my log book is! Can't be helped. We gotta call the cops."

Lone Arranger was about to tell the Goose that he wasn't about to do that. Then Mary and Mona pressed their bloody, evil, wild-eyed faces to the rear glass and grinned at him.

The Lone Arranger screamed like someone had just stuck a rattlesnake into his boot.

When he finished cussing and hollering he picked up his mike and called the Goose. "Yeah. I see what you mean. You been on nine, Goose?"

"Ten-four. But I can't raise a soul."

"I'm hearin' you ol' boys jabber," another driver cut in. "I'm on the north side of Tepehuanes. You want me to call the cops and give them a message? Come on. They call me the Cowboy."

"Yeah, Cowboy. This is the Lone Arranger. Call the cops and tell them there's a dark blue Lincoln Town Car comin' dead at them. Naked people inside. There's blood all over the inside of the car, and splattered on the rear window. You ten-four all this, Cowboy?"

"Man, are you puttin' me on?"

"Hell, no!" Goose hollered.

"OK. I'm pullin' into a service station now."

"Tell the cops me and the Lone Arranger will be right behind them," Goose radioed. "We'll keep them in sight."

"Ten-four. I'm out of the truck now."

About two minutes later, the Lone Arranger radioed to the Goose. "The crazy son of a bitch is signaling for a left turn, Goose. What do you wanna do?"

"Let's stay with them, Arranger. You got a gun?"

"Damn right. You?"

"We ain't supposed to carry them, but I do. Got a shotgun. I'm right behind you. If there's a county mountie listenin' to all this, you better answer me!"

"Calm down." The voice came out of the speaker. "I'm listening. I just caught the call from the city dispatch. What's your twenty?"

"We're about three or four miles north of town.

313

Turnin' southwest on a dirt road. There's a billboard on the southbound side of the highway advertisin' a motel."

"I know where you are. I'm rolling."

Mona and Mary held up the body of the young man and grinned out the rear window.

Lone Arranger grabbed for his mike. "Deputy? They got a dead body in the back seat with them. He's got blood all over him. And I don't think this is any college prank, Deputy."

"Ten-four. How many in the car?"

"Four or five. Alive. I can't be real sure on that."

"Stay with them if you can. But don't put yourselves in a position to get hurt. Ten-four?"

"Ten-four on that."

The deputy, a ten-year veteran on the force, and aware of what was taking place in and around Tepehuanes, was rolling wide open and saying a little prayer he hadn't spoken since childhood. He cut off at the intersection, fishtailing upon hitting the dirt and sand, and with the truck lights in sight, went roaring down the road.

He had to stand on his brakes when the car and the two trucks braked suddenly. After he got his unit under control, the deputy bailed out, a riot gun in his hands. He kashucked a round into the chamber and yelled for those in the car to step out, hands high.

Both truck drivers had dismounted from their cabs and were standing close to their rigs.

"We got shotguns in the cab, Deputy," Goose called softly. "You want us to get them?"

"All right. But don't use them unless I give the order, understood?"

314

The drivers nodded and climbed up to grab their shotguns and climbed back down.

"I said get out of that car!" the deputy yelled. "Now do it!"

The back door of the big car opened slowly, the drivers and the deputy tensing.

The body of the young man was shoved out onto the ground.

He was headless.

"Good God!" the Lone Arranger muttered, tightening his grip on the pump shotgun.

The young man's girlfriend was pushed out the other side of the car. She fell naked to the ground, her throat and neck bloody. She appeared to be alive.

In a way.

"Get out of the car!" the deputy hollered.

An object was flipped out of the Lincoln. It landed at the feet of the deputy. He stared in horror at a mouth-open, eyes-open bloody head that appeared to have been torn from a torso.

Goose and the Lone Arranger both fought hard to keep from puking.

The engine of the Lincoln roared into life. Back tires spinning, the car turned around, its headlights catching the men in full glare.

"Fire!" the deputy yelled.

Shotguns roared in the night, buckshot whanging and sparking off metal. The headlights were knocked out. One front tire was blown off. The windshield was shattered.

Yet the car kept coming at them.

The three men jumped out of the way as it crashed into the deputy's unit, knocking it to one side, and leaving the radiator punctured, steam hissing white in the night air.

The heavy car backed up and tried to run over Goose.

Squalling, he jumped up between his tractor and trailer and fired once. A side window exploded as the buckshot tore into the back seat and struck flesh.

Goose watched in horror as part of a woman's face was torn away, exposing the whiteness of jawbone and a row of teeth.

She grinned at him.

Lone Arranger and the deputy fired at the rear of the fast moving car, knocking out the tail lights and part of the rear window. The deputy ran into the center of the road and watched as the buckshot-riddled car turned toward Tepehuanes.

He ran back to his unit and called in, alerting his substation and the PD.

As he tossed the mike to the seat, the Lone Arranger started screaming.

The deputy looked. Then he stood rooted by his car, eyes unbelieving, hands clutching the shotgun.

The bloody young woman was walking toward the truck driver. Her throat had been torn out. Her arms were outstretched, her hands clawed, reaching for the man. Her face was very pale. Her lips red and full. She smiled, exposing unusually long teeth. Very sharply pointed.

She was speaking in a language none of them could understand.

The Lone Arranger lifted his shotgun and yelled for her to stop. "I'll shoot you, lady. Stay away from me."

She spoke again. One word. They all understood that. "Blood."

"She's one of them things that ain't supposed to be real!" Goose yelled.

"Tell her, not me!" Lone Arranger said.

The woman grunted.

Kept coming.

Lone Arranger pulled the trigger. The charge hit the woman in the shoulder. She was knocked down. Got up. Grinned at him.

There was no blood coming from the hideous wound.

Screaming his fright and disbelief, the Lone Arranger climbed back into his cab and locked all the doors, hollering for someone to get that crazy woman away from him.

Goose bailed out on the other side of his rig and tried to reload his empty shotgun. His hands were shaking so badly he dropped all the shells onto the ground. He got down on all fours and frantically began searching for them.

The bloodied, throat-torn, wild-eyed woman turned slightly, upon spotting the deputy.

She held out her arms to him, beckoning him to come to her.

The deputy backed up.

He could see the whiteness of bone at her shoulder. No blood.

He could not recall ever being so scared in all his life.

The woman screamed at him, a chilling scream. Then she began to walk toward him.

He had seen that shooting her did no good. He ran

317

around his unit.

She kept coming, following him, grinning at him, motioning for him to come to her.

Still on his hands and knees, not knowing what was going on, the Goose felt a hand close around his ankle, over his cowboy boot.

"Turn loose of my foot, Arranger!"

"I ain't got your foot!" the Lone Arranger yelled from the cab of his truck.

"Well, if you ain't got it . . . who has?" Goose was afraid to look around.

Slowly he turned.

The headless body of the naked young man was behind Goose, one pale hand holding onto his ankle. Cordlike tendons hung down from the gaping wound where his neck had been. Like Goose, the headless man was on all fours in the dirt and sand.

With a shriek that would have been the envy of any Indian on the warpath, Goose jerked his foot out of the boot, and he climbed up the Lone Arranger's rig, onto the hood, and then onto the top of the cab.

The headless man pushed himself to his feet and then stumbled around the area, running into trucks and trailers and the deputy's car.

The deputy jumped into his crippled, steaming unit and grabbed up the mike. Calling in. Frantically.

"Bring a net out here!" he screamed into his mike. "Two nets."

"Bring a what?" dispatch replied.

"Some big nets! Nets. Like you'd use to catch a bear or something. Just bring them, and don't ask questions. Man, I'm in trouble. Hurry up. Officer in

318

trouble. Shots have been fired. Respond code three."

"Are you being attacked by a bear, Fifteen?"

The glass on the driver's side was splintering, the woman pounding on it with a rock.

"I'm being attacked by a zombie!" Fifteen screamed into his mike.

"A zombie!"

No reply.

"Repeat that last transmission, Fifteen. Did you say you were being attacked by a zombie?"

Fifteen was in no position to reply. He was fleeing his unit, out of the passenger side. A bare bloody white arm was sticking through the broken glass on the driver's side.

Fifteen ran slap into a naked, bloody, headless horror that grabbed him in a cold deathlike embrace. The naked flesh smelled of the grave.

With a strength born of pure fear, Fifteen broke free and jerked out his .357, emptying it into the horror, the slugs knocking the thing backward, away from him.

The woman came after the deputy then, at a stumbling run, grinning and grunting as she came.

The deputy ran toward the Lone Arranger's truck and climbed up onto the top of the cab, joining Goose.

"Y'all get off my truck!" Lone Arranger squalled, almost out of his mind from fear. "Hurry up! Them things is comin'!"

"We would if we had some place to go," Goose screamed.

Lone Arranger grabbed up his CB mike. "Halp!" he screamed.

A pounding stopped his yelling. He turned his head. Looked directly into the eyes of the naked woman.

He screamed in terror, and tried to drop the rig into gear. But she splintered the glass with the rock, stuck her arm through the hole, cold bloody fingers reaching for the Lone Arranger.

The Arranger bailed out the other side and jumped, landing right on top of the headless man, both of them rolling on the sand.

Lone Arranger got to his feet first and took off for Goose's truck, the headless man, waving Goose's boot, right behind him.

"I'll send help!" Arranger hollered, climbing up into Goose's rig.

"Come back here, you coward!" Goose screamed, trying to keep his bootless foot out of the clutches of the wild-eyed woman.

Arranger rolled up all the windows, and quickly locked the doors.

The headless man was right behind him, climbing up onto the long hood of the truck.

Fifteen and Goose were stomping on the fingers of the young woman as she tried to climb onto the top of the truck on which they were trapped. She was howling insanely, snapping her jaws together and slobbering as she reached for their feet.

Arranger dropped the rig into gear and took off, across the desert, swinging in a wide half-circle, heading back to the dirt road.

Maybe.

The headless man was standing on the hood, holding onto the twin airhorns on top of the cab.

320

Arranger just couldn't see where he was going.

"Get off there!" Arranger screamed.

The headless man hunched his naked hips against the windshield.

"Ain't this a hell of a note!" Arranger muttered. "I'm quittin' truckin'. If I get out of this mess, I'm goin' to work at the shoe factory with Bubba."

He grabbed up the CB mike. "Halp! Somebody—anybody—halp!"

Around and around the desert they roared, Arranger yelling and the naked headless man on the hood hunching his hips against the windshield.

"Kick her in the head!" Fifteen hollered to Goose.

"I can't get no purchase!" Goose yelled. "I ain't got but one boot on."

Holding onto the airhorn with one hand, the headless man pounded on the windshield with the heel of Goose's boot.

The windshield began to splinter under the hard strokes.

Red and blue flashing and revolving lights appeared in the distance as a half-dozen police and sheriff's department cars howled up the dirt road.

"Finally!" Arranger said. He locked the rig in a tight left turn. The trailer sheared off from the fifth wheel, to go rolling into the darkness and break open, spilling Mother Martha's Yummy Yummy Good for the Tummy candy bars all over the ground.

The police cars slid to a halt by the disabled unit and the rig. Arranger headed for them, the headless man still hanging on to the windshield.

Suddenly he stood on the brake pedal and slid to a stop, then bailed out, landing on his belly in the sand. He scrambled for the protection of the cops.

Some of the cops had ropes in their hands.

"Get that thing off the truck!" Lone Arranger hollered, pointing.

Mike looked. Blinked his eyes. "That's impossible!"

Lone Arranger stuck out his chin. "Oh, yeah? Well, you get on up there with him then."

Peter made a loop and tossed, the loop settling around the screaming naked woman. He jerked and she came tumbling off the hood. Another cop roped her legs, and the two men then tied her up securely. Carefully avoiding her snapping teeth, they also cuffed her wrists and ankles.

The headless man had been roped and hauled down. He, too, was cuffed, hands and ankles.

A deputy held out a boot to Goose. "You want this?"

Goose recoiled as if he'd been handed a live cottonmouth. "Hell, no!"

"Just get me back to Missouri," the Lone Arranger said. "I ain't never leavin' again."

The sun finally came bubbling up out of the east, spreading light over the besieged little city of Tepehuanes, and the cops breathed a collective sigh of relief.

The headless man and his screaming girlfriend had been taken to the hospital, admitted through the basement, and placed in isolation. Along with the snarling and biting head that had rolled up and attached itself to a cop's boot. That officer, though frightened out of his wits, had managed to free his foot without injury.

But the damage to his mind was yet to be determined.

Both rigs had been towed into town and stored at the impounding area. Their drivers, hospitalized for observation, were in isolation—to keep them away from the press, once more gathering like flies on a dead carcass. The drivers' companies had been notified that the men had been involved in an accident—not their fault—and they would be released in a few days. No cause for any alarm. No charges. No tickets. The county would pay for any and all damages.

Mary Beth and Belline sat in the lab with Larry Carleson and stared at the bloody head, encased behind thick heavy wire.

The head snarled and howled and cursed and spat at the doctors.

They were careful to remain at a safe distance from the spitting, wild-eyed horror.

"It has to be destroyed," Mary Beth finally said. "I guess by fire."

"Not yet," Carleson said. "I want tissue samples to study. You all know what we're witnessing is absolutely impossible."

"How do you propose to get those tissue samples, Larry?" Dr. Belline looked at his colleague. "Ask the damned thing's permission?"

The head laughed at them. "Die!" Its grotesque mouth formed the word and spat it out. "Die. You'll all die."

Which was what the head had been saying for the

323

past hour.

Mary Beth stared at Hell's creation. "You have a very limited vocabulary."

The lips peeled back in a semblance of a grin. "If I were you I'd keep my mouth shut, bitch."

Her back stiff and her lips compressed in anger, Mary Beth rose from her chair and walked out of the room, ignoring the laughter pealing from the head.

The eyes of the head shifted to Belline. "What about you, Frenchy? Got anything to say?"

Belline got up and left the room.

Larry Carleson sat alone in the lab and stared at the head.

The head spoke. "Ask and ye shall receive."

"What was your name before the . . . accident?"

"There is no before. Only now."

"Why aren't you dead? You're a medical impossibility."

"Don't be stupid, Carleson. You know perfectly well where I get my life."

"I want to study you."

"So come closer."

"I'm not that stupid."

The head laughed at him, curving its lips back to expose needle-sharp teeth and a very red tongue. "How would you like eternal life, Carleson?"

"You can do that?"

"Oh, yes. A favor for a favor."

"At what price?"

The head grinned.

"No, thanks. I'll find eternal life with my Savior."

"Then the hell with you!"

"If you won't tell me your past name, what is your

324

current name?"

"Henny Penny. Maybe Lucy Goosey."

Carleson stood up.

"Where are you going?"

"To arrange for you to be transported into the desert and burned. Destroyed."

"I thought you wanted to study me?"

"I changed my mind."

"Worse than a woman."

Carleson stared at the head.

"Let's make a deal," it said.

"I'm listening."

"Come closer."

"I can hear you very well, thank you."

"Coward!"

"Say what's on your mind."

"Attach me to my body."

"Medically impossible."

"Don't be naïve. Just stitch my head back on and I'll take it from there."

"I think I'll pass."

"That makes you a fool."

"Perhaps. But it insures me of something."

"Oh?"

"Staying alive."

FIVE

Stanford stepped out of his room early, just after the sky lightened. He walked to the dining room and enjoyed a hearty breakfast, lingering over coffee, which he assumed would be his last cup.

He then drove about the town for the better part of an hour, making his peace with God, steeling himself for the ordeal he knew awaited him.

He also knew there was not one chance in ten million that he would ever see another dawning.

Not on this earth.

At seven-thirty on a beautiful Western morning, Stanford parked his rented car in front of the Kelly house and walked up to the porch, ringing the bell. Janis opened the door and smiled at him.

"Good morning," he said.

She greeted him and invited him in, walked toward the den. "I don't have any coffee to offer you. I don't drink it and neither does Linda. Mother is still in bed. I think they gave her a real strong pill last night."

"That's good. She needs her rest. Janis, I want you to do something for me."

She shrugged. "All right. If I can."

327

"I would like you to wake up your friends and Linda, and then go to the playground at the end of the block, all of you. Wait for me there."

"You'll come for us?"

"Someone will."

She stared at him.

"Will you do that for me, Janis?"

"I'm not going to ask any questions."

"That's good."

"I'll go get the others out of bed. How about Mother?"

"I don't believe she'll wake up." Stanford felt that Paul would take care of that. The boy wanted a showdown. He would set the stage for it. "I don't believe this will take very long, Janis."

Only forever, he silently added.

Janis nodded her head, meeting the tall man's eyes for a moment. Then she walked out of the den.

Stanford sat quietly, waiting as the girls were awakened. They dressed and gathered briefly in the kitchen, to have toast or juice or cereal. They did not speak to him, and he did not attempt to engage any of them in conversation.

They all knew why he was here. Even Linda. He supposed Janis had quickly briefed her.

And he did not see Paul.

Stanford didn't have to. He could feel Paul's presence. Knew that the devil-boy was wide awake and waiting eagerly for him.

To destroy him.

The girls walked through the den toward the front door. They looked curiously at Stanford, but said nothing to him on their way out. Only Janis paused for a moment at the door and looked back.

"Will I see you again, Mr. Willingston?"

"I . . ." Stanford hesitated. No need to lie to the girl. "That is rather doubtful, Janis."

"I . . . see. I think. You don't believe you are going to win, do you, sir?"

"That is also doubtful, child."

"Then . . . ?"

"Don't you see, Janis?" He looked right at her. "Someone has to try."

She nodded her head, her eyes very serious. "Can anybody beat him, Mr. Willingston?"

"I don't know."

She turned and walked outside, quietly closing the door behind her.

Stanford rose from the chair and walked slowly up the hall. He looked in at Connie Kelly. She was sleeping very soundly, very deeply. He took a book from her dresser, and dropped it on the floor.

She did not even stir at the sharp sound.

Stanford stepped out of the room and closed the door. While he had been in Connie's room, the door to Paul's room had opened.

Stanford doubted the boy had moved to do it.

He could see Paul, sitting in the center of his bed, smiling at him.

Stanford stepped to the open door.

"Come on in." Paul's deep, well-hollow voice made the invitation. "My mother will not wake up unless I call her. I can assure you of that."

Stanford stepped across the hall, walked into Paul's room.

"Close the door, Pig!"

Stanford pushed the door closed. Staring at Paul, he could feel hot evil pulsing from the boy.

329

Paul clenched his right hand into a fist and extended his middle finger to Stanford. With a laugh, he said, "A salute to you who are about to die!"

Leo banged on Stanford's motel-room door. No response. With a curse, he looked around him. Stanford's rented car was gone.

"Losing my touch," he muttered. "I should have looked for that first thing."

As he was walking toward the car he'd rented, a dark sedan pulled into the motel's parking lot, Father Gomez behind the wheel. The priest parked, got out, and walked swiftly toward Leo.

"I awakened this morning from a terrible dream." Gomez's words came in a rush. "I dreamed that Inspector Willingston was dead."

"He's not in his room. And his car is gone."

"You think he's gone to face the boy? Alone? My God, why?"

"Because somebody had to do it, Father. Yeah. I think he's gone to face Paul."

"Have you called Mike?"

"I was just going to do that. Come on, let's use my car. We'll find a phone and call on the way."

Walking toward Leo's car, Gomez glanced at his watch. "How long has he been gone?"

"Don't know."

"Pray for his safety."

"Pray that he shoots straight while you're at it."

"One of us is going to die, for sure," Stanford told the boy.

"It isn't going to be me. You should have stayed on the island, Pig."

"Call it destiny, but we had to meet, Paul. Or whatever your name is."

Paul grinned. The lip-curving contained more evil than Stanford had ever witnessed. "Did you enjoy killing your wife, Pig?"

Stanford maintained his composure. With an effort. "Not particularly."

"You know she screwed Mantine, don't you?"

Stanford remained silent. Not trusting his voice. He knew Paul was trying to anger him into making a sudden and deadly move.

Paul laughed. "I was there, you know? In another form, of course."

"Of course."

"She was with child when you shoved that stake through her heart."

"I suspected that."

"I suppose the child would have been a cousin of mine. Destroying it is reason enough for you to die. Tell me, why hasn't Mantine killed you?"

"Mantine isn't strong enough to overpower my faith. He's tried, and always failed."

"I wondered about that," Paul muttered in that strange voice. He lifted his burning eyes. "But I'm strong enough, right, Pig?"

"Perhaps."

"You know I'm not alone."

"Of course. You're a coward. Like all of your kind."

Paul showed no emotion.

"I know your plan, Paul. I will not—cannot— allow you to commit the ultimate evil."

"You can't stop me. Not now. You might have when you first arrived. But it's far too late. You know that. My human mother will have my child."

Stanford grimaced. "Hideous. Disgusting."

"That's the breaks of the game, Pops."

"Janis?"

"I have plans for her. I'll have a good time with her, I assure you of that."

"No doubt." Stanford's reply was as ugly-sounding as Paul's thoughts were evil.

The insult bounced off Paul like a velvet BB. He pointed toward the TV set in the corner of the room. It was off. "I've been reviewing some past events, Pig. Now it's your turn."

"I'm sure that will be entertaining."

"Watch."

The set clicked on. The screen lightened. The islands.

Stanford kept his expression bland. He knew what was coming at him.

Figures filled the screen. A tall man in a police uniform and a naked woman. Stanford held a sharpened stake in his hands. Sound filled the room. The man's hard breathing. The woman's wild shrieking and cursing.

She leaped at him, her mouth open, a terrible fanged aperture. Stanford swung the heavy stake, striking the woman in the face. She fell back, her face bloody. Stanford tried to ram the stake into her chest. She rolled away and tried to get back on her bare feet. He swung the stake again, hitting her on the back, once more knocking her down. Then he held the stake with both hands, raised it high, and drove the point downward. He was screaming out his rage and disgust.

It missed her chest, drove deep into her naked belly. She screamed in pain, both hands gripping the wood, trying to pull the hurt from her.

Stanford kicked her in the head, and jerked the stake from her bloody belly.

She rolled away, the ground slick with her blood, and came to her feet, screaming and spitting at him, attacking him with fingers like claws, ripping his face.

He fought her back, both of them bloody. She leaped at him. Stanford held the stake like a spear, the point catching the woman as she jumped. She impaled herself on it, and howled insanely. She wrapped her legs around his waist.

Stanford fought her to the ground and, with all his strength, forced the stake deeper into her chest, the point finally touching her black heart.

The struggle ended abruptly when the stake was driven through her heart. The woman's hands fell to her sides. She trembled, and was dead.

A man stepped out of the tropical darkness. A priest, carrying a large can of kerosene. He poured the flammable liquid onto the woman's naked, bloody body. Turned her over and saturated her from head to toe. Stanford had walked away, to get another five-gallon can of kerosene.

The priest looked at him. "Now, old friend?"

Stanford nodded. "Yes."

The priest struck a match and tossed it on the woman's head. She exploded in flames. Flesh bubbled, hair ignited, eyeballs melted and ran down charred flesh. More kerosene was poured onto the pyre. Flames leaped into the warm night.

The men continued to douse the body with kerosene, for an hour, until there was nothing left except cooked bits of flesh and charred bones.

The remains were carefully stirred into a pile, then shoveled up and placed in a large steel box. The lid was locked.

The scene shifted. A small cemetery behind a church. The men worked hurriedly, as if fearful of the dawn that was but an hour away.

They mixed concrete in a wheelbarrow. Lined the grave and then placed the locked steel box into the hole, covering it with more cement. Finally earth was shoveled into the pit.

Exhausted, Stanford and the priest both slumped to the ground.

The priest was praying.

Stanford was openly weeping.

Rain began to pour from the sky.

The earth seemed to tremble.

"Oh, my," Paul said sarcastically. "How touching!"

Stanford jerked out his pistol and shot the boy.

Leo stopped at a pay phone and called Mike's office. The chief had just walked in, after snatching a few hours' sleep.

"It's Stanford. I think he's gone to the Kelly house to face Paul alone. To kill him if he can. Gomez and I are on the way. Meet you there." He slammed down the phone and raced back to his car.

As they roared through the streets, Leo asked, "Can he kill the boy? Any hope at all?"

"I doubt it. He might hurt him. But it's doubtful he can kill him. The best we can hope for is that he'll weaken him."

"And if that's the case?"

"Someone will have to finish it."

"Who?"

"I don't know."

"All right—how?"

"With God's help."

"You know who, don't you?"

"I think I do."

"You won't tell me?"

"The person has to find out first."

Paul rolled off the bed onto the floor just as Stanford pulled the trigger. The slug just grazed his shoulder.

Paul screamed. Not a scream of pain, but of rage and black hate.

The room filled with a stinking yellow smoke, almost blinding the inspector.

Paul's brother materialized, in all his hideousness. He leaped through the yellow haze, onto Stanford's back, his long, stained teeth biting into Willingston's shoulder.

With a scream of pain, Stanford hurled the demon from him. Blood pouring from his torn shoulder, he lifted his pistol and shot the creature in the chest, knocking it back. Swinging the muzzle in the direction he'd seen Paul roll, Stanford pulled the trigger.

"Mother!" Paul yelled, his scream ripping through the yellow, stinking murk.

Stanford fired again, at the sound of the voice. "Setup," he muttered. "And I walked right into it."

"Mother!" Paul shrieked.

Stanford fired again.

The demon leaped at Stanford, its clawed hands ripping his face, shredding the flesh. Blood dripped onto the carpet.

Abruptly, the yellow haze vanished. The demon was gone. Stanford stood in the room, tall and bloody, a gun in his hand. Paul huddled in one corner, appearing to be no more than a frightened little boy.

The bedroom door opened. Connie stood there, her eyes dulled from hard sleep, both pill induced and mind controlled.

She held Mark's shotgun in her hands.

"Mother!" Paul wailed. "He's trying to kill me. Stop him, Mother!"

Stanford turned, pistol in hand, to face the woman.

She lifted the shotgun and blew Stanford's head all over the room.

"How is he?" Leo asked Mary Beth.

"He's all right. The bullet just grazed him. He's healing so fast it's defying medical explanation."

Leo shook his head. Felt a myriad of emotions. He had not known Stanford long. But in a very short time the men had become good and fast friends. With a sigh, he looked at Mary Beth.

"Now is the time, Mary Beth. And the best place

336

Kill the boy."

She shook her head. "I can't do that, Leo. I just can't."

"You know what he is." He felt like grabbing her by the shoulders and shaking her.

"I know what you and Mike and Father Gomez suspect him of being. But I cannot cold-bloodedly murder an eight-year-old child."

"You've seen the head?"

"Unfortunately."

"The headless man?"

"You know I have."

"The woman?"

"This conversation is pointless, Leo. There is nothing to link Paul with those people . . . things. Whatever they are."

Leo stared at her. With a silent curse, he turned and walked away.

But he stopped and turned around. "You've seen the book. You've seen the mark on Paul's arm."

"A birthmark. It could be nothing more than that."

He had to keep trying. For Stanford's sake. For everybody's sake. "His sister is convinced."

She stared at him.

"Mary Beth, I myself saw, in Paul's bedroom, his demon brother. I shot it. Both Father Gomez and I were pinned up against a wall by some invisible force, and held there. Why would we both lie about something like that?"

She remembered the dead-but-alive cop in the back seat of her car. "It's been a stressful time, Leo. For all of us."

"I tried," Leo said. He walked off. This time, he did not turn around.

"I can't explain it," Mary Beth muttered.

She understood Leo's frustration and felt sorry for him. She had liked the tall inspector from the islands.

And she felt Paul was responsible for the deaths of Jenny, Mrs. Cauldman, Mr. Cauldman, Stanford, and all the others. Felt it—couldn't prove it.

But she just could not bring herself to kill an eight-year-old boy.

Her eyes followed the ex-New York City cop. A group of press-types tried to stop him at the end of the corridor, to throw questions at him.

Leo brushed them off with a curt slash of his hand, and kept walking.

They didn't pursue him because they didn't know who he was.

Mary Beth walked to the doctors' lounge, which, like most areas of the hospital, was now off-limits to the press. She poured a cup of coffee and sat down.

Like most of her colleagues, she was sure that sooner or later somebody was going to talk, spill the beans to the press. Faced with a constant barrage of never-ending questions, somebody would get angry and let something slip.

She had no idea what might happen after that.

Chaos, surely.

But that might be a good thing. Expose the horror to the public.

She lifted her eyes as a very tired-looking Mike Bambridge walked in and poured a cup of coffee. He sat down at the table with her.

They were alone in the lounge.

338

"You look tired," she said.

"I am."

"I can arrange for a bed here. You can get a few hours of uninterrupted sleep. God knows, you look like you can use it."

He shook his head. "I could, but when I closed my eyes something else would break loose."

She met his tired gaze.

"I put an end to the truck drivers' complaining about being released. I told them they could either stay here and get fat and keep their mouths shut, or go to jail under a protective-custody order. They suddenly decided the hospital was a really great place."

Mary Beth smiled. "Goose and the Lone Arranger. They certainly are a couple of characters."

"They are that. But you can't fault them when it comes to courage. That scene out in the country would have frightened anybody. Sure scared me."

"We've had to keep Jake heavily sedated. He's really having a bad time of it, drying out."

She remembered the disgusting and impossible head in Carleson's lab. Reached across the table and touched Mike's hand. "Mike, what are we going to do?"

He gently squeezed her fingers. "I don't know. God help me, I just don't know. I hate to admit it, but I suppose that depends on Paul, doesn't it?"

He's been talking with Leo, Mary Beth thought. "Paul is just a little boy, Mike."

"Are you trying to convince me or yourself?"

She refused to reply. She didn't know the answer.

"Mary Beth, he isn't just a little boy. I'm not even

sure he's human. You said yourself it was medically impossible for a gunshot wound to heal that quickly. And by the way, he's being released now. I passed him in the hall."

She could not suppress a shudder. "At least he's gone from here."

Mike pressed her. "If you believe your own words, why should you be afraid of a child?"

She side-stepped that. "When Leo left a few minutes ago, he was very upset with me."

"I know."

"I'm afraid he might try to do something to Paul."

"I hope so."

"You don't mean that, Mike!"

"The hell I don't." There was as much heat in his reply as there had been in her objection.

"Mike, can't you just lock the boy up? Can't you get a judge to declare him legally insane?"

"It isn't that easy, Mary Beth. I think the boy would breeze through any sanity hearing. Besides, without Connie's permission it would be practically impossible to do that. And from what Janis tells me, the boy has his mother in his pocket. No"—he sighed—"we'd be wasting our time."

"So what are you saying we should do?"

"It's like a boil, Mary Beth. It has to come to a head."

"Speaking of heads . . ."

The chief of police shuddered. "I saw that thing outside of town, remember? I want to take it out into the desert and destroy it. But sooner or later, the press is going to bust this story wide open. If we don't want to come off looking like a bunch of fools, we've got to

340

keep those . . . things intact—in a manner of speaking—to show them."

"The hospital is being filled with the macabre and the impossible, Mike."

He rubbed his face. "It's got to break, Mary Beth. And soon. It has to."

"I just wonder what is coming next?"

Carla Weaver's parents found their daughter in her room. Hanging by an extension cord from the clothes hook on the closet door. From the condition of her body, it was assumed she'd been hanging there for about twelve hours. There was no note to indicate why the child had committed suicide.

Janis and her group, along with Mike and Leo and Father Gomez and many others on both sides of the dark line, knew that it wasn't a suicide.

Knew it, but couldn't prove it.

"More souls for the Master, sister dear," Paul whispered to Janis, then laughed at the expression on her face. "You'll see her again, sis," he promised, his breath foul on her face. "I promise you that. One way or the other."

Janis slapped him.

Paul recoiled, his face ugly with hate. But the intense light in his eyes softened as he regained control. He smiled at her. "I'll make you watch when I take Mother. Then I'll turn you over to Lisa's gang . . . and I'll watch. Don't you think that will be fun?"

She spat in his face, then ran to her bedroom, closing the door and locking it.

341

Janis now knew what she had to do. Not Leo or Mike or Father Gomez or Deputy Loneman.

Janis.

She had to do it.

She touched the cross that lay cool on the skin of her chest.

It seemed to throb under her fingertips, as if telling her something.

She threw herself onto the bed, sobbing.

"It's just too much," she whispered, her tears dampening the spread. "It's just too much to ask me to do."

You won't be alone! The voice sprang into her head.

The tears stopped, and Janis sat up in the center of the bed. Her eyes were wide and frightened. "Who said that?"

Silence greeted her. Both real and imagined. She didn't know what to believe.

"I can't do it. I'm not strong enough. No matter how much I hate him, Paul is my brother."

He is the child of Satan!

"Even if I were strong enough, how would I do it?"

You will know.

Janis lay across the bed and cried herself to sleep. She did not hear the voice again.

Stanford's remains were shipped back to the islands, to be buried beside his wife's. The police told the press it had been a horrible accident. Nothing more. By some miraculous happenstance, the press bough the story.

342

"Maybe our luck is changing," Sheriff Sandry muttered.

"Don't count on it," Mike cautioned. "I think Paul is just taking a breather. Letting things calm down for a while."

To the cops it also seemed that some divine intervention had calmed the town. The stink vanished. Domestic violence returned to normal; that is to say the cops could just about name those couples who were prone to hammering on each other on any given night.

Mark Kelly was buried, and on the next afternoon, Carla Weaver was laid to rest.

Father Gomez had fought to have both bodies cremated. But Connie had resisted as had Carla's parents. The priest had watched the services with a grim expression on his face.

He had a horrible feeling that the community had not seen the last of the dear departed.

There was a bright note, however: No more was seen of Andy and Mary or Darrel and Mona.

Coyotes dragged the bones of the salesman out into the desert, and scattered them. It would be weeks before a California detective traced the man to Tepehuanes.

The truck drivers were released from the hospital. By this time, they had convinced each other that the horror-filled night had never happened. Impossible. They had both suffered from food poisoning, or something like that. But headless zombies? Naw! No way.

They climbed into their rigs and pulled out, happy to do so. And certain if dispatch ever tried to

343

route them through Tepehuanes again, somebod
was gonna get punched in the mouth.

Linda was sent home from the Kelly house. Sh
didn't want to go, and Janis didn't want her to leav
But Paul convinced his mother it was the best thin
to do. They could now get on with their lives, he said
as a family unit.

Becky and Sam Matthews put their house up fo
sale and moved away from Tepehuanes. No e>
planation offered.

None was needed by those who knew what wa
going on.

Old Jake was finally released from the hospital.
judge agreed that he could return to the ranch ar
look after things until probate settled the estate of th
missing Mary.

Old Jake bought three cases of rye whiskey, locke
himself in the bunkhouse, and got raging drunk. S
far, he'd stayed that way.

Jenny Cauldman died. Of old age. Her remai
were cremated.

Summer drifted slowly toward fall.

The head remained locked in its wire cage. St
quite talkative.

The headless young man and his girlfriend we
alive, and strapped down securely in isolation. Af
the horrible, gut-wrenching experience with G
Holland, none of the doctors wanted to be a part
anything like that. Not again.

They often said as they looked in on the imp
sible, "Die, goddamn you. Just die!"

Rather redundant, since both creatures were de;
Sort of.

Lisa and her gang kept out of sight and behaved

least on the surface, like little angels.

Mantine and Nicole seemed to have dropped off the face of the earth.

Gillette stayed close to home.

Leo rented the Matthews' house and settled in. He waited, keeping a low profile.

The press left Tepehuanes. No news there.

Janis prayed a lot.

And Paul smiled a lot.

Connie settled down behind her word processor, and inserted the software. She had a book due in a couple of months and had to finish it. Two months had passed since the family's return from the islands.

It was time to put the past behind her and get things back to normal.

She was working on a historical romance, set in the mid 1800s, in Mississippi. Much researched history and subtle sex.

Her fingers flew over the keys. She wrote several pages, then reviewed them.

Her mouth dropped open at what she'd written.

Connie blinked her eyes. Rubbed them. Shook her head. Surely she hadn't written that!

She could visualize her editor lying on the floor in a dead faint.

She erased that part of the floppy disk, and clicked off the word processor.

She knew she had not written the words she had reviewed on the screen. She was a good writer. Her books sold well, and were translated into many languages.

She had never—would never—write such trash.

But, she pondered, if she hadn't written the words, who had?

She rose from her work station and walked to the rear of her study, located at the back and to the side of the house. From the window, she could see Leo Corigliano sitting by the pool behind the Matthews' house. It seemed to Connie that he was always there, day and night, waiting. Sometimes watching the house.

In the two weeks since he'd rented that place, Leo had never once tried to engage Connie in conversation. But Janis spent a lot of time over there, as did Linda and Melissa and Jean and Carol and Roy and Bing.

But never Paul. He would not go near the ex-cop.

She leaned against the wall and stared out the window at Leo.

She sensed that he blamed Paul for the death of Inspector Willingston, that he believed Paul—an eight-year-old, nine next month—had conspired to have Stanford killed. And she knew how Janis felt, how Mark had felt about his own son.

They all believed that Paul was evil. Connie had heard Janis and her friends talking. They said Paul was the Son of Satan. A devil-child. The spawn of Hell. That his brother was a demon. That Paul wanted to kill them all and sexually assault his mother.

That was the most ridiculous thing Connie had ever heard of.

Paul was just a little boy.

She sighed.

A strange little boy, she admitted. Brilliant. An

with a well-hollow, deep voice.

But a devil-child?

Utter nonsense.

Movement caught Connie's eyes. She stared as Paul crept silently up to the stone fence that separated the two properties. But what in God's name was that beside him?

She peered at it more closely. It was a mist. She blinked. The mist was gone.

Paul was standing up, staring at her, an odd light in his eyes. The light vanished. He smiled and waved and moved toward his bicycle, pedaled off.

Had she imagined the mist? Surely she had.

Connie watched as Father Gomez walked around the Matthews' house to join Leo by the pool. The men shook hands, and the priest sat down.

Then he and Leo looked toward the Kelly house.

Instinctively, Connie drew back, even though she knew they could not see her.

Janis was with her friends. Her group, as she called it, was congregating at Melissa's.

Connie struggled within herself for a moment, finally reached a decision.

Let's bring this out in the open. To a head. Face it. Talk it out. Settle it. Once and for all.

She turned out the lights and walked out of her office, through the den and the back door, to the fence that separated the large plots of land. When she approached the gate, Leo and Father Gomez stood up, facing her.

"Mrs. Kelly," Leo said.

The priest smiled at her.

"Mr. Corigliano. Father." Connie pushed open

the gate and went over to the men. "We've been neighbors for a couple of weeks now, Mr. Corigliano. My daughter and her friends think very highly of you. Yet you and I have not exchanged a word since you moved in. I find that very strange."

She stared at him, putting the verbal ball in Leo's court.

Leo batted it back. "What is there to say, Mrs. Kelly?"

"Connie, please."

"Leo."

She smiled. "It seems we've covered this ground before, haven't we?"

"I believe so."

"May I join you, gentlemen?"

"Please do, Connie." Leo pointed to a chaise lounge and Connie sat. "Something to drink? I just fixed a fresh pot of coffee."

"That would be nice. Black, please."

Coffee poured, the three of them sat in silence for a time, none of them knowing exactly what to say or how to say it.

Connie tried a wan smile. "Paul is just a little boy, gentlemen. Very bright. Perhaps too bright for his own good—if that is possible. I do not believe that he is evil. Nor do I believe that he is some sort of devil child. I don't believe in those sorts of things. Some . . . well, odd things have occurred; I will admit that. But I do not believe that my son has anything to do with them. And to tell you the truth, Leo, I resent your presence here."

"Your right, Connie."

"What has Janis told you about Paul?"

"Everything she could remember about his behavior. She said Paul could always manipulate you, work you."

"That's nonsense!" But, with a sinking feeling Connie knew it was not. Paul had always had that ability.

Or she had just let him manipulate her.

"Janis told me . . . us"—Leo indicated Father Gomez—"about Paul's night-creeping. About the various pets he's killed. Your own, and those belonging to neighbors. And she's told us about the times he's threatened to kill her, the many times he's said he wished she were dead. Raped. She described his strange behavior on the island." He met her gaze and did not back down. "Connie, I followed Paul on the island. I saw him meet with Mantine and Nicole."

She paled, started to protest, but closed her mouth. Leo had no real reason to lie.

Then Leo cocked the verbal hammer and let it drop. He leveled with Connie Kelly, leaving nothing out. He told her about Janis peeking into Paul's bedroom on the island, watching the sand change. About Stanford burning the death cottage. About Stanford having to kill his own wife.

"Janis is a very bright kid, Connie. She's overheard you and Mark talking. She's heard you both admit that something was, is, wrong with Paul. It doesn't surprise me that you can't remember all that clearly. Paul has simply ordered you to forget; he's instructed you to block it out. Why he can work you that way, and not Janis, is something I don't know."

Connie looked at the priest. "Do you believe all

this nonsense, Father?"

"Yes, Connie. I do."

"Then I think you're both quite mad!" she declared, but she couldn't put that strange mist she'd seen out of her mind. She elected to say nothing about it. For the moment.

"Have you seen the book Melissa brought to Janis?" Leo asked.

She struggled silently. A book? What book? It seemed she had seen a book left at the house by one of the kids. But the memory was vague and shadowy. A book? She just didn't know.

She shook her head. "I don't remember. Is it important?"

"Very." Leo told her about the book, adding, "And Mantine and Nicole are in town. They've been spotted, riding around with some fellow named Gillette."

That brought her head up. "I know that name. He's a convicted child molester. And he's been accused of dealing in kiddy porn, right?"

"Correct. And Lisa Arnot and her gang have been seen entering and leaving Gillette's house. From there, they report straight to Paul. You want to put all that together, Connie?"

She stared at her coffee cup for a moment, then lifted her eyes to Leo's. "You put it together, Leo. And bear this in mind: You are talking about my son."

"Stanford told me Gillette is a caco."

"A what?"

"Simply put, a person who was born to do evil, answerable to Satan. Stanford said the Harveys, the

350

Simpsons, the Yardleys—all those at the Harvey house that night—were cacos. Their true nature was just now breaking through."

Connie rubbed her temples with her fingertips. "I don't know what to believe. I will admit that I am confused. Someone . . . something has been manipulating me. I guess that's the right word. I sit down to work, to write, but the words are not mine. Filth comes out. And I can't remember things. Leo, Father, I absolutely can't recall discussing Paul's behavior with Mark. That's frightening." She sighed. "But Paul is my baby. I suppose, to some degree, he's always had his way, in most things. The baby in the family usually does. But does that make him evil? Not in my mind."

"What do you remember of the island vacation, Connie?"

"Very little."

Father Gomez decided to take a chance. Looking at Leo, he said, "Perhaps it's time to show her the . . . objects at the hospital?"

Leo exhaled slowly. "I wasn't going to do that just yet. But perhaps you're right."

"What is it you're going to show me?"

Leo stood up. "Hell."

SIX

"De girl knows," Nicole told her husband. "I tink it's time for us to leave dis place."

"Bah!" Mantine scoffed at her. "I lak dis human form we in. Woman, you warry too much."

"I'm tellin' you, Mantine, dere is plenty cause for warry. Too many peoples is knowin' 'bout us. Too many peoples is involve. And dey not weak peoples. Dis cop wit de stupid name is big trouble."

Mantine cut his hard mean eyes to her. "Dat's simple. We figures out some way to kill him, dat's all."

"Dat ain't gonna be easy. And Paul jus' tinks he's gonna kill his sister. You been lyin' to de boy, Mantine. It's time to admit dat and to tell me why you been lyin'."

Mantine stood up, a tall handsome man. His eyes shone with an evil that encompassed centuries. "I ain't been lyin' to de boy. I just ain't been tellin' him true, dat's all."

"Same ting."

"Ain't neither." Mantine paced the bedroom at the rear of Gillette's house. He and Nicole had gathered enough strength through sleep and collected evil to function in human form for many hours. But in human form, in the living world, they were vulnerable. Mantine turned slowly, to look at his wife of more than a hundred years.

"De boy was born to die, Nicole. You knows dat. Each time he dies, a stronger force take his place in de scheme of tings. Dats de way it's been foreber."

"Yeah. I knows dat. But all de others knew it. Dey knew it from de start. How come you don' tell Paul the truth?"

"Damn it, woman! 'Cause de body and de mind dat was 'posed to be ready to receive Paul's power ain' ready. You know all dat as well as me. How come you all of a sudden ax such dumb questions?"

"Dat's de point I'm makin', Mantine. Why ain't i ready? You know de answer to dat well as me. 'Cause somebody is blockin' de power. Now, you listen to me! I ain't gonna mess around wit' God, Mantine We knows better dan dat. God squash us lak a bug.'

"Woman, you talk nonsense. God ain't nebe interfered afore, not directly. Not neber. How com you all of a sudden tink He doin' it now?"

"I din' say He was doin' it. But somebody rat clos to Him is."

"Who?"

"Don' know. But I take a guess and say dat damne old Michael is guidin' someone's toughts. Dat's wha I tink it is."

Mantine brushed that off. "God don' permit non of His people to leave dat place."

"I neber said Michael was here. I said he's talkin' t someone. And you know as well as me dat he dor have to leave dat place to do dat."

Mantine thought about that. It made some sense to him. Things had not been going as smoothly here as he had at first predicted. He had been confused as to why that was so. This explanation made sense. "Who he talkin' to, woman?"

She looked at him.

"No!" Mantine recoiled, unbelieving.

"Yeah."

"Dat's against de rules! Dat just ain't allowed. God got to play by de rules."

"Mantine, I done tole you and tole you: God ain't doin' dis."

"Yeah. But He ain't stoppin' it neither."

"No. He ain't. But you got to 'member, He don' have to stop it."

Mantine gave that some thought. Shook his head in agreement. "How strong you tink she is?"

"Ver' strong. Mantine, let's get out of here. Leave. I got a bad feelin' 'bout dis place. Tings ain't workin' out here."

"She strong enough to kill de boy?"

"Maybe. Don' know."

"What you tink we ought to do?"

"I tole you: Go home."

"'Sides dat?"

She shrugged. She would stay with her man. Even though she had a strong sense of impending disaster. "Maybe turn Gillette loose on her."

"Yeah." Mantine smiled. "Dat's a good idea. De boy can take over after dat."

Nicole opened the door and called for the caco.

Gillette listened. Licked his lips in heady anticipation. Such a pretty little girl. Soon to be all his.

"Do I have permission to take pictures to remember her by?" he asked.

"Not dis time," Nicole told him. "Maybe next time."

"Do I just go to her house?"

Gillette was expendable. He didn't know it, but he was. Besides, he was beginning to irritate Mantine and Nicole. "Of course. Paul will be dere."

"When?"

"Dis afternoon, mon."

Connie was first shown the headless man. Alive and well, and strapped down securely. She looked, then ran to the ladies' room and threw up her breakfast. Taking a deep breath, she washed her face, swallowed hard, then pushed open the door, returning to the isolation ward.

She was shown the woman, also strapped down. Snarling and snapping and cursing and grunting.

She looked at the doctors' faces. The strain was beginning to show on all of them.

She touched Leo's arm. He could feel her fear through the touch.

"How . . . ?" Connie managed to ask.

"Ask Paul," she was told.

A sharp retort died on her tongue. She realized that she was definitely in the minority concerning her son.

She was taken to Carleson's lab.

The head greeted her.

"Hi, baby! Come here and give me a great big

356

juicy kiss."

Connie felt she would faint. She gripped Leo's arm and stared at the horror grinning at her. When she started to walk closer to the dirty, slobbering head, Leo stopped her. "Don't get too close, Connie. He'll spit on you. The spittle is highly contagious."

"What has my son to do with you?" she blurted.

"All praise the young master!" the head screamed. "All bow down to the Son of the Dark One." The head laughed and laughed, green slime leaking out of its mouth, slicking the red lips. The smell in the lab was very nearly overpowering.

Connie stood, numb with shock. She bit at the knuckles of her hand, almost drawing blood. Then she screamed at the head. "Tell me! What about Paul?"

"He wants to screw you, baby!"

Connie almost lost control. The room spun wildly for a moment. "Paul is my son! He's only eight years old!"

"He's a thousand years old. Ten thousand years old. He's as old as sin."

"Why are you suddenly so cooperative?" Dr. Belline asked.

The head cut its maddened eyes to him. "What have I got to lose?"

"I've seen enough—heard enough." Connie's voice was low, but filled with dread and near panic. "Get me out of this . . . place, Leo. Please!"

The head was still hollering, cursing, and spitting as Leo led Connie out into the corridor.

He walked with her to a small lounge and sat her down in a chair. "You want some coffee, Connie?"

357

She looked up at him. Leo thought he had never seen such fear and confusion. She nodded her head, not trusting her voice.

"Back in a minute."

Mary Beth had followed them out of the chamber of horrors. "I'll stay with her," she offered, and sat down beside the badly shaken woman.

"All right," Connie was saying, as Leo returned, cups of coffee in his hands. "I've seen it. Now what am I supposed to do about it?"

Mary Beth seized the moment. "Let us confine the boy, Mrs. Kelly. Give us permission to conduct a sanity hearing. I'm one of the few who doesn't want to kill Paul."

The mother turned to Leo. "You would agree with that?"

He shrugged his shoulders. "It wouldn't prove a thing. Nothing at all. The boy is too smart. He'd breeze right through it. But you do what you want to do. He's your son."

Connie kept her eyes on him. "Could you really kill an eight-year-old, Leo?"

"I don't know. Maybe. But we're not talking about your average eight-year-old. Paul is a devil. I'm firmly convinced of that. So . . . yeah, I think I could. And while we're leveling with each other, I also think you made a very bad mistake in sending Linda home. I wish you'd call her, right now, and get her back to your house to stay with Janis."

Connie stood up. Her eyes had lost much of the fear. "Why, Leo?"

"Because I sense—call it a cop's hunch—that matters are rapidly moving toward a head. And don't like the idea of Janis being left alone. That's one of the reasons I moved next door, to keep an eye on her. She's a good kid. Would you please call Linda?''

Connie hesitated. She had witnessed so many impossibilities, such horrors, that her mind had clicked off. She nodded minutely.

Mary Beth pointed across the hall. ''Use the phone in that office,'' she said.

Connie walked out of the lounge and across the short hallway.

''We've made a small step, Leo.''

''Not much of a one.''

''What do you mean?''

''Paul is still alive.''

''You really could kill him, couldn't you?''

''Yeah. I really could.''

''Will you?''

''Father Gomez says no. He says someone else will do that.''

''Who?''

''He wouldn't tell me. He said the person has to find out first.''

''I wonder who it is?''

''I'm afraid I've already figured that out.''

Without Janis, Connie, Linda, or Paul knowing—he hoped—Leo had arranged with Mike and Sheriff Sandry to have two city cops and Peter Loneman stationed not far from the Kelly house during the early afternoon. Leo had a gut feeling that something bad was about to go down.

And he couldn't shake that feeling.

Peter had slipped into Leo's rented house while Connie was with the ex-cop at the hospital. He watched the Kelly place from a side window, staying in touch with the other cops by walkie-talkie.

Sheriff Sandry and Mike had warrants drawn up. With two deputies and two city cops, they were going to force Mantine's hand, charge him and Nicole with illegal entry into the country.

If it came to that.

Linda had arrived at the Kelly house, carrying a suitcase, and Paul had promptly left, to sit by the pool, pouting, an angry look on his face.

From behind binoculars, Peter smiled. "You were right, Leo. The kid is really mad."

"I didn't think he'd be too happy about Linda returning. I just wish I knew what was going down. And more importantly—when."

"Relax. Eric and Fifteen and me have been assigned here permanently. We're here to stay, Leo."

"Doesn't Fifteen have a name?"

Peter laughed. "Raymond. But he's always been called Fifteen. First time he went out on a trouble call alone he got so excited he forgot his name when he called in. All he could holler was his unit number. Fifteen. The name stuck."

Leo smiled as Peter's radio crackled. "It's confirmed. Movement at the Gillette house. Mantine and Nicole have been spotted. The sheriff thinks Gillette is up to something on his own."

"If he heads in this direction, we'll sure know what's on his mind."

"Yeah," Peter said grimly.

The men waited.

The walkie-talkie popped. "Gillette is pulling out," Peter informed Leo. "Alone. Heading in this direction. Soon as he's out of sight, the sheriff and Mike are hitting the house."

"I hope Sandry realizes that in this case he's got to shoot first and ask questions later."

"He may be a politician, Leo, but he's a good cop. Believe it."

Leo grunted.

Peter looked at him and said, "He and Mike are both carrying throw-down guns. Of course, being one of New York's finest, you've never even heard of anything like that, right?"

Leo rolled his eyes. "Heavens no!"

The tension vanished as Peter laughed.

They waited.

"Now!" Sandry ordered. As he spoke the words, he was leaving his car, running toward the Gillette house. Two young deputies were running in front of him, one of them carrying a sledge hammer.

The deputy swung the twelve-pound sledge, striking the doorknob squarely. The knob flew inward, the door slewing open, one hinge broken. The police raced into the house, guns drawn.

Mantine and Nicole were caught totally by surprise in the den. They whirled around, shock on their faces, fear in their eyes at being caught in human form.

"Freeze!" Sandry yelled. "You're both under arrest."

361

Nicole hissed at the men.

Mantine's face changed into a mask of hate.

Then the couple began to change before the startled eyes of the men, a horrible transfiguration overtaking them. The smell of the sea filled the house as Mantine and Nicole were caught halfway between human and inhuman form.

Wriggling, squirming coils of seaweed flopped on the carpet.

One slithering rope of seaweed latched onto a cop's leg and quickly wound its way up his leg, past his waist, and coiled around his neck. The cop cried out and dropped to his knees on the carpet, the seaweed choking the life from him. He managed to get his fingers between the slick stuff and his neck, to break the snakelike coil. He tossed it aside, coughing.

Sheriff Burt Sandry and Chief Mike Bambridge opened fire on the hideous things that now stood before them. Two creatures that numbed the mind, and defied description. Creatures like nothing either man had ever before witnessed. Sandy, wet, scaly, hairy, ugliness.

Sandry pumped five rounds into what had been Mantine, each slug knocking the spawn of Hel backward. A foulness oozed from the creature.

Mike put two slugs into the chest of the thing that had been Nicole. The misshapen howling creature stumbled backward, its open, fanged mouth-hole gushing a greenish stinking fluid. Fighting back nausea caused by the stench, Bambridge stepped closer and emptied his pistol into the thing's chest. The slugs stilled the devil's heart.

As dead life began to leave the man and woman,

wind whipped through the house, screaming, over-turning tables and smashing lamps, pushing the men backward against the wall.

A city cop fought the wind and stepped forward with a sawed-off riot gun. He shot Mantine in the chest. Three times he pumped and pulled, the buckshot ripping open the creature's chest cavity and forever stilling its evil heart. Mike had managed to reload, using a speed-loader, and he emptied his pistol into the heart of Nicole.

The creatures began to change, to work their way through a hideous metamorphic transformation. Within seconds, Mantine and Nicole had sped through centuries, as the creatures within them changed and materialized, lived and then died.

Now two human forms, bullet and buckshot shattered, lay on the floor.

The sheriff and the chief ordered their men out of the house.

Then they looked at each other, their faces slick with sweat and shock.

In unison, they dropped their pistols beside the bloody bodies, Sandry saying, "I have never done anything like this in my life, and I feel you haven't either, Mike."

Mike shook his head. "No. I haven't. But can you think of a better way to handle this?"

Sheriff Sandry slowly shook his head. "I just want this over with."

Both men pulled search warrants from their back pockets.

And Mike called for the men to enter the house. "Tear this place apart," he ordered. "I want this to look as legal as possible."

Connie was in her study, writing. She carefully studied each page before she stored it on a disk. She wanted no repeat of what had taken place earlier.

She knew she could never completely put what she'd seen at the hospital out of her mind. Nor could she push aside her growing suspicion of her son. But she had written through good times and bad, and had a writer's ability to detach herself and work.

She lost herself in writing.

In the den, Paul smiled at his sister. "Why don't you go outside and play, sister darling?" he suggested.

"Why don't you jump into the pool and forget you know how to swim?" was her response.

Paul whirled, stared at Linda. "You must know I resent your presence in this house!"

"That's too bad, kid."

The boy, his eyes filled with evil and hate, turned and walked up the hallway, to his mother's study. He pushed open the door and stared at her back.

"Mother!"

She turned, meeting his eyes.

Paul smiled at her.

Connie's fingers froze over the keyboard. She was utterly motionless.

Paul closed the door and stepped back into the hall. Something had gone wrong. He had experienced a feeling of something leaving him. Something terrible had happened. He had no idea what it could be.

But he knew something was wrong.

And where was Gillette? The caco should have been there by now.

The boy walked slowly up the hall, back toward the den.

Janis's friends had gone home. Paul had only Linda to deal with. He smiled, a cruel curving of his lips. An idea formed in his brain.

He was strong enough now. He could do it.

He slipped to the archway of the den. Good. Janis was in the kitchen, fixing something to stuff into her face.

"Brother!" he whispered. "Come."

A mist formed beside the boy.

A dark rotting odor hovered about it.

Paul looked at the yellow mist, then cut his eyes to Linda and smiled.

The mist moved, sinking to the floor. Snakelike, it slithered over the carpet, then slipped under the sofa.

Paul closed his eyes and his feet left the carpet. He stood suspended a few inches off the floor. Silently, he began moving, in air, toward the kitchen.

A scaly hand slipped out from under the couch and clamped onto Linda's ankle.

The teenager screamed.

Janis whirled around from the counter, a sandwich in her hand. She was face to face with her brother. His eyes were very bright. His breath was foul on her face.

The house began to stink of sulphur.

Paul was quick, but Janis was quicker. When he grabbed for her, she shoved the sandwich in his face and pushed him backward with all her strength. He stumbled back, fell down the steps, into the den. His head banged against the floor, momentarily stunning him. Peanut butter and jelly covered his face.

Linda was screaming hysterically. Janis cut her eyes to the girl.

Then she stood, numb with fear, and gazed at the thing that had grabbed Linda. It had materialized into a full-blown horror and was tearing at the teenager's clothing.

Outside, Gillette was panting up the sidewalk, his thoughts as dark and evil as Hell could make them. He did not know that Mantine and Nicole had been destroyed. But he did know he was free of something and also that he had lost something. With the death of Mantine and Nicole, the caco had lost their control. Now he was very nearly mindless, except for one thought—to do what he had been ordered to do. And to accomplish it in any way he could.

Linda's hysterical screaming broke Janis's numbing paralysis. She grabbed a butcher knife from the counter and ran toward Linda, stepping on her brother's head as she jumped down the steps to the den floor.

The hideousness had forced the teenager onto the couch. Head bent, it was trying to kiss the lips of the howling girl.

Linda twisted away, trying to avoid the slobber. Her eyes were half-crazed from fear.

Janis struck, driving the long-bladed knife deep into the demon's back. Its scream rattled the windows, and a noxious corruption flew from its mouth, spraying the couch. Clawed hands released the teenager. She rolled to the floor and scrambled away just as the front door flew open and Gillette, wide-eyed and red-faced, ran into the foyer.

Janis struggled to free the knife, finally working the blade out of the demon's back. Using both hands, she then plunged the blade deep into the creature's neck. It howled its agony and flung her away. She lost her grip on the knife, but the scaly horror ran up the hall, turned, and jumped through a window. It vanished into the back yard.

Linda was screaming and crying, crawling around on the floor, trying to gather up her torn clothing to cover her nakedness.

Paul struggled to his hands and knees on the floor. He looked around, his eyes dazed.

He found Gillette and pointed toward his sister. "Her!" he screamed.

Gillette ran toward Janis.

When Paul heard a car screech to a halt in the driveway, he fell back onto the floor, pretending unconsciousness.

Gillette grabbed for Janis and she kicked him hard.

He screamed out of pain as she whirled and ran toward the fireplace to grab a poker.

Gillette was furious. "I'll make you pay and pay for this," he shouted.

Peter and Leo reached the doorway. They had guns in their hands.

Screaming his near-mindless rage, Gillette ran toward Janis.

A .357 and a .44 roared, together. Gillette was stopped abruptly and flung backward. He hit the back of a chair and flipped over it, landing on the floor, a hole in his head and a hole in the center of his chest.

He jerked once, drummed his heels against the floor, then finally realized he was dead.

Connie staggered out of the hallway, to stand looking down at the bloody confusion in the den a few feet below her.

"Paul!" she managed to shout. "Paul! What's happened to my baby?"

She staggered, trancelike, toward the seemingly unconscious Paul.

But Janis had had quite enough of her mother and of Paul. She halted Connie halfway across the den and spun her around.

Facing her mother, she pointed a finger at Connie Kelly. And the ten-year-old, almost eleven, said "Now you listen to me, Mother. Damn it, listen!"

Paul sat up and fired visual hate at his sister. But with a very odd smile on his lips.

Connie drew back her hand to hit the girl.

SEVEN

"Connie, no!" Leo shouted.

The woman let her hand fall to her side.

Slowly, she recovered from the shock of hearing profanity from the lips of her daughter. She took a long look at Janis, and for the first time, she backed away from her.

Paul bounced to his feet and ran from the den, to stand on the landing above it. "You'll all be sorry!" he screamed at them.

Then he ran down the hall to his bedroom, and slammed the door.

Paul pressed against the inside of the door, a wide smile creasing his cruel mouth. Everything was working out just fine.

Those left in the den looked at each other, saying nothing. The expressions on their faces told it all.

Linda had found a robe and had slipped into it, covering her nakedness.

Peter was calling in to the station house.

Leo put a hand on Connie's shoulder. "You want to talk now, Connie?"

"Let's all talk!" Janis said, considerable heat in

369

her voice.

Mother smiled at daughter. Cut her eyes to Leo. "I guess it was, ah, the shots that jarred me out of the . . . trance, I suppose you'd call it. The last thing I remember was turning around from my word processor and seeing Paul standing in the door."

"And then?" Leo asked.

"Nothing. A total blank. Blackout." She looked at the bloody, cooling body of Gillette and shuddered. "When I came out of . . . it, my arms were stiff and hurting from hovering over the keys."

Peter hung up the phone and walked to Linda, who was sitting on the steps. He talked quietly to the teenager, taking notes on a small pad.

Janis told her mother about what Paul had done. About his pointing her out to Gillette. And she told her about the creature from Hell attacking Linda.

"Describe this creature to me, Janis," Leo said to the girl.

Janis closed her eyes and described the demon.

"That's the same damn hideous thing that was in the room with me and Gomez." Leo met Connie's worried yet unbelieving eyes. "It's true, Connie."

Connie walked across the room, away from Gillette's body, and sat down in a chair. Her face was drawn, her eyes were weary. She raised her hands in a gesture of defeat. When she spoke, her voice was low but filled with a new resolve. "Paul is obviously mentally ill. I guess I've known that all along. The devil possessing him? I don't know about that. Demons and monsters?" She shrugged. "Whatever whoever, is doing this to my son, well, obviously they've taken control of him. He needs help, and

370

needs it now." She looked at Peter. "Contact a judge. I'll sign the commitment papers."

In his room, Paul laughed softly. "Fools!" he whispered. "Stupid fools. Playing right into my hands. I love it!"

The press once more rolled into Tepehuanes, and this time many reporters vowed to stay, to ferret out the truth. Just too much had happened in this small city for any of it to be no more than coincidence. Too many strange events could not be explained away.

INS officials flew into town and talked at length with Sheriff Sandry and Chief Bambridge about the deaths of Mantine and Nicole. They went away satisfied that the lawmen had acted in self-defense.

The bodies of Mantine and Nicole were cremated, the ashes sealed in steel containers and locked. The boxes were buried in concrete-lined tombs. It was a very private service. Conducted at night.

No mourners.

At least none that those in attendance could see. Or wanted to see.

It appeared that Darrel and Mona and Andy and Mary had vanished.

But no one believed it.

The sand people had seemingly returned to the earth.

No one believed that either.

Old Jake got raging drunk and stayed that way. He knew where Darrel and Mona and Andy and Mary were hiding, but as long as they left him alone, damned if he was going to bother them.

371

The horrors at the hospital continued to live on in death.

And Paul, without any fuss on his part, was committed to the small mental ward at Tepehuanes General.

"And Jesus Christ really lived?" the fascinated psychiatrist asked Paul.

"Oh, yes. He lived, wandering about, spewing his rot to any who would listen. I was there when he died."

The shrink sat in his chair and stared at the boy with the deep, hollow voice.

Paul seemed perfectly relaxed. Almost happy.

The psychiatrist finally found his voice. "You were . . . there?"

"Yes. With my brother."

"Where is your brother now?"

"He's around."

"While you were . . . there, were you in your present form, Paul?"

"Don't be stupid. Of course not."

"I see."

"I very much doubt it."

"All right. Tell me, if you are so powerful, the Son of Satan, why are you allowing yourself to be subjected to these questions? Why are you taking your confinement so passively?"

"I find it amusing."

"Ummm. Would you like to go back home?"

"Not particularly."

"Why?"

"The journey is a long one."

"What? Oh. Yes. I see. Getting back to the death of Jesus. What were your thoughts after the crucifixion?"

Paul smiled. "I said, 'Well, now it will be A.D.'"

Janis was in her room, with Melissa. Leo sat with Connie in the den, having after-dinner coffee. Since Paul's confinement, the two of them had gotten close. Very close.

"The whole summer has been like a bad dream," Connie said. "And before you say it, I know. While summer might be nearing an end, our . . . situation is not yet over."

Leo thought: She still does not realize what must be done to end it. Or will not accept that is perhaps a better way of putting it. "Did you see Paul today?"

She sighed, her face tightening. "Briefly. He asked me some obscene questions. I walked out."

"He's playing a game, Connie. Paul could bust out of that ward anytime he wishes."

"Yes. I believe that. Now."

"And . . . ?"

"I choose not to dwell on that."

Naturally. "A few members of the press are still hanging around town."

"I know. I avoid them at the hospital. Mary Beth has arranged for me to enter and leave through the basement. But I won't be going back there. At least not for a long time. He's got to show some signs of

373

improvement before I subject myself to any more of that."

He smiled at her and touched her hand. "I'm glad you've reached that decision. What surprises me is that Paul has not tried to control you from there."

She met his smile. "Oh, he has, Leo. But I've learned to fight him. With the help of Father Gomez."

"So that's where you've been going each afternoon. I wondered. Felt you'd tell me in time."

"He says you're a hopeless backslider. But a good man in your own peculiar way."

"Yeah. He's given up trying to get me to church. I'll shock him one of these days and show up for confession."

She studied his face. "You've got a worried look in your eyes, Leo."

"It isn't over, Connie. Paul's playing a game, but he's going to tire of it. When he does, all Hell is going to break loose. And I mean that quite literally."

"It's been so quiet and nice."

"It won't last." Leo rose from the couch and walked up the short flight of steps to the kitchen. After pouring another cup of coffee, he held up the pot to Connie. She shook her head.

"Too much coffee might keep you awake, Leo," she said with a smile.

"Is that right? Oh, I intend to stay awake for at least an hour . . . later on."

"That long, huh? I can hardly wait. You've improved."

"Well . . . fifteen minutes, at least."

They shared a relaxed laugh that felt good to both.

of them. It had been nice and quiet. But Leo knew it wouldn't last. He just couldn't figure out what the boy was waiting for. And he could not understand why Paul was taking his confinement with such grace. It wasn't like him.

Connie rose to still the ringing of the phone. As she listened, Leo watched her face pale. She steadied herself by leaning against the edge of the table. Then tears began to stream down her face. She muttered something that Leo could not make out, and gently replaced the phone on its cradle.

"Paul?" Leo asked, hoping against hope.

She shook her head. Wiped her eyes and took a deep breath.

"Connie?"

When she did not reply, Leo walked down into the den and went to her side. "What's wrong, babe?"

She shook her head and blinked tears away, then went into his arms, pressing herself against him for a long moment. Finally, she pulled back and looked into his eyes. "That was Mike Bambridge. His department got a call that some vandals were tearing up the cemetery."

Leo felt his guts begin to churn.

The waiting was just about over. Paul had decided to make his move.

"Dispatch sent a unit over there. It wasn't vandals, Leo. Two graves had been broken open. Leo . . . they weren't broken into. It looks like they were both broken out of. From the inside."

"Which graves, Connie?"

"Mark's body and Carla's are gone."

"Oh, no!"

"It's started, Leo? It's begun?"

"Yes."

"But . . ."

From up the corridor came sounds of breaking glass and Janis's and Melissa's screams filled the hallway and ripped into the den.

BOOK THREE

While from a proud tower in the town
Death looked gigantically down.

—Poe

ONE

Leo told Connie to stay put and ran up the hallway. Since Paul's confinement in the hospital, and the general quieting down, he had not been wearing his pistol.

Now he realized what a terrible mistake that was.

And within the span of a few seconds, with a sinking feeling in his gut, he began to realize a lot of other things.

Paul had conned them all.

He hit the bedroom door with his shoulder, knocking it open, and literally fell into the room, landing on the floor, banging his knee.

The scene that greeted his eyes and the stench that filled his nostrils momentarily stunned and sickened him, freezing him to the carpet.

Janis's clothing was ripped. The girl's shirt, torn from her, was hanging in shreds. She was keeping her jeans up by clutching the waistband. She must have been standing by the window when the thing grabbed her.

Mark Kelly, his burial suit dusty and dirty, had one leg over the window sill, and was struggling to climb

379

all the way into the bedroom.

The room stank of the grave.

Melissa sat in the center of the bed, her eyes wide with fear, her face chalk white.

Mark grunted and grinned. His mouth was filled with maggots. One crawled over his bottom lip and down his chin, to fall silently to the carpet.

The walking, living dead reached for his daughter with wormlike white fingers. Janis seemed rooted to the floor, unable to move.

Leo jumped to his feet, his aching knee almost giving way under him. He grabbed a brass lamp from Janis's nightstand and lunged toward the walking dead, hitting Mark in the center of the head with the heavy lamp, knocking him backward, out of the shattered window. Mark howled in anger; his breath crypt-cold, fouled the night air.

"Get out of here!" Leo yelled to the girls, as Mark began to climb back through the window.

The girls ran.

Leo jerked the spread off the bed, and tossed it over Mark's head. He balled his right hand into a fist, then popped the zombie on the side of his jaw, just as hard as he could.

Mark's fingers closed on Leo's bare arm, digging in, trying to pull the man to him. Leo smashed the monstrosity again, broke free of the cold fingers.

Behind him, up the hallway, Janis and Connie and Melissa were screaming.

Leo hit the undead again, the impact of fist against jaw hurting his hand; but he was too keyed up to notice. He swung a short left hook that caught Mark on his bedspread-covered nose. The bridge crunched under the blow and flattened.

Mark threw off the spread.

There was no blood on him despite the battering he'd taken.

He reached for Leo. His dead eyes were bright with rage and the life beyond the darkness of the grave.

Leo had always been a brave cop. Never a stupid one. In the span of about three seconds, he decided it was time to haul it out of there.

He turned and ran out the open door, heading for Mark's study and the gun cabinet there.

Grunting and snorting and leaving a trail of worms and maggots and dirt, stinking of the grave, Mark lumbered and stumbled after Leo, staggering from side to side in the hallway, bouncing off the walls.

"Get the kids out of here!" Leo yelled to Connie, as he turned into Mark's study.

"Where to?" Connie screamed from the den.

"Father Gomez. Go to the church. I'll meet you there. And don't stop for anyone."

"What?"

"Just go—now!"

Leo smashed the gun-cabinet door with his fist, the glass cutting his hand. He jerked out a shotgun and jammed in shells, turning when he heard Mark breathing behind him.

He leveled the gun and began pulling and pumping. The medium loads blasted into Mark's dead body, the force of them, at almost point-blank range, knocking it backward, out into the hall. Leo reloaded, this time with buckshot, and fired again.

Howling ancient curses that originated from the

dark and sour side of the grave, Mark screamed and lurched away, heading up the hall, toward the den.

Leo heard Connie's car back out of the garage, the tires protesting as she raced away.

Leo stood for a moment, listening. He was alone in the house with Mark.

He breathed through his mouth. The stench in the house was sickening. He stepped on a crawling maggot and felt the thing crunch under his shoe.

He could hear nothing.

He turned to the gun cabinet and stuffed his pockets with shells, magnum loads, buckshot. He loaded up again, chambering a round and adding fresh round to the tube.

He longed for his old sawed-off riot gun.

He paused, listening.

The house was silent.

But Leo could sense that Mark was still in it. Hiding. Waiting.

He jerked up the phone in the study and punched out Mike's number, figuring the chief would be home at this time of night. He was, having dinner with Mary Beth.

Leo spoke for about ten seconds, then hung up. Mike was on the way, with reinforcements.

Leo remained silent for a moment, thinking and listening. What could he do? He decided the shotgun was very nearly useless against Mark. How does one kill a person who is already dead?

Stanford had told him. Leo hadn't believed Willingston at the time. Now he did.

What had the inspector said?

Yeah. He remembered. Just like in the books and

the movies. He laid the shotgun aside and looked around him, saw a small fireplace that looked as though it had never been used. Leo picked up a brass poker and unscrewed the hook. Stanford had told him that the only way to kill one of these things was to pierce its heart.

All right. He'd try it.

He walked to the study door and paused, gripping the poker tightly. No strong grave smell greeted him. He could still smell the tomb, but felt reasonably sure that Mark was not in the hall.

The little bit of doubt remaining didn't do very much to calm his rattled nerves, however.

He stepped out into the semidarkness of the hallway, the poker held like a bayoneted rifle, ready to be driven deep into the walking horror's chest.

The hallway was empty.

The floor creaked behind him.

He whirled around.

Nothing.

Taking a ragged breath, Leo slipped silently up the hall, pausing just before he reached the archway that opened into the brightly lighted den.

Only the den was no longer as brightly lit as Leo remembered it being when he and Connie were having coffee and talking.

Only one small lamp was burning, and that was placed in a far corner.

Shadows loomed long in the sunken room.

Leo gritted his teeth, reluctant to face the darkness that yawned before him.

The undead creature had enough sense remaining to turn off the lights. Then a more disturbing thought came to him: Mark could see as well in the dark as Leo could in the light of day.

Wonderful.

Outside, the night seemed unnaturally quiet, with no sirens cutting the darkness, no flashing red and blue lights.

Leo wondered about that.

And within a few heartbeats, he suddenly realized why Paul had gone to the hospital so willingly, even cheerfully. Why he was taking it all so calmly.

Every little thing began to click into place until the macabre puzzle lay exposed in Leo's mind, in all it ugliness.

It was horrifying.

Disgusting.

It came to him with such a soul-wrenching jar tha he was almost numbed.

Everything the boy had been doing was an act. Hi screaming tantrums over what the others, includin Leo, had perceived as his failures, had been, i reality, personal victories. Paul had quietly an calmly, and quite brilliantly, conned them all. H had worked it all out in his twisted and hate-fille mind. With more than a little help from a muc darker power.

In the gloom of the den, Mark laughed.

Leo's hands were sweaty as he gripped the hand of the poker. Could Mark intercept his thoughts? I guessed so.

Jesus, Joseph, and Mary!

Leo wiped his palms on his pants' leg.

They were alone.

Alone!

Sure they were. That was the way Paul planned

all along.

There would be no cops racing to the rescue. Well, maybe two or three. At most Mike, Peter, Burt Sandry, and perhaps Raymond/Fifteen. Leo felt that would be just about it as far as badges went.

He leaned against the hall wall and fought back a hard trembling as the awful truth struck home and settled in his mind.

Stanford had warned him, cautioned him repeatedly, that everything Paul did might not be what it appeared to be at first glance. He had dealt with the Devil and his minions and servants before. He had known that one must always be ready to expect the unexpected.

The inspector had been right, of course.

And now, Leo thought, Paul had the entire town in his pocket.

Nearly everybody. Leo would bet on that. He was betting. His life.

While Leo and the others had been running around willy-nilly, their thoughts on destroying the devil-child, Paul had been quietly taking control of nearly everyone in the town.

But how had the boy done it?

How! Leo mentally berated himself for not spotting what was going on. How could just one person manage to accomplish such a task?

Then it came to him.

Very easily, that's how.

Because the people in the town were already a part of the Dark One's scheme. They probably hadn't even realized it. Not until Paul returned from the islands.

They'd all been waiting for the young master.

But nagging doubts tugged at Leo's mind. Was Paul the end or the beginning? Was he the mainspring, or simply a minor cog?

Leo didn't know. Might never know.

But he was certain of one thing: They were alone. Alone.

The thought chilled him.

Connie. Connie and the kids. For the first time in his life, Leo had found someone he wanted to spend the rest of his life with. He wasn't going to lose her now. He had to get to them. Had to prevent them from making contact with anyone outside the tiny group he was reasonably sure of.

Leo took several deep breaths. He could smell the rancid stink of the grave. The sour odor of rotting flesh. Of flesh-eating worms.

Suddenly, Leo screamed and charged into the den.

And ran right into the solid grave-stink of Mark Kelly.

His unexpected charge had startled the living dead. The collision had knocked the creature sprawling to the den floor. Leo maintained his grip on the poker as he leaped to his feet and stood over the stinking creature from the satin-lined mouth of the grave.

Mark looked up at Leo, his undead eyes burning like coals of hate.

"Die, damn you!" Leo screamed, holding the poker with both hands, high over his head.

Mark hissed a long sigh of icy-cold death-breath at Leo.

Then he laughed.

Leo brought the poker down with all his strength

the tip driving deep into the man's chest.

Mark screamed, a banshee's wailing; ten thousand voices ripped from the bowels of Hell as the metal tip plunged deep into his body. Mark tried to roll. But Leo held him firm, impaled on the poker. Mark hunched his hips, attempting to work loose. He could not. Leo worked the poker deeper, sweat dripping from his face.

A corruption sprang from Mark's ruined chest, a vile, stinking greenish fluid erupted in a gush from the maggot-eaten body and the blackened heart. Mark's hands gripped the shaft of the poker; curses rolled, in a dozen languages, from his mouth. But his weakened arms were unable to pull the offensive metal from his chest.

He gripped Leo's ankles, trying to bring the man down. He could not. Leo kicked the undead on the side of the head, in his mouth. Worms gathered on the tip of his shoe.

He shook his foot, dislodging the worms. He had a horror of them crawling up his pants' leg and eating into his flesh.

Straddling Mark, standing over him, one foot on either side, Leo summoned all his strength and drove the poker deeper into the zombie's chest. Oblivious to the green, stinking filth that squirted from the enlarging hole, he worked the poker from side to side, always driving it deeper.

Mark howled. Howled like a rabid monster caught in a death trap. He hissed like a huge snake. Shook and trembled as the hissing faded into nothing when his second soul winged away into eternity, never to return.

Leo hoped.

Leo looked down. No metamorphosis had taken place. Mark was peaceful in death. He had not been one of *them*. Only an unwilling and unwitting participant. A pawn for his son to play with.

That was a relief to Leo, for he had been wondering about Mark and Connie.

Now, standing over Mark, looking down at his peaceful face, he was sure of Connie.

But what was he to do with the body?

"What am I thinking of? Jesus—leave it!"

His chest heaving from his exertions, Leo took a moment to calm his racing heart; then he staggered back to the study and grabbed up the shotgun. He stuffed his pockets full of shells, and grabbed a .38 pistol and a rifle from the cabinet. Pockets bulging with ammunition, he ran toward the back door and raced to his car. Tossing the guns onto the seat, he locked all the doors, then backed out of the drive.

He saw many people milling about in their front yards or on the sidewalk or along the curb. They seemed disoriented, not sure of what to do next.

Leo felt their orders would soon come.

He drove off, picking up speed.

He almost collided with Mike's unit at an intersection. Tires smoking, the cars slid to a stop. Mary Beth was sitting next to Mike.

Leo backed up and rolled down his window. "It's busted wide open!" he called. "This has been Paul's plan all along. I'm sure of it. Find Peter and Raymond and Sheriff Sandry. Don't count on anyone else in this town. I believe nearly everyone else has rolled over and joined Paul. Willingly or

388

unwillingly. But that makes no difference now. I just killed Mark. I'll get Connie and Linda and the girls. We'll meet at the hospital."

Mary Beth's eyes were round with fear. She opened her mouth to speak, then closed it.

Mike appeared stunned. He shook his head. "Everybody in the town?"

"Near as I can guess, yes."

"The doctors and nurses?"

"Possibly. I don't know. We can only hope that a few are still with us. I guess we're just going to have to find that out the hard way."

"Jesus Christ!"

"That's one of the people I've been quietly calling on during the past ten minutes or so," Leo admitted. "Let's get going, Mike."

A thrown brick spider-webbed the rear side window of Mike's unit. The impact caused him and Mary Beth to jump.

Then, from one end of the street, a chanting, humming, evil sound drifted to them.

Mike looked up toward it. When he spoke, his voice was hoarse. "Dear God in Heaven!"

Mary Beth put her face in her hands and began slowly shaking her head back and forth.

The humming and chanting intensified, coupled with the sounds of marching feet.

"There's two of my men in that crowd," Mike said.

Leo twisted in his seat, looking behind him. He grimaced, swallowed hard. Fear touched him with a cold slimy hand that seemed to tangle in his gut and hold on tight.

The street behind them was filled with people,

walking, marching, shoulder to shoulder. They waved guns and clubs, and shouted hatred and profanity as they chanted praises to Satan.

One phrase stood out from all the rest: "Die! Die! Die!"

Leo dropped his car into gear and wiped his sweaty palms on his shirt. "I've still got the walkie-talkie, Mike. We'll stay in touch that way."

Mike nodded his head.

"Roll it!" Leo shouted above the hate-filled voices. He floorboarded the gas pedal and squalled off.

Mike jammed the pedal to the floor and spun the wheel, doing a cop turnaround in the middle of the street, his rear tires smoking. He followed the taillights of Leo's car.

Mike keyed his mike. "I wonder if we can get out of town?"

Leo picked up the walkie-talkie. "I don't know. I wouldn't bet on it."

"What's the plan?"

Driving one-handed, Leo said, "I told Connie to take the kids to Father Gomez. You know where Carol Hovey and Jean Polk live?"

"Ten-four."

"Pick them up. And be careful when dealing with their parents. You know what I mean."

"Ten-four. And you'll be . . . ?"

"I'll go get Linda and then pick up the boys, Roy and Bing. I'll meet you at the church."

"Ten-four. I'll get in touch with Peter and Fifteen."

"Pete here," the speakers in the cars popped. "I've got Fifteen right with me, on my tail. Stay away from the station, Mike. The personnel have turned."

"All of them?" Mike radioed, disbelief in his voice.

"All of them, Mike."

"Sheriff Sandry here," the speakers crackled. "Same with my substation. We're all alone in this thing, people. I had to kill one of my deputies, but I picked up a back seat full of weapons and other gear. I'll head for the church and secure that area. See you all over there."

"Ten-four, Burt," Leo radioed.

"One more thing," Sheriff Sandry radioed.

Mike and Leo waited.

"Don't try to leave town. They've got us cut off and boxed in tight. I don't know what they think they're going to gain by this. Deputies and state police all over the county are monitoring these transmissions. This place will be crawling with cops in a couple of hours."

A strange voice rattled the speakers. "A couple of hours is all we need."

Another voice added to the confusion. "What's going on over there?" Only Leo could not hear it on his short-range walkie-talkie. "This is the state police. I—"

The voice was cut off.

"The bastards jammed the frequency!" Burt hollered into his mike.

"You can bet dispatch will broadcast a ten-thirty-three now," Mike's voice was calm.

"What's a ten-thirty-three?" Mary Beth asked.

"Emergency situation in progress. Keep the frequency clear for local and emergency traffic only. That will give those who've rolled over even more time. Maybe until dawn."

"Thirty-eight point two is requesting ten-thirty-three." Dispatch's voice was cold and clear. "Please use teletype for communications and disregard any radio transmissions. We have a one-oh-three M with a police band radio disrupting regular communications. Do you ten-four, State Police?"

"We ten-four, Tepehuanes PD. Are you requesting additional assistance in this matter?"

"Ten-fifty. We can handle it."

"Ten-four. State police clear. Switching to tach frequency for our calls."

"Ten-four. Thirty-eight point two out and clear."

"What was all that about!" Dr. Fletcher yelled.

"One-oh-three M is a mental case. Ten-fifty means negative, no assistance needed. The state police just switched to an alternate frequency. They'll disregard any call that does not come from our base station."

"We're going to have to survive this night!" Burt radioed.

"Ten-four," Leo replied. "I'm gone."

He laid the walkie-talkie on the seat and peeled around a corner. Screaming up the street where Linda lived, he tore into the drive and braked hard, just before wrecking the rental car. Jumping out, shotgun in hand, Leo ran across the yard and onto the small front porch.

He could hear frantic and near-hysterical screaming coming from inside the lovely home. The sound of a blow, of a hand striking naked flesh, drifted out to him. Leo cursed the night and what it had brought.

The front door was locked. And it was a stee

security door. No way Leo could kick it in. He jumped off the porch and ran to peer through a front window. He cursed again, low. Linda was naked, pinned to the floor, her father attacking her.

Leo smashed the window with the butt of the shotgun and crawled in, disregarding the shards of glass that cut his hands as he climbed into the living room.

"Get away from her," he yelled, his voice cold with rage.

The wild-eyed man, a savage look on his broad face, turned from his daughter and faced Leo, snarling like a maddened, rabid animal.

Linda scrambled away and frantically grabbed at her torn clothing.

Leo leveled the shotgun and shot her father. The magnum-load buckshot caught the man in the lower belly and spun him around, knocking him backward. He fell over a couch and lay screaming on the floor. Even dying, his words praised Satan and damned Christians.

The roaring of the shotgun had sounded enormous in the room. It had momentarily deafened Leo.

Crying, but not hysterically, Linda had managed to tug on jeans and a shirt. Leo grabbed her by the hand and pulled her toward the front door.

The small porch was filled with wild-eyed men and women, their hands claw-like, the fingers curved. They reached for Leo and Linda.

Linda screamed in panic, and Leo leveled the shotgun, pulling and pumping, the slugs tearing into the bodies of those blocking the doorway. He cleared the porch of those who chose to devote what time they had left to the teachings of the Dark One.

Then he and the teenager stepped over the moaning and the dead, and waded through the gore, to the car. Others had gathered in the street. Screaming hate and filth, they blocked the driveway with their bodies and poison-spewing mouths.

Leo dropped the gears into reverse and backed over them, giving the car gas, slamming into them. He felt nothing as the tires crunched the life from those who refused to move out of his way.

Linda closed her eyes and tried to keep from puking at the sounds of breaking bones and squashed flesh.

She was successful at fighting back the hot bile, but just barely.

A screaming woman held onto the door handle. Dragged along the street, she howled out her pain and rage, blood and bits of flesh and mangled clothing marking her trail.

Leo pulled out the .38 he'd taken from Mark's gun cabinet and shot her between the eyes.

The screaming ended in a choking bubble.

Linda finally found her voice. "What's happening here?" she wailed, fear touching the words. "My father killed my mother and then attacked me. He knocked me down and jumped me."

"The boil has erupted." Leo spoke through tight lips as he turned onto the street where Bing and Ro lived, close to each other.

Paul sat in the center of his bed and smiled. He looked at the heavy steel door to his room, locked from the outside. He blinked his eyes. The lock clicked, and the door swung open.

"Thank you, Father," the boy said.

And he wasn't speaking to Mark.

A mist formed beside the bed.

"Hello, brother." Paul looked at the mist. "How do you feel?"

The mist must have felt just fine. A grotesque laugh sprang from the yellow miasma.

Paul rose and walked to the open door. It was time to have some high ol' fun. Humor from the Dark Side.

The devil-child looked up the corridor to the nurses' station. Most of the women were with him, although he doubted they were aware of that. Yet.

He saw one who wasn't a part of his plan. She was, Paul recalled sourly, one of those rare "good" people. Not perfect, but trying to be. She had resisted his silent callings. She had also tried to comfort the boy she thought him to be, murmuring stupid things to him, stroking his hair.

He stared at her for a moment, as she leaned up against the nurses' station, attempting, without much success, to engage the other nurses in conversation. Her feet suddenly flew out from under her, and she sailed across the corridor to slam against the wall. Screaming in fear, she was bounced, on her behind, up and down on the floor, her head jerking back and forth like a rag doll. Her lips were cut by the impacting, and blood dribbled from them, staining the front of her white uniform.

The other nurses sat and stared at her, their eyes shining with perverse pleasure.

"Take her," Paul ordered the mist.

The mist became a creature born in the smoking pits. It grabbed the nurse by the hair and banged her head against the wall, again and again. Flesh split and blood squirted, and her cries became weak, small mewing sounds of helplessness.

The other nurses looked on impassively.

The demon released her, and she slumped over onto her side and died with her face pressed against the coolness of the tile.

The demon, suddenly transformed back into a mist, slithered along the floor to gather at the feet of its earth-brother.

Paul waved his hand at the nurses. "Go!" he ordered.

They moved out in single file, walking up the corridor, vanishing around a corner.

Paul walked to the nurses' station and found the bank of switches, electrically controlled, that locked and unlocked all the doors to the psychiatric wing of Tepehuanes General.

With a bark of laughter, he flipped switches and released the half-dozen mentally ill patients.

"You're free!" he shouted, his hollow voice echoing around the empty corridor. "Come! Give your miserable lives to the True Father."

The men and woman shuffled out of their rooms, some grinning, some slobbering.

Paul walked away. Leaving them to whatever mischief they might decide to pull, he strode out of the wing, a smile on his evil face. The mist trailed him as he walked up the stairs to the first floor, the

the second. He came face to face with Dr. Jack Thomas.

"What are you doing out of your room?" Thomas yelled.

Then his feet flew out from under him. He landed heavily, on his backside, on the floor, the breath knocked out of him. Paul waved his hand, and Jack Thomas began spinning on the floor like a human top, faster and faster, the seat of his trousers smoking from friction.

Paul waved his hand again. Jack's spinning stopped. He lay on the floor, confused and dazed. A force he could neither see nor comprehend jerked him to his feet and sent him sailing down the hall. Jack screamed as he crashed out a second-floor window. His screaming ended abruptly when he impacted on concrete at ground level.

One of the mentally ill had followed Paul to the second floor. Grinning and slobbering, he grunted and pointed to the window.

"You want to go, too?" Paul asked.

Grunt.

"All right."

Paul waved his hand and the man followed Jack Thomas to the concrete.

Splat.

Paul looked out the smashed window at the broken and bloody bodies sprawled below.

He rubbed his hands together. Grinned wickedly. It was going to be a fun night!

TWO

Those reporters who had elected to remain in town, snooping and prying and nosing about, had gathered in the lounge of their motel for a nightcap. One was a particularly odious fellow, Matt Maguire. Matt believed that he and he alone knew what was best for the country. Certainly no president ever had. Matt also believed that no one had any rights except members of the press.

Not even his colleagues liked him.

He was a pompous ass who would ruin anybody to get a story, and then loudly proclaim his right to do so under the first amendment.

It amazed the other members of the press that Matt had managed to stay alive this long.

Matt leaned back in his chair and shouted, "Another round, barkeep! Make it snappy, and put some booze in the drinks this time."

The bartender looked at Matt. His eyes were flat and shiny. "Stick it, man!" he called.

Matt flushed. Balled his fists. Looked at his equally startled colleagues. What was going on in this crazy town? No one talked to Matt Maguire in such a manner.

He didn't have to take that kind of talk from som‹ nobody.

"Get your butt over here and wait on us!" Mat‹ shouted.

The bartender told Matt where he could shove hi‹ orders.

Matt jumped up. "Do you know who you'r‹ talking to, Bub?"

The bartender did. Told him so. Using variou‹ loosely strung together four-letter words. He ende‹ his assessment of Matt by shouting, "All praise th‹ Dark One."

"All praise who?" the lone female reporter in th‹ group questioned. Marta. From Los Angeles.

"The Dark One!" a cocktail waitress screamed. Sh‹ then picked up a heavy ashtray and hurled it ‹ Marta.

Marta ducked just as the other waitresses and th‹ bartender began throwing glasses and ashtray‹ bottles of booze and cans of beer at the reporters.

Marta decided that the place was dangerous, ar‹ split.

Jeff, from San Francisco, ducked a bottle of be‹ and yelled at her. "Where are you going?"

Marta waved, but didn't stop.

She ran right into the sweaty arms of a half-doz‹ wild-eyed men in the lobby. She didn't even ha‹ time to scream when she saw the desk clerk sprawl‹ over the counter, his belly sliced open.

The men carried her, squalling and hollering a‹ telling them that she'd sue them all, to a motel roo‹ where they proceeded to physically abuse her.

Matt and Jeff and Harrison, who was from New York City, had backed up and were engaged in throwing various articles at the bartender and the waitresses, who proceeded to toss them right back.

None of the reporters really had any idea of what was going on, but when an ashtray hit Matt on the side of his face, splitting skin and drawing blood, they all decided to follow Marta's lead and vacate the premises.

"I'll sue you!" Matt hollered over his shoulder as he loped out of the room. "I'll sue this rat-trap motel and everybody connected with it!"

The bartender pulled out a pistol, and began throwing lead in all directions. One slug just missed Matt as he rounded a corner and entered the lobby.

"Good God!" Jeff hollered, spotting the bloody mess that was the desk clerk.

They could hear screams coming from down the hall.

"That sounds like Marta!" Harrison panted.

"Everyone for himself," Matt yelped. "I'm getting out of this crazy place." He ran out into the hot and dangerous night.

Jeff and Harrison ran toward Marta's squallings.

Matt looked up and down the street. People were milling about; most had chains and clubs and guns in their hands.

"What is going on in this town?" he said to the dark night.

But when he heard gunshots, journalistic inquisitiveness was overridden by cowardliness.

Matt ran toward the motel parking lot, jumped into his car, and locked all the doors. He thought of the tape recorder, portable typewriter, and luggage back in his room.

"Hell with them," he said, cranking the car and dropping it into gear. "After I get through suing this place I'll own the town."

He pulled out into the street.

A milling crowd blocked his way.

Matt honked his horn, but nobody paid any attention to the incessant blaring. He rolled down his window.

"Get out of the way!"

A rock smashed his rear window as a crowd gathered around his car, pushing and shoving and rocking the vehicle.

The driver's-side window was shattered with a club. Hands reached inside for him. Gripped by near hysterical fear, Matt floorboarded the pedal and knocked a half-dozen people sprawling, the tire running over some of them. The agonized wailing of those hurt grated on his nerves like sandpaper being ground against raw flesh.

He roared off wildly into the night, not knowing where he was going, just that he was going.

Jeff and Harrison hit the motel-room door together, splintering it. They both pulled up short at the sight that greeted them.

Marta, lying naked on the bed, was being attacked by three men. Jeff and Harrison battled briefly with the men while Marta grabbed a blanket to cover her nakedness. Then the three reporters ran to the rear exit of the motel and lit out into the night.

Feeling safe for the moment, they paused to catch their breath and to assess their situation.

"Whole town has gone nuts!" Harrison panted.

"But why?" Jeff asked.

"Write the story later," Marta said, her voice rembly with fear. "Right now, let's see if we can find ome cops."

"Yeah," both man agreed. "Let's get to a police tation."

"Good idea. We'll be safe there."

eo backed up, took a deep breath, and kicked in the ront door of Bing's house.

Even after years as a cop, seeing man's inhumanity oward man, Leo was not prepared for the sight that reeted him.

Bing and Roy were being abused by a group of men nd women.

Leo leveled the shotgun and began to fire indis- riminately.

Howling and wailing filled the room as buckshot ore into flesh.

"Run to the car, boys!" Leo shouted, shifting the notgun to his left hand and pulling the .38 out of his aistband with his right.

The boys ran past him, limping badly, blood reaking their legs as they ran into the night.

Leo put two more shots into the floor, then backed ut the door and jumped off the porch, heading for e car.

He was tackled in the yard by one man, kicked in e side by another. Leo fought free, shoved the .38 to the belly of one of his assailants, and pulled the igger. The man screamed as lead tore into his guts.

403

The second man jumped onto Leo's back and rode him to the ground, hitting him with his fists. Those left alive in the house ran out onto the porch, then leaped to the ground and headed toward Leo.

The engine of Leo's car roared as Linda scooted behind the wheel and dropped the car into gear. The rear tires smoked and squealed as she gave it gas and spun the wheel, angling toward the men and women who were now running across the front yard, toward Leo and the man he was fighting.

The car knocked several men and women onto the grass. They sprawled there, their bodies mangled.

Leo smashed his attacker's face with the butt of the empty .38, then rolled free, reaching for and finding his shotgun. He jumped into the back seat of his car.

"Go!" he yelled, as he frantically reloaded his weapons.

The car bounced across the yard, jumped the sidewalk and curb, and screamed up the street.

"Go where?" Linda shouted, above the roaring of the laboring engine.

Strangely, Leo had to fight to suppress laughter. I'm losing my mind, he thought.

He was just about emotionally drained, momentarily on the verge of breaking. "Get thee to a nunnery," he muttered.

"What?" Linda shouted.

Leo reached deep within himself to draw on his inner strength. "The church," he told her. "We're gathering at the church."

Jeff, Harrison, and Marta were certain they were

404

going to die that night. They had made it to the police station, but had been handcuffed to the steel bars of the windows, and stripped naked.

When two policewomen grinned and got out knives, they knew they'd made a bad choice.

Matt guessed he had tried every street in town, and he'd hit some sort of blockade on every one. He was very close to the breaking point. Then he saw the sheriff's department cars go screaming through an intersection.

He followed them. Matt wasn't crazy about cops, but they could be useful on rare occasions.

He pulled in behind the cars as they slid to a stop in front of a church.

Then he found himself looking down the muzzles of sawed-off shotguns.

"It's that loud-mouthed reporter," Peter said, lowering his shotgun.

"I just cover the news," Matt said wearily. He knew most police officers despised him.

"That's one way of putting it," Fifteen said. "What do you want?"

"To be safe," Matt admitted. "I'm scared."

"Then go inside the church," Peter told him.

Tepehuanes General began to stink like an unwashed and untended slaughterhouse. One of Carleson's assistants had been strung up like a pig, gutted, and left to die slowly.

Belline, Carleson, and Clineman had sought

refuge in the basement, but they knew they must get away from the hospital, and soon. A search for them was underway.

They were just about ready to make a run for it.

"Find them!" Paul shouted from the second floor.

The headless man stood beside him, holding his head in his hands.

"We'll look." It was the head that spoke, peeling back its lips in a macabre grin as it did so.

The head noticed its intact girlfriend and winked at her.

She opened her fanged mouth and smiled.

Belline, Carleson, and Clineman chose that moment to run for their lives. They got clear of the building and found an ambulance with the keys in the ignition. Pulling out of the hospital compound, they headed for safety. Somewhere.

The commander of the state police detachment in Phoenix had a bad feeling in his gut. And as the night wore on, he couldn't shake it. With a sigh, he finally picked up the phone and called in.

"How's the situation over in Tepehuanes? They catch that nut?"

"I don't know, Captain. There hasn't been a thing on the air or the teletype."

"I don't like this!" the commander stated flatly.

"Neither do I. And Burt Sandry can't be located. His office is really getting antsy."

"How about Mike Bambridge?"

"Can't get in touch with him either. All we're getting is a lot of bull from the Tepehuanes P

Burt's office has admitted they've been working on some sort of devil worship thing in and around Tepehuanes."

"I don't recall being briefed on that."

"We weren't. SO admits they've deliberately kept a lid on it to muffle the news. But it's beginning to add up in my mind."

"How so?"

"Reports of creatures in the night. Those truck drivers. That cop's body that disappeared. Missing persons. It's all adding up, Captain."

"What's our man—Langston—in Tepehuanes have to say about this?"

"I don't know, Captain. We can't reach him either. And he hasn't been heard from since going ten-eight."

"How long has that been?"

"Hours."

The captain was silent for a moment.

"You still there, Captain?"

"Yeah. Roll a SWAT team. It's probably over-reaction on my part, but I just don't like the feel of this. You know what I mean?"

"Yes, sir, I do," the watch commander said. "I've had one standing by for an hour."

Lisa Arnot and her followers had a good time torturing a young man. But when he died all the fun went out of the game.

"Let's go link up with Paul," Lisa suggested.

The others thought that was a good idea, so they headed for the hospital.

407

On the way, they found an elderly man and set his clothing on fire. They laughed as he screamed and staggered away into the night, a living firebrand.

"I can't understand it," Matt said to Leo. "There' not one ounce of sense to it. These people who've chosen to follow Paul have nothing to gain by this and everything to lose."

He was in the rectory, where they had decided to make their stand.

"That's true," Father Gomez said.

"Well, that's probably the point," Linda replied

"What do you mean, child?"

The girl cocked her head to one side. "I may b young, but I'm somewhat of an authority on matter such as these. I mean, I've studied everything I coul get my hands on about this stuff, ever since I coul read. The devil masks his true intentions under laye of raw violence and senseless actions. Don't yo agree, Father?"

"Yes."

"But the mark on Paul's arm . . . ?" Mike pr tested.

"Meaningless," Gomez said. "Since it was fir brought to my attention, I've looked into that. If read it right, Paul was put here to die. And he refusing to cooperate. Someone else has been pr pared to receive his powers. But I don't know wh Yet."

The priest did not see the hot look of pure hate th was directed at him.

But Leo did.

THREE

ate Trooper Kyle Langston was found by the lead
r of the Tepehuanes bound SWAT team. The
ghway cop was bent over the steering wheel;
peared to be sleeping. He was. Sort of.

He was chalk white. His eyes were wide and staring
d very dead-looking. His hands gripped the
ering wheel so hard that the skin around his
uckles had split open. No blood. His hair was
ow white.

Kyle Langston had been twenty-eight years old.
'd had a full head of coal black hair.

'Holy Mother of God!'' a SWAT member whis-
red.

The sergeant in command took a deep breath and
allowed hard. He kept telling himself that he'd
n worse.

But he couldn't remember when.

'Get a camera and take some shots,'' Sergeant
lson ordered. ''Jimmy, get on the horn, tach freq,
d call in. Get Captain Madison out here. Tell him
le three.''

'Right, Sergeant.''

Sergeant Wilson touched Langston's neck with h[is]
fingertips. The flesh was very cold. He shone h[is]
flashlight onto the body. Grimaced when he sa[w]
teeth marks on the man's neck. And knew somethin[g]
was very wrong.

"There isn't a drop of blood on him, and from th[e]
looks of things, none in him, either."

"What!"

"Take a look, Ned." Wilson stepped away from th[e]
car.

When Ned stuck his head inside the car, Troop[er]
Kyle Langston lifted his head and kissed the youn[g]
SWAT member right on the mouth. Then [he]
grabbed Ned in a cold grip, and dragged t[he]
screaming young man into the car with him.

"The chanting is getting louder," Leo said. "H[ere]
they come." He was very calm. "Everybody who c[an]
pull a trigger, grab a gun and get to a window.['']

Father Gomez looked out into the night a[nd]
crossed himself.

They were facing what at first glance appeared [to]
be several thousand citizens of Tepehuanes. Actua[lly]
the mob was smaller, but large enough to [be]
terrifying to the few defenders.

Many people had remained in the town. They w[ere]
busy fighting other small pockets of resistance.

"There must be more like us," Linda said.

"I agree." The priest picked up his shotgun a[nd]
chambered a round.

"Probably. Judging by those shots we've b[een]
hearing off and on," Burt Sandry noted. He [was]

ading a spare shotgun he'd taken from the
bstation.

"We know how to shoot," Bing said. He tried to
in. "Sure would be more comfortable than sitting
wn. If you know what I mean."

Leo smiled at the boys. They both had spunk.
rab a gun," he said to them.

"We don't know anything about guns." Janis
oked at Melissa and Carol.

The chanting from the outside was louder, nearer.

"You girls go into that small room and lock the
or," Father Gomez told them, pointing.

Fifteen picked up the phone, again, and held it to
s ear. Dead. With a low curse, he slammed it down
to the cradle.

"Paul worked it all out, didn't he?" Peter said to no
e in particular.

"With some outside help," the priest reminded
m all.

And then there was no time for anything other
n survival.

Connie, Mary Beth, and Linda took one side of the
use, shotguns in their hands. Leo and Father
mez took the other. Burt Sandry and the boys took
rear. Peter and Fifteen manned the front.

A staunch advocate of gun control, Matt was
htened of guns. He joined Janis and the other two
ls in the small room.

or a full five minutes, hearing was shattered by
roaring of weapons and the screaming of the
ng and the badly wounded. Several times those
sessed managed to breach the windows. They
e shot to death inside the rectory, or had their

411

heads beaten in by gun butts. Eyes smarted from th
sting and stink of gunsmoke. Nerves were frayed ra
by tension and by the howling of those maddened b
Satan.

Weapons became too hot to handle and we
exchanged for fresh ones from the piles place
around the room. Leo was slightly wounded in h
left arm. Gomez took a cut on his head. Sandry wa
hit in the left side but stayed on his feet. Bing's sca
was nicked, and a bullet creased Roy's shoulde
Though clubbed on the forehead and knocked to t
floor, blood pouring into her eyes, Connie lifted h
shotgun and shot the squalling woman trying
climb in the window, in the face. A chunk of flyi
brick caught Mary Beth on the jaw, slicing it ope
And Linda was hit in the mouth with a gun butt, a
lost several front teeth.

But the embattled little group hung on.

Then, as if on some silent signal, the fighti
ceased, those possessed racing off into the night.

"What happened?" Peter questioned. He a
Fifteen were the only ones who had not been injure

Someone in the rectory knew, but that pers
wasn't about to say a word.

Another person suspected the truth, however.

It was almost time for a transference of power
stronger, more stable person would take over. A
Paul would die.

Mary Beth began patching up the wounded w
what she could find in the medicine cabinet.

"Hospital ambulance coming in!" Leo shou
his hearing still impaired from the roaring gunfig

Connie looked out. "Doctors—Belline and Cli

412

nan and Carleson."

They watched as the men stepped over and
hrough the dead and the dying.

Leo opened the bullet-pocked, axe-scarred door
hat was barely hanging on its hinges. Right then, he
nade up his mind. Even before he greeted the newest
urvivors, he said, "We can't stay here. We've got to
hift our location."

The doctors began to assist Mary Beth, using
nedical supplies they'd carried in from the am-
ulance.

"And go where?" Burt asked as the doctors worked
n the wound in his side.

"Back to my house. It doesn't have as much glass as
onnie's, and the roof is tile." He had other reasons,
ut kept them to himself. "What do you say?"

"Walther's Sporting Goods is on the way," Peter
id. "We'll stop there and get more ammunition.
n for it."

"Let's roll."

ooper Langston ripped at Ned's throat, greedily
cking his blood, feeling new and strange life flow
to his own body. The young trooper howled and
ked and tried in vain to break free.

For a few seconds, the other SWAT members stood
shock and stared.

Sergeant Wilson broke out of the paralysis first,
d stepped up to the unit, emptying his .357 into the
iling, bloody-faced Langston.

Langston continued smiling at him. Despite
oking holes in his uniform shirt, he slowly opened

413

the door, stepping out into the night. His lips wer
slick with blood and his teeth, very sharp, wer
needle-pointed.

Wilson looked at his empty gun, then at th
grinning Langston.

He knew he was in big trouble.

Another trooper ran up and shot Langston in th
chest with a riot gun. Another put a load of buckshc
in his belly. The buckshot knocked Langston bac
against the car, but did not stop him.

A third trooper knocked Langston down with
wild swing of his shotgun, and then proceeded
beat in the back of the man's head with the butt.

"Grab Ned!" Wilson shouted. "Get him to th
hospital at Tepehuanes."

Langston suddenly began laughing, his brai
hanging out of his skull. He grabbed the neare
cop's ankles and hung on with a cold steely grip

The trooper screamed and emptied his pistol in
Langston's back at almost point-blank range. Lan
ston released his hold and the trooper stumbl
away.

Still not done in, Langston crawled around on t
highway, snarling and grabbing at any leg he cou
see.

Yet another member of the team realized what
was seeing and ran to the trunk of his car. Jerking c
a small axe, he raced back to the impossible sce
and, with a horrified look on his face, beg
chopping at Langston's arms, rendering th
useless.

No blood flowed. Langston flopped his shatter
arms on the pavement.

Wilson got it then. He didn't believe it. But it was the only thing that made any sense. He grabbed the axe and chopped at Langston's chest, opening the cavity to expose the dead but still-beating heart. As he chopped, he yelled, "Handcuff Ned's hands behind his back. Be careful. Don't let him bite you."

"What?" a trooper screamed.

"Just do it, damn it!" Wilson shouted. He lifted the axe high and brought the head down, chopping through Langston's heart.

The trooper screamed in real pain, then cursed them all as he lay dying on the highway, his dark soul winging away. Again.

The troopers stood in the deserted and moon-swept road and struggled to get their emotions under control. Finally, one said, "I don't believe none of this. But if I was to believe it, I'd have to ask who done this to Langston—and where are they? Or it?"

The troopers nervously looked around them, scanning the seemingly empty landscape.

Then Ned began to speak in a language that none of them could comprehend. He now appeared to be completely free of pain.

They all knew that was impossible. But then, everything they'd witnessed in the last thirty minutes also was impossible.

The men looked at Ned. Looked at each other. "I didn't know Ned could speak Russian," one said.

"He can't," Wilson said. "And that isn't Russian. I was stationed on the border in Germany. I learned some Russian. I don't know what that gibberish is; nothing I ever heard of. Put Ned in the cage and be careful doing it. Donnie, get on the horn and get

Captain Madison. Tell him to move it. Advise the troop to order all roads into this area closed. Immediately. For at least a twenty-five-mile radius in all directions."

"Now what, Sarge?" he was asked.

"We wait."

The night yawned huge and silent around them.

The small group made it to the sporting goods store, got guns and ammo, and rushed to Leo's house. The vehicles now had a few nicks and dents from thrown rocks and bricks, but they were all running.

And, curiously, they had not been pursued. No one knew what to make of that.

All took up positions and waited, the lights in the house turned off so they could better see outside.

Leo broke the silence in the den. "I think it was screw-up. I think Paul went too far, too fast. I think he lost control."

"I tend to agree with you." Gomez spoke from one of the near darkness. The street lamps the only illumination. "It's winding down."

Most felt they knew what had to be done to stop the spreading madness.

Only two people knew for sure. Leo was one them.

"I wonder what happened to my mother," Melissa asked.

No one offered a reply.

The girl would never see her again.

Flames shot up into the night sky, from

lowntown area.

"Burning parts of the town," Burt observed. "I agree, Leo. The kid's beginning to lose it."

"I think if we can hold out until dawn, we've got a chance," Gomez said.

"You mean those . . . out there, the possessed, fear he dawn?" Burt asked.

"No. But most of them will be so tired by then hey'll be unable to put up much of a fight. Outside elp can come in, or we'll be able to get out."

"All the books I've read and the movies I've seen tate that the undead fear the light," Matt put in.

"There is sometimes truth in that," Linda stated. But Satan can do anything he wishes, whenever he rishes. You all know, you must understand, that this just a game to Satan. When he tires of it, he'll eave."

Good God!" Captain Madison blurted. He stared at angston's body, bullet- and buckshot-pocked, axe-auled, the arms broken in many places, then peered ito the cage of a highway-patrol unit at Ned.

Ned hissed at him.

Madison recoiled from the shiny skinless skull, the ng, needle-pointed teeth.

He wiped his face with a handkerchief and joined Wilson.

"That's impossible!" he said. He pointed to Ned.

"Yes, sir," Wilson agreed. "We know. Did you ose the roads, sir?"

"Yes." The captain slowly regained composure.

Shook his head. "That was a good move on you part. Troopers and sheriff's deputies are rerouting traffic."

After receiving Donnie's near-frantic transmis sions, the captain had ordered all available highway patrol personnel into the area. He had debated whether or not to call the governor. Had called hi superior instead. Let him notify the Gov. But now Captain Madison realized he had one big problem or his hands. A situation unlike any he had ever faced Sergeant Wilson had spoken of zombies and undead Madison could just hear himself telling such thing to the governor.

A trooper walked to his side. "The boss is on th radio, Captain."

Here it was. Something Madison had been dread ing. He walked to his unit and picked up the mike

"Captain Madison here."

"What's going on out there, Tom?"

"I don't know, sir."

A short moment of silence.

"Well, Tom, if you don't know, who does?"

"God."

A short moment of silence.

"Ten-nine, Tom?"

"Sir, we're going to have to go into Tepehuane And I have a hunch it's going to be bad. With losse Our situation here is . . . well, unbelievable. U godly. Impossible. But it's real."

"You're not making any sense!"

"Not over the air, sir."

"Have you taken losses, Tom?"

"Two men."

Another short period of silence. "Very well. I'm choppering in. My ETA is one hour."

"Yes, sir."

Madison tossed the mike onto the seat and rejoined the knot of troopers. In the cage of the unit, Ned was howling like a maddened dog. Banging his shiny skull against the window.

"The boss coming in?" Wilson asked.

"In all his glory!"

Paul felt ten feet tall. He was undefeatable. Victory was his. The town was his. He looked at the sobbing girl, and calmly ordered Lisa to cut the child's throat.

With a smile on her evil face, Lisa pulled a knife out of her boot and did what she was told.

"I never did like that one," she said, wiping the blade on her jeans.

A deputy from Burt Sandry's tach team had heard all. He stepped around the corner and into the corridor. He was bloody from numerous gunshot wounds, but still on his feet. Dying, he knew, but strong enough to still be effective. His friend Eric was dead. Whole damn town had gone nuts.

Painfully, he pulled the riot gun to his shoulder and blew Lisa's head all over the filthy floor.

Pumping another round into the chamber, the deputy ended the short evil lives of Sally Rees and Rex Grummen before a nurse ran up behind him and drove a pair of scissors into his neck. With a burbling scream of pain, he dropped to the floor, still holding onto the riot gun. Twisting, he shot the nurse in the stomach as life ebbed from him.

The last thing he recalled was a strange voice saying, "Enter now, for thou art a good man."

The deputy died with a smile on his face.

What was left of Lisa's gang scattered, running for their lives, oblivious to Paul's shrieked commands to return.

"Either they don't know where we are, or they just don't care anymore." Leo offered these explanations for the hours of relative peace.

"I wonder where Carla is?" Melissa asked. "I mean, they both busted out, didn't they?"

Leo held his tongue. He had encountered quite enough of those . . . things for one night. For one lifetime. And he didn't know if he could take much more.

But he had more horror to face. He was certain of that.

"No more fires have been set," Gomez pointed out. "And the others don't appear to be spreading. It appears they're burning out."

The priest lifted his arm to check the time. His watch was gone. He had lost it. "What time is it?"

"Quarter to four," Connie told him.

Gomez laid his shotgun down on a table and went in search of the bathroom. He paused in the kitchen by the back door. Thought he heard a whispering. He'd seen Linda leave the room moments before. Yes. He thought he recognized the voice. He opened the back door and stepped out into the night.

He smiled. "Guess we both needed some fresh air," he said.

The last thing he would remember in this life was a wishing sound, a hot moment of very intense pain, and a saddened feeling that he had been betrayed.

"Very disappointing, is it not?" He heard the voice peak to him as a peaceful blue filled him and he ntered into his second life.

His head and body were shoved over into the vaters of the swimming pool.

The long-bladed butcher knife was tossed over the ence, into the desert.

A figure ran back to the house, slipped in through n open window at the rear. The window was silently losed and locked from the inside.

state police helicopter did a fly-by of the town. The ootter took in the burning buildings, the bodies that ttered the streets. He got the hell out of the area hen bullets began zinging around him.

"There's a war going on down there!" the copter ilot yelled into his mike. "I don't know who's ghting who, but it's bad."

"Get out of there!" Captain Madison ordered.

He did not have to say it twice.

Leo was sitting on the couch, sharpening stakes. ne stake looked more like a spear.

Hearing the copter circling, Peter ran out to his r, and radioed.

"This is Deputy Peter Loneman. I'm with Sheriff ndry and Mike Bambridge and several others. e're safe for the moment. For obvious reasons, I n't give you our location. Just listen to me. I don't ve time to repeat this."

Very briefly, Pete outlined the situation.

Captain Madison, the head of the state police, and half-a-dozen sheriffs and deputies from surrounding counties listened, stunned and shaken, not knowing whether to believe the deputy or not.

"I know Pete Loneman," Wilson said. "He's a good, solid, steady man."

"I don't know him," Madison said. "But I went through the academy with Burt Sandry. Get him on the horn to confirm this . . . situation."

It was confirmed.

"Jesus!" Captain Madison whispered.

"We've got to go in," Wilson said.

"Now wait a minute!" the commander of state police yelled. "Zombies! Walking dead people! Devils and demons! This is crazy!"

"You saw Langston and Ned, didn't you?" Madison asked him.

The commander nodded his head wearily. "Yeah, OK, OK. I'll call the governor and ask him to send in the nearest national guard unit. That'll be in Tucson. It's an infantry outfit, I think. We'll have them cordon off the town; then we'll go in. Wilson, you and your men will spearhead. Get geared up."

Peter found the body of the priest half-submerged in the pool. It was light by then. After seven.

Leo was sure, now, finally, who it was the power was to be passed to.

And it sickened him.

"You're sure," Mike asked him.

"Yes. It's logical, and I feel it in my heart."

422

"Then . . . this person will soon try to destroy the rest of us?" Peter asked.

"No. I don't think so. But the bloodlust got too strong. It became uncontrollable. Probably jealousy figured in, as well."

"Ah!" Mike nodded his head. "Now we're getting on the same wavelength."

"I'll alert those that need to know. Watch your backs."

Mike and Peter walked off. Leo looked around him. Then he walked about the house, speaking softly with the survivors.

Peter was outside, in his unit, in contact with the state police. The national guard was in place. And the SWAT team, headed by Wilson, was getting ready to take off.

The town was very quiet. Overhead, in the clear blue of the sky, vultures were circling, eager to feast on the bloating bodies that lay in the streets.

The next few hours were going to be rough.

Mike had been watching the Kelly house. He called out, "That little devil-kid and some girl just walked into the place, big as brass."

Leo's eyes found Janis's.

"It's going to take two of us," she said.

"I know. Are you ready?"

Connie sat on the couch, watching, listening.

"I guess so, sir."

Leo handed her the shorter, sharpened stake, keeping the spearlike one for himself.

"You're going to have to kill Paul's other self," the girl reminded him.

"Yes."

423

"You have to do that," Janis pressed. "That's the only way Paul can be killed."

"I know. Janis?"

"I'm ready."

The man and the girl walked out the back of Leo's place, heading for the Kelly house.

They did not speak to one another on the short journey.

At the back door, they paused.

"Ready, Janis?"

"I'm ready."

Leo pushed open the door. They could hear Paul laughing.

They stepped into a tiny bit of Hell on earth.

FIVE

one moment the spearheading SWAT team was
ving to fight their way ahead, inch by inch, then
e people attacking them laid down their weapons
d fell to the street, holding their heads, as if
ffering from agonizing headaches.

And the same thing was occurring all over the
wn. Wilson radioed for the others to come on in,
it to be careful. "Something very weird is hap-
ning," he said.

"He thinks we don't know that?" Captain Madi-
n asked.

Madison's walkie-talkie crackled. He lifted it to his
r. "Yeah. Go on."

"Burt Sandry here, Tom. It's over. The demons are
ad. I don't think you're going to have any trouble
ting to us. But come on. You're gonna have to see
s to believe it."

nnie was crying, so were Linda and Mary Beth.
ggie had been handcuffed by Fifteen and stowed
the cage of his car.

427

The Kelly house was filled to near capacity with cops.

And Leo was sitting on the floor, just about drained.

"That can't be her!" Mike was saying, pointing to the old hag in stinking rags on the floor. "My God she was so young and pretty."

"It's her." Leo's voice was husky with exhaustion "Took me awhile, but I finally figured it out."

"I don't know that I could have done it," Pete said. He could not take his eyes from the horrible looking hag on the den floor.

Connie looked like she was about to faint.

Mary Beth led her outside and placed her in the back seat of a police car.

Then Leo turned to the commander of state police "Is it over?"

"Not another shot fired. They just gave up and la down in the street. Weirdest thing. None of them seem to remember anything that happened."

"Would you, if you were in their shoes?" Leo ask him.

"Good point. Yeah, I see what you mean." He looked at the dead hag on the floor. "About the lit girl, Mr. Corigliano . . . ?"

Leo nodded. "Stanford—Inspector Willingston suspected her all along. I just didn't buy it. I . . ."

His eyes caught something behind the back-ya fence; something that should not be there. He look at Mike and pointed. "Mounds of sand out the Mike. Could it be?"

Belline and his colleagues moved swiftly, Belli saying, "We'll take samples—carefully, this time

428

nd check to be sure."

"You were saying, Mr. Corigliano?" Captain Madison prompted.

"What finally convinced me was the death of ather Gomez. The murderer had to be someone uch shorter than he was. From the angle of the cut. nd left-handed. That pretty well narrowed it own."

A trooper entered the house and whispered omething in Captain Madison's ear. Madison imaced. To the group: "Four naked bodies have st been found outside of town. They've been entified as those of a couple who owned a large nch in the county, and your missing cop and his ife, Mary. All four are dead."

"Drive stakes into their hearts and burn the dies," Leo said.

"Now, see here, Mr. Corigliano!" the top gun of e state police protested.

"Just do what I tell you, you windbag!" Leo ared.

Madison nodded at Wilson. The SWAT leader dded in return and, with Peter beside him, left the use. They had some stake-driving to do.

"Carla Weaver?" Burt asked, tossing out the estion to anyone.

'No sign of her."

'What are you going to do with Ned?" top gun ed Captain Madison.

'That's up to you," Madison fired back. "But bear mind that he's one of . . . them."

Top gun nodded wearily. "I'll order it done right w."

429

"We have creatures in the hospital," Fiftee reminded them.

Leo pointed to the blanket-covered body of Mark "Somebody, get that body out of here so Mrs. Kell won't have to look at it. Hasn't she been throug enough without that?"

The body was swiftly removed.

"How about other pockets of defenders in th town?" Matt asked. He had recovered some of h bluster.

"Who are you?" Captain Madison asked.

"Matt Maguire, a member of the press. No answer my question."

Madison had twenty-five years in on the force. H retirement papers had already been okayed. H smiled, then did something he'd wanted to do f twenty-five years. He hit a smart-ass reporter rig smack in the mouth, knocking him cold.

The other cops in the room applauded.

Madison took a bow.

Then Leo stood up. He ached in every bone a muscle, but he headed outside. He had to see woman and try to explain the death of a little gi

SIX

ne Week Later.

o sat between his two favorite women. Connie on
s left, Janis on his right. A big bowl of hot popcorn
the coffee table.

Leo hugged them both, pulling them close.

"You did think it was me for a time, didn't you,
ster Leo?" Janis asked, munching on popcorn.

"Yes, I did, honey. And I'm sorry about that."

"Let's talk it out, Leo," Connie said, reaching
oss him and grabbing a handful of popcorn.
low did you put it all together?"

"Well, something was always happening to the
er girls, but never to Melissa. She just got a little
er, that's all. She was the one with the book, and it
t seemed like she was always around. I got
picious. And when Gomez was killed . . . well,
lissa was the only left-handed person in the house
t night. Besides, I saw her look at the priest, and
d it right."

"By eager, you mean she was so impatient she just
l to see Paul die?" Connie asked.

"Yeah."

"I'm glad it's over," Janis said.

But all three of them knew it wasn't.

Too many people were still missing. The report ers, Marta and Jeff and Harrison. Old Jake. Some of Lisa's gang were still on the loose—somewhere. And Maggie had hanged herself in the jail, but her body had vanished.

There were still too many loose ends for Leo to feel comfortable.

The people in the town, those who had taken Paul's side, all maintained their innocence. Something had taken control of them, they said.

Yeah. Sure.

Connie stood up and stretched. "Well, it's going be a big day tomorrow. We've got a long drive ahead of us. Time for bed, Janis."

She stood up and looked back at Leo. "You' staying here tonight, aren't you?"

"I'll be right here, honey," he assured her.

The girl went off to bed.

Connie met his eyes. "It's Janis they want, isn't Leo? Now damn it, don't lie to me."

"Yeah. That's what Father Gomez told me about an hour before he was killed."

"That's why you're in such a hurry for us to lea right?"

"Yeah. We're going on a long trip, Connie. May for a year. I'm a rich man, I can afford it. We'll h tutors for Janis. Then we'll settle up in Westcheste

"And hope for the best?"

He didn't reply.

Something pecked on the windows of the hou something that blew out of the desert.

"It's just sand, Connie," Leo said. "Relax. It's j grains of sand."